QUANTUM Ball

Write My Wrongs, LLC, P.O. Box 80781 Lansing, MI 48908
United States
www.writemywrongsediting.com
Copyright © K.A. Wood 2022

ISBN: 978-1-956932-01-0

All Rights Reserved. No part of this book may be reproduced, stored in a retrieval system, or transmitted by any means, electronic, mechanical, photocopying, recording or otherwise without written permission from the author.

K. A. WOOD

This is a work of fiction. The names, characters, places, and incidents are the product of the author's imagination or are used fictitiously. Any resemblance to actual events, locales, or persons, living or dead, is entirely coincidental.

*This book is dedicated to my family and friends.
Without their support, who knows what I might have written.*

Prologue 20 25

Every day, programmers and developers rely on specially coded libraries, modules, and packages to help them create advance programs and applications with ease. They do this by using easy-to-understand functions that convert their ideas into parallel code streams, which run faster on today's computers and high-performance computing clusters. Many processor core computers rely heavily on parallelism and distributed computing designs. This approach basically encapsulates the knowledge and genius of different people and makes traditional high-performance computing clusters easier to use without understanding completely how they work at the cost of true efficiency.

The field of quantum computing will need to employ the same principal at a more extreme level of abstracting away the required understanding of the underlying physics. There are a few computer scientists, mathematicians, and quantum physicists who truly understand how quantum computing works internally today. But they will not be able to explain it in a way that everyday developers can become immediately productive with the new technology. So, they must capture as much of what they know into well-defined and structured sets of routines for others to use, reuse, and share.

This is the way it's been since the first code compiler was conceived back in 1952, by Admiral Grace Hopper, on the first electronic room-sized computers. The reuse and inclusion of commonly needed routines is what jump-started the computer and application programming industry, more than the invention of the electronic computer itself. Making computer programming languages human readable as text with syntax and grammar rules, then converting them into machine executable programs, spawned a surge of new people into the fledgling computer industry. This simple idea drove mankind's technological advancements for the next seventy years. The requirements of having an electrical engineering degree or a mathematics degree to program a computer were no longer a necessity. Instead, the new field of computer science was born.

These new programming languages became so robust and structured that the grammar was considered real languages worthy of study in and of themselves. Some university doctorial curriculums required the study of two foreign languages as a requirement for completion. Studying a computer programming language eventually became one of the valid languages the doctoral student could choose. This, in turn, transitioned students from their original field of study to the computer sciences.

Over a short period of time, the languages became very powerful. A simple programming function could generate hundreds or thousands of machine-level operations. Thousands of man-hours were spent developing these routines to perfection. They would run flawlessly each time, to the point where it would never be questioned or tested again. This encapsulated years of knowledge and precision into reusable functions. Eventually, the details or knowledge of this code was forgotten or taken for granted. Those individuals and teams who created these original routines moved on to other projects, retired, or simply passed away.

Funny things happen when humans and society disregard history. One of those funny things happened in the computer industry. Programming languages had become so well developed and built upon themselves by using the previous generation's languages to develop the next generation of programming languages. These "generations" literally defined the advancements and indirectness of the new languages. The higher the generation, the more removed from the computer hardware. As computers became faster and cheaper, more effort was put into making programming easier, which made using computers easier, but making anything easier requires a lot of effort in the underlying layers of abstractions.

Subsequent advancements in languages are generating tens and hundreds of thousands—sometimes millions—of machine-level instructions to perform a single, high-level task, all in the attempt to abstract the complexities away from the developers and users. In many cases today, these functions span multiple computer systems over abstracted network layers. Rather than making the underlying codes more efficient, faster computer hardware was designed and manufactured. New and more complex machine-level instruction sets were built into the computer hardware as well to help streamline and make the execution of these operations more efficient.

For over forty years, the race between computer hardware architectures and performance hungry programming robustness pushed both to new advances in speed and capacity and ease of use. Some programming language functions were built into the hardware processor instruction set for more speed on critical operations. First-generation languages were used to develop second-generation languages. Second-generation languages were used to develop third-generation languages, and so on. Today, you can create complete and robust applications by drawing pictures that translate into programs, which translate into hardware instructions.

Very few knew how some language functions were actually written, and those who did knew there were going to be problems in the future. Just like the Motorola 68000—the last microprocessor understood and designed by human hands—was used to design future microprocessors, previous generation programming languages were used to design future programming languages.

"Time" was one of those problems. Specifically, the "time" and "date" data structures. Memory, storage, and processing power were expensive and precious resources to consider when developing programs, so some ingenious programmers figured out a way to use half the memory required when representing date as data. They used a trick—a shortcut—where "19" was used as a constant to represent the twentieth century. The rationale was that, in the future (based on trends in hardware advancements), there would be more memory and processing power to go back and rewrite these date and time routines to more accurately represent real data—rather than only using the last two digits of the year and prepending a constant "19" for the century.

By the time the year 2000 was approaching, many in the computer industry realized no one had gone back and recoded those decades-old date and time routines several generations of programming languages were all built on—and were still using. Those original date routines and data formats were still in use in every program-running industry and commerce, from video games to flight plans.

Like peeling onion layers, computer scientists unraveled decades of programming codes through programs and languages. In some cases, the routines were built into the hardware of the computers and needed to be bypassed and rewritten in software to avoid the anticipated catastrophe. Without this global software update, from applications to operating systems, when the clock struck midnight on January 1, 2000, the world of computers would send society back to "1900"; ironically to a time when computers didn't even exist.

One of the largest economic booms—and busts—was caused by the lead-up to the great "Year 2000" bug fix, more commonly known as the "Y2K buildup." Companies were buying more and more computer hardware and storage capacity to replicate their data and applications in order to work on updating and testing their systems, applications, and just-in-case scenario testing. The effort paid off, and airplanes did not fall from the sky. There were a few fringe stories of one-hundred-year overdue books at local libraries and videos tapes at neighborhood video rental outlets because of the computer problem, but the electricity grid did not shut down and nuclear missiles stayed in their bunkers.

After that infamous date came and passed, the surplus of computer equipment buildup caused a temporary industry depression. Eventually, an innovative way to use the excess computing capacity as a shared resource was created that would eventually become "the Cloud."

For every technology glitch, there is an equal and opposite innovation.

Chapter 1

The sound of the front doorbell ringing was heard from the stairwell in the middle of the house. The security app on his phone also chimed and displayed a notification message on the screen. Tyson McNally had been waiting for this ring for what felt like hours but tried to occupy his mind with other work.

He just about finished setting up a suite of burn-in test jobs on a new system he and his team set up in his company's lab in Santa Clara when the doorbell rang. He looked down at his phone and opened the security app to see a delivery guy standing at his door. Next to the delivery guy was a large package. The pointless distractions worked, but now it was time. He quickly launched the suite of programs he was in the middle of configuring, which would take about an hour to fail since he wasn't finished with it. He didn't care; it was busy work anyway. It must be the package he'd been waiting for. The FedEx package tracking service stated within the hour, and this was about thirty minutes from then.

Ty had been expecting this package since last week and was monitoring the delivery schedule since the missed delivery time came and went. It seemed to never fail that once the normal tracking system missed a scheduled delivery time for any reason, any information beyond that point was useless—if any was provided. It was as though all misfit deliveries were no longer allowed to be included in the tracking system and only human actions were permitted, which also included no updates to the shipping company's system. An information blackout. Apparently, they finally synced up the delivery data in the last couple of hours.

Ty got his six-foot, two-inch, wiry frame out of his desk chair and lifted his arms above his head to quickly stretch out, then bent over to extend his legs. It was a bad habit of his to sit for too long, so he extended his extremities as often as he could; he was still working on curbing this habit. Walking out of his office, he quickly ran his hand through his thick, dark-brown, easy-to-maintain hair.

Ty opened the door to a FedEx "Custom Critical White Glove Service" delivery guy looking down at his tablet with a box on its end standing next to him. There wasn't a dolly or any other type of carrying aide with him.

"Tyson McNally?" The delivery guy asked, looking at Ty and holding out the ruggedized tablet for him to sign.

"Yeah, that's me. How's your day going so far?" he asked, taking the stylus and placing his hand under the tablet for support while he signed it.

"Good so far, but then, it's early," the delivery guy said without really caring about the greeting.

Ty could see the name "Jimmy" on his name tag above the FedEx logo on his company shirt. The FedEx "Custom Critical White Glove Service" was used for specialty equipment and safe transportation of sensitive shipments. Why this package was late by a week was baffling him, and Jimmy never mentioned or apologized for that fact. He guessed the primary goal was to treat a fragile package with care rather than rush it.

Ty returned the stylus to Jimmy, who was already retrieving the tablet from him.

Jimmy verified the signature, touched a couple of places on the tablet's screen, placed the stylus back in its slot at the top of the tablet, and then jammed the tablet up into his armpit, holding it there.

Jimmy picked up the large package with ease and handed it to Mr. McNally.

Since Ty observed Jimmy's build to be somewhat larger than average, and athletic, he expected the package to be heavier than Jimmy was showing. He braced himself to accept the package, incorrectly estimating its weight as Jimmy handed it off to him. To his surprise, the package was even heavier, and with his poor judgement, he ended up slightly dropping the box down out of Jimmy's hands. Overall, it wasn't that heavy, but it did surprise him with its awkward weight.

Jimmy must live for these moments, Ty thought, because he noticed an ever so slight smile in his eyes as if knowing that his strength always caught customers by surprise.

"Sorry about that, Mr. McNally," he said with an undetectable smirk.

Ty considered himself to be in pretty good shape, so it was a little embarrassing to get caught off guard like that. He chalked it up to poor judgement instead of weak muscles.

"Have a nice day," Jimmy said without waiting for a response.

"No problem. Thanks, you too, Jimmy!" Ty was able to get out a return farewell while Jimmy was midway through his pivot on his way back to his delivery truck.

The mention of his name caused him to give a slightly tilted head nod back at him as he continued into his truck and on to his next delivery.

Ty backed up into his doorway, facing the street, and closed the door slower than he usually would. He picked up and pulled the package against his body, half hugging it and half cradling it. He'd been waiting for this package for a while, having convinced the research team and his friend in Saitama to send him one of the five prototype devices to experiment with and test on their behalf. He promised them test results and performance information on how the device worked and behaved; what kinds of problems he could solve; even a couple of application demonstrations based on it. That would all be invaluable material for marketing the device in the future if it was ever productized. But being honest with himself, he just wanted to get his hands on the new device to play with it and try it out. He studied quantum computing by taking courses and reading articles and papers but possessed no practical experience with a real one.

He used to joke that everything he knew about quantum computing he learned from reading Michael Crichton's book, "Timeline," but that was no longer the case. Based on some online courses and time with early training systems offered by big tech companies developing their own version of a quantum computer, in theory, he was more knowledgeable today. Today's quantum processing units worked nothing like the description in that story.

These educational machines were mostly software simulations of quantum computers and didn't have the true advantage or provide the phenomenon expected from a real quantum computer. Though, even this device was a special hybrid of software translation and conversion, and quantum mechanics, but it was supposed to be more quantum than simulation. Where that distinction was, was what he wanted to find out. While it wasn't a large quantum computer, it would be interesting to see what it could really do; or not do.

Everything about this new machine was different from the current state of the young quantum computing industry, starting with its size, weight, and environmental requirements. Hand delivered without a dolly? While not like the quantum computer as he understood it, there were enough quantum mechanics built into the device to exhibit true quantum phenomenon and quantum productivity, at least based on the earlier version demonstrations he had seen. At least that's what he was able to understand from the researchers in Saitama.

The software and hardware components actually made the device easier to use, giving the system a more traditional, useable interface and feel. Probably the most important part of this device was in the translator, converter, and code compiler, and a modified programming language closely based on python, called quantum translation Python—but everyone at Saitama just called it QtPython. The special collection of libraries and packages used to bridge the conversion from the human readable python-like code to the quantum computer's instruction set in the QPU could be a game changer. He was still debating with himself as to which was more valuable: the hardware or the programming language.

The software part of the quantum computer could be one of the most important developments in this fledgling industry. It could either be the path of the future or a stopgap solution until programmers and developers learned to program quantumly as opposed to the traditional computing style the way it's done on classical computing designs today.

Chapter 2

Ty was not a quantum physicist, but he was a computer scientist and a data scientist. He took the package into his home office located on the first floor of his two-story home. The house was too large for a single person, but he was too busy to downsize into another one. He didn't really love the house, especially after his wife passed away seven years ago, but it met his needs. The downstairs den he used for his home office was large and spacious; perfect for his needs and life at the moment.

He had a main desk for his remote work with a company laptop there and an area in the corner where he set up a large workbench with shelves for tools and various parts storage, complete with test equipment. Aside from his bedroom upstairs, the family room where he watched TV, and the kitchen, he spent the majority of his time at home in this room either working or experimenting with different projects and technologies for fun. Most of the time, the two activities were one in the same.

Now, he had a new toy to work with. This was the closest he'd come to using a real quantum computer. The specifications were moderate to small compared to the current state-of-the-art in quantum computing. While the big technology companies were building and claiming larger quantum computers at 130 and 160 quantum bits, called "qubits," this device employed a modest 36 qubits. Qubits represent either a one or zero, or a one and a zero simultaneously using a quantum mechanics condition called superposition. There were industry rumors of a functioning prototype of two thousand qubits deep in the research labs at IBM. Other companies had marketing claims of machines with sizes of ten thousand qubits, with future plans for one million qubits, but it was unknown what that really entailed.

The primary reason for the increase in the number of qubits was to implement error checking and correction into the QPU pipelines in order to ensure stability of the quantum states, or at least detect the lack of stability. It was all about improving the accuracy, reliability, and prolonging stability; designing in more predictable, useable behavior.

The advantage of this device was that it could operate at room temperature and on house power. The large quantum computers in use today, mostly for experimentation, development, and education, needed to be hosted in large voluminous-sized spaces with the machine sitting in the middle. They were mechanically and environmentally isolated as much as possible to help keep outside interference from breaking down and destabilizing the quantum fields. This, and the fact that components in these machines needed to be cooled to near zero degrees kelvin, employed superconducting materials and used over twenty kilowatts of electrical power.

This new device used a different approach that could propel the fledgling industry forward, out of the labs and into the enterprise. At 36 qubits, could a cluster of these machines work in unison to solve bigger problems at a fraction of the cost in the future? Ty's mind was wandering off into details. He focused on the task laying in front of him.

"Let's see what we have here." Ty placed the package in the middle of his office floor and began opening the box carefully. While the box was somewhat large, it felt well packaged, nothing flopping or sliding around inside, as he would expect.

Good solid packing material, he thought to himself. Leave it to the Japanese to package something well. He pulled out a couple of smaller boxes and packages and set them aside. Probably power cables and other miscellaneous stuff. Once he uncovered the largest part in the box, he noticed something he'd never seen before, an aluminum shell wrapped around the inner large box.

"Whoa! That's different," he said out loud to himself. Stuck on the aluminum foil wrapping was an orange sticker with the word "FRAGILE!" printed on it, along with some kanji characters above the English word which he assumed meant "fragile." He now remembered the same sticker on the outside of the package when it was delivered, but he really didn't pay attention to it since it was delivered by FedEx Custom Critical White

Glove Service and the box didn't look damaged. In fact, it looked freshly packaged.

Now that he was exposing the full sight of the aluminum covered box, he slowed down his handling of the next part of the unpacking. He was now very aware of the warnings. The aluminum shell was thicker and smoother than normal kitchen foil, but thinner than an aluminum soda can. It seemed like there was a good chance he could cut his hand on the edges of it. The "FRAGILE!" sticker was placed right next to a rounded plastic pull tab. About a third of the tab bent up from the flat surface and had the words, "PULL HERE" stuck to it. Above that, the kanji characters probably gave the same instructions.

For some reason, he was feeling more anxious than normal, and he couldn't tell if he was excited or nervous about what he would eventually find inside. During his meetings at the Katoshi Research Facility with the research team, they had shown him pictures of an earlier version of the device during one of the tours of their labs.

The first version, the Mark 1, was a huge machine, similar to all the other quantum machines he had seen pictures of currently in the industry. They only showed him pictures of this device; once they exhausted their research with it, they destroyed it and moved on to the Mark 2 version.

When they showed him that device, it was laying on a workbench hooked up to a bunch of test equipment, all lit up under a large spotlight. The scene seemed like what a robot on an operating table having surgery might look like. It definitely wasn't production ready.

His friend, Yuichu, explained to him that the next version of the device would be more polished and closer to production quality. Though, it would still be a working prototype as they worked their way toward a minimal viable product candidate. Yuichu was having a new type of enclosure designed to house the device's internals better. It wouldn't look like a box of parts.

Ty pulled on the tab, and the aluminum sheet covering that area peeled up with it. He didn't even notice a seam where the edges began to open, but it was opening along a predefined patterned path. He heard a small gasp of air as the sealed covering opened. He kept pulling on the tab slowly, almost waiting for the next instruction to show up and tell him to "STOP PULLING" in both English and Japanese; there wasn't.

Being careful not to cut himself on any part of the edges, he continued to pull the plastic tab beyond the reach of his arm and adjusted his position on the floor to kneel in order to keep pulling. Finally, the aluminum sheet reached a point where he could tell it would stop; it did stop. The entire top of the box was now open, and he could see plastic covering a basic cardboard box inside. He let go of the plastic tab and the peeled aluminum flap quickly curled down toward the box into a nice, neat tube and out of the way.

"Huh, that was cool," he mumbled to himself.

The plastic bag inside used regular packing tape, which he proceeded to peel without any instruction. He moved the excess plastic out of the way to find the cardboard box flaps taped closed with the same kind of tape as the plastic bag. He peeled the tape off and flipped open the four box cover flaps. Inside was a large hunk of injection foam wrapped in plastic sheets. Lifting the whole piece of formed foam carefully, so as to not break it or make a mess, he set the chunk of foam aside to see something he wasn't expecting.

Inside the box, situated diagonally from corner to corner, was a large, matte-black cylinder. There was a glass window-like panel at the mid-point of the cylinder. Lines of thin vents ran along the sides of the clear window along the length of the cylinder, stopping about two inches from the ends.

"Wow! Now that's what an enclosure should look like!" Ty was now freely talking to himself as he continued to release the two-foot or so monolith from its packaging. Next to the cylinder, embedded in the bottom half of the injected foam protection, was a folded frame mount. Ty removed that first and laid it on the floor next to the other part packages he removed earlier. In the space left by the framing part was another sticker in two languages. On the sticker was printed, "NOTE: SET UP THIS STAND FIRST BEFORE EXTRACTING DEVICE," as well as the Japanese equivalent of the English instruction.

"Huh? Okay," he mumbled to himself.

On the other side of the matte-black cylinder was another package of parts with a sheet of paper draped over it. As nice as this equipment was packaged, he could tell it was hand packed, probably by someone at the lab. Looking at the sheet of paper, there was a simple diagram illustrating that the cylinder was to be placed on the mounting frame in an upright position. He pulled the bag of parts out of the injected foam slot and laid it on the floor next to the mounting frame. There were no additional instructions in the cavities left by the parts bag.

Realizing these simple instructions were important, he grabbed the folded mount, looked at it carefully, and examined it from all angles. It looked like a tripod, but with four legs and feet; it was a pentapod stand. It was actually a quadpod with the fifth foot coming down from the bottom center for five points of contact with the ground. The feet on each leg were much larger than he would have expected. There was a lot of rubber material—he assumed it was rubber—between the bottom of the rubber feet and where the feet mounted to the frame. The frame itself wasn't any kind of metal or plastic; it was a hard and rigid, smooth and shiny material. It looked like black glass, but it was lightweight and didn't seem to be as breakable as glass. He had never seen material like it, at least not used for this purpose. Grabbing two of the opposite legs of the frame, he pulled them apart. The frame opened up to its pentapod form with a coarsely threaded stud looking mechanism pointing up from the top center. When fully expanded, the frame clicked and locked in; sturdy and stiff.

He set the pentapod down, making sure all five contact points touched the ground. To his surprise, the pentapod was very stable on the five large feet and five-point contact. Normally, a tripod would be more stable since there would be no way for three points to teeter or wobble.

Changing his mind, he decided to move the mount to a different location instead of in the middle of his office. He placed the mounting pentapod off into a corner location near his desk. He then dragged the box containing the black cylinder closer to the new location of the stand. He located the bottom of the cylinder, finding a large threaded hole at one end of it, and checked that the other end didn't have a hole. Taking a deep breath, he dug his hands under the cylinder and lifted. It was large in circumference at about eight inches.

Again, he overestimated the weight of the device. It was lighter than it looked. He kept looking at it as a big iron pipe or something, but in reality, it was plastic and he lifted it effortlessly. He carefully corrected his grasp and tilted the cylinder upright, then he lifted it up and toward the mount. He tilted the cylinder ever so slightly to help locate and align the hole on the bottom over the threaded protrusion of the stand. Carefully, he slid the cylinder downward onto it. It stopped about halfway down on the stud and situated itself correctly. The device seemed to want to start turning on its own, to self-thread itself onto the mount. He removed his hands from the cylinder and watched as it slowly turned clockwise, each rotation lowering it further, until it finally stopped with a slight bounce back at the end of its journey before settling.

He looked at the picture on the instruction sheet again. It showed a turning symbol above the cylinder and a bubble labeled "Click" in both languages. He assumed he would be the one to thread the device onto the mount.

He placed his hands on the cylinder and carefully continued turning the device in the direction it self-threaded. To his relief, he felt and heard a satisfying click. The device was secure and locked on the mount. The whole process was peculiar but satisfying.

"Now that's some precision machining," he muttered under his breath.

He carefully situated the device so the glass window-looking portal faced his desk and chair. He assumed this part of the device was the front, and if there were any lights or other indicators, they would show up there.

It was a strange looking configuration. The stance of the mount was wide enough that the device was sturdy and stable. It wasn't going to accidentally tip over unless knocked over intentionally. The material of the frame and the feet seemed to provide some kind of nonconductive isolation from the ground. It looked awesome. It stood there like the depiction of an old virus model.

He began opening the miscellaneous packages and boxes to see what was in them. The writing and instructions alternated between English and Japanese to a common panel of quick-start drawings.

"A quick-start installation guide? How is this not a production candidate?" he questioned himself.

Someone once told him, "Perfection is the enemy of good-enough," and this always stuck in his mind.

"If you wait until something is perfect, then you waited too long," was another antidote someone once told him. These seemed appropriate at the moment.

Basically, the quick-start guide instructed him to plug the power adapter into a standard wall outlet, then into the power input port of the device. The power adapter was a large power brick with a standard electrical cable plug on one end and a standard power jack that plugged into the power input located toward the bottom of the upright cylinder. On the power adapter brick were the words, "INDUCTIVE COUPLING POWER SUPPLY."

"I get it! I'll bet this cylinder is completely isolated and shielded from its surroundings!" Ty was still talking to himself, solving the puzzles as they came up.

The power brick was basically like a wireless power adapter. It was similar to how a wireless phone charger worked by using induction to power the device without directly connecting wires.

"So that must mean…" He quickly grabbed another parts package and carefully opened it up. Just as he'd thought, there was a five-meter-long fiber optic cable coiled up in the package. He also found a USB adapter with a fiber optic port on it.

"Even communication with the device is mechanically and electrically isolated!" Ty could feel his heart rate increasing. This meant the device really was more quantum than simulation.

As he stood up to stretch his back and legs and survey everything, he carefully assessed the packaging and packages on the floor. He took both halves of the injection foam material and inspected every inch of it, looking for additional embedded parts, instructions, or notes; nothing. He looked into the boxes and layers of wrappings for more parts; clear. Then he carefully repacked the boxes, starting with the foam injection molds. It was little like putting a Russian nesting doll back together, but not really.

When he was satisfied that all the packaging was nice and neat like when it arrived—albeit a little bit lighter—he picked up the box and walked through his house and into the garage through the kitchen door. There he found an open space near his workbench and carefully placed the box down. He wasn't sure why he was being careful; the box was empty; habit. The only thing left of any value was the aluminum wrapping that he uncurled as best he could and taped down. The material could be useful for another project someday. He kept the packaging in case he needed to ship the device back.

After making sure the box wouldn't fly away, he turned to admire his girlfriend. There, in the left stall of the garage floor, was his silver-gray 2006 BMW M3 ZCP Coupe. He loved looking at this car. It was the start of his car collection, and the only car in his collection. He bought it over seven years ago and initially made a bunch of restorations and some tasteful modifications. It was still mostly stock, aside from a larger set of performance tires, which gave the wide body a very aggressive high-performance stance. There wasn't much to do to the car without over modifying it or changing the engine configuration. The ZCP designation meant it was already configured with the BMW Motorsport team's competition package. With the naturally aspirated engine and his software modifications, the car had 347 horsepower, from a stock slant 6-cylinder engine that could rev up to 8,500 rpm comfortably. This car was special in that it was the last lot manufactured of the E46 M3 platform. Supposedly, all the kinks were worked out, including the factory reinforced subframe, LED lights, and more, just in time to stop making them. There were only a few hundred made to this mid-year specification.

He squeezed out as much performance from the engine through computer software, electronic modifications, and a few hundred pounds of tasteful deletes. He didn't care about gas mileage, he wanted as much power to weight performance as the stock platform could provide—no superchargers or turbochargers. The power to weight ratio of this car was nearly perfect and was by far the most high-performing car he'd ever owned both in speed and handling. He even bypassed the electronic limiter built into the car's computer software that capped its speed at 155 mph—a limit imposed by German automobile makers to help slow cars down on the German autobahn. With his software modifications, and other unnoticeable physical mods, the car was able to reach a speed of 177 mph of the 185 indicated on the speedometer when he had it on a dyno. He'd never driven it on the open road at that speed—the fastest he'd ever had the guts to do was 140 mph out on deserted stretches of highway—but it handled so smoothly.

As a force of habit, he pulled on the driver-side handle and cracked the door open. The window dropped down about an inch, the cabin light came on, the dashboard lit up, the head unit began initializing with the modified start screen he installed while updating the car's software. The SMG transmission pump primed up with a whirling sound that lasted a couple of seconds. He could tell the battery needed to be connected to the charger again as the pump's vibrance slowed down toward the end of the priming cycle. Had it been four weeks since he last took the car out for exercise?

Ty opened the door completely and bent down to push a button. The trunk popped open while he went to one of his storage cabinets and retrieved his battery charger. He lifted the trunk lid and the floor panel up and latched it in place. He lifted the battery cover on the passenger side, exposing the battery compartment and battery. He loved that the car's battery was located in the rear trunk and out of the engine compartment up front for weight distribution. Details. He connected the charger to the battery terminals like he'd done nearly a hundred times before and plugged the charger into the nearby outlet. The low hum of the charger told him that everything was setup and connected correctly, and by tomorrow at around this same time, everything would be topped off and good to sit for another four or five weeks.

In the other parking stall of his garage was his 2017 Tesla Model S plugged into the charger on the wall. Though he worked from home most of the time, he did drive into the office a couple of times a month, so it seemed silly to call this his daily driver, but it was the car he used for everything else but fun. It was bought used from a colleague at work a few years ago at a very good price due to his friend's hasty revenge divorce sale.

He upgraded the batteries to the newer, higher performance battery configuration, and updated it to the latest Tesla software. He made some software modifications and hacks where he could. He even enabled some of the recent Easter Eggs that Elon Musk revealed when participating in the Joe Rogen Experience podcasts, but he hadn't tried them out yet because he didn't plan on racing an electric vehicle. Everyone was always telling him about how fast this car was, but he only ran errands in it and never explored what was fast about it.

Ty left the garage and headed back to his office. The first thing he did was to go over to his desk. He looked at the laptop's screen to see the tests he started a while back—when the delivery guy rang his doorbell—had indeed failed at about test number thirty-four of fifty. There was a listing of red output logs all over the terminal window he opened to do the test run.

"I'm done with this for now."

He closed the MacBook, unplugged the power cord, the USB dongle, and the HDMI cable connected to the external monitor on his desk. Picking up the laptop, he placed it on a shelf on the wall next to his desk. From there he grabbed a different laptop. This one was much larger and bulkier than the sleek new MacBook he just stored away. This was an old personal gaming laptop he named "Tomahawk." Today, he used this laptop to do deep learning and artificial intelligence development work. On occasions, some crypto currency work, but that wasn't his specialty.

Beyond being physically larger than the streamlined MacBook on the outside, it was larger inside as well. Ty made some modifications to the laptop for his needs, like 128 gigabytes of memory and 4 terabytes of solid-state storage. The 8-core processor could be overclocked to 4 GHz, but he normally ran them at the prescribed 3.6 GHz specification. There was a built-in graphic processing unit with over a thousand graphic cores and eight gigabytes of RAM. But his artificial intelligence workhorse was an external graphics processing unit in a separate enclosure that he named "Bazooka." This unit was an old ASUS card with a Nvidia A100 graphics processor that he picked up during a recent data center upgrade. It had over six thousand graphic processors and forty gigabytes of graphics memory. He bought an external enclosure as an empty build kit and modified it to accommodate the powerful graphics card which included liquid cooling. "Graphics card" was what everyone still called them, but no one actually used these types of cards for video viewing or game play. They were used for graphics rendering, crypto-mining, and in his case, the card was used to train and infer artificial intelligence models.

He didn't need to use Bazooka today for this work. He had another bazooka to work with. He paused and thought for a moment. He needed a name for the new device. He didn't want to keep calling it "the device," and calling it a quantum computer wasn't going to work either. It needed a name, a project name, a cool project name.

"MOAB? MOAQ?" Ty talked out loud, letting the words marinate in the air of his office as though there might be someone listening and jumping in yelling, "That's a great name!" Instead, he just shook his head slightly, getting the sound out of his mind. He was playing on the famous acronym, "Mother of All Bombs," MOAB, as "Mother of All Bazookas," or "Mother of All Quantum." Stupid, why did it have to be a weapon again? He thought for a moment, and it struck him—"Q-Tip?"

"Q-Tip!" He practically yelled in excitement. "That sounds cute and cool! Definitely nonthreatening."

He turned and looked at the two-ish-foot-tall cylinder perched on the funky looking pentapod. It looked a little alien, or worse yet, a black squid, or a virus model, but it also looked harmless.

Ty walked toward the device and examined it for the first time up close. Mounted on its pentapod stand, he could see the reason it had a matted black finish was because the external case was 3D printed. The layers of plastic formed tiny grooves that didn't allow for a smooth and polished finish, but a fine, nonreflective satin finish that caused the surface to be matted, unable to reflect light properly or efficiently. The device seemed to absorb light, giving it an almost shadowy appearance that lacked dimension and depth.

"Q-Tip! Project Q-Tip." He lowered himself to one knee and bowed his head slightly, silently.

"I bestow upon thee the title Q-Tip, and all the rights and privileges pertaining thereto…"

He stood up, looking down at the device with a sense of pride. Ty turned back toward his desk, flipped open Tomahawk, and pressed the power button.

Chapter 3

There were two USB devices in the supplemental packaging. The first was the USB adapter with an optical port, the second was a USB flash drive, which he assumed contained the software he would need to set up his laptop. He decided to look at the flash drive first to see if there were more instructions or a "README.md" file stored on the file system.

Browsing to the top-level folder of the file system where the USB flash drive was located on his system, he found what he was looking for.

"Yep! There it is."

There were a few other files at the top-level location and about a dozen subfolders of various names—mostly standard installation software labels—including an installation program. He double-clicked on the "README.md" file. Another window appeared on his main screen with instructions on how to start and what to do.

The list of instructions was moderately long and was a little broken up in what was affectionately called "Jinglish" in the company. Jinglish was either Japanese translated to English language without a review, or sometimes written in English by a Japanese writer. The latter was more understandable. The reverse version of this was "Englanese," which was an English speaker either writing in English for Japanese consumption, translated from English to Japanese, or an English speaker attempting to write some poorly crafted Japanese. Normally, everyone just sent all

English communications to their Japanese colleagues, which was still referred to as "Englanese," as they spoke and understood English a hundred times better than anyone could speak or understand Japanese from his U.S. based company.

Ty started reading the document, which opened with licensing agreements, legalese, and other junk he wasn't interested in reading—basic standard opening form. He scrolled down until he reached "Installation Procedure."

He stood up from his desk and did as the instructions stated. The first thing he needed to do was plug in the device, Q-Tip. The instructions stated that if everything was correctly done, there would be two green LED lights on the brick, located in line with the power cord. Though red lights might show temporarily as well, which was normal. While picking up the other end of the power cord, he noticed the cord itself was stiff and larger than a power jack cord normally would be. It was coiled into a couple of loops and showed no kinks or bends. It looked a like a coax cable.

Ty stood up and went back to his laptop, he scrolled down further and saw a note stating to not bend the coax segment beyond thirty-five degrees.

"Hmmm? Seems like these sorts of warnings should be listed at the top of the file document," he muttered.

He quickly scrolled up to the top of the document and there it was.

"*Please fully read these instructions before taking any action*," He read out loud in a disappointed voice and dropped his head in an animated gesture of defeat. Tricked again! This probably happened more often that he realized, but he started ignoring these types of warnings a while ago. Software installation and setup instructions were pretty straightforward, and most of the time, this type of warning was put there because the author of the document just wanted you to read it, so they felt like they hadn't wasted their time. All the important information was written into the installation scripts, prompting what to do next. This was a prototype, so maybe there were some non-standard, not production ready steps he needed to do.

The first time this happened to him was early in high school, where his teacher passed out a test for the entire class. Before passing it out, she instructed everyone to read the entire test before starting. She placed a test face down on each student's desk. In his defense, everyone in the class failed, as everyone did the same thing.

As soon as the teacher placed the last test on the last desk, she walked to front of the room and said, "You may begin."

Everybody in the class filled in their name at the top righthand corner of the first page, like they had been taught to do. Other students began answering the questions. The problems on the test itself were oddly simple.

It took a few minutes before there was a loud groan from the back of the room, "*Crap!*"

Everyone looked up and back, but only a few students knew who said it. Then another grunt from the front of the class and a pencil slammed on the desk. Confused, the rest of the class began flipping to the last page, and a collective moan filled the room.

The last page had one instruction in the middle page, "*Do not answer any of the problems on this test. Write your name backward on the front of your test and hand this in.*"

That was a fun lesson on following instructions, but apparently, it didn't stick.

Ty sat down and began reading the entire document. He still bypassed the software use agreement, but he read the six pages of instructions completely. When he finished reading it, twice, he scrolled back up to where he left off. There were no other "gotchas."

He went back to Q-Tip, looked behind it, and located the power input port. Then he picked up the power jack end of the power adapter and untied it carefully; it nearly straightened out on its own. He plugged the power plug into an available outlet on a power strip near his desk. He glanced over at the power adapter brick as he pushed the plug in. A red LED came on, on the power side of the brick. He took the power jack and plugged it into the port of the device. Both LEDs were red for a moment on both sides of the brick, they each blinked a couple of times, then both turned green and stayed that way.

Ty went back to his laptop and began typing in the command for starting the software installation process. This step needed to be done before connecting his laptop to Q-Tip. According to the instructions, this step would take about an hour. The entire package included installing a virtual machine and the provided hypervisor to run it, which contained a python-like programming language developed by the research team in Saitama called "quantum translator python"—QtPython. He was surprised they didn't just call it QPython. It seemed like everything in the quantum computing world—actually in quantum studies overall—contained the word "quantum," a "Q," or some variation of this in front of it.

Scott Lang nailed it in the movie "*Ant-Man and the Wasp*" when he asked the quantum physicists guys if all they did was put the word "*quantum*" in front of everything to describe what they did. Then he remembered a QPython already existed in the world for programming mobile phones and tablets.

Everything would be installed from the USB flash drive. For whatever reason, he decided to ensure this was the case and disconnected his Ethernet cable from the back of the laptop and turned off his Wi-Fi while the installation ran. The instructions stated whether there was network access or not, the installation would run to completion. He didn't want anything to vary from the installation procedure with some random, unexpected, automatic update.

Ty started the installation process and watched his monitor for a moment to see that everything was going fine, then he headed upstairs to his bedroom to change. It was late in the day, but there was still a lot of sunlight left outside. He was going for a run around the neighborhood to clear his head and get the blood flowing through his body before he really started digging into getting Q-Tip up and running.

Chapter 4

The train heading north barely left Yokohama station on time. The attendants on platform thirteen had been pushing the crowds into the train cars, trying to get the doors to close, and cutting off additional passengers trying to sneak on board the overcrowded cars.

In a comical, coordinated scene—and in an attempt to keep the train on time—each attendant began to pull people who were keeping the doors from shutting out of the doorway until each door closed. In each case, they rapidly bowed their heads to the passengers in apology with a quick explanation and instructions to catch the next train. Normally, it was a matter of getting the passengers to move from the doorways and into the middle of the cars, but from 6:30 to 9:00 in the morning, Monday through Friday, the trains were already packed with passengers heading north into the most crowded city on Earth, Tokyo.

The Japan Railway express train strained to attain speed on the seventeen-minute segment of track to its next stop, Shinagawa station. Five minutes into the train's cruising speed, an eerie omnipresent sound swelled inside the cars. A tone that sounded like it was coming from inside one's head. One sound, in unison, with no way to determine where it was coming from. Passengers who were reading a book, looking out the window, or sleeping while standing up began looking around, momentarily confused. Those passengers who were on their phones playing games, messaging with friends, or watching whatever was on their Facebook page knew what was happening. Just as the commotion was beginning to gather momentum, the train began aggressively braking and came to a compete stop in the middle of the track that took about twenty-five seconds to complete. Everyone onboard lurched forward during the deceleration, but since the train cars were packed to the point where people could barely move, bodies just leaned on each other. Those passengers who were standing grabbed at safety poles, handrails, handholds, and safety straps hanging from the rails. Those passengers sitting watched as the human mass shifted forward toward the front of the car as though they were watching a demented parade briefly go by in front of them.

***

In February of 2007, the country of Japan launched a nationwide early warning system called the J-Alert. The system was designed to inform the public of different types of threats and emergencies, such as tsunamis, severe weather, flooding, volcanic eruptions, ballistic missile attacks, and earthquakes. The J-Alert system used a satellite that enabled authorities to swiftly broadcast warnings and alerts to local media and the public through a countrywide system of loudspeakers, television, and radio broadcasts, transportation and highway messaging, and internet and cellular communication alarms. It took approximately one second to inform local authorities, and between four to twenty seconds to dispatch the warning message to the public across all communication mediums.

In March of 2019, an upgrade to the J-Alert receivers reduced the entire process down to two seconds. Today, there are over six thousand seismometers throughout the island country of Japan.

The J-Alert system is integrated with the Japan Meteorological Agency's, known as JMA, Earthquake Early Warning system, known as the EEW. There are two EEW systems produced by the JMA, one for the general public and the other for the National Meteorological and Hydrological Services. An EEW is issued to the general public when an earthquake of five or higher on the Japan seismic scale is detected or calculated. An EEW prediction is issued to the National Meteorological and Hydrological Services when an earthquake of three or higher is detected.

The JMA monitors and analyzes the over six thousand seismometers located throughout the island nation. By detecting pressure waves from two or more seismometers, known as a P-Wave, the JMA analyzes and forecasts the approximate location of the epicenter, allowing the JMA to engage the EEW to alert the public in the affected prefectures.

Depending on the severity of the earthquake analysis, trains in the affected prefectures either slow down or stop. Slowing a train down during a moderate earthquake greatly reduces the likelihood of derailing. Stopping a train during a severe earthquake greatly reduces chances of bodily injury to passengers. Normally, trains will continue their journey after a brief system's check throughout the railway system.

The JMA, EEW, and J-Alert systems are used to reduce the chances of chemical spills, to protect patients in hospitals, prevent fire ignition and explosions, shutdown high risk factories like foundries, and warn the public to increase the speed of any evacuations. The systems are also tied to all the nation's transportation systems, especially the many train systems and networks. Within sixty seconds of the detection of a five or higher earthquake, every mobile phone in Japan will sound the alarm tone, and every train will stop where it is, all within minutes of activation.

***

The passengers who were using their phones knew it was an earthquake as the emergency notices and messages popped up, overriding any app they were using. The passengers who were not on their phones took a moment to realize and recognize what the sound meant—it was an earthquake. The omnidirectional sound was coming from everywhere, so no one could locate its source, even on their own phone. As the train came to a stop, everyone waited for the earthquake to come. Depending on where the epicenter of the earthquake was located, the time could be a minute from now, or the area was not in danger.

Without additional warnings, the train began lurching up and down and side to side, tossing a few unlucky standing passengers to the ground, where they could be trampled. The passengers who were lucky enough to be wedged in the middle of the mass of humans were just held there and moshed. The overcrowded areas of the train were too dense for anyone in the center to fall, but on the outer edge of the hunk of passengers, they fell into sitting passenger's laps and crashed onto the windows beyond the seats. The higher speed trains had state-of-the-art magnetic levitation suspension to smooth out the high-speed ride over the system of tracks, but the suspension system couldn't smooth out the violent upheaval of this earthquake. The chaos lasted for over two minutes with no easing of the violence.

This would be a devastating earthquake and the aftershocks would continue for months. If the epicenter was sea floor based, then there would soon be another J-Alert alarm warning for all of the coastal prefectures to prepare for a tsunami.

***

The heart of research and development for Katoshi Corporation was located on the outskirts of the Saitama prefecture northwest of the center of Tokyo. The Katoshi Research Facility, efficiently referred to as KRF, had two main buildings that blended harmoniously with the surrounding hillside of trees and landscape on the large campus in a suburb of Saitama. Conveniently located, it was about a ten-minute walk from the nearest train station. Spring caused the landscape to blossom on the lush campus. The cherry trees were in full bloom, while the other one hundred species of trees and shrubs on the premises were also in different stages of blooming or in full spring foliage. It was a peaceful and tranquil environment for doing advance technology research, a stark contrast from the crowded concrete jungle and noisy streets outside the distant front gate.

The morning status meeting was about halfway done. The large screen monitor was mounted flat on the opposite wall of the outside window. The conference room was larger than the other conference rooms that lined the meeting room hallway, but it was still only large enough to comfortably host ten people, enforced only by having ten chairs situated around the table in the center of the room.

The large screen was currently showing the status of the six prototype Mark 3 machines. Each unit was simply labeled one through six down the first column of the displayed table. The heading stated, "Project Shinsei Mark 3 Status, New Star." The information on the screen indicated what departments they were at, what teams they were assigned to, the name of the team lead, and a brief description of the type of work that was being conducted—except for number five, which simply stated, "special." The status column all stated "in progress" except for the last one, number six, which stated "en route."

Dr. Takashi sat at the center of the conference table facing the screen. The first five units were all assigned to different teams in his department located downstairs. He pointed his shaky, wrinkled finger down at his printout of the presentation in front of him on the table.

"What about number six? Where is that one at?"

He put his hand down and turned to look at Yuichu Norigawa, who was sitting at his laptop and conducting the meeting.

"I wasn't aware there were six units." Dr. Takachi asked confused.

"Ah! Takashi-san, that unit is en route to a development lab in the U.S., ran by Tyson McNally's team. The status is 'en route' because it should have arrived last week. There was a delay in the delivery. We are waiting for confirmation by the shipping service of the delivery and by Ty-san that the unit arrived in working condition." Yuichu slightly bowed toward Dr. Takashi since he thought he was done.

"No, I mean, why is a device going there? I can see that it is going to Tyson McNally and his lab for testing and experimentation," Dr. Takashi tried to clarify.

Dr. Takashi rarely attended researcher status meetings. He had a standing invitation to all the weekly status meetings related to the development of all the projects in his department, but this was only the second time he attended a meeting for this project, so he wasn't up to date on all the details of the technical progress of it.

Chairman Nakatori himself requested status of this project directly from him, so he decided he should attend this morning's status meeting.

Dr. Takashi leaned toward Toshi Narioshi, who was sitting next to him.

"Did I approve this?" He asked loud enough for everyone else to hear around the table.

"Hai! You were briefed in your office about two months ago after the meeting with Ty-san back in February. You agreed the justification was compelling and approved one of the next versions of the Mark 3 prototypes would be assigned to him, while the other four devices would remain here. However, due to the upcoming special meeting next month with Dr. Lancer and his team, and the tight schedule, we assembled a sixth device late to send to Ty-san using the remaining spare parts from the last forging." Toshi slightly bowed in respect when he was finished.

It was always irritating having to remind the old man of his previous decisions.

Dr. Ashito Takashi was a legend at Katoshi Corporation, but that was many, many years ago. Dr. Takashi was continually promoted out of appreciation and respect for his earlier contributions. Eventually, he was promoted to the general manager of the company's top research and development organization, where he had been in charge for the past fifteen years. The department ran well because of all the dedicated and passionate researchers, but Dr. Takashi received all of the credit. He rarely understood the ins and outs of the operation, yet no one had the courage to have him replaced. It was hoped, long ago, he would get bored and retire to great fanfare and benefits, but he didn't seem to have anything else he would rather sleep through. Hope was never a good strategy.

Dr. Takashi gave a slight groan. "I do not recall approving this action. It is not our procedure to send off any early prototype to our American counterparts. I know Ty-san is a very capable researcher. Our department has worked well with his team in the past on other projects, but not with something this early in our process."

"Takashi-san, this batch of devices are still in the prototype phase and in experimental condition. While these are not production quality, they are high quality. We wanted to see if there is a market for them in North America and Europe. Ty-san has deep relationships and connections in both regions, so we only needed to send one unit outside of our department. We will also be able to use the collateral he develops in our markets as well, here in Japan. Besides, we still have the full allocation of devices for our purposes, with one extra one built for this specific need," Yuichu explained again.

Yuichu had the idea of building a sixth unit out of spare parts in order to send it to his friend in the U.S. He almost didn't list it in the status report because of how confusing it would be for Dr. Takashi.

Tyson McNally was well respected within the research and development divisions of Katoshi Corporation, especially here at KRF. He had delivered valuable insight and additional features to prior projects. He was also a good global ambassador of the research teams.

"All of the devices will be collected and destroyed once testing is done, and we move on to the next versions. We are scheduled for a six-to-nine-month window of testing, experimentation, and development activities with the Mark 3 prototypes. Toward the end of this activity window, we should have a batch of Mark 4 units built and ready to be tested with roughly the same experimentation window. We should have double the production of these next units to help develop our manufacturing processes. If everything goes well, the Mark 5 design will be our first production ready candidate in about sixteen to twenty months and ready for manufacturing on a limited scale."

Yuichu continued, "With Ty-san's help, we believe our schedule can be improved by twenty percent, barring any unplanned setbacks." Yuichu advanced the presentation to a slide displaying the current planned schedule that showed side-by-side timelines with and without Tyson McNally's help.

"It hasn't been determined yet, but at the end of the Mark 3 development phase, either a team will visit Ty-san's facility, or he will visit here with us for a briefing on his findings. This will be a very insightful meeting, and I hope you will be able to attend." Yuichu explained to Dr. Takashi.

"If Ty-san can develop demonstration applications with this device that can prove the existence and advantage of quantum productivity and quantum speedup in a commercial practice, then it would be invaluable information going forward," Yuichu continued.

"But are we not doing the same thing here?" Dr. Takashi asked, frustrated.

"Hai! We need all the innovative thinking we can quietly access for this project. That special team with the special requirements are not open to sharing their progress as you are aware. They only ask for help, and provide no insight in return, so it has the same effect as being short one team and one unit. Plus, they spend more time in the U.S. than here with us." Yuichu was getting tired of explaining the situation, again.

This was the same justification he'd used before with the old man, but this was a new justification, again, for the moment.

"Quantum computing is a very new field and needs to be approached from a different mindset. Most of the researchers and developers working on this project are physicists, engineers, and computer scientists. Ty-san is a computer scientist and a data scientist, but he has a keen mind when it comes to proving customer value. He has a global following on social media and is a respected influencer and thought leader for the company. When the time comes for our announcement, he will be one of our key spokespersons outside of Japan. He has a way of always making us look good to the rest of the world." Yuichu finished with approving nods from around the table.

"Let's continue with the mee—"

The tone had a faint sound, like a delayed audio shadow. The phone sitting on the conference room table was easily heard and located, but all the other phones were stored in jackets hanging up near the door or in shirt pockets. Its sounds were muffled, but still in unison.

"It's an earthquake!" Toshi stood up and yelled.

The earthquake hadn't arrived yet, but in the past, when the J-Alerts came, the earthquake was a minute or less away and meant it was going to be severe.

Everyone in the meeting room looked at each other for a few seconds, then Yuichu spoke up, "We are on the fifth floor and not close enough to the staircase to evacuate. We should all get under the table."

The five of them got on their hands and knees and began crawling. Toshi helped Dr. Takashi down to the floor and under the large conference table. There they would wait out the oncoming earthquake.

A few seconds later, a low rumble could be heard, rapidly getting louder. The roar now had sharp clashes of glass and metal crashing into each other with the sounds of alarms and sirens mixed in, and still the rumble approached. Simultaneously, the lights went out and the room violently shook. It wasn't just the conference room; the entire building was bucking ferociously.

The building was over sixty years old, built to the highest standards of construction, and designed to withstand earthquakes. All buildings in Japan were built this way and newer buildings incorporated newer earthquake resistance techniques, but this was different. It wasn't just the building, the ground the Katoshi Research building was built on was on a hillside overlooking the Arakawa River. While the building was winning the battle with the earthquake's attempts to destroy it, straining to withstand the fierce shaking, the ground supporting the building was not holding up its end of the fight. Up and down the hillside, above the building, and down toward the river, the ground was cracking—breaking.

After what felt like an hour of the powerful rolling and tumbling, the shaking slowly stopped until the ground was calm again. The conference room was a mess. The entire ceiling came down, including lights hanging by their wires. Ceiling panels fell on the conference table and floor, exposing the subceiling and the network of cables, pipes, and ducting. The windows were broken. The large, wall mounted TV monitor crashed to the floor, and dust filled the air. The emergency lighting system kicked on as soon as the lights went out, but since the emergency lights were still on, that meant electrical power to this part of the building was out—more likely the entire building was dead. Moaning, coughing, and voices could be heard in the hallway outside. The public sirens were starting to fade outside, but car alarms were still screaming, which were louder now that the windows were blown out.

Toshi checked on Dr. Takashi's condition. The others tried looking at each other, finally removing their hands from their heads and looking up from the floor.

Living in Japan meant you lived with earthquakes. Japan leads the world in construction practices and architectures to withstand earthquakes.

Dr. Takashi was seventy-six years old and had lived in Japan his entire life, but he had never experienced a more furious earthquake. This was going to set records, and there was going to be a lot of damage.

The group began crawling out from under the sturdy conference table and stood up. Toshi helped Dr. Takashi up to his feet. Everyone began patting themselves off, causing more dust to fly from their bodies and filling the air around them. They began coughing again.

"How is everyone? Anyone hurt?" Yuichu looked around at everyone.

Heads nodded, letting him know they were alright and uninjured. Everyone was shaken up and still collecting their wits, but no one looked dead.

He looked at Dr. Takashi and put his hands on his shoulders, "Takashi-san, are you okay? Can you walk?"

Dr. Takashi looked up at Yuichu and nodded as dust swirled around him from his hair.

"Hai. I am good." He was beginning to shake off the shock.

Yuichu walked toward the meeting room door and opened it slowly, looking up at the door frame as he pulled. The door needed extra force to free itself from the frame.

"Structural damage?" Yuichu mumbled to himself. "It can't be."

Then he shook that thought out of his head. The interior offices and meeting rooms were not part of the building's support structure, these were just partitioned walls and not load-bearing, they were just out of position.

Yuichu stuck his head out of the door and saw similar damage as was in the meeting room. Light fixtures were dangling from the ceiling, ceiling panels had fallen to the ground, there was exposed subceiling, emergency lights were on, and dust filled the air. He had never seen this much damage to this building after an earthquake—or to any building.

Some people were wandering the hallway, moaning, bleeding, or both. There were shouts for help in the distance. More meeting room doors began to open, and more heads started popping out to look up and down the main hallway. It looked promising. Everyone must have sheltered under the meeting room tables for protection. For the most part, people were moving and walking, dodging the light fixtures dangling from the ceiling by their wires. The emergency lighting system was bright and helpful. EXIT signs were lit up brightly.

Yuichu stepped back into the room and looked at everyone. "Can you all walk?"

The group already started toward the door before he stepped back in.

"We should evacuate the building as soon as possible. From here, it doesn't look dangerous, but I have never seen this much damage before. I think we can get to the nearest staircase and head down," Yuichu informed the group.

Heads all nodded in agreement to a cloud of dust.

Yuichu pulled the door completely open, forcing it past the debris on the floor, which helped move one of the hanging lights out of the way of the opening. They started walking in single file toward one of the doorways with an EXIT sign lit up; Yuichu led them. Even though the electricity was dead, they avoided touching anything electrical hanging down from the ceiling. The team began helping others as they passed by other rooms. Everyone appeared to be able to walk, though some had blood on their heads or clothing.

"We should hurry and evacuate the building. We can tend to your wounds outside. Does anyone need help walking?" they were telling everyone they encountered.

Only a couple of people needed help walking, and after several steps, they were able to proceed on their own with urgency.

Yuichu realized this was taking too long; aftershocks were guaranteed to follow.

He had never been in an earthquake like this. He was in this very building during many large earthquakes, including the Great Tohoku Earthquake in 2011, and the building always survived and endured. They needed to get moving.

"Everyone!" Yuichu shouted, looking back at the long line of people following him. "We need to hurry and evacuate this building now! I don't think it's safe to be in here, and we have a long way to go."

He could see the despair in their faces, but everyone seemed to understand and started walking faster.

Yuichu decided to get as many people outside as he could, immediately. He felt energized and strong. He would come back into the building with others who were in good shape in order to help others, but he wanted to get outside to assess the situation. He could also get emergency personnel back into the building with him to lead rescue efforts. The campus had its own fire station and emergency team on the premises, so they were lucky in that the response time should be minimal—assuming everything was fine outside. There was another large building near this one, and three smaller buildings on the campus, but this was the main building.

Nothing prepared them for the devastation they were seeing. In one of the open work areas, everything was knocked over and covered with ceiling debris and broken glass. Filing cabinets, printers, copiers, cubicles, and computers were all unrecognizable. Bookshelves were tipped over, spilling their contents all over the floor.

"Good, no one's here," Yuichu muttered to himself.

They must have all escaped before them. The staircase was just on the other side of the open door on the right-side wall.

"It looks like everyone here has already left. Come, this way!" He rallied everyone to follow him.

They all made their way to the door. They could hear many voices and steps echoing from the staircase. The staircase was a safe place to be since the stairwells were part of the reenforced building infrastructure design to help with its strength.

As they started toward the stairwell door, they all heard the oncoming rumbling.

"Aftershocks? Already?" someone yelled, and they all seemed to try to brace themselves against the wall in anticipation of the oncoming tremors.

This was different. The building was not shaking, but it felt like it was moving. Sliding. Dropping.

Yuichu looked back at everyone, "Run! Now!"

He started grabbing people by their shirts, arms, clothes, whatever and whoever he could grab, and started throwing people into the stairwell. As people started running past him, he pushed them forward into the doorway. "Hurry!"

He paused for a moment. He could feel the weird motion speeding up. He looked down at the floor beneath him. It was undulating, but not breaking. The building was completely intact, but it was moving.

Through a distant blown out window, Yuichu understood what was happening; the scene in the glassless frame was panning across the opening. The entire building, foundation and all, was sliding down the hill. No, the building wasn't sliding down, the earth was sliding downward. The earthquake caused an enormous landslide that was taking the whole building down toward the river.

Then he felt it. The floor and the building began to tilt down toward the direction it was sliding.

Yuichu fell to his knees where he stood. He put his head down and stooped over onto his hands, the floor still heaving up and down. Now it also began to heave upward on one side. He could hear screaming and crying, and the rumbling of concrete and steel from everywhere. Then nothing.

***

The seven-story building, with three sub floors, uprooted like the surrounding trees, was going to flip end over end. The building was built before the development of seismic isolation, dampening and energy absorption techniques, so it was built with brute force strength. The building was so strong that it wasn't going to collapse in an earthquake, it was going to tip over and tumble as a whole into the Arakawa River from a landslide.

That was what the surrounding town's observers thought as they watched the building beginning to tip. It was a disorienting sight, still trying to clear the shock from the powerful earthquake out of their heads, then trying to focus on the spectacle off in the distance. That building was going to tip over, but it would not stay together long enough to tumble end over end. As soon as it tilted to a critical angle, the entire structure collapsed like it was built with playing cards, toppling and crumbling into a single solid hunk of concrete, rebar, steel, office equipment, and flesh. The landslide continued downward to the lowest point it could seek. The structure and its ten slabs of flooring starting to slide apart, pulverizing everything in its path and disintegrating itself.

The river below was only two hundred meters away, but the landslide and the demolished building seemed like it took forever to reach the lowest point. Earth, trees, cherry blossoms, automobiles, roads, and building overran the riverbank and disrupted the flow of the water. The core movement of the landslide finally stopped amid a cloud of dust.

Water began to build up and find alternate ways through or around the blockage, causing additional flooding to the surrounding areas. The flowing water attempted to wash away dirt, debris, and anything else in its quest to find the path of least resistance to continue its journey to the ocean.

The entire building and its contents were destroyed, leaving a strange hole in the landscape where it once stood watch over the surrounding suburb for over sixty years. Like something came and cropped the landmark out of the scene.

Chapter 5

Tyson had been running for about thirty minutes and was approaching the small minimart and gas station in his neighborhood. He worked up a good sweat and was catching his breath before heading in. He glanced up at the lottery display boards above the store's doors to see what the current jackpots were at. Powerball was at a record high of $3.743 billion and growing, and the Mega Millions jackpot was also high at $2.392 billion, but not yet at a new record.

The Mega Millions record was $3.1 billion set nearly three years ago. That jackpot was split by six tickets. Back then, the lottery display boards couldn't handle the billion-dollar numbers, instead it used to show "999" for all amounts over one billion dollars. Billion-dollar jackpots were more frequent since both the Powerball and Mega Millions lotteries went to a three draws a week format a few years ago; enough that the lottery commissions needed to address the board displays, so they replaced them. They added an additional digit, going from three digits to four, and added a decimal point.

This also provided a more accurate jackpot total at all the lottery retailers. The Powerball jackpot was a new world record, and it wasn't done growing, so it was unknown what new high it would reach by the time it was finally won. Personally, he didn't think they would ever need a fifth digit on the display boards.

He wiped the sweat from his face before entering the store. Pulling out his phone, he fished around for his last Powerball lottery ticket located in the attached storage pocket on the back. He ignored his message notifications for now, it was getting late. Unfolding the ticket, he placed the barcode under the lottery scanner.

"Winner! $4! Please see the clerk," showed on the device's display.

He knew this was a four-dollar winning ticket, he already looked it up, but it was a habit of his to scan tickets at the store just in case he missed something or there was a promotion of some kind—though it never happened to him. He'd always hoped, someday, they would give a consolation prize for not having a single number picked on a ten-ticket slip. The odds of not picking a single number had to be just as unlikely as picking a jackpot winner.

He always felt that if he ever won the jackpot, he would feel something: intuition, a tingling, a sense of divine joyfulness, or that something abnormal happened. He knew it was bullshit, but it made him feel better about wasting money like this. A tax on the statistically challenged was what it was called. However, he had been using lottery numbers in his work as a source of excellent random numbers, or as an excuse to play the lottery professionally, though the numbers were an excellent source of random numbers.

He always played the lottery more when things weren't feeling right at work, which meant he had been playing a lot recently. He also believed the motto, "You can't win if you don't play." He wasn't stupid. He knew the odds of winning the jackpot, but he also felt someone had to win at some point. He chuckled at himself every time he saw an ad saying, "Chances of winning are 1 in 25." In his mind, winning two dollars was not winning, but the marketing and messaging took a little of the sting out of playing.

He spent a lot of time and energy a while back analyzing lottery numbers and techniques for predicting them or not predicting them. A lot of statistical analysis overlapped his work in machine learning, and it felt good to stretch out some old, unused mathematical passions. He even used some of his predictions of the game to get more information and tune his machine learning models, and of course, try and win the jackpot—any jackpot. What a joke. You couldn't predict a real random number sequence. No, discernable patterns existed that could be processed with today's computing capabilities.

People have been trying since the lottery began. In 1992, Stefan Mandel won twenty-seven million dollars in the Virginia jackpot by buying blocks of lottery tickets in a tight range of numbers. It cost him thousands of dollars, but it paid off. Through mathematics and statistics, Stefan Mandel won fourteen jackpots. It was a little like the roulette wheel or baccarat games in casinos, where the house displayed the last twenty numbers to show the "trends" of the game, or at least let people believe there was a trend to be observed. The lottery commissions continued to evolve the game's parameters to make the odds impossible to predict.

The predictions Ty made were just as random as the drawing itself. After doing some analysis on his own calculated predictions, compared to the numbers provided using the Quick-Picks options, showed that the Quick-Picks picks had a slight edge over his calculated picks. This work cost him a lot of cash, but he got to play the lottery and call it work, and he learned a lot about the lottery system and random number theory. He still used the outcome from this work as workloads to test new systems for performance and stress testing. That was some of what he was doing before Q-Tip arrived.

Things weren't going as planned at work, again. Especially this quarter, and rumors of big cuts were making the rounds again, this time with a lot more anxiety in colleague's voices. With new changes up in the executive suite, including yet another new CEO, again, changes were coming down the line. This division of Katoshi Corporation, Katoshi Systems Services—"KiSS," as everyone was fond of saying—wasn't performing well this year, again. Which meant more stupid outside changes would fix the problem. What he couldn't understand—what nobody understood—was why bringing in failed executives from other failed companies was a good idea. It had been happening this way his entire career. He facetiously referred to it as "an executive garage sale," picking up another company's failed and discarded executives.

He always felt the best people to fix a broken ship were with the people who knew how the ship worked and what was wrong with it. The employees who worked with the company's problems daily knew what to fix. Developing leaders and rummaging for leaders were two very different approaches. One was inspiring and built loyalty, the other just felt sleazy and fake.

Poaching was a different tactic—a better tactic. He didn't mind attracting real successful talent to lead a company. Persuading successful leaders from successful companies they built up or fixed always felt like, "If they came "here," they must see great potential," as opposed to an "I'll take anything" hire.

The "I'll take anything" type of hires were like a cancer in a company. Once one got in, they started getting rid of good employees to make room for their unqualified cronies. It wasn't a horrible thing when the churn happened at the top executive levels, but when it bled down into the daily operational staff, it became obvious these weren't business decisions.

Ty always felt his position in the company was safe, and his contributions were what propelled the company through rough patches many times over during his career there. New products, new markets, leading everyone to the next big thing, vision—all based on the work he and his small team provided. However, he couldn't get over the feeling something was brewing. When a new CEO wanted to pivot, they pivoted hard and in their own image.

Plus, his new boss from the last executive garage sale hadn't held a staff meeting in a couple of months and hadn't communicated with him for much longer than that. He was fine with it; those staff meetings were short and pointless. Nobody on the call would get to say anything, just Rick relaying the corporate message of the month, then done. It was better for him, he had always been self-directed, and he had a long list of projects for his team, and himself, to do. They were always busy, and he was always receiving requests to talk about the next big thing his team was working on.

This guy only cared about promoting his brand on social media. Rick didn't know anything and spewed the same technical buzzword garbage over and over. It was his confident delivery that made Ty sick to his stomach when Rick talked. If the guy had pointy hair, he'd be the manager in the Dilbert cartoon strip. But this recent lack of communication was bugging Ty. It seemed ominous. Could an incompetent boss ruin someone's reputation; career?

Ty tried to clear his head of meandering troublesome thoughts and focused back on reality and the task at hand. He walked up to the counter.

"What's up Drew?" Ty placed his ticket on the counter to parlay his huge winnings in the next lottery drawing.

"Hey, Ty. Good, things are good. How about you?" Drew replied.

"Meh, I could complain, but I don't think it would help anything."

He looked around the store, there were only two other people inside, both looking at beverages in the refrigerator. He chuckled.

"Besides, you look too busy to listen. I'll save it for the bartender."

Drew smiled back; thankful he wasn't going to have to listen to someone else's problems.

"This is a four-dollar ticket. Could you exchange it into two Powerball tickets? And give me another ten Powerball tickets for tonight." He placed a twenty-dollar bill next to the four-dollar lottery ticket on the counter and slid it toward Drew.

"It's pretty light in here for these large jackpots. What's up with that?" Ty tried chatting it up with Drew.

Normally, with one jackpot of this amount, there would be a line of people outside waiting to buy tickets. This was two games with multi-billion-dollar jackpot amounts.

"It just got quiet a few minutes before you showed up. The crowds come in spurts. If you hang around for another ten minutes, this place will be packed."

"Ha! Good timing on my part then."

Drew picked up the money and the ticket, looked at the ticket, put the twenty-dollar bill on the register, and placed a brass paper weight on it. He side-stepped to the lottery machine and inserted the ticket into the slot. A second later, a slip of paper slid out. Drew grabbed both the winning lottery ticket and the slip, then grabbed a stapler and stapled the two pieces of paper together. He started tapping on the touch screen and two tickets came out of the slot, one longer than the other. Grabbing everything, he side-stepped back to the counter, handing the two tickets to Ty. He pressed a couple of buttons on the cash register and inserted the twenty-dollar bill into the money tray, then lifted the tray and tossed the stapled ticket under the drawer.

"Good luck, Ty. Have a nice day." Drew completed the transaction efficiently.

"Thanks, Drew. See you later."

Ty looked down at the tickets as he started to walk out of the store. He checked that the last set of numbers started with the letter "J" for ten tickets. The other ticket just had two lines of numbers. He also scanned the ticket and the numbers, noticing there were three 19's in the Powerball column, and there seemed to be several 13's on both tickets. This looked interesting. Random number patterns, no such thing, but it intrigued him. Then he stuffed them into the pocket on the back of his phone.

"Hey, Ty? Don't you work for a Japanese company?"

Ty stopped and looked back a Drew.

"What? Why? Yeah." Ty stuttered as he was caught off guard by the strange question.

They had extended talks a few times in the past, and one time, Drew asked about the Katoshi company logo on a shirt he was wearing.

"Haven't you seen the news?" Drew was now pointing up at one of the two TV monitors mounted in the upper corner behind the counter. "It's on every channel."

Ty looked up at the ceiling mounted monitors to see chaos and shaky videos. The volume on the televisions were turned all the way down, but the closed captioning was on. The headline on the news channels simply stated, "Powerful Earthquake Strikes Near Tokyo, Japan!"

Ty's jaw dropped. He quickly grabbed his phone out of his pocket and unlocked it with his face; it was blowing up.

"Holy shit! I gotta go, man!"

He glanced over at Drew, turned, and bolted out of the store. He immediately started running, taking the most direct path home, and reached his front door in fifteen minutes. He unlocked the door and headed straight to his office. He grabbed his work laptop from the shelf, quickly glancing at the installation process running on his desk: "Completed!" Then he looked at the device in the corner.

"I'll get back to you later."

He headed to the family room and powered on his large screen TV and turned it to one of the news channels, then turned up the volume.

***

News of the earthquake that hit Japan spread around the world almost instantaneously through news outlets and social media, though most of the news media was just replaying on the spot social media feeds and adding their comments and analysis. At this point in the news cycle, there was only news and information to report; opinions and analysis would come in the next few days. Everyone was trying to get information about which prefectures were hit the hardest. The JMA was providing information and graphics showing the location of the epicenter of the earthquake. There was no real strategy yet as to how the news outlets were covering the disaster other than playing videos uploaded from social media users. It was difficult for loved ones, friends, and colleagues to get any useful information. Live information was mostly in Japanese, and it took time for good translations to be provided. The video feeds from personal camera phones were coming in slowly because much of the telecommunication infrastructure in the hardest hit areas were offline.

A couple of large buildings collapsed, including a high-rise—buildings that were built to sustain severe earthquakes. This earthquake was a 9.8, the worst in recorded history. Business's marketing departments with global divisions in other parts of the world were sending updates to employees and the media as best as they could. This disaster could cost a trillion dollars or more and would take years to clean up and rebuild from just from watching this footage.

Ty watched his TV screen while catching up on text messages on his phone, emails on his corporate laptop, and news feeds in his internet browser while sitting on his couch in the family room. Family room? What kind of single person had a family room? Besides a widower. He shook his head, no time for self-pity or reflection. He had friends and colleagues in Japan. Hell, corporate headquarters, the company mother ship, was in Japan. He knew the news channels weren't really going to report on the status of corporate businesses, but if people were dead or dying, they should report something. Even the business channels for the news outlets were broadcasting the main news feed. He browsed to the company website to find the same condolences every corporation was sending out. Then he navigated to the main Katoshi website. There he found a link to local information on corporate status and the different businesses Katoshi ran.

"The Katoshi Research Facility in Saitama!" he clicked on the linked and gasped. "Oh My God! The main building was destroyed?"

The building was destroyed in a landslide shortly after the main earthquake stopped. It was currently estimated that 150 employees died as the building slid down the hillside into the Arakawa River. The building began leaning further than he'd ever seen a building lean, then it collapsed on its way down the hillside halfway before reaching the river. Only a few survivors who were in the main first floor lobby or near other first floor exits were able to escape the building during the earthquake, or shortly before the building buckled.

Ty reread the announcement and watched the shaky video of the building beginning its death slide several times. Screaming filled the audio, with a faint thunder of concrete, steel, earth, and trees rumbling in the distance.

He saw that the time in Japan was approaching noon. It was Thursday in Japan and Wednesday in the Unites States. The earthquake struck just a few hours ago, at about nine in the morning, which meant the research campus was near full occupancy. At that time of the morning, status meetings were kicking off or halfway done, starting the long day. All the researchers and developers worked on the upper floors. The first two floors were for guests and visitors with nicer meeting rooms and their executive briefing center. No one expected an earthquake to knock down this building, but a landslide? He wondered if there were any VIPs visiting. He feared the worst for his friends who worked there. Yuichu always arrived to work earlier than the others and usually worked late.

He was just visiting that very building two months ago, meeting with Yuichu and Dr. Takashi to discuss testing and development plans for their new quantum computer. Narioshi-san was there too, taking notes. They were meeting in Dr. Takashi's office on the fifth floor. He was the general manager of KRF, who agreed to send him one of the Mark 3 prototypes to get a head start on looking for ways to productize the new machines; the one now sitting in his office waiting to have its installation procedure completed.

"In a fifth-floor office. I would have never made it out of the building," he thought out loud.

He continued to click on links relating to company news and information about the earthquake, damages, destruction, and statements from company executives. As far as he could figure out, the only company structure destroyed was the main KRF building. There was other minor damage to other facilities, but these could be repaired. Other employee losses were unknown. The majority of the human loss for the company was at this research campus.

Other parts of Japan suffered major damage as well. Other companies also suffered property damage. There was one other tall high-rise building that collapsed, and by luck, didn't cause damage to other surrounding structures. These incidents were based on a broad assessment of damage. There were other reports coming in of a railroad bridge that collapsed, structure fires were everywhere, roads and highways damaged and some small homes in many of the residential areas were either on fire or had some type of damage.

Ty continued to watch the news, flipping channels between news outlets looking for the most up-to-date information. He was responding to text messages from colleagues and friends, even customers were sending condolences and looking for more information. No messages from his boss. He quickly started texting his boss to see if there was any company information or what he had heard; no response. Then he called him and left a voicemail; like that would ever be heard.

Then, there it was, on his television, video of the Katoshi Research Facility building sliding, tilting, and collapsing down the hillside, the earth and trees sweeping it away. The images were larger on the large screen; now it looked much worse. One of the news channels, he didn't know which one he was watching, gained access to the footage and was talking about the building and the company. They didn't announce the casualties or the function of the building, but they were talking about the landslide triggered there and in other areas in Japan. This was by far the worst damage caused by any of the half-dozen landslides triggered by the record earthquake.

Yuichu was a close friend of his. They had known each other and worked together for nearly ten years. Ty knew his family and attended a couple of birthday parties for each of his two girls when he visited Japan. During longer trips, when he needed to stay the weekend in Japan, Yuichu and his family would take him out to lunch or dinner to help him pass the time. He enjoyed that.

During Yuichu's trips to the U.S., they would meet and discuss what was being worked on and where they could collaborate together. They would plan and attend customer meetings together in Japan and the U.S., and Yuichu even attended his wife's funeral.

It wasn't like him to cry, but he could feel his throat tightening up, his nose was beginning to burn and run, and his eyes were swollen. He knew his friend was working today, and he would be in meetings on one of the top floors. Ty was supposed to confirm the device finally arrived after missing the original delivery date.

Grabbing his phone, he sent a text to his friend. After several minutes, there was no response. Then he gave his friend a call—voicemail. This disaster was going to cost a lot more than dollars.

Chapter 6

In the two weeks following the earthquake, Katoshi Corporation closed operations for a few days worldwide to mourn the loss of fellow colleagues and evaluate the damages at other facilities. Other large corporations were doing the same thing. All businesses in Tokyo and surrounding prefectures were closed until further instruction. This helped in a lot of ways by easing the stress to the power grid and other crippled utilities while inspections were made. Trains that could operate did so on a limited schedule, mainly for emergency personnel and essential workers, and it allowed citizens to assess their own property, neighborhoods, and families. Grocery stores and essential retailers, like hardware and supply stores, were given the option to open as soon as their buildings were inspected and certified safe in the most damaged areas—if they had enough employees able to report in for work.

Confirmed casualties were currently at 3,212 and rising. Estimates predicted the number would continue to rise as rescue crews and inspectors worked their way through the destruction. An accurate count of how many perished could still take weeks to arrive at a final tally. The one blessing was that the earthquake was land based and didn't trigger a tsunami. The epicenter was located in the mountains north of the Ibaraki prefecture, nearly seventy miles northwest of central Tokyo, and officially registered as a magnitude 10.0, which was revised up from the initial 9.8, and lasted for almost three minutes. The earthquake could be felt at the Korean peninsula, the shores of mainland China, in Taiwan, and in the Philippines. Another blessing, but curious behavior, was the relatively few and much less severe aftershocks following the main earthquake. This oddity greatly helped rescue efforts and cleanup operations.

All the infrastructure and buildings needed to be inspected for structural integrity and safety before they could be cleared for entry and use. The Japanese government was very well equipped and manned for these situations. The most obviously damaged buildings were inspected first. Emergency and essential facilities like hospitals, the train systems, bridges, roads, and critical utilities and services had the highest priority. Next were the buildings of essential businesses.

Prime Minister Handoka Nakanishi declared a state of emergency for all of mainland Japan and some of the surrounding islands. He also deployed the Japanese Armed Forces to maintain civil order and help emergency personnel and essential workers.

International help and financial aid poured in from around the world. U.S. Navy ships in the area arrived within a week of the earthquake, including an aircraft carrier; faster ships arrived in a couple of days, docking at different ports throughout Tokyo Bay to provide supplies, equipment, manpower, and electrical power where needed. Most of the U.S. military bases throughout Japan that were undamaged deployed personnel, equipment, and supplies to provide relief. The effort was similar to Operation Tomodachi following the Great Tohoku Earthquake and Tsunami in 2011. The U.S. formally named this humanitarian effort Operation Mikata.

Similar military help was provided by nearby countries, Australia, New Zealand, South Korea, and Taiwan. China, in a surprise humanitarian gesture, sent an enormous amount of equipment and supplies. European countries were too far away to send in navy ships in a timely manner, but they did fly in medical and emergency personnel and supplies to help rescue crews and staff hospitals.

***

The assessment, clean-up, and clearing of roadways, railways, and subways took weeks to get into a state of reasonable useability. Businesses started opening up slowly. The further away from the epicenter and in the least damaged areas, life returned to some state of normalcy sooner. Large businesses began to open and conduct business where they could. Factories began to manufacture products; stores and services were all coming back to life. Employees were going back to work after addressing their needs at home.

Business hours and work weeks were shifted and staggered. Through coordination with Japan's Ministry of Economy, Trade, and Industry, major companies that employed the most people shifted workdays and hours to lower and level the stress on utilities, services, power, and infrastructure. Heated toilet seats were turned off everywhere. Escalators were powered off at all train stations and subways. The train systems were rescheduled to balance out the load and match the modified work schedule shifts. These measures greatly limited wasted capacity and efficiently utilized resources overall.

All of Katoshi Corporation's business units in Japan were assigned the work week schedule of Wednesday through Sunday for the next six weeks. Since air conditioning was turned off in office buildings, employees were allowed to dress more comfortably while reporting into the office. Factory workers still needed to dress safely for their work.

Throughout the rest of the world, Japanese businesses were back at work the following Monday after the earthquake struck. These businesses managed their inventory exported from Japan. Technology businesses, especially software and consultancy divisions, were at full operations.

***

Katoshi Systems Services was a United States based company that operated worldwide, except in Japan, and one of the largest divisions by revenue and employee headcount in Katoshi Corporation family of companies. The product portfolio had an even blend of software and product development, consulting and services, cloud technologies, advance analytic solutions, and information technology infrastructure hardware. The hardware portion of their product portfolio was only 25 percent of their business, but it laid the foundation for most of the solutions they provided based on it, and it all came from Japan.

Katoshi Systems Services had four consecutive years of economic downturn with double-digit revenue decline forecasted again that year. The company would still see revenues of six billion dollars at the end of the year, but growth was currently not in their future with next year looking bad as well. Lack of an executable strategy and a believable vision had forced the floundering division to change executive management five times in the past four years, including five chief executive officers.

Each time, a new entourage of executives, with a hundred years of combined industry experience at other failed companies, would come in and change the direction of the company. There would be a small acquisition or two to demonstrate their commitment to the new direction and vision. After bonuses were paid out, they would either leave or be restructured out because of poor company revenue performance, milking the company of guaranteed money for overall poor performance, but overachieving on assigned key performance objectives; basically, being awarded bonus money for failing.

There was an ongoing joke in the company that you could set your calendar for the beginning of the financial year by the changes in management at the top. It was a sad joke, but one that everyone understood. Long time employees couldn't understand the rationale of the constant moves and how executives at Katoshi Corporate headquarters could continue letting one of their top divisions perform so poorly and allow such instability in management without some type of heavy-handed intervention.

There was an unsubstantiated rumor floating around that several other divisions in Katoshi Corporation hated Katoshi Systems Services. The rumor started many years ago when a young hotshot Katoshi Systems Services executive embarrassed several corporate executives during a Katoshi Corporate board meeting. This was when Katoshi Systems Services was at its peak making well over twelve billion dollars a year in revenue and growing. The young executive insulted executives at other Katoshi Corporation divisions during the board meeting and embarrassed them in front of their peers and leaders. Worst, as the rumor went, this cocky executive called their products garbage, worthless and dumb. In Japanese culture, and especially in business culture, this was the worst thing a westerner could do. These vindictive executives had been secretly conspiring to sabotage and oversee the financial collapse of Katoshi Systems Services since. It wasn't enough to ensure the executive and the whole executive team was removed, the whole company needed to disappear. Such were the origins of rumors.

There was a saying in the business world about Japanese culture and business, "They always play the long game." They were patient, focused, committed, and smart, and they had plans on top of plans. If they wanted to do something or enter a market segment, they researched it thoroughly and invested quietly, and they always planned to dominate it. The foundational companies of Japan's economy were not startups. Many of these companies had been part of Japan's economic engine for over a century. A ten-year business plan was a quick idea to try something new. Likewise, if they wanted to remove a competitor, rival, or offender, there was a well-thought-out plan. They were not proud enough to forgo twelve billion dollars in revenue all in one year because they were offended. No, they would bleed it away slowly, causing suffering, redirecting those revenue streams across other divisions, their divisions, methodically and carefully without drawing attention.

So, while Katoshi Systems Services was half the company it once was and spiraling downward, having shrunk almost six billion dollars in revenue, the overall financial standing of Katoshi Corporation showed good financial growth and stability.

These were the conspiracy theories told by employees to each other to help explain and comfort themselves as to why the company, with its superior products and technology, was performing poorly compared to their competitors in the same market space. It was also why Katoshi Corporation wasn't stepping in to help fix their leadership problems. No, the Katoshi Systems Services board of directors would continue to flounder on their own in the only way westerners knew how, by hiring their friends to take a turn at the helm of a sinking company, all the while looking for a contractual way to milk a payout before their incompetence became public knowledge.

***

After a long week of reflection and mourning, meeting with his team and colleagues at work—except for his manager who didn't answer his calls or respond to his messages—Ty spent Saturday morning working out at his gym and running for a couple of hours. After cleaning up and eating lunch with the news on the television, he took his M3 ZCP out for a mountain drive.

Enjoying the drive and escape only this car could provide, he drove it hard. It had been a while since he'd driven it. The M3 ZCP never failed to lift his spirits when he took it out, and he enthusiastically experienced it.

His wife used to love going for rides out on the back mountain roads but didn't especially like the spirited driving. With no music playing on its high-end sound system, just the therapeutic feel of the naturally aspirated engine and the sound of the rumbling, raspy exhaust as he accelerated out of turns and opened her up on the straightaways, his mind was on auto-race, and he thought of nothing else.

The car was the flawless blend of class, handling, performance, and power. It never failed to turn heads even though it was as stock and plain as the day it came off the assembly line, aside from the aggressively wide tires and stance. There was a saying in the auto enthusiast world, "If you don't turn back to look at your car after you've parked it, you bought the wrong car." He bought the right car.

Ty was nearly done with the route he usually drove to stretch out his M3 ZCP. The roughly forty-mile course of twisting mountains turns, uphill straightaways, no stop lights or stop signs, and very light traffic was a familiar outlet for him. Whenever he needed to rejuvenate his spirit or when he thought the car needed to stretch out, and he didn't have anything pressing to do, this was his track of choice.

He actually hated using the car for errands and running around town. He would park his car alone in the deserted back area of a parking lot and walk the long walk to the store entrance, glancing back at his girl. Inevitably, someone would park uncomfortably close to his isolated car.

He only took it up to about 120 miles per hour for a brief moment on one of the straight stretches and only redlined it once at about 7000 rpm. He felt exhilarated after the technical stretch of road, but now he was back in civilization and drove the rest of the way home courteously. The drive took about forty-five minutes. He checked all the gauges to ensure everything was still at specification; nothing overheating. He stopped at a Shell station near his neighborhood to top off the gas tank with the ninety-one octane V-Power fuel blend that was recommended for the S54 engine. Then, he drove home and backed the car into the garage.

While in the garage, he walked around to the back of his Tesla and unplugged the charging cord and let it retract back into its cradle. He thought he would be driving this to the office sometime that week.

He grabbed a bottle of water out of the fridge, went to his office, and sat at his desk. It was the middle of the afternoon, and there was still lots of daylight outside. He thought about Yuichu and his family and the other guys he'd worked with, like Toshi and Ichimoto-san, who were part of Yuichu's team; the research facility he had visited many times throughout his career at Katoshi and just visited a couple of months ago; and his job. It was Sunday in Japan, and the rescue efforts and cleanup operations were ongoing. A lot of the undamaged areas of Japan could open if they wanted to, but in the heart of the destruction, everything would be shut down for some time.

He checked his work laptop for any new company emails regarding the earthquake. A lot of condolences and "We will endure" messages from heads of divisions, but nothing substantial. He wasn't sure what he wanted to see, but he thought he'd know it when he saw it; this wasn't it.

He clicked on the browser page he recently saved. It was a company-wide internal webpage with a list of the names of confirmed lost colleagues in alphabetical order. The webpage design was beautifully adorned with images of Japanese culture and Katoshi achievements, tastefully arranged and subtle in its presentation. The names of 159 employees were listed in four columns dominating the center of the webpage. At the top of the webpage, written in three forms was:

尊敬と記憶において、私たちは亡くなった家族を称えます

Sonkei to kioku ni oite, watashitachiha nakunatta kazoku o tataemasu

In Respect and Memory, We Honor Our Fallen Family Members

It probably reads more poetically in Japanese, he told himself. The list had been at 159 since yesterday. All of them from the Saitama facility. He didn't know if they were counting today, if this was everyone and recovery operations were complete, or if the number was much larger and they just didn't want to announce the greater loss of life. He recognized at least a dozen names on the list, including Yuichu and his team, and Dr. Takashi.

Ty had mixed feelings about the list of fallen employees being displayed on a webpage. On the one hand, it was a nice touch and it let family, friends, and colleagues know the fate of those in the earthquake. On the other hand, it seemed cold and too soon to put the names of the dead on a webpage. The webpage was company internal access only, so it wasn't public information and would have to be intentionally leaked out, but still, it just felt not cool. He wasn't sure if this was business or some part of Japanese culture he hadn't experienced yet.

Fourteen years ago, during the catastrophe of the Great Tohoku Earthquake and the tsunami that followed it, all eyes were focused on the nuclear disaster unfolding in front of the world's view. The tsunami generated by that powerful earthquake had swept away an entire coastal community into the sea with video replaying the nightmare scene over and over. Ty was working at a different company then and wasn't monitoring how Japanese culture handled the loss of life. He, as well as the rest of the world, was mesmerized by the nuclear disaster being broadcast live. Life's realities were in the details one observed.

***

Ty sat at his desk thinking about what was going to happen next. He sent out emails to his small team of three letting them know what he knew, added a few links to sites with information, including the Katoshi "death page," and added a few personal thoughts and encouragements. He also set up another virtual meeting for Tuesday morning to talk about the disaster and discuss plans going forward. His team had been to the research lab in Saitama and knew many of the researchers there as well. He had been sending out short bursts of information in his team's group message board, but those were informal and chatty. He needed to get his team thinking about what to do now that KRF was gone. Half of the work they were doing was with the KRF researchers, but now, that function needed to be replaced. His team was the only group in KSS that worked directly with KRF.

He glanced over at the orphaned machine. He just realized this was likely the only one left in existence with the other four units destroyed. Not only were they destroyed, but everyone who knew how they were built was probably dead, including the project lead, Yuichu.

Ty considered this for a moment and then thought, *This project is dead.* Or at least suspended for a very long time.

He didn't know if they would be able to recreate it from their notes and plans, reverse engineer this one, or if they even wanted to. It would definitely take a long time get back on a release schedule.

The initial market analysis for developing this type of product showed a very healthy revenue stream for many years to come if they could build a competitive alternative to the "Big Quantum" players in this new field. Their approach was groundbreaking. This was going to be disruptive to the entire computing industry—classical and quantum.

But now, would they want to start over? For all the advanced research KRF did, they weren't very good at project management. There was a very good possibility all documents on this and other projects were destroyed and lost, including their backups. It was a strange circumstance in that this facility wasn't a profit and loss department, so the information generated there was not treated like a revenue generating organization or "business critical." Code, including chip designs and the like, was protected, but records, inventory, even laptop data, was loosely managed. Since they were advanced research, nothing was in the cloud or saved to other information and code managing services like Github. Nothing they worked on was open source and nothing ever showed up in the public domain. Maybe further down the development cycle once their development matured and went through several phases of productization, but never directly from this organization. No, this facility was the equivalent of a skunkworks operation in the commercial world.

Piecing everything back together was going to be tough, even with this one remaining device sitting in his office. The software they sent with the device was not the source code. It was the high-level binaries that would call the lower-level functions of the device. There had to be dozens of layers of abstractions and removed details of the underlying device. As he thought through the situation, it was starting to sound impossible to reverse engineer.

Maybe if he could build a killer application using this technology it would trigger interest in resurrecting this project sooner rather than later. That was it, he needed to do some more research—tomorrow.

He decided to call it a day and got up from his desk and left his office. He poured himself a large glass of wine and spent the rest of Saturday evening watching Adult Swim. There should be a new episode of *Rick and Morty* later on tonight. Numbing his mind and emotions for a while and grabbing a few laughs before heading to bed would be a wasteful use of the time, but reenergizing his soul and entertaining the heart, that was good use of his time.

Chapter 7

Dr. George Lancer removed his glasses with one hand and with his other, he rubbed the bridge of his nose, then massaged his temples, and leaned back in his chair. The meeting was in its third hour and nothing really new had been discussed since the first hour. The six other participants in the meeting were his direct reports and were discussing what was left of the Katoshi Research Facility in Saitama, Japan. They started to review the investment they put into the research and development of the new quantum computer being developed there. The five new Mark 3 devices, as well as the existing four Mark 2 machines—though the Mark 2 machines were supposed to be destroyed soon—gone. Everything was destroyed, including all records, hardware, software, and most of the personnel.

This meeting was meant to discuss their contingency plans. The Mark 3 device was going to potentially be a limited availability product, combined with a special version of the software, a new computing platform for the Central Intelligence Agency to test and experiment with. Quantum computing was going to change the cyberspace landscape for all government intelligence agencies and the "company" was first in line. The current approaches to quantum computing were not delivering on the performance, phenomenon, and other promises expected by now. Plus, the costs and instability put a viable and reliable market ready quantum computer at least another five years away. The device Katoshi Corporation developed was a completely new approach that could've disrupted and reignited the entire industry. Their next device was on target to be ready for general availability in eighteen to twenty-four months. Room temperature, cheap quantum computing—small, agile, enterprise class at enterprise volumes, initially.

Most U.S. government agencies realized long ago that the reliance of one-off specialized technology was an unsustainable economic model, and open market forces needed to be a part of any new technology decision, investment, and strategy. The days of building their own equipment and technology just wasn't cost effective. This situation had been exacerbated in the computing and analytics industry. There were new ways of investing in commercial enterprises to create what they needed at a fraction of the overall costs. Also, keeping up with the fast pace of today's technology advancements was impossible for a bloated lumbering government to stay competitive. In most cases, they could modify the products and technologies to meet military specifications or protocol requirements with a tiny fraction of the investment compared to building something from scratch that only specialized personnel could support and maintain.

The various government agencies created and funded venture capitalist civil service units to take their requirements and specifications to the open market. Recently, they started going global within the framework of the new trade agreements with friendly countries and invested in these new joint venture partnerships.

Intel-Q was one of these organizations within the U.S. government—arguably the most successful one. Intel-Q was the venture capital arm of the "company." Its successful track record attracted other agencies to seek their services much more than their own equivalents of investment firms. The name "Intel-Q" was a whimsical concatenation of the elements "Intel" and the name "Q"—the omnipotent fictional character and race from the TV series Star Trek the Next Generation. Intel-Q employed their own scientists, researchers, developers, and engineers, even financial and investment experts, lawyers, and they had access to outside consultants, advisors, and academics on retainer whenever needed. They advised and guided other enterprises and startup companies, then funded them to create the cutting-edge technology they required, providing the capital these companies needed to sustain themselves or sustain an emerging market.

Dr. George Lancer was the director of advanced computational platform investments at Intel-Q, a position he had held for the past ten years. Coming from Purdue University, where he was the dean of the Computer Science department for over twenty years, he made the transition from academia to government work when a longtime colleague and friend of his retired and asked him to take his place. A spry and brilliant man hidden from the world by his lackadaisical leadership attitude and relaxed approach to authority, he was a little off-putting to those uniformed, chain of command types—especially with his long, semi-kept hair and casual attire. For a man of his experience and legacy, they all expected someone more polished and conforming. He never understood that kind of thinking. It had always been his experience that if you wanted change, not to conform to norms. Spending all of his legendary career in institutionalized employment, he always managed to excel at everything, except compliance.

Since coming to Intel-Q, Dr. Lancer had been pursuing and influencing the promise of quantum computing. He spent a significant amount of time at Purdue tracking the progress of the fledgling industry. He even developed an introductory course at Purdue in his department on quantum computing to mixed reactions. Not that the course wasn't popular, on the contrary, there was a waiting list to enroll in the once-a-year course taught by him, but they also didn't have a "real" quantum computer on campus; real being one of the developmental machines currently used for experimentation.

There would be three career paths in the quantum computing industry in the future: the physics or industrialized side, where physics students—especially quantum physics—mechanical engineering students, electrical engineering students, and chemical and materials engineering students could apply their knowledge in making and advancing the new hardware; the software side; and the applied side. Computer science students, mathematicians and statisticians, and programmers and developers could find highly sought-after careers in the new industry. Then there was the management of these new systems in the information technology field. Interested students could find careers in this field.

Without one of the experimental quantum computers on campus, most of the course study was theoretical and based on simulators. He would persuade his colleagues from the other science departments to guest teach a few classes on the specific subjects of material science, quantum physics and mechanics, mechanical engineering, and all the related disciplines required. He would sit in on these guest lectures to expand his own knowledge.

The big tech companies that were attempting to develop the new machines would provide shared time on some of their machines, but it wasn't enough to provide the experience and knowledge needed. He was successful in getting funding from the tech companies, but never enough to obtain a fully "operational quantum computer" donated to the university with support personnel. The total costs were unsupportable, which included a new building on campus. Plus, these new machines weren't stable enough for productive, meaningful work. No, quantum computing was still not a real commercial industry.

Even the National Science Foundation applauded his requests for funding, but until real, positive progress was made, they could not fund the "too experimental" endeavor.

News of the disaster in Japan and the destruction of the research facility in Saitama was a major blow to his personal number-one priority. He had other projects in different stages of development, but none of those were going to be as disruptive as this one. The KRF researchers, with the guidance of some of his scientists, were testing the cryptographic functions of the device and the special software with extraordinary results. He was scheduled to visit KRF next month with his team for a live demonstration, which would have sealed the approvals for another round of funding to start development on a final production version. He also requested additional demonstrations of other capabilities. It never occurred to him to ask how they protected their work in the case of a "hole in the ground" disaster.

He looked around the table at his team. "Look, I want to see options by tomorrow afternoon on where we go from here. We have invested heavily in KRF to deliver this for us, and we were so close. Now we have nothing."

While Dr. Lancer paused, his phone vibrated on the table. "Excuse me." He picked up the phone and answered it. "Moshi-Moshi. How are you doing, Nakatori-san? You must be very busy to be working at this hour."

The room fell still, and all eyes were on George to determine if they needed to leave. He looked up at everyone and motioned them to stay seated.

"I understand… No, we have not decided yet, we are just looking at options… I'd be willing to do that and reassess the situation… By the way, were there any patents filed in Japan or here in the U.S.? I see… Okay, thank you for the call and the offer… Please secure the area seven, twenty-four… Yes, it would be a good plan if this project could be continued, we could show it as a technical delay in the schedule… The entire floor? …I understand… Okay, I'll set that up and let you know… Thank you and good night." Dr. Lancer disconnected from the call.

"Well, that was chairman Nakatori," he said as he looked around at his staff. "It seems the destruction of the building in Saitama isn't a total loss. He received reports from the rescue and recovery supervisors that many of the servers and laptops might be salvageable, and there are documents intact and laying around. It hasn't rained there since the earthquake and the current forecast is for clear skies for a few weeks." He looked thoughtful as he spoke.

"Chairman Nakatori is allowing us to search the site for one week before they need to start major cleanup operations, so this needs to happen quickly. The site has been searched looking for survivors and the deceased, but he assured me nothing from the area has been removed aside from a few personal items."

He folded his hands on the table in front of him and looked around. "If there's something there, we might still be able to continue the work to some degree. He is giving us an entire floor in one of the other buildings on the campus to store the equipment and work on extracting anything we can find. There will be a few researchers from adjacent projects available to assist us."

Looking to one of his directors, he said, "Dana, put a team together and get them to the site. Get some computer forensic experts on your team. If there are computers still around and the storage modules are intact, they might be able to salvage the data from them. The first priority is to collect and store all the equipment, computers, documents, and debris in that other building. You'll need a team to prepare that workspace during the salvage operations. Anything to help restart this project somewhere else."

"I'm on it. I assume I can use company assets to get there?" Dana wrote down some notes. "We could land at Yokota Airbase and use personnel there and set up forward operations." She waved her pen while she spoke.

"And I can get extra personnel from Kinser Marine Base to assist in securing the site and the preparation. They're both near Saitama. They should have some heavy equipment to help with salvage," Dana added.

"Excellent! Yes, on the company assets. I need them there ASAP. Good idea with the military bases and personnel, let's use them and their facility, but make sure they're in civilian clothes when they're at the site and no heavy weapons. We need more manpower than firepower. This is not a military operation and it's not a matter of national security, so we don't need that kind of unwelcomed attention. It's just a time-sensitive operation before anything starts disappearing or deteriorating." George was fully engaged in the train of thought Dana was proposing.

George looked at Dana, snapping and wagging his finger. "But nix the military heavy equipment. They're probably being used for other earthquake operations anyway. We should get local light-duty equipment, no military markings. Think archeology, not earthmovers. And no helicopters; I don't want the locals thinking we found an alien spaceship or something."

A quick thought entered his head. "Dana, see if we can get some of the Marines there now. I think two teams could start preparing the storage area and another to secure the site. I do want our people there to supervise the collection of material and data. Concentrate on the third, fourth, and fifth floors, and the basement where the server room was; I don't know what that will look like. And get a plane with communications capability. You'll need to coordinate from the air."

Looking around the table George asked, "Do we have any images of the device, or the components used? It will help the search efforts if they know what they're looking for."

Placing his hand on the table in the direction of another one of his managers, he said, "John, Chairman Nakatori said they did file some patents for the project. They are early and theoretical patents. They haven't gotten to the implementation filings yet, but he wasn't a hundred percent sure of that. Have a couple of your patent researchers find whatever they can dig up. There might be something there to help restart this. And find out if there are any images or drawings of final candidate products."

"Good idea. I'll get right on it." John confirmed and immediately was on his phone.

"The rest of you, I need you to look into your portfolios and find me something promising with the other companies. Anything that looks like an extra twenty-five to fifty million dollars of infusion might get us closer to what we need if this doesn't work out. If there's nothing useful at KRF to continue on with, then we'll be able to divert those funds somewhere else, but I want us to really push this course of action as hard as we can before moving on." George paused for a moment. "Any other ideas? Am I missing something?"

Phil spoke up. "George, why is this project so important? We have just as much invested in the other programs as this one. There seems to be something critical about this one that I don't think we're all aware of." He left his statement hanging in the air, not really sure if he was done saying what he completely wanted to say.

George looked around at everyone. "Because this quantum computer works. It's not the fastest or the biggest, but it's fast enough. Speed isn't the issue; quantum phenomenon is what's important. It is—was—stable and could repeat its results. And the most important part of it is how it's programmed. We'll be able to use all the current talent and skills to program it. That's a huge leap forward in being immediately productive with this type of computing. Or at least it was."

George sat back in his chair and continued, "The other projects have started down the path of bigger machines with more qubits just to stabilize the results. It will take them five to ten years to balance out that equation. The end result will be a machine that'll require its own large building, dozens of people just to keep it running, cost twenty-five to forty million dollars, and there'd be only a thousand people in the world who could program it. The device in Saitama could be redesigned to run in your phone in ten years for a dollar, along with all the application developers you would need. This device could literally be the Apple II of the quantum computing industry."

George took a deep breath. "Our meeting there next month was to confirm their findings along with our special software versions for the device and our customer's needs, and to bump the schedule up. The goal was to have them produce more of the current Mark 3 devices and get them into our own labs to prove to the "company" that this will solve their immediate tactical needs. What they have accomplished was nothing short of a technical miracle."

With a heavy exhale, he said, "All swept away by an act of God. Any other concerns or questions?" George paused and looked around for a couple of seconds. "Okay, I'm calling this meeting. Jane will send out meeting invites to you shortly for tomorrow's follow-up, except you, Dana. Let me know if you have any questions, suggestions, or ideas."

No one said anything else, and they all got up from their seats and left his office. It wasn't that they were intimidated by Dr. Lancer, quite the opposite. Everyone liked and admired him. They were actually disappointed they didn't have any better answers for him. In the back of everyone's minds, they all wanted to assist in the recovery operation, but they knew they had their part to play somewhere else.

George stayed in his chair and wrote down some notes before finally getting up and walking to his desk on the other side of his office. He didn't really care about his job, he worried about doing a bad job, which he felt would let the world down. They were so close to his dream of seeing a practical, affordable quantum computer on the market, available to the world—of everyone having access to this new computational power and thinking quantumly. What advancements could be developed in the future with such ubiquitous capability?

He turned his chair around to stare out toward the horizon from his sixth-floor office window and the rolling landscape of Langley, Virginia.

The "company" and all the other agencies and military branches would weaponize it for their purposes—as would everyone else in the world—but that would be a short-term necessity. It was a part of his plan, his strategy, that these mainstream technologies needed to be disrupted—broken down. When traditional cryptography was finally rendered obsolete and insecure, quantum cryptography would take its place. Quantum encryption would replace it and be unbreakable; not because of harder math problems to solve, but because quantum pairing using entanglement would be singularly unique.

Quantum computing would be transformative with accelerated advancements in the fields of robotics, artificial intelligence, compression, communications, space exploration, propulsion systems, planetary colonization, the environment, energy and battery technology, transportation, human life sciences, and more. It would provide a clearer understanding of natural forces, like gravity. New problem-solving techniques, answers to problems humans didn't even know how to begin answering, new questions, everything would be a whole new frontier of opportunity. Quantum computers designing the next generation of quantum computers, and the languages used to program them, would push mankind forward into a new future.

There would still be a market for the classical computing machines for a long time; maybe forever. No one expected a quantum computer to completely replace a classical computer for mundane tasks and simple devices, but those simple devices would have access to quantum computing-based services. Just like many people still rode horses or hand wrote letters, classical computing technology wouldn't completely disappear. But the days of building gigantic, power-hungry supercomputers to do hard math problems needed to end. It was this transitional period that would help make everything feel normal as the world completely changed.

He still held hope for this vision while he was still alive, but now it was looking like it might be another ten years before it happened instead of a year from now or even based on a meeting next month. He initially thought he could make this happen by teaching, but that was moving too slowly, so when this opportunity came up, he saw a new, faster, more straight-forward path to a new future.

He wasn't a lunatic or a mad scientist angry at the world, just the opposite. He cherished humanity. He had done the research study himself, but never published it. He deduced the current technological trajectory in computational sciences had hit a plateau and had been on this plateau for some time. A plateau that would keep humanity's progress stagnant and lethargic for another century.

He didn't want humans to wage war on each other to change humanity, he wanted industry to battle it out, humanely. A disruption to the way information was processed, the way insight was calculated, and the way knowledge was derived. Humans needed to be humans, not computer and data scientists. There needed to be a change in the way humans relied on today's computers to make decisions, better decisions. It would all be peaceful, sane, and natural. It could be globally profitable for everyone.

Let the free markets fight it out. The rich would become poor trying to sustain a losing legacy battle, or they would become richer by embracing the next phase of this technological revolution. The economy would see a worldwide sustained growth never before seen in human history. A new, larger, and growing wealth class, more wealth for more people. Another possible outcome from his research study was that poverty, over population, and racism could be eliminated; just the human race.

"Shinsei"—New Star—that was such a fitting project name, he thought.

Dr. George Lancer didn't want to be the one to usher in a new renaissance for mankind to explode, he just wanted to be the one to light the fuse.

Chapter 8

Ty flipped open Tomahawk to see where he left off in the installation procedures of the machine. It was Sunday afternoon, and he spent the morning hanging out with his friend and neighbor, Tim. They went to the archery range to practice and have a little friendly competition—he lost again.

The installation completed almost two weeks ago, installing itself on his system, complete with hypervisor and a virtual machine, which should contain all of the tools, utilities, and libraries for communicating with Q-Tip. He switched back to the "README.md" file to see what the next steps would be. Carefully reading the instructions again, he ensured he didn't have another close call of messing up. If he messed this up and bricked the device, there was no replacing it or help to recover it.

The next step in the procedure was to make sure the virtual machine was shut down, then to connect the USB optical adapter into an available port on the host system. Picking up the USB optical adapter, he plugged it into the side of Tomahawk, pointing toward Q-Tip so the cable would lay straight toward the device. Fiber optic cables worked best when there were fewer bends in them, and a kink destroyed the cable.

Scrolling down to the next step and reading it, he then took the fiber optic cable and plugged it into the port on the USB adapter. He pushed it in until there was a click that indicated it was secure and properly in place, then he got up from his chair and carefully uncoiled the cable, laid it across the floor, took the other end, and plugged it into the optical port in the back of Q-Tip. He pushed it in until there was a satisfying click. He looked down at the cable where it laid on the floor, gently flowing from his laptop to the device, no kinks or crossing of the strand. There was more than enough cable length, so he rerouted the extra out of the way so there was less of a threat of tripping over it. He walked out of his office and into a closet and grabbed a small throw rug. Walking back into his office, he placed the rug over the cable between his desk and Q-Tip to protect it from getting kicked or kinked.

Ty sat back down at his desk and began reading the instructions again. He was reading several steps ahead each time to make sure there wasn't some timing gotcha that might mess up the installation. This was the moment he had been waiting for—the next step was to power on the device. There was a small switch located near the power connector at the base of the machine. He walked over to Q-Tip and, looking at where he plugged in the power cable, bent over and toggled the rocker switch to the "ON" position. He stepped back, not knowing what to expect. The top of the cylinder enclosure—a ring that encircled the top of it—lit up red. No fan noise or humming—nothing else.

Okay, he thought. *The instructions said there should be a red indicator on top, so everything is going along as it should.*

He hoped something more interesting would happen. The next step was to power on and boot up the virtual machine. He clicked the "Power On" button on the virtual machine's control panel and watched the window display a sequence of power up diagnostics and virtual power-on self-tests. Standard stuff and unnecessary since those tests were originally designed to check hardware status. Then the operating system began to load. A Linux distribution displayed, then an Ubuntu banner splashed across the window.

He smiled out loud; he loved running Ubuntu on Ubuntu.

Clicking the full screen button, the display on the screen expanded to immerse him in the virtual machine desktop environment. It was as though he was running on a physical system. When the system completed its boot-up sequence, a single terminal window appeared in the center of the virtual desktop screen with a shell prompt waiting for instructions and commands to be typed in.

He exited the full screen mode of the virtual machine, then grabbed and dragged the program displaying the "README.md" document to his external monitor. This way he could continue reading it while the virtual machine was running in full screen mode on his laptop's screen.

Ty read the next few steps before proceeding, the first of which was to make sure the USB flash drive was still plugged into the same USB port as when the virtual machine was installed. He hadn't removed it since he plugged it in, but that was good information. He wondered if there was a crypto key somewhere on it that protected the software or access to the device. He began typing the list of commands shown in the instructions. There were several, and each time the responses were expected. Everything was going smoothly. He read a few more instructions and typed a few more commands until he came to the "start device" command.

He carefully typed in the command and hit the enter key. The terminal window displayed nothing for a few seconds, then output:

```
bash$ start device

Connection to Shinsei Mark 3, s/n: 0006 successful!

starting initialization [=====            ]25%
```

Ty heard a weak click come from Q-Tip. He looked over at the device to see the red ring on top changed to a blue ring on both the top and bottom of the cylinder, and a very faint hum could be heard coming from it as though something was starting up. Then the sound disappeared, and the device went quiet again. As the progress bar advanced, blue lights began coming on through the vents and the small window on what he always assumed was the front of the device. Q-Tip stood there with three sets of glowing blue stripes straddling a small blue window with two blue rings on the top and bottom of the cylinder. It looked awesome. Yuichu must have hired a professional enclosure designer from Apple or something. If it looked alien before it was powered on, then even aliens would think the device looked alien now that it was powered up.

Ty could barely see inside the small window portal. He stood up and walked over to Q-Tip to look inside of it. The initialization progress bar was only at forty-five percent. He bent down to get a better look. In the center was a metal cylinder protruding up toward the window—about the size of an 8.4 ounce can of Red Bull—he assumed was made of copper or a similar metal. It was hard to tell with the blue lights illuminating the inside. From the sides of the metal cylinder were eight small metal tubes coiled once and going into the surrounding surface the metallic cylinder was mounted on. Above the attachment point of the metal tubes were eight steel branded lines, or cables, connected to the cylinder and out onto the mounted surface. It looked simple, elegant, and clean—unlike the current pictures of quantum computers that looked like copper and gold chandeliers hanging down from the top of their voluminous enclosures.

As he was admiring the inside of the device through the window, light indicators around the edge of the window started to flash and sequence through different colors and patterns, then, the window went dark. It wasn't that the blue light inside turned off, it was that the window glass darkened until it was nearly blacked out. He could still see inside the window, but it was hard to make out any of the details.

"Well, that was rude!"

Ty stood up. He wondered if the window was just self-dimming or if it was an LCD panel and part of the display indicators for status and messages.

Walking back to his desk, he noted the progress bar was at eighty percent as he sat back down. The excitement was getting thick in his office as the progress bar continued on to its completion.

Then he wondered if it would always take this long to start up, or is this was a first-time initialization, and the next time it would start up faster. It felt like it was taking about five minutes, then the progress bar jumped to a hundred percent and a new prompt came back, ready to accept a new set of commands. It was a standard python interactive prompt—the QtPython prompt. He carefully studied the status output:

```
bash$ start device

Connection to Shinsei Mark 3, s/n: 0006 successful!

starting initialization [=====================]100%

completed initialization and startup of Shinsei Mark 3

startup procedure time, 4 minutes, 45 seconds

Ready!

QtPython 0.0.3 (May 11, 2025, 17:54:48) Katoshi Corp.

Type "help," "copyright," "credits," "license," or "samples" for more information.

>>>
```

"Alright!" Tyson was giddy as he clapped his hands in front of himself.

He looked up at the time in the corner of his laptop screen. It was nearly 6:00 p.m. Before he got started, he decided to go into the kitchen, grab some snacks, make himself a sandwich, and grab a Diet Coke to enjoy in his office. He opened the bottle of Diet Coke and took a long drink from it; the first swig from a freshly opened soda always felt the most satisfying to him. Taking a couple of huge bites out of his ham sandwich, he began typing with his mouth full.

Ty spent the night reading documentation and running the sample programs provided in the samples folder, learning how to use the programming interfaces to the device, the different libraries and functions provided, and programming guidelines. He ran a couple of sample programs, then read the code to see what was going on, starting with "Hello World!" He thought this was an interesting program to run on a quantum computer, but when he looked at the code in the program, he realized it was much more complex than a simple print statement of "Hello World!" It was a "Hello World!" from the "quantum realm." He laughed out loud; he loved that movie.

He would run some of these programs and watch Q-Tip's window and the surrounding indictor lights flicker. The window itself stayed dark and tinted. He spent some time looking for a map or key as to what the surrounding indictors meant but decided it might not be that important right now. It was still interesting that this device had external and observable indicators at all.

After familiarizing himself with the basic coding of Q-Tip, he explored the rest of the sample folders, looking at what seemed like categories: statistics, chemical materials, quantum annealing, mathematics, combinatorics, and others. Eventually he found what he was looking for, an "AI" folder.

Now we're getting somewhere.

He browsed into the AI folder to find a large selection of machine learning techniques for classification and regression, anomaly detection, clustering, association, neural networks, reinforcement learning, and more. Standard machine learning stuff, but he was sure there was a quantum approach to these.

He looked inside the QNLP folder. There were a lot of natural language processing samples. He doubted there were any examples for cleaning and prepping the data—that would seem like a waste of resources for a quantum computer. That data should come in already cleansed and prepared by a classical computer. He thought about that for a moment. *This is a good hybrid case for combining classical and quantum computing together.* After thinking about it further he wondered, *Wait. Why would a quantum computer even need data to be cleansed?* He wanted to come back and explore this later.

Natural language processing was a subdomain of artificial intelligence that fascinated him. He always felt artificial intelligence would see a giant leap forward in mimicking human behavior and interaction if a computer could finish someone's sentence or thought. Today, phrases must be completed, paused, or batched up, then processed—no matter how fast— to understand the question or context. There were some editing applications that could suggest sentence completion as someone wrote. But to have a conversation, like with an old friend or between a longtime married couple and be able to complete each other's sentences or thoughts, well that just might require a quantum computer to realize it. The Alan Turing test would need to be revamped if that ever happened.

He clicked out of that folder and moved over to the content of the AI folder again. He opened one of the sample programs in the regression folder to look at the code. Aside from the different imported modules and the special calls to and from the device, the code didn't look much different than something he would code. Yuichu's team did an amazing job of abstracting away the complexities and device specific interfaces in their routines. It looked like standard python programming code with only a few interesting lines of code for setting up datagrams and metadata. He assumed those would translate to the QPU's instructions on the device through the code converters and transformers.

He popped back up in the folder hierarchy and down into the classifiers subfolder. There were programs for traditional machine learning samples, including the Pima Indian Diabetes dataset example. This was a very popular dataset and machine learning education example. With machine learning, the artificial intelligence part of it was in the learning or training to recognize data patterns. Once the model was trained to output a prediction, you would give it the same type of input it trained on but had never seen before. Then it would make a prediction. In this case, given a few body measurement parameters like Body Mass Index, Glucose level, Triceps skin thickness, and other medical measurements, a machine learning model could predict if someone had or was going to have diabetes.

There were other popular educational examples and case study datasets in the folder. He wondered why these were on the machine, as they were pretty basic, beginner-level type examples for machine learning. He also wondered if the training of a model was done on the quantum device and whether the model was only inferred on the device.

Then he realized why these might be there. The samples appeared to get more complex. It was like the old 1983 movie *WarGames*, where the "WOPR" mainframe computer started out playing tic-tac-toe in order to learn gameplay, strategy, and how to win. Subsequent games like checkers, then chess, all the way to "Global Thermonuclear War," increased in complexity and challenge, teaching itself winning strategies.

These sample programs appeared to follow the same pattern of getting more and more complex, at least in the artificial intelligence field. He didn't believe the device was learning from every sample program—each machine learning model was standalone and a separate program. But he could see how the developers were building more complex artificial intelligence programs, most likely to determine if there would eventually be something quantum to be revealed—or discover some resource limit.

Before opening the Pima Indian sample program, he copied one of his old development folders from Tomahawk and copied it into the virtual machine's file system, then he opened another terminal window and opened one of his old machine learning programs. He copied and pasted some the lines of code from the Pima Indian sample program into it and modified it to fit what his program was doing. After renaming the final model file that would be trained and created, he saved the new program and executed it.

Quickly, he looked over at Q-Tip, nothing happened. Looking back at his program, it was already done. The program had an execution timer that output the time to complete which displayed "0.0000s."

"Okay! So, it's very fast," he mumbled under his breath.

That program usually took about five seconds to complete. Editing the program again, he adjusted his execution timer to output a higher number of digits for more accuracy. This was already at ten thousandths of a second. He wasn't sure how granular he could make the time on this laptop. Or could it be the modules in QtPython that weren't working correctly with his code? If that was the case, then maybe there were special functions for doing timers in QtPython. He was sure the concept of execution time might not mean the same thing on a quantum processor and getting that kind of information might require special coding statements.

He found what he was looking for in the documentation and programmer's guide. Adding the timer function to his program, he typed it up to re-execute it. Before pressing the enter key, he turned his head to look at the indicator panel light on Q-Tip, then blindly pressed the key.

The tinted window quickly let the blue light out of the enclosure. The eerie opening and closing of the window creeped him out, almost like an eye blinking. The auto-dimming of the window wasn't like a light blinking on and off, it seemed to open from the bottom up, then close from the top down, like an eyelid; a very sleepy eyelid struggling to wake-up. The window dimmed dark immediately, almost slamming shut.

Ty blinked, trying to figure out what just happened. It must be a characteristic of the dimming mechanism of the window—he felt a little hypnotized. Looking at his terminal window, the execution time now displayed "0.00000000000+s."

"Okay, that's different. Not sure how to interpret that," he grumbled and decided to move on and worry about the timer issues later.

It could be a bug in the module, or he just needed to read the documentation more carefully. It shouldn't matter. He browsed to the location of the model file he trained and created and found it.

"Thirty-six hundred bytes! What the hell!?"

He looked at the file size, thinking something was wrong. That model should be a couple of megabytes in size. Then again, it wasn't generated on his laptop, it was created over there on Q-Tip.

"I wonder if the thirty-six hundred bytes has anything to do with the number of its qubit size; thirty-six times one hundred or something? It is a product of the device. This could be interesting." He was talking himself through any confusing obstacle.

He started editing another program. This program would actually use the model, score some data, and make a prediction from it. There was always a minimum of two parts to machine learning development, at least for supervised machine learning: training and building the model, then using the model to make or infer predictions. There was also a verification phase after the training part, but this was being done simultaneously with the training.

After finishing his edits, he saved the program. Next, he created some data from a dataset file he had and saved that. He accidentally glanced up at the time.

"One forty-five a.m.! I gotta get to bed."

It had been a while since he'd been so engrossed in something that made him lose all track of time. He quickly typed up the commands to execute the program, and again, he placed his finger over the enter key and turned his head to watch Q-Tip. He pressed the key.

The device, once again, opened and closed its window like an eye waking up. For the brief time the eye was open, he could see the blue light inside the device leak out of the enclosure's window, bathing the area in front of the device in more blue tones. The dimming window slammed shut again—which snapped him out of his mild trance.

Looking at his screen, the output for the dozen sample data records displayed like they normally would, except for a weird set of symbols: "$\Delta\lambda\varphi.\alpha\alpha$" for the probability. Garbage characters typically meant he had a memory overflow error somewhere. Interesting that it wasn't caught during runtime or didn't crash his program.

"I'm tired. There's too many bizarre things happening to think about while I'm tired." He rubbed his face. He looked at the time again, "Two-o-five a.m.! What happened to the time? I need to get some sleep."

He wasn't sure what to do with Q-Tip, so he just left it powered on. He would read the instructions for shutting it down tomorrow, which meant later today. He stood up from his chair and stretched his back and legs, then walked to the door. He turned off the lights, leaving only a low blue glow emanating from Q-Tip lighting his office, then he walked upstairs to his bedroom and fell asleep thinking of what he would explore next with the machine.

Chapter 9

Ty woke up the next morning alert and energetic. He slept in to seven o'clock and jumped out of bed to get washed up, taking care of his personal hygiene, and dressed in some serious hacking clothes—which included a t-shirt, jeans, and running shoes—then headed downstairs to the kitchen.

There, he loaded up his tandem Keurig coffee makers with his favorite K-Cup pods: Italian Roast. He set up the two coffee makers and rigged them together to pour one large twenty-ounce coffee. It was a professional looking arrangement. He received several compliments on it, so he built the same for several of his friends. It could be used as a single cup serving, two servings at a time, or the twenty-ounce pour, which was how he used it.

Placing his large coffee mug under the dispenser and pressing the two buttons, the coffee machines began their cycle in harmony. Grabbing a packet of Pop-Tarts from the cupboard, he popped them in the toaster. Reaching for a paper towel as he walked toward his freshly squeezed coffee, he picked up the oversized coffee mug and headed over to the toaster just in time for the pastries to pop up. Placing them on the napkin, he picked them up, and with his coffee in his other hand, headed to his office. The entire process was nearly automatic, well-rehearsed, and only took a few minutes. Breakfast wasn't an important part of his day, but he needed to have his coffee. The Pop-Tarts just seemed like the right thing to do for his stomach.

Setting breakfast down on his desk, he sat down in his chair, took a careful sip of the hot coffee, then a bite out of one of the pastries. Another sip of his coffee, then he woke up Tomahawk. Everything was where he left off from earlier this morning. Glancing over at Q-Tip, there was no smoke, and the lights were still on. His office wasn't even warm. One thing Ty admired about Japanese craftmanship was the quality. Even an advanced, experimental prototype was quite polished and safe.

He picked up where he left off, bizarre results he couldn't explain without blaming it on a glitch or bugs in the system or software. He decided to accept the fact that he was new to this field at this level and the modules and device were in working order. That, and he didn't quite understand or know how to use the device or the software yet.

Then he remembered, it was Monday morning. He looked over at the time, 7:45 a.m. He spun around and grabbed his work laptop off the shelf, placed it on a clear area on his desk, opened it up, and logged in. He grabbed his phone off the wireless charging station and looked for any new messages or notifications.

"Good. A slow start to the week," he sounded off to himself.

He turned back to the project at hand. He began browsing around the samples folders again, wanting to try something more advanced—more quantum. Timing a program's execution wasn't going to be as interesting as doing something quantum.

Looking around he saw a folder named "Cryptography." This should be interesting. Then he hesitated. One of the early concepts that encouraged the start of quantum computing was the theoretical ability to break current encryption technology. Modern communications and internet protocols, password and content protections, crypto-currencies, digital signatures and fingerprints, device security, just about all aspects of today's privacy mechanisms relied on the same cryptography technology.

Today's encryption approach was to base crypto keys on multiplying two large prime numbers together. This made breaking down the products into its constituent factors extremely difficult on today's classical computing technologies. Much of the supercomputer and high-performance computing build-up were, in some large part, attempts to break down these types of huge numbers and completing the math problems in a useful amount of time.

In theory, according to mathematician Peter Shor, a pioneer of quantum computing, a quantum algorithm should be able to break down these huge numbers into their prime factors, thereby breaking the key, almost instantaneously using quantum superposition.

Cryptography, the science of making and breaking encryption codes, relied on this fluke of math and computational deficiencies. Knowing that by the time a classical computer could finish breaking down the encryption key, the keys would change or expire, thereby sending powerful, and expensive, computer systems solving for useless answers late. The duel between encryption code makers and code breakers had advanced forward by continuing to incorporate larger prime numbers. There was even a race of creating supercomputers and algorithms searching for larger prime numbers. If it were true that a quantum computer could break modern, or even future encryption codes, then this device was…

"Oh shit!" He gasped. He clicked open the "Cryptography" folder, fearing what would be inside. In the folder were three subfolders: "encryption," "decryption," and as he suspected, "ShorsAlgo." He clicked open the "Shors Algorithm" subfolder only to find it empty. A sigh of relief swept over him. He made certain there were no hidden files or subfolders. He inspected the "encryption" and "decryption" folders to find them empty as well. Then he looked at the back of his laptop again to ensure that his Ethernet cable was still unplugged, and his Wi-Fi was turned off.

"Whew!" These must be stubs for sample content in the Saitama lab. The problem was this kind of technology couldn't be imported or exported to or from the United States if this device had the programming code to break encryption keys. It would be dangerous to have, even if it was just an example of how you could do it. If he wanted to see any programs to break encryption keys, he was going to have to do it himself. He felt a little better thinking that the relatively small number of thirty-six qubits wasn't sufficient to break the really large and most complex codes. Right? The continuing development of large quantum computers with more and more qubits was in some part due to working with these large numbers for this purpose. Then again, this was the equivalent of just thirty-six qubits. Now he wasn't really sure what that meant.

Currently, the largest known prime number is a Mersenne prime number, with 24,862,048 digits when printed out in based ten numbering. It is "$2^{82,589,933} - 1$." It is known as a Mersenne Prime Number because it's a number based on a power of 2 minus 1. This prime number is designated as "M82589933" and took twelve days of nonstop computing to discover. The eight largest known prime numbers are Mersenne prime numbers. That's not to say that every large prime number was a Mersenne prime number, but the last fifty-one discovered prime numbers have been Mersenne prime numbers.

Ty wondered if Q-Tip could discover the same number faster. Or could it find the next prime number in a shorter amount of time. Would thirty-six qubits be enough to work with these types of numbers?

Ty's racing mind was calming down now that the panic of the NSA or FBI breaking into his house and arresting him was subsiding. The fact that he still had a quantum computer that could break encryption codes in the right hands was disturbing to him. Then again, an off-the-chart genius with a classical computer and/or a GPU would be able to do it so long as they created a never-before tried algorithm. He was more relaxed after convincing himself that having the device was okay; it was the included capability that was the problem, and he didn't have the included capability.

He also wondered if the special modules and packages included with the QtPython language had any special math functions for accelerating the development of encryption algorithms like hashing or digital fingerprinting. He guessed, and hoped, Yuichu's thorough understanding of the situation meant these functions were also withheld from this specific device and distribution.

Still, the fact that those folder stubs were present bothered him. Were these types of experiments and development being done in the Saitama facility before it was destroyed? Ty decided to delete them and remove any trace existence of that folder and its empty content, just to be safe.

Maybe actually looking for large prime numbers would be a safer experiment. He was familiar with the Great Internet Mersenne Prime Search—or GIMPS—software for discovering Mersenne prime numbers. If it took twelve days to find the largest known prime number, how fast would a small quantum computer find the same prime number or the next prime number, he wondered. Many of these types of tasks were used for stress testing systems and computer builds. A twelve day burn in test would definitely flesh out any hardware problems.

Then, Ty realized he had his own stress and performance testing suite of programs that he always used to shake out a system before moving forward on any of his development projects. That was as good a place as any to start. The test should be long enough to wall clock time it, initially. If it was too fast for that, then, well that would be something worth pursuing. He was working on stressing a new system when the device was delivered to him a week or so ago. The suite contained several computationally intensive routines and had many machine learning tasks in it. He would remove the ones that needed a lot of external data since that wasn't the purpose.

He would start by removing any input and output routines used to test network and storage performance throughput, this needed to be purely processor based—specifically calculations. He assumed the code converters built into the QtPython routines would translate his programming code into properly formed quantum code. He could start with his lottery number work from several years ago.

That reminded him. He picked up his phone, opened the pocket attached to the back of it and pulled out his Powerball tickets. He then unlocked his phone and opened the lottery app. He scanned the barcode at the bottom of the first ticket and waited.

The notice popped up, emotionless. "Sorry, this ticket is not a winner," appeared on his display. He scanned the second ticket—no luck there either—then he navigated back to the homepage of the app to see the Powerball jackpot was at $3.958 billion. The Mega Millions lottery game was at $2.445 billion dollars, though he wasn't currently playing that game. Maybe he should start playing both.

Ty looked at the display of both lottery games on the main page of his lottery app—over six billion dollars in jackpot money. He quickly read the subtext below the jackpot numbers. The Powerball estimated cash value would be $2.967 billion for the Powerball jackpot and $1.834 billion for the Mega Millions jackpot.

The idea finally came to him. He searched on his laptop for his old lottery and random numbers project. It was a couple of years old and resulted in finding out that his predictions sucked, but now, for a chance at winning nearly five billion dollars cash value before taxes warranted another look at these routines with a quantum computer. If anything, it would give him something to aim toward and stay focused on instead of wandering around looking for something to try. Besides, what could be more quantum than making future predictions from random numbers?

***

Ty's phone rang and vibrated, a notification on his work laptop slid open while playing the default ringtone showing a call coming in from Rick Michaelson, his boss.

"Interesting, he never calls me or talks to me," Ty mumbled to himself.

This was probably bad news. His gut feeling was that the new executive team from this most recent executive garage sale wanted to restructure and reorganize to make room for their incoming buddies. Which meant layoffs were coming, and this performing buffoon needed to tell Ty himself. He had been anticipating this for some time, and with the recent disaster in Saitama, this was probably good timing for another round of futile changes.

"Hi, Rick. What's up?" He answered the call from his laptop.

"Hey, Ty. How have you been?" Rick's voice sounded insincere and automatic.

"Still dealing with the loss in Saitama. I have, er, had, some good friends there, and we had a few projects the team was working on together with them."

"I understand. That's good to hear. Look, I need you to be available for a call in about an hour. I'll send you the invite for a video meeting in a minute."

"What's the meeting about? Is this the 'we're making some changes' call, and I'm being laid off?" His voice was sarcastic, but stoic.

"Sorry, yes. There are some big changes coming. Your role, function, and team are being eliminated. Even I'm being let go and so is my boss, Byron. This entire business unit is getting whacked. The new executives want to take the company in a different direction."

Ty felt the weight of years of frustration lift from his shoulders, and the fact that this guy was being let go too lifted his spirits. He had been with this company for a long time and continuously contributed and managed to create cutting-edge technology for them for years. With all the constant changes and lack of transparency, he knew at some point, nobody would remember or be aware his contributions. He knew Rick wasn't reading his status reports or forwarding it up the line. Otherwise, this wouldn't be happening to him and his team. His team would have moved to another business unit or division.

"Okay, so what's next then?" Ty held his emotions in check but wasn't going to talk in pleasantries.

"Like I said, there's a meeting in about an hour. You and I will be on with HR to lay out the details and terms of your separation agreement."

"Can I inform my team?" Ty asked emotionlessly.

"No, at this time this is confidential, and HR will handle the meetings with your team directly without you. If you give them a heads up, it would be grounds for immediate termination, and you would forfeit any severance benefits coming to you." Rick sounded like he was hiding something.

"Well, that's screwed up! Then why are you telling me?" *Keep the emotion in check*, he told himself.

"Hey! I'm being let go too! A lot of people are caught up in this. At your level and status, you're being given an executive exception for a higher severance package. HR has all the separation details for you in the upcoming meeting."

"Yeah, well you deserve to be let go. You are the worst manager I have ever worked for, and I'm not the only one that feels this way. It's worth getting laid off if it means you're getting booted! Actually, I don't even know how you got that job without blackmailing someone."

There was silence on the line for several awkward seconds.

Then, "Just be on the call," Rick said before disconnecting the call.

The "end call" tone sounded, and the conversation was disconnected.

Ty closed the app and sat back in his chair. Even though he had a hunch something was brewing for some time, it still stung. He had never been laid off before. He'd talked to colleagues who had been let go and tried to console them. They would tell him about the severance packages and would ask for him to write them a reference, which he gladly did. But now, he was the one who needed consoling. Who was going to console him? Just about everyone he had worked with in the past were gone or being let go. Why couldn't he give his team a heads-up, even if it was just about him? Something was not right about this. It was going to make him out to seem like an asshole, but he didn't want to jeopardize the severance package.

It bothered him that Rick didn't say anything back. He was just a spineless, worthless, show boater. Then he recalled some senior managers getting bonuses for peaceful and issueless transitions as they were also being let go some time ago. It was highly stressful and some of his friends at the time opened up to him about it. It seemed pretty sleazy, but at least they were getting an incentive to perform. Paying upper management extra to stay long enough to recommend who on their staff should be terminated sounded fine back then, but now that it was being done to him, the whole situation sucked.

"That's it, Rick is going to break the news to my team himself because he's getting paid extra to do so!" Ty exhaled.

Rick rarely talked to him since he came on board two years ago, he sure as hell didn't know who Ty's team members were or what they did. There were so many attempts to engage this guy and include him in their activities, but Ty finally gave up after a while of being ignored. Did he even know that two of his people weren't in the U.S.? Ty wondered if there was a quota he was trying to meet for his own severance package. Rick came across as being a weasel and continued to excel at it every chance he got.

***

The meeting invite came to his company laptop email—an 11:00 a.m. meeting. The invitees were Rick and someone he didn't recognize. He assumed it was the human resources guy. There was a video link in the invite for the meeting. He looked at the time, this meeting was a little over an hour and a half away. He thought about changing his clothes and going out for a run, then decided to spend the time looking at Q-Tip and getting his lottery program working. He doubted the KSS administration knew anything about this device, but if they did and they were looking to retrieve it from him, he wanted to get some time on it to see if there was anything interesting to come out of it. There was a good chance they wouldn't need him to turn in company assets for a week or two. They would also have to specifically ask for it by name. He wasn't going to volunteer its existence to them if they didn't know anything about it.

Ty stood up from his chair and walked over to Q-Tip. He bent down and examined the device thoroughly from top to bottom. He used his phone's camera to look underneath, so he didn't have to tilt it. He scanned the pentapod. Nothing, not a single asset tag, serial number, or company sticker. Not even a brand name. It was still a prototype and probably two more iterations away from being a commercial product, but he had never received an advanced prototype this early. Finally, he went out into the garage and examined the packaging again for any sign this unit was recorded somewhere. Zilch. Just standard looking packaging stickers.

Ty turned his attention back to Tomahawk and where he left off. He began exploring his project folder from three years ago. He opened the last python program he worked on and started refamiliarizing himself with the code. Then he went back to his work laptop and opened his internet browser. He went to one of the lottery number repositories to download the latest set of drawn numbers. It had been three years since he last worked on this, so his lottery numbers were out of date. He downloaded the Powerball and Mega Millions datasets. He liked this particular dataset because the numbers were listed in the order drawn, where most datasets were sorted by number value. As the files downloaded, he wondered how many people were downloading these files since the jackpots were at and near record highs and doing their own analysis. Did anyone even do this kind of work anymore since the lottery parameters were changed to make it nearly impossible to calculate a prediction or simulate the drawing?

According to lottery statistics and analytic sites like www.lottonumbers.com, there was a list of the most drawn balls, the least drawn balls, and the most overdue balls. So, some players played the favorites and others played the underdogs. When looking at that distribution, every number had been drawn. It was a similar premise as a set of balls having been drawn before, except for the timing and combination.

After downloading the datasets, he plugged in a USB flash drive and copied the files to it. When it was complete, he unmounted the flash drive and unplugged it from the laptop, then he plugged it into an available USB port on Tomahawk and copied the new set of numbers to the folder where his previous, out of date numbers were stored.

Doing a quick comparison of the files, there were 546 additional new records compared to the old datasets. At three drawings per week, there was roughly about three and a half years of new drawings to work with for both games.

Ty quickly executed a program that ran a data preparation operation on the Powerball dataset that removed all the drawn numbers prior to October 4, 2015. On that date, the Multi-State Lottery Association changed their double-matrix structure to increase the number of winners, but it ended up actually increasing the odds of winning the jackpot, thereby increasing the size of the jackpots. That was the last game format change that was still in use today for Powerball. There was no point in teaching a computer to learn how to predict random balls that no longer existed. The format changed from drawing five "white-balls" between the numbers one through fifty-nine up to one through sixty-nine. The Powerball pool decreased from drawing one ball between the numbers of one through thirty-five to one through twenty-six. This meant it was easier to win a prize, but also increased the odds of winning the jackpot from 1 in 175, 223,510, to 1 in 292,201,338.

He ran a similar data preparation program that did the same truncating of the drawings for Mega Millions. The Mega Millions Consortium adjusted its double-matrix structure format on October 28, 2017. Like with the Powerball—only with somewhat higher odds—it increased the chance of winning the jackpot from 1 in 258,890,850, to 1 in 302,575,350. Both had the desired effect of increasing the sizes of their respected jackpots.

On August 23, 2021, the Powerball lottery started drawing numbers three times a week, on Monday, Wednesday, and Saturday. This also had the effect of increasing the size of the lottery jackpot and it grew faster. Within a year, the Mega Millions Consortium also started drawing numbers three times a week, on Tuesday, Friday, and Sunday.

Ty wanted to try something different. In his previous work, he'd tried predicting the next possible set of jackpot number occurrences, suspecting the previous drawing sets were somehow related to the next drawing set and how the group of balls were drawn as a whole. After a few years of thinking about what a failure this effort yielded, he continued considering different ways to approach this problem in the back of his mind.

When predicting random draws from a pool or drum of a fixed set of balls, could there be a continuum as a sequence of the drawn balls in order with time as a factor or parameter? Five numbered balls were drawn from the one to sixty-nine drum, the white balls, therefore, once a number had been drawn, it could not be drawn again. Only one number was drawn from the Powerball drum between one and twenty-six. This was actually easier to predict or guess. In fact, it would only cost a player fifty-two dollars to cover the Powerball draw. The problem was the five white ball draws, as well as combining the two matrixes. This also meant there could be two identical numbers, or labels, on a single ticket: one white ball and one Powerball ball, but they weren't related. So, was there a time correlation to numbers drawn in the past to numbers drawn at the present, or in the future?

Was there a rhythm to the process? Ty began to think in terms of music, in the beat or rhythm of the draws. Pull away from the details and play the game from a timing approach similar to music. Draw white ball, draw white ball, draw white ball, draw white ball, draw Powerball ball. Pause. Put everything back. Repeat.

Or da, da, da, da, da, la, rest, reset, repeat.

Or more appropriately, Do, Re, Mi Fa, Sol, La, rest, reset, repeat.

"This is good!" he told himself.

He wondered though, were the two ball pools related? Maybe there were two beats going on. One beat of five draws and the other beat of one draw. Or one beat with two different instruments.

Like, Do, Re, Mi, Fa, Sol, Honk, rest, reset, repeat.

Ty chuckled to himself. It was still a single song, but in practice, he probably would need to code it separately.

Was there music in random numbers that were forced to repeat within a bounded cadence, like a song? Like the lottery? Could that rhythm be detected and forecasted? Like a good musician who could listen to a song and improvise or play along without the need of sheet music. One who could even take the lead, knowing where the song was heading, but never having heard the song before.

This wasn't about numbers being randomly drawn, it was about a physical object being in a certain place at a certain time in a confined space.

The balls could have letters or symbols on them, they could even be blank, it wouldn't change the premise. There was no quantity or weight associated with a single ball other than one ball. It was just a label. And there was a rhythm to the process if you added time and order. And a rhythm could be played ahead or repeated. A musician should know where the next "Sol" was played in a song by learning when it was played in the past or where it should be played in the future.

Ty began looking at his code differently. He wanted to add time as one parameter, or as a dimension. Time always seems to be an omitted factor in random number analysis, or more precisely, the date. Time had a funny way of making itself known when it was least expected, or worse, when it was ignored. However, time also tended to break down when included in quantum physics, when time equaled infinity or when anything included infinity.

Another parameter that was disregarded in statistical analysis was sequence or order. Mainly because the game's rules disregarded it. When the balls were drawn, the order was ignored, but was there a sequential pattern embedded in the draws based on the boundaries of the problem? Rather than only looking at the results as a one-off draw of six balls, the drawn numbers could be treated as a continuous draw. This would result in every fifth draw with time as a variable at three times a week.

Ty started contemplating this scenario. There would definitely be some quantum algorithm that could be put to use for this. He began looking at the sample folder in the virtual machine again. There it was!

He found what he was looking for. A sample folder named "FQML." He clicked on the folder to open it up. The content included a lot of subfolders of sample programs using fully quantum machine learning techniques and functions.

Ty could vaguely remember from an online quantum computing course he took a while back that, "...*one type of problem that can be solved with fully quantum machine learning is that of 'learning' unknown conditions... That quantum computers are able to inherently resolve complex problems with associations between inputs that don't exist...*" or something like that? What was a more unknown condition than predicting random numbers? Ty asked himself.

He needed to teach Q-Tip to learn an unknown quantum state from a known quantum state from a nonquantum state. He started looking at one of the sample programs to see if he recognized what he was looking for, which was a function that would take his problem, his dataset—with its time dimension—and translate it into a numeric landscape of peaks and valleys. Ty would then train the system to the rhythm of the numeric landscape—the music. It wasn't that the landscape had fixed values for the peaks and valleys, the heights of the peaks and depths of the valleys changed with every draw.

Ty found what he was searching for and began coding his own program with the quantum learning and transformation functions he saw in the sample program code. He also took his datasets and truncated the last twenty draws from both games. He saved these in a separate file and would use them later to test his quantum learning model.

Chapter 10

Ty lost all track of time. He quickly looked up and saw it was the top of the hour. Just in time. Not that he was excited about this meeting, he was scared, but he considered himself a professional and this was business.

He took a few deep breaths to clear his head and switch gears. He needed to get his mind ready for this meeting. Going from time-based quantum machine learning algorithms to being laid off from a bullshit company seemed like a good way to strip the gears of his brain if he didn't take the time to push in the clutch.

He turned to his work laptop, where the meeting reminder was displayed, stating he was now one minute late. He took a few more deep breaths and waited. Then he clicked on the link and his company's video conferencing application opened up and automatically joined the meeting in progress. Perfect timing. He would have been pissed if he was the one having to wait in the online virtual lobby.

There were two video panels on his screen and two faces. One was his boss, Rick, looking anxious and stupid. It looked like he was doing this meeting from his home office too. The other face was trying to look empathetic, concerned, and comforting, but was insincere in the attempt. He quickly wondered if everyone in human resources—or "talent management" as they like to be referred to now-a-days—rehearsed the "We're here for you, but we're letting you go" face at their team meetings.

"Hello Mr. McNally. I'm Scott Richardson, and I'll be handling your severance case. Can I assume Rick has informed you of the purpose of this meeting?"

He wondered how many of these meetings this guy had done so far. Scott was pretty polished in his delivery.

"Yes, a little over an hour ago."

"An hour ago? You were supposed to be informed last week. In fact, this meeting was supposed to be held last week. Have you been on vacation or unreachable for some reason?"

Ty could see Rick squirming in the other video panel.

"No, I've been working on a few projects here and there. And with the disaster in Japan, I've been keeping my team up to date, talking to customers and colleagues as to how we are going to keep moving forward. Basically, all on my own using information and messaging from the various corporate emails and from other division's messages from their websites. I haven't received any guidance from Rick, he's been unreachable and unresponsive to my calls and messages. So, I figured he's been busy with other pressing issues; besides, I know how to handle my job. It's been like this since he took over."

Ty didn't care about how Rick was being perceived. He was not only going to throw that prick under the bus, but he was going to drive the bus himself and drive it back and forth over that worthless waste of a vice president position. What was he going to do? Give Ty a bad performance review? Not approve his next vacation request?

"I see. That shouldn't have happened. All executives and upper management were given specific instructions to share the official corporate message about the disaster with their direct reports. There should have been staff meetings to go over these instructions."

Ty was enjoying this so much. He never complained to HR about anything; he always just went with the flow. But to hear that this loser was sabotaging him, his career, and his team on purpose pissed him off. At least he was going to have an audience with someone before he left.

"That's not true, he just doesn't respond to my correspondences or join any of my staff meetings," Rick blurted out.

Why did Rick sound panicky? It shouldn't matter since he was getting dumped too. Ty was enjoying this.

Ty quickly pulled up his email app, did a quick sort on "from Rick Michaelson," then clicked on the "Share My Screen" button in the video conference window.

"These are the emails and meeting invitations sent to me by Rick. As you can see, the last item I received from him was about ninety minutes ago for this meeting. Then seven weeks ago, and that was just a forwarded email to his staff's distribution list to get our expenses in before the end of the quarter. The message prior to that one was two weeks before that. Similar kind of forwarded corporate email. Actually, that also means he's only sent out two staff emails in the past two months. At least using his staff's distribution list."

Ty then clicked on another sorting request. The screen updated with a new list.

"And these are my emails to Rick asking for information about the disaster. My team's weekly status reports. Requests for how to message our customers, and other things. The most recent messages, four of them yesterday, and so on."

Then he clicked on a phone screen mirroring app. His phone's screen now showed on his laptop screen and shared in the video conferencing window. He picked up his phone and started swiping.

"These are all the phone calls I've made to Rick since last week with no answers. These are all the phone calls from Rick: none. And these are all the text messages I've sent directly to him, and these are all the responses: not even one. One explanation is that he doesn't know how to use any of the software, or read and write, but then that would be impossible. There's no way he could have been hired for this role. He doesn't even know how to pronounce or spell what we're working on." That last part made him chuckle.

Totally unprofessional. *Bad Ty*, he scolded himself.

"Well, you must have my number wrong or something because I never get anything from you!"

Oh, that lying sack of shit. He could tell his face was screaming a thousand obscenities and his eyes were burning a hole in Rick's bulbous forehead. Rick was saying this in front of someone else, HR, and trying to say this was Ty's fault. Ty touched the phone number on his phone.

With the video conferencing app still sharing his phone screen, it changed to the familiar phone app, "Calling Rick Michaelson." A loud ringtone could be heard over the computer speakers. Rick's eyes looked down, then a hand gesture, and the ringing stopped. The shared screen in the video conferencing app showed Tyson's phone app with the notice, "Call disconnected, do you want to try again?" For fun, Ty touched the "Retry" button while smiling from ear to ear. He wanted to keep his emotions under control during this meeting, but he was beginning to lose it. This lowlife was the cause of his problems. The same ringtone sounded on the laptop's speakers again.

This time, Rick's hand movements were more pronounced. The ringing over the laptop's speakers stopped, and he picked up his phone and turned it to silent mode, then set it back down.

"Okay, so what? We're all getting laid off. What difference does it make?"

The annoyed shame on Rick's face was worth the effort, and to have HR on the line was priceless. At least he wasn't going down without a fight. He was getting laid off with what he anticipated would be a pretty good severance package, and he was able to get a few well-deserved blows in on this phony. Even if he forfeited his severance package because of the way this meeting was going, he was fine with it. He had a decent amount of money saved up to find another job elsewhere. Ty wondered why Rick didn't abruptly leave the meeting and go cry in the corner somewhere.

"What fucking difference does it make? You just called me a liar in front of HR by lying about it!" Calm down. He took a deep breath.

"Sorry about that, Scott." He was actually sincere about the apology to Scott for the outburst. "But I'm a little surprised I'm the only one that's being treated like this by Rick."

Ty took a deep breath before talking again. "This guy has been sabotaging me and my team ever since he joined this company. He's probably sabotaging others as well. I've saved everything relating to this starting three months after he took over. It was obvious he was incompetent for the job. Heck, give me two days and I bet I can prove that thirty percent of this past year's revenue decrease is caused by his ineptitude and irresponsible leadership. All you care about are 'likes' on your social media accounts." Ty leaned closer to his laptop camera. "Your leadership is embarrassing." Then he sat back, took a deep breath, and continued, "All he does is regurgitate technology buzzwords that don't make any sense. He doesn't even do his own work; someone else does it for him. I'm amazed I'm the only one who can tell. I don't even tell people who I report to because it would reflect poorly on me and my team."

Better, good control, good tempo, no stuttering over words, no cursing.

It was then that he noticed Scott's video panel. Scott wasn't wholly paying attention to the discussion, or he was and taking notes. He didn't blame him. Scott probably heard these types of rants all day long when people were being laid off and upset about it. Ty wasn't upset about getting laid off, he was upset about everything else.

Although, it wasn't that he was only taking notes, Scott kept looking up past his camera in two directions. It was then he realized Scott was doing this meeting from his office and there were other people in the room behind his camera.

Ty felt this kind of information should have been disclosed at the beginning of the meeting, though he was a minute late.

"Is there someone else in this meeting, Scott?" He felt like his privacy had been violated. "I thought this meeting was supposed to be confidential." What did it matter anyway?

"One last thing, since I now have an audience, why am I not allowed to inform my team of my being laid off and of their being laid off and of the dissolving of this function? It seems like an unprofessional move and sleazy of the company to forbid that I share the information." Ty was done with what he wanted to say and mentally checked that item off his list.

Scott refocused his eyes at the camera.

"We never said you couldn't inform your team of this information. In fact, you were supposed to inform your team last week of this situation. You and I were to have this type of meeting with each of your team members and inform them of the reorganization. We're a bit behind schedule with you, but as soon as you were informed of this meeting, you were supposed to start scheduling meetings with them."

Ty was seething. His face was red with anger. He looked at the video panel with Rick's bulging head in it. His face was red too, but for a different reason.

"I was threatened by Rick with immediate termination and told I would forfeit my severance package if I mentioned any of this to my team. He said it was his job to handle my team directly," His voice was trembling with rage. His eyes were getting bloodshot and swollen, not because there were tears coming, but because he was about to scream. Oh, it was a good thing this meeting was virtual, or he might be going to jail.

The meeting was awkwardly silent for too long. Ty said what he needed to say, plus more. He hadn't even heard the terms of his separation agreement or what the actual severance package consisted of. He couldn't wait to end this chapter of his life.

As best as he could, he tried to gain control of his composure. It was time to move on from this dumpster fire. The sooner the meeting was over, the sooner he could stop looking at Rick, the sooner it would be over.

"So, what are the terms of my severance? I have a resume to update. I also have a good team of people to inform," Ty broke the silence stoically, with control, and professionalism. He exaggerated looking at his phone for the time. The meeting had already taken forty minutes and they hadn't even started talking about him yet.

He could see Scott's head shake toward someone beyond his camera and his lips moved without any sound, then he noticed that Scott's microphone was muted. Then it was unmuted.

"Mr. McNally, please hold off on informing your team of the restructuring. This is now an official corporate request. We'd like to revisit this, and we will get back to you first thing next week. Please continue with whatever you are working on until then. And, if you have any questions, concerns, or just need something, contact me. After this meeting ends, I'll send you my direct number and a meeting invite for Monday morning next week. Finally, could you forward to me your last status report sometime today?"

Ty was a little stunned. He guessed they needed to rework his severance package. After the revelation of misinformation and being threatened by upper management, they might have to sweeten his severance package by quite a bit. In thinking a bit more about it, he might have a legitimate lawsuit to pursue.

"Do I need to get a lawyer?" Ty decided to poke at this a little to see where this was heading.

"I don't think that will be necessary, Mr. McNally. Now, Mr. Michaelson on the other hand might consider calling his."

Ty couldn't get to his screen capture function fast enough to save Rick's dumbfounded face when hearing that last statement.

"Mr. McNally, would you mind leaving the meeting now? And please expect my emails to arrive in a few minutes. Mr. Michaelson, stay on the call."

Ty went ahead and clicked on the "Leave Meeting" button in the video conferencing app and clicked "Yes" on the "Are you Sure You Want to Leave this Meeting?" confirmation message. He thought about what just happened. Maybe he and his team weren't getting restructured out. Since the entire business unit was getting whacked, he suspected they were getting transferred to a different business unit or something along those lines.

He got up out of his chair and stretched. That was stressful. He bent over and forwarded the status report from last week to Scott. Ty wasn't sure he wanted to stay employed at this company anymore, anyway. Could he ask for the package, maybe get a sweeter deal out of it after of all this garbage? Or would he have to quit with nothing to show for it? What would happen to his team if he left or got let go? They were all quite a bit younger than him and they had families.

The best place to think this through was while on a run. So, he headed upstairs to change his clothes. There was still a lot of adrenaline and anger lingering in his body, he could feel it in the shaking of his hands. He needed to go burn it off. He decided to not stop by the minimart to buy more quick-pick lottery tickets. The next time he did go, he was going to pick his own numbers.

Chapter 11

After his adrenaline cleansing run, Ty felt better and a little more normal again. That meeting drained him, but there might be some good things to come out of it. It was an emotional and cerebral confrontation with him as the victor, whether he was still with the company or not. He checked the time. It was almost two o'clock in the afternoon. He went upstairs to clean up, grabbed a quick, late, light lunch, and headed to his office.

"Where was I?" he asked himself while entering the room.

Sitting back down with a clear head, he remembered he just cut out the last twenty draws out of the Powerball and Mega Millions datasets. He unlocked Tomahawk and began looking at the program he started writing. He scanned it from the top to where he left off, checked his comments to figure out if he needed to add something and fix some code he hadn't figured out yet.

"Damn!" He was frustrated that the meeting changed his mentality so much that he needed to refamiliarize himself with where he left off. He needed to get back in the zone. He decided this was going to be an all-nighter, or at least, a long nighter. He stood back up, went to the kitchen, grabbed his standard all-nighter snacks and a Diet Coke, and headed back to his office.

"Oh yeah! Now I remember."

He figured out what he was trying to do by reading his comments and the code he started. He was going to treat the draws as a single continuous string of draws, resetting the balls every sixth draw. In a way, this was going to be much harder to calculate, and the odds of pulling out the next string of numbers was going to be astronomical because the numbers would be predicted in draw order; position was now a key factor. He was going to incorporate time into the algorithm in order to adjust the numeric landscape he was creating, kind of like a drummer providing the beat to a song. That triggered something in him...

He grabbed his phone, opened the music app, and selected a playlist he liked to listen to when he was going to pull an all-night coding session—his personal hack-a-thon playlist. The music played in the background on the Bluetooth sound system in his office. All instrumentals and not too loud. This playlist would play for over three hours, then repeat.

When he reached points where he needed to know how to use the FQML methods and functions to make sure he set it up correctly, he would read the documentation. He opened all the sample programs in the FQML folder. If there was a reference to another QPU specific function, he would go read about that one and open the related sample programs for it. Sometimes, he would look up some quantum algorithm using the internet by using his work laptop, which was still connected online. There wasn't a whole lot of online help for what he was trying to do; he couldn't google QtPython and FQML functions, and Stack Overflow was useless.

This process went on for hours. His Notebook development environment would let him know if there was a syntax error, typo, or some other ill-formed code. He was especially pleased that the QtPython language was integrated well enough into the development environment to recognize errors in the quantum specific code. That made this process much easier, and probably safer. He wasn't sure what would happen if a coding error made it to the device undetected. He had read old stories of early computer hardware and peripherals catching on fire or just burning out because of a software error overdriving a component or making a device do something it wasn't designed to do.

***

"Yes!" Ty clapped his hands and excitedly rubbed them together, then pumped them victoriously over his head. The program was finished after one last save. It had taken him several long days of development, testing, research, and coding to complete this program. He designed his program to work with either games dataset by passing in a few parameters when running his code.

Technically, the program could work on just about any lottery game with a double-matrix game structure. The program also did both the machine learning training on a learning dataset and the prediction using the models. He decided to approach the problem as two games within each game. One game used five draws so there were many more data points to work with. The other game was the single draw with four times less data points to work with, but each with the same beat. Both draws were combined together at the end as a single predicted lottery ticket, complete with the predicted date of the ticket.

This was something he wanted to try. The dates and days were a repeating pattern of every Wednesday and Saturday for Powerball, and every Tuesday and Friday for Mega Millions. Then, several years ago, the days changed to Monday, Wednesday and Saturday for Powerball, and Sunday, Tuesday and Friday for Mega Millions, but he wanted the device to figure that out. He still felt the device, or quantum computing, had a problem understanding time related constructs.

He coded his program as a continuous retraining approach because new draws would always be added to the end of the training dataset, then used to train and create the next iteration of models instead of using transfer learning. He would use the training dataset as input for the game's past draws, train, then output the predicted sequence of the set of numbers.

He withheld twenty draws from both game's datasets, so the predictions should be for about six weeks ago. He opened the Powerball training dataset and scrolled down to the last entry. It was the Monday, March 31st drawing. So, when he ran his program, the resulting prediction would be for the drawing held on Wednesday, April 2nd. He would check the accuracy of the prediction by confirming the draw from the withheld data. Then, he'd add that draw to the training dataset increasing it by one draw—more accurately, six draws—and make the prediction held on Saturday, April 5th.

"I'll repeat this process nineteen more times until I get to yesterday's Powerball drawing."

Ty was talking through the process out loud while diagramming the process on a pad of paper. He could have coded this process into his program, but decided it would be better, or at least more fun, to step through this last phase of testing by hand. It would also give him a sense of how the algorithm was performing, and he could diagnose his program or the device in case anything interesting happened.

He quickly copied the two withheld twenty draw files to the still plugged in USB flash drive, then unmounted it and pulled it out. Plugging the flash drive into his work laptop, he dragged the two files to the printer icon on his desktop screen and dropped them there. The printer started warming up and calibrating itself. It had been a while since he last printed something. It would be a good idea to have the list of draws printed out so he could check them off as he went through this process. He could also make quick notes if something weird were to pop up.

Ty was ready to run his program for the first time through Q-Tip. He looked at the time on his desktop, 10:41 p.m., and he felt really good. He developed a good habit of standing periodically to stretch and walk around for a few minutes every hour. This allowed him to work longer and not get too stiff. He would run through the Powerball data's twenty draws through to completion tonight. Depending how long that took, he'd either run the Mega Millions data's twenty draws tonight or first thing tomorrow morning.

He typed in the command to run his program, added the parameters for game type, "Powerball," and the Powerball dataset file name to use. He took one last look at the time and made note of it: 10:45 p.m. Like before, he hovered his finger over the enter key, turned his eyes toward Q-Tip, and blindly pressed down. The auto-tinting window panel on Q-Tip opened up, and that familiar blue light briefly escaped from the inside of the enclosure. The window turned dark again, then it opened up again. Ty forced himself to turn back to look at the terminal window where he started his program. The only thing that printed out was the time when the program started. Since he hadn't figure out how to get the execution or processing timing to work internally properly, he would wall clock time how long the entire program would execute. He'd worry about timer details later. So right now, either his program was still running, or it was hung.

He looked back at Q-Tip. The window was smoothly opening and closing. It seemed faster than once per second, but not by much. He stared at the device and the window panel for a moment, mesmerized. He finally blinked and shook his head slightly. The window stayed closed.

"Whoa! I still can't get used to that weird feeling."

He looked at his terminal window again. The program finished and outputted the predicted results and something that looked like a date and the completion timestamp. He quickly did the math between the two timestamps,

"Forty-five minutes? What the…" He couldn't finish his sentence.

He looked at the time on Tomahawk's desktop clock. 10:47 p.m.

"What the hell is going on! That felt like ten minutes, but only two minutes? Umph, I give up trying to figure out the time functions of this thing."

It was probably a bug and time functions apparently weren't a priority to get right in this early version, so he dismissed it for now. Besides, it was never going to get fixed.

He studied the output and ignored the timestamps.

```
bash$ qtpython -S predict_numbers.qtpy -g powerball -f datasetPB.csv

Thu May 15 10:45:19 PST 2025

---Prediction -> "wE!d AP#r 2} 2025.3, 31 20 2 54 9 - 3"

---Probability -> "Δλφ.αα"

Thu May 15 11:30:32 PST 2025

bash$
```

At least he had his prediction. The date looked weird, so did the probability of the prediction. There was definitely something broken with the time package, and he couldn't figure out what was wrong with the probability output format. It might be an unprintable value. He'd have to do more testing, but it felt like it only happened when the device was engaged. It didn't matter, he knew what the date was supposed to be, and it seemed that was an attempt to output a date. Maybe he should take out the code to predict the date and just output the probability. Could be why the timestamps didn't make sense. He'd deal with that later.

He looked down at the output for the twenty Powerball drawings and looked at the results for Wednesday, April 2nd.

"Holy shit!" It was a perfect match. Right numbers, right order.

"Oh my God! Crap!" His heart skipped a beat and was pounding in his chest. His armpits were drenched from excited sweat. His office suddenly felt warmer.

"Okay! Calm down and finish the process." He put a checkmark next to the first set of numbers and made a couple of notes, especially about the time. He edited the Powerball training dataset, added the March 31st drawing to the end of the file, saved it, and executed the program again.

This time he didn't stare at the device, he kept his eyes focused on the program. The starting timestamp was back too normal, displaying the correct time: 10:50 p.m. A couple of minutes passed, and the program was done with the same output format.

"Well, that felt more normal. Okay, note to self, no more staring at Q-Tip while its busy."

He was in a very good mood, and he actually wrote that note down on the printout. The completion timestamp showed another forty-five minutes of elapse running time again, which he just ignored, as well as ignoring the predicted date and probability output. He examined the new prediction.

```
bash$ qtpython -S predict_numbers.qtpy -g powerball -f datasetPB.csv

Thu May 15 10:50:05 PST 2025

---Prediction -> "#sA,T a%pR ,5 2025.1, 45 6 33 10 63 - 7"

---Probability -> "Δλφ.αα"

Thu May 15 11:35:57 PST 2025

bash$
```

He looked for the Saturday, April 5th drawing on his list and matched the numbers perfectly and in order.

"Bingo!" He couldn't help himself. His heart wasn't racing anymore, but his excitement was impossible to contain, and his office was starting to cool down.

This time, he decided he didn't need to step through the remaining eighteen drawings. He opened the training dataset file and added the remaining drawings, except the last one, to the end of it. He kept yesterday's drawing out for one last prediction that he could validate with.

He pressed the up-arrow key to recall the last command he typed in and pressed the enter key. The timestamp again showed the current and correct time, 10:55 p.m. He was trying to not let this bug him. After several minutes this time, the program printed its output in the window and printed the weird timestamp and completed. This time, the bogus complete elapse time was fifty-two minutes.

"Hmmm, something weirder with time. Go figure." Seven minutes more by adding seventeen more drawings, but only about fifteen seconds longer in actual time. He assumed if he looked at the outputs of the first two first two programs and their elapsed times, the second program would be slightly longer from the first run after adding the one drawing to the dataset.

He scanned the printout to the last drawing; yesterday's drawing.

```
bash$ qtpython -S predict_numbers.qtpy -g powerball -f datasetPB.csv

Thu May 15 10:55:37 PST 2025

---Prediction -> "+W/ed M=Ay 14 2025.9, 34 1 57 5 67 - 15"

---Probability -> "Δλφ.αα"

Thu May 15 11:47:49 PST 2025

bash$
```

Another perfect prediction. He kept checking the same probability output garbage symbols; so that must mean 1.0 in quantum probability. Maybe it wasn't garbage, but something meaningful, just not interpretable, yet. He made a note to keep an eye on that in case it ever changed.

If he played these numbers yesterday, he would be the Powerball jackpot winner. He typed on his work laptop and pulled up the lottery webpage to check the status. The Powerball and Mega Millions jackpots were still growing due to growing ticket sales. The Powerball jackpot was currently at $4.107 billion and the Mega Millions jackpot was currently at $2.802 billion.

Ty looked at the real time, 11:02 p.m. He still needed to train and test the Mega Millions game prediction model, though he felt confident it would work the same way, and there was no way he could sleep right now. He would do the same thing as with the Powerball prediction. He reached for the Mega Millions drawing printout.

***

Everything worked perfectly throughout the Mega Millions validation steps. His program generated similar output with the same probability shown as the same strange symbols and the delta between the timestamp not making any sense. The timestamp difference was shorter than the Powerball, probably because there was about two years' worth of fewer drawings between the current version of the two games. He was now ready to get tomorrow's Mega Millions drawing and this Saturday's Powerball drawing predictions.

This was the moment of truth. How quantum was this device? All of the other predictions already happened. The answers already existed. There was a difference between knowing the past and predicting history versus knowing the future. There was no such thing as a past random number. Once the numbers were known, it was just a bad guess.

You couldn't change history. You could put your hand on the past. You could hide the past. You could ignore the past. It could be described in any way you wanted. It could even be lied about. But it was what it was—done.

A future that hadn't happened yet. There was no evidence or information, only speculation—theory. You couldn't prove the future until it became the past. Was there a door between the past and the future; a boundary where water drained in the opposite direction when you crossed it; where the past and the future are divided, or overlapped?

"Crap! What the hell am I worrying about? It's only two bucks a game. I'll spend twenty dollars on the ticket to hide the fact that I'm only betting on one set of numbers." Ty laughed at himself. He probably lost a couple of thousand dollars playing the lotteries over the years. He'd definitely lost a lot more money than he'd ever won. The lottery wasn't a tax on the statistically challenged, he had a background in statistics and mathematics, and yet he still played before he knew the answers. It was a tax on the hopeful.

He added the last lottery drawings to the two training dataset files. He recalled the command for running the Powerball version of his program. He hovered his finger over the enter key and looked over at Q-Tip. This time it was a very different run than the previous tests, this was a production run—the money run. He wanted to see if the device behaved differently.

He pressed down. The window began opening and closing at the same frequency as the last time he watched. It went on for some time without deviating from the rhythm. It was therapeutic watching the way the light came on and off, flooding the area in front of it momentarily in a blue glow. Like an eye blinking, not flashing. There was something soothing about the way the down cycle looked like an eyelid closing, then the on cycle like the same eyelid opening.

Breaking the hypnotic rhythm, the window shut dark; off rhythm. This time the indicator lights surrounding the darkened panel blinked a pattern of colored lights briefly before the device completely took its normal, inactive posture.

Ty blinked a few times and shook his head to clear it and wake his conscience. He felt like he was watching Q-Tip for about a half hour. He was less disoriented than before and quickly came out of it. This time he remembered the indictor lights flashing a colored pattern at the end which snapped him harder back into reality. He knew it! There was something different about predicting the actual future. He looked down at the note pad and made notes of the differences. He looked up at the output from his program.

```
bash$ qtpython -S predict_numbers.qtpy -g powerball -f datasetPB.csv
Thu May 15 11:02:17 PST 2025
---Prediction -> "S#At M=ay 1}7 2025.0, 59 51 34 2 10 - 2"
---Probability -> "Δλφ.αα"
Thu May 15 11:04:49 PST 2025
bash$
```

He had his numbers for this Saturday's Powerball drawing. There was no way to validate the results; no way to prove it until the future became the past. Could he act on this observation without changing the result; changing the future? He checked the rest of the output. The probability symbols didn't change. That was either a good sign or it was still just broken.

The timestamp, why was the timestamp only showing two minutes? Did predicting the future take less time, less effort than predicting the past? The time on his desktop indicated it was about twenty minutes real time. Still unable to get his head around the time issues, he thought about this. He started writing down more notes. He felt like he was watching Q-Tip process the prediction for thirty minutes, but it took ten real minutes, and his program indicated that it only took two minutes. He wrote down more notes and decided to disregard his *feeling* of time and noted only the time values he had. There was definitely a different behavior when predicting numbers that didn't exist yet. He saved the output to a file, and for good measure, he decided to write the predicted numbers down on a blank sheet of paper. Observed, recorded and soon to be used.

59 51 34 2 10, PB 2

He then recalled the Mega Millions command to run his program. He decided not to watch this time. His mind was still fuzzy from the last run. He pressed the enter key and watched the program output and the desktop time. About seven minutes later—it felt like seven minutes—the program outputted its prediction and was done. He examined the output, it showed only about ninety seconds of timestamp delta. He quickly wrote down some more notes.

```
bash$ qtpython -S predict_numbers.qtpy -g mega -f datasetMM.csv
Thu May 15 11:45:03 PST 2025
---Prediction -> "Fr)i maY^ 1%6 2025.0, 9 7 43 57 22 - 17"
---Probability -> "Δλφ.αα"
Thu May 15 11:46:39 PST 2025
bash$
```

He quickly saved the output and wrote down the Mega Millions prediction below the Powerball prediction.

59 51 34 2 10, PB 2

9 7 43 57 22, MB 17

Ty grabbed his pad of paper and began writing down numbers. He wrote down his birthday date, Janet's birthdate, and the date of her passing. He paused for a moment, the anxiety flushed out of him, and his throat tightened up a little. He missed her and wished she was here to share this with him.

Taking a long breath, he wrote down the date of the earthquake in Japan. A teardrop landed on the paper below his scribbling that he left there as a reminder that he wanted to do something good with this. He could change the world, do something good for the world. He smiled at the thought and felt a new sense of pride and purpose for what he could accomplish with this...*power*? He hadn't thought of it as a power. It seemed irresponsible to be gambling with this kind of power, but he needed to start somewhere. He wasn't even sure this was going to work.

Refocusing, he arranged the numbers, and manipulated them to fit the five-pick format, like using eleven and twenty-nine. Instead of repeating twenty-nine, he came up with four sets of additional picks he could use to fill in the lottery forms, including his Q-Tip predictions. He would just call it a random pick of numbers to fill out the form.

2, 11, 29, 19, 8, PB 8

7, 1, 5, 19, 13, PB 3

2, 21, 20, 1, 8, PB 18

4, 24, 20, 2, 5, PB 25

59, 51, 34, 2, 10, PB 2 / 9, 7, 43, 57, 22, MB 17

He didn't know why he was so nervous and why he felt like he needed to hide these picks. People ran programs to choose lottery numbers every day. Even the lottery provided number picks, though he doubted quick-pick numbers attempted to predict the drawing. Other gimmicks provided users with attempts at predicted numbers. Shit! Even fortune cookies provided lucky numbers to play.

It would be midnight soon. His neighborhood minimart would be open for about another hour. This might actually be a good time to go since there might not be a crowd. The lottery frenzy was at an all-time high with these record jackpots hanging in the balance. He took the paper he wrote the numbers on, folded it, and put it in his back pocket. He decided to go upstairs and freshen up quickly. He changed his dried sweat t-shirt and sprayed himself with some Axe.

***

Ty pulled his Tesla into one of the parking spots near the front door. He looked at the lottery jackpot display boards. They increased a little since he last checked at home: $4.123 billion for the Powerball jackpot and $2.993 billion for the Mega Millions jackpot. The Mega Millions was going to be drawn later tonight. He looked inside the store window to assess what was happening. It looked like three people were inside: one in the snack aisle, the other two standing at the front of the refrigerator together, and one clerk. Looking behind him, he could see two nice cars at the gas pumps and two dudes pumping gas.

Thinking about it, he probably looked suspicious scoping things out, so he leaned forward and started distorting his mouth in his rearview mirror, arbitrarily stuck a finger into his teeth, then swiped them with his tongue, and finished off the vain performance with an exaggerated smile. He then leaned back a little and tussled his short, dark-brown hair for no reason. He was blessed with very low maintenance hair. Opening his door and stepping out, he walked into the store and headed for the lottery counter off to the left.

"Good morning!" He smiled at the clerk behind the counter.

"Welcome," the young woman acknowledged him.

He couldn't remember ever coming in here this late, so he didn't know her. She would probably be closing the store soon.

He reached into his pocket to fetch his folded piece of paper and placed it down in front of him. He reached for a Mega Millions and a Powerball pick form and placed them on the workstation's surface. He grabbed a couple of extra forms, folded them, and put them in his back pocket. Using his own pen, he started filling in the numbers. There were five plays on a slip. He finished filling out the Powerball slip, then finished the Mega Millions slip. He looked them over a couple of times to make sure they were correct, then proceeded to the counter.

"Hi there!" Ty greeted the young lady behind the counter, again.

He put the two slips on the counter.

"I would like ten quick-picks of Mega and Powerball along with these."

"Do you want new quick-picks or preprinted tickets?" she asked, looking at him.

"I'll take preprinted tickets."

During lottery frenzy times like this, lottery retailers would sometimes preprint ten drawing quick-pick tickets to speed up the transactions at the counter.

She picked up the slips and walked over to the lottery machine and inserted the first of two slips and touched the screen a couple of times. The slip was pulled into the machine and came back out, and out came his lottery ticket for one of the two games from the printer slot. She left the ticket where it was and inserted the next slip and touched the screen. Out came another ticket. She grabbed the two lottery ticket printouts, his two slips, and one ticket each from the two preprinted short piles of tickets in front of the machine. She placed the pile of paper slips on the counter in front of him and touched the screen on the register.

"That'll be sixty dollars."

Ty pulled his phone out of his pocket; opened the back, pulled out three twenty-dollar bills, and handed them to her.

She touched the register screen again and the cash drawer opened up. She lifted the drawer, tossed the twenties under it, set it back down and closed the register drawer.

"Good luck," she said as he picked up the tickets and slips.

"Thank you. Have a good night."

He paused at the front door to quickly examine the tickets. He really didn't care about the other twenty-eight tickets he just bought, only the two. Satisfied, he left the store, got into his car, and drove the short dark drive home.

He was excited, exhausted, and tired simultaneously. It had been a very long and emotionally complicated week. He wasn't sure if he would be able to get any sleep tonight, but he'd go through the motions and try.

Chapter 12

Ty woke up after about two hours of total sleep, but he wasn't tired. He jumped out of bed and got himself ready to face a new day. Even though he was certain his life was going to change this evening, this weekend, this was the feeling he always expected to have if he won the lottery and didn't know it yet. There was an extra energy to everything he did. If he was looking into a spectrum analyzer, he would've bet there'd be a positive raging aura around him. He laughed to himself, even Rick couldn't mess this day up.

Jumping down the stairs and into the kitchen, he checked the time, 7:00 a.m. Thirteen hours to go before he would know if what he had done worked, then another twenty-four hours for the second ticket to be confirmed. What was he going to do all day with himself?

He turned on the news to see what updates there were from Japan as he had his coffee and breakfast.

Later, he went to his office to sit there because that was what he always did. He looked at Q-Tip and the work on his laptop. He wouldn't know the full result of his prediction until tomorrow night. Even if the predictions were half right, life as he knew it would change. Then again, if he was only half right, then that would mean something was very broken in his algorithm. What good would that be going forward? Fifty percent right or 50 percent wrong wasn't useful, except for gambling, and the world didn't need a better way to gamble.

He began looking at his code again. What else could he do with something that could shortcut math problems and peek into the future? Was it really looking into "the" or "a" future? Or as machine learning implied, extrapolating a learned trend? He wondered if the FQML functions internally worked with statistics and trends or if there was something else. The way the functions were set up seemed different than other types of supervised machine learning algorithms, but he couldn't put his finger on it. Then there was the whole weirdness with time. That alone had him wanting to figure this out.

Last night spooked him a little. He needed to check the mirror a couple times this morning to make sure he wasn't prematurely aging or reverse aging in some time bubble science fiction way. He did have an overactive imagination and watched and read too many science-fiction stories for a man of his age. Reading was just reading, right? Of course, his favorite genre was based on time travel or time anomalies.

That's it, I'm just over thinking it, he thought.

Though, there was no denying it, there was a problem with time. Either he didn't understand how to use the functions in this modified language or the functions were broken, never to get fixed by its developers.

He decided to start looking into this further. His understanding of quantum computing was pretty weak. So, he'd start there. He began looking up papers and articles on the subject. He wanted to understand more of the physics behind a quantum computer, the quantum mechanics versus how to use one as a calculator. If he wanted to help the world, he needed to get smarter about the power in his hands. Otherwise, he could just be Superman playing with nuclear bombs not knowing the damage they could cause everyone else. Besides, according to his predictions, he had plenty of time.

The thought of having nothing to do for the rest of his life scared him. What would motivate him? Drive him? Make him get up in the morning? Adding another car to his one car collection was one reason he currently worked so hard. After Saturday, he'd be able to buy Jay Leno's entire car collection. What was the excitement in that?

Trying to find that special person to start a family with was something he had been thinking about recently. He still missed Janet and wished she was here, but only recently had the thought of moving on showed up in his heart.

But who would marry a billionaire without any charm? How did dating work like that? He hadn't dated much since Janet passed away. Nothing serious; nothing clicked. He knew his first impressions on a first date didn't warrant a second date. Even if he did get that far, he would probably be just as bad on a second date. He had no game. No style. But who would actually let him know that? He didn't think he was that interesting. He liked being who he was from the get-go. He had no date face.

That was the way it started with Janet. She was who she was, and he was who he was. It probably helped that they knew each other before their first date. He didn't really know anyone now.

He stared off into the distance—looking at nothing. Why couldn't he just close his eyes when he wanted to think? He'd always had the habit of looking toward something but never really *looking* at it when he was thinking things through. He wasn't searching for answers, just thinking things over—playing a storyline in his mind with no ending.

No, he wanted to think of something the world needed that he could address with a few billion dollars—maybe many billions of dollars. How much would fixing the world cost? You can't just give everyone money, people are stupid, and people are ruthless. The cold-hearted would take from the naïve and good natured. It would all just end up back where it started. How much did he need to make, or win, to overcome that inevitability? Could that cycle be broken? Winning lottery jackpots would dry up fast. How many times could someone win before a new rule was made up and put in place to thwart him? Or an outright ban?

There were other ways to make money with numbers and math. Funny, it seemed like everything he could think of involved some form of gambling—legal or otherwise. Games of chance, risky business, betting on something. It all boiled down to the same thing: did numbers tell you to bet on one thing or another, and how much was the reward? It all assumed that no one knew the results ahead of time before placing a bet or making an investment, beating everyone else to the inevitable answer. That didn't seem like the best approach to helping the world. Just a means to an end.

Investments? Well, there were sleazier ways to make money than playing with Wall Street. After all, stocks could be looked at as just a landscape of numbers with more dimension to work with, each with a direction that could be predetermined, predicted, or forecasted. There was a rich history of numbers and data to work with—historical data.

Venture capitalist! Now there was a more interesting way to save the planet in a capitalist way. That was an exciting way to spend billions of dollars.

He blinked a few times, then closed his eyes to gain back his reality. He looked over at Q-Tip, the device's window port was closed. So, there was no hypnotic trance he was caught in, just him and his imagination in deep meandering thought. He looked at the clock, 8:45 a.m.

"Oh man! This is going to be a long day."

He'd already spent all his imaginary money, planned out the rest of his life, and saved the world somehow, and the drawing wasn't for another twelve hours.

He took a sip of his coffee and decided to go look up what kind of data there was to work with in the stock market. Not really a world-saving endeavor, but it did have the advantages of making lots of money and not hurting anyone. The issue he always hated was the decisions made based on investment and return. If you're going to do something good, you shouldn't have to worry about making a profit or losing money. He'd wondered how many people or organizations actually set out to solve a real-world problem without having to worry about the cost or if there was a return to be made.

He looked at the time again: 8:50 a.m. This was worse than Christmas Eve.

Chapter 13

The search team at the Saitama site extracted tons of broken equipment, computers, documents, and other materials in just a matter of days after arriving. They created a classification system and stored the bits of parts in different rooms according to how they were cataloged.

All of the recovered servers were put in one storage office; laptop computers and tablets were in another. This area of the building hosted the computer forensics team. There were stacks of pelican cases full of their equipment. Tools were set up at different workstations, where people were pulling apart and extracting storage modules from the different broken devices. There was an equipment rack set up that included their servers and a large storage array system they used to centrally store and catalog all the pieces of data they could extract from the broken computer equipment. They would clean the parts up and refurbish them as best as they could, test them to determine their functionality, and then connect the parts to their equipment. There they would run diagnostics on the parts, then run a program to scan and extract all the information they could from the recovered storage modules, errors and all.

The team would do several passes through the modules—a raw byte-by-byte crawl of the entire storage module—a file level crawl through the module's file system if they could. Once they extracted that data, they would attempt a file system check on the copied data and create another repository for it. Finally, they would package up the storage module, label it, and store it in a container unchanged.

Occasionally, one of them would run into an old disk drive used as external storage or some other type of archive. These had the dual dilemma of having ten times more storage capacity and being ten times slower to transfer data from it if they worked. The ones that worked went through the paces of getting the data off them, and the ones that didn't work were placed in a special bin for a more intrusive data extraction process at a later time. The team always knew when someone started a hard disk drive data extraction process because they would get up and take a break for a while.

When the data was uploaded, they would input additional metadata to the retrieved files that included type of equipment, make and model, and anything else that seemed useful. At the moment, they didn't know what was in the data, but they were extracting a lot of it.

All the workstations were dumping the information to the central object store. Another group of technicians were monitoring the ingestion and indexing rates. At the moment they collected over fifteen hundred terabytes of unique pieces of information and growing. A team of two data scientists were developing queries and processes to sift through the hoard of information, adding layers on top of layers of filters, translators, error correction algorithms, and other types of cleansing processes.

Other sections of the operation were less complicated. Test equipment and cables, enclosures with components in them, racks of various equipment, robotic parts—basically anything that didn't have a storage module in it went into a different area of the first-floor storage and work area. This area was where the engineers and scientists examined the parts, looking for particular materials, uncommon metals, elaborate cooling or venting systems, and any other kinds of exotic equipment. They didn't actually know what they were looking for, but they knew that they needed to find it.

Then there was the documents section of the floor. Every piece of paper, folders, filing cabinets, desk drawers, printer equipment, books, magazines, notepads, and sticky notes. Anything that had paper in it went into the documents section. There, a team of KRF employees, Marines, Air Force, and Intel-Q personnel worked on examining everything. This area by far had the most people working in it. Some of the documents were in English and could be examined alone, but the majority of them were in Japanese and needed a Katoshi employee to help with the translation, sorting, and cataloging. Some of the Marines were set up to use a translation application on secure tablet computers with ultra-high-resolution cameras, but that only helped classify the piece of information for one of the Katoshi researchers and an Intel-Q scientist to examine it further later.

Dana was in charge of the entire operation in the storage building and at the collapsed building. One of her reports was outside at the destroyed building site overseeing that operation at the moment, another was supervising operations in the storage building somewhere. There was a main staging area near the entry doors where everything collected from the extraction site outside was brought there to await sorting and examination. Basically, if it was man-made, it was dropped off there.

At that moment, she was hovering around the documents section, observing that process and looking at the different heaps of documents. One stack was for papers and articles on a wide range of subjects. Later, that stack would be further sorted down to topics and relevance. One area of piled up papers was actually manilla folders, some with a few papers in them, others in their own pile, empty but with writing on them. Another stack that caught her attention was of printed-out presentations. A lot of them were duplicates and they formed their own piles. They were handouts for meetings. She worked in Japan many years ago while in the military. She was even stationed at Yotota Air base for six months working with her Japanese military counterparts in intelligence as an analyst.

One quirky thing that always amused her about Japanese businesses—if there was a presentation on the screen, there was a printed-out presentation for guests and VIPs. She picked up one single presentation placed all by itself. Maybe the others would show up eventually and the pile would eventually start to grow like the others.

It was tattered but still stapled. It looked like it originally had about a dozen pages. The title slide was almost completely gone except for a quarter corner of it still stapled to the remaining sheets. The last page was in similar condition. She carefully flipped through the printed-out slides. This was a good document, and it was a mix of English words and kanji—she could read some kanji. She recognized the word "Shinsei," or at least she knew what "shin" looked like. It usually meant "new." The word "Shinsei" was also on the page spelled in English phonetically. She quickly grabbed her phone and entered "shinsei" into her translation app. The translation app displayed "shinsie" and an arrow pointing to the English translation—"new star."

She continued through the document to a slide that looked like a status table. She examined it and realized there were six lines of status. She walked over to one of the Marines using one of the few secure translation tablets.

"Marine, could you scan this page for me?" Dana asked.

"Yes, Ma'am." She looked down at the page and placed the camera over it.

The page in the screen of the tablet began transposing the kanji words into the English translation, in the same font size and same format, overlaying the translation over the page, adjusting as the live image changed with the Marine's arm movements. The Marine touched the screen, locking the translated image in a screenshot.

The Marine handed the tablet to Dana. "Here you go, Ma'am." She stood stiff and erect.

Dana got a better view of the Marine's rank and name. "Thank you, Corporal Wallis, please relax. And please call me Dana. I am not active military."

Dana looked at Corporal Wallis standing at attention. She was tall, almost as tall as she was. She wasn't used to standing next to a tall woman, it made her feel a bit normal in a good way. While Dana was shorter than some of the men she worked with, at five foot, nine inches, she was as tall as many of them. She estimated Corporal Wallis was five foot, seven or eight inches, a good sturdy Marine size.

"Yes, Ma'am. Dana, Ma'am," She knew she couldn't say it right and it showed on her face. Corporal Wallis was nervous. This was her first assignment working with the "company."

"Corporal, please relax. There's no reason to be nervous. I'm not a company agent. I'm just an investor. An analyst. I work for Intel-Q." Dana was trying to assure the corporal that there was no secret agent shit about to happen. "Don't worry, this is not a matter of national security, we're just looking after an investment."

"Thank you, Dana." Corporal Wallis actually relaxed with a disappointed tone in her voice.

Dana read the newly translated document. "Corporal, can this translated page be sent to me? To my phone from the tablet?"

"Yes, can you hand me your phone?" Corporal Wallis held out her hand.

Dana put her phone in Corporal Wallis's hand, who then placed the phone on the screen in the upper right corner. She touched a couple places on the tablet's touch screen and the screen on Dana's phone came on and showed a smaller view of the page.

"Here you go," Corporal Wallis said, handing her phone back to her.

"Thank you for your help, Corporal. Keep up the good work." Dana turned and started to head out of the area when she stopped and pivoted back.

"Corporal, can I see your tablet?" Dana took a few steps toward the piles of documents.

"Sure," Corporal Wallis handed her the tablet.

"Can these translations be saved and used to search other documents?" Dana was showing her the specific translations she was interested in.

"Yes. I can save them and create a search query out of them." Corporal Wallis knew where Dana was going.

"Good. I'd like for you to use these when you continue cataloging these documents." Dana was pointing at the symbols and translations. "Make me a special pile of anything with these keywords in them. In either English, kanji, or both."

"Got it, Dana." Corporal Wallis looked down and started setting up the special search requests.

"And Corporal, do you have my phone number?"

"Yes, I got it when I connected to your phone for the document transfer." She looked a little ashamed.

"Excellent. Call me or send me anything you find that looks interesting. You have an idea of what I'm looking for."

"Yes, Ma'am!" Corporal Wallis almost saluted her.

With that, Dana nodded an acknowledgement and headed out.

As she walked, she touched the document image to zoom in on some of the details of the image still on her phone. She encrypted the page and sent the file to Dr. Lancer's phone. Then she called him.

The phone rang for some time before he finally picked up the call. "Sorry to wake you, George," she apologized.

"Not a problem, Dana. Thanks for getting to me with an update. What've you got for me?" George sounded tired but was quickly waking up. The only reason he'd be called right now was if there was something important to report.

"Check out the encrypted file I just sent to your phone." She waited for Dr. Lancer to open the file.

"Okay, what's the code?" He sounded nonchalant. It was normal business as usual.

"Lima, Tango, Romeo, four, two, nine," Dana said while continuing to walk down the hall.

"What am I looking for? It looks like a translated presentation slide with a table on it." George was looking at the image of the translated page now with the speaker phone turned on.

"What did you say the project name was?" Dana was egging him on to find it for himself.

"New Star or Shinsei. Ah, now I see it. Sorry Dana, it's three ten in the morning here. Good, you've found the right area or something." George still hadn't fully awakened.

"How many prototypes did you say they built?" Dana still wanted Dr. Lancer to figure this out himself.

"Five. Good lord! There's status for six devices?" George was now very awake. "Why can't I read the status of number six?" He was fully engaged in what he was looking at.

"The document I got this from is part of a presentation deck. It's in pretty bad shape and it's the only presentation printout that we've found so far. No other copies. Which means there was probably only one VIP or guest in the meeting." Dana was deducing what she thought had gone on.

"Given the timing of the earthquake, it was probably one of their morning status meetings, and this one had an important attendee."

"So, this status of 'en route' for number six means that one device could be somewhere else and not destroyed with the building." A sense of hope could be heard in George's voice.

"That's exactly where my thinking is taking me." Dana was feeling pleased with herself.

"The header has department heads on it. Do we have a clue as to who this department head is? There's a good chance they don't know this is the last one. We need to find this device." Dr. Lancer sounded confident the project wasn't dead just yet.

"No idea yet. Let me keep pulling on this thread. I'll get someone from my team to take over operations here and brief them on what to look for. I have one of the Marines keeping an eye out for more documents like this one. I'll start looking into what departments were working on this project outside of KRF. You might want to give chairman Nakatori a call to see if he knows of an outside department that would do work with this project, or if he knew there was a sixth device. I'll check in with you later. Sorry for the early wake-up call, but I knew you'd want to know this information ASAP. Try to get some sleep, Dad." Dana disconnected the call and looked up at the operation.

Things were moving along, but this was their first breakthrough. They still weren't sure what they were looking for. This device was different than the others she researched. It would have been easy to spot five or six of those giant gold and copper chandeliers, but this new quantum computer, no one really knew what it looked like or what to expect.

Dana walked over to the staging area and studied the piles of debris. She smiled at herself. "I can't believe my job has come down to rooting through trash." She took in a deep breath of air through her nose and exhaled. "Well, maybe not trash."

She squatted down and lifted a random cable harness, looked blankly at it, then dropped it. She clapped her hands together to clean them off and headed for the door.

***

"Okay, sounds like a good plan. Good job over there, Dana, and thanks for the call." Dr. Lancer disconnected from the call.

He paused and smiled hearing his daughter call him "Dad." It was all business, but the last part was personal and sincere, and he loved it. Bringing his daughter onto his team was one of his best management decisions, even if it was mostly professional. He looked at the document on his phone again. Then he swiped the screen and touched it.

He changed into some clothes and headed to his home office. He walked over to the printer and grabbed the printout he'd sent over and set in on his desk. Before sitting down, he turned on a desk lamp that brightened the area and the entire office. Putting his glasses on, he studied the document more intently. The entire center of the page looked like it was scraped diagonally, leaving only a couple of corners of information legible.

He reached into one of his desk drawers and pulled out a large magnifying glass. Looking closer at the page, he placed the glass on his desk and grabbed his phone. He pulled up the file again and looked at the translation overlay layer. He swiped the screen a couple of times and touched a few buttons to separate and set aside the translation layer, leaving only the original document image. Another swipe and touch, and the printer momentarily came to life.

Getting up from his desk, he grabbed the page from the printer and placed it down on his desk as he sat back down. Using his magnifying glass and scanning both pages side-by-side, he could make out additional details. There was more information, faint information on the nonaugmented document. It was scuffed up a bit, but readable to a human eye. The translation application couldn't detect it, so it didn't translate it. He couldn't read the words on the page and a translation app wasn't going to *see* the words there. He'd bring the page into to the office with him later for someone to examine it.

There was another revelation that came from this piece of information. There was another organization that knew about the device enough to work with it. Maybe they helped develop it or helped build it. There was a sense of hope again that this project could be salvaged with minimal delays.

He picked up his phone and called Chairman Nakatori.

Chapter 14

"Tyson McNally, *Billionaire*!" he shouted. Ty was watching the live stream of the Mega Millions drawing online when his numbers were drawn, in order. He jumped out of his chair and was bouncing around the house, running into rooms he hadn't seen for months. He turned on every light. He flushed all the toilets in the bathrooms he never used; he didn't know why. All he knew was that he just won the Mega Millions jackpot. It was one kind of feeling knowing he was going to win. It was a whole other type of feeling when he actually did win. He couldn't contain himself.

He looked at the lottery app on his phone again. The final jackpot was $3.211 billion with an estimated cash value of $2.408 billion. Even after taxes, that could still be over $1.3 billion in the bank. He was a bonified billionaire. It wasn't a new record jackpot, but it was a top three. No, the record jackpot win would be for tomorrow night's Powerball drawing. But no matter what happened tomorrow night, money was, would be, in the bank tonight.

"I am now a member of the 'Tres Comas' club!" he proclaimed as a tribute to one of his old favorite shows, "Silicon Valley."

He screamed in his unused living room with his arms stretched out over his head, spinning in circles. His mind was racing on what to do next and the steps he should take.

The first thing he did was fill in and sign the back of the Mega Millions winning ticket. The slip had only five tickets on it, so it was shorter in length than the ten ticket slips he always bought. There were only two areas to fill in his information. He filled in all the blank lines and signed it twice. He took a picture of it with his phone, then a video of the ticket with him turning it over to show his information on the back.

Using the lottery app on his phone, he read about the process of claiming a prize over six hundred dollars. He downloaded the claim form and printed it out. He thought it was strange there was only one claim form for any prize over six hundred dollars for any game. It seemed like there should be more paperwork for a three-billion-dollar jackpot than a six-hundred-dollar prize.

After filling out the form, he went ahead and printed out two copies of the ticket, then went to his printer and made two copies of the claims form. Taking one of the ticket copies, he folded it up and put it in the storage pocket on the back of his phone and gathered up the rest of the forms and the original winning ticket. Using a paper clip to hold everything together, he walked down the hall to the closet where he opened his gun safe and placed the forms and tickets on the shelf inside.

He looked inside the lit compartment at his unused gun collection. *Has it been over a year since I've been to the shooting range?* he wondered.

He picked up one of his 1911s and cocked the slide, smooth as silk. He spent a lot of time and money building these guns as a hobby, but lately, was too busy to enjoy them.

He wasn't paranoid, he was just following the procedures he'd read on "what to do after winning the lottery" he'd found online earlier in the day. The list of "what to do" included calling your financial advisor, your tax attorney, your lawyer, your accountant, your doctor, a priest, a magician, your plumber, and your landscaper.

He thought, *Who has all these people working for you unless you're already rich?*

It was Friday night, how was he going to find all of these professionals? Seemed like anyone taking a cold call on a Friday night or the weekend might be someone he didn't want to have represent him. No, this could wait until Monday. He did have a tax guy he'd used for ten years, but he wasn't too sure about using him for this situation.

Besides, this wasn't over yet, there was still the Powerball drawing tomorrow evening. When that occurred, all kinds of crap would start happening. His neighborhood minimart would be the center of the universe for a while. It was already going to get a lot of local attention tomorrow once it was announced where the Mega Millions winning ticket was purchased. He thought about what it was going to be like after tomorrow night. He'd met the owner a couple of time over the years. Hopefully, the owner would take care of his employees with his lottery bonuses, especially after tomorrow. If the owner didn't, Ty might have to step in and do something.

Now that he was a winner, he realized it was a mistake to buy the two tickets from the same retailer, but what was done was done. One thought crossed his mind, he could give away winning lottery tickets, but he'd have to be smart about where he bought them. That way he could take care of family and friends, his team at work, and charities he wanted to help. That seemed like it would be easier to share this power in the short term and less paperwork for him. It would definitely help take the attention off of him. They all could manage that process themselves. Or he could just give everyone the numbers to play themselves. He didn't know if that would really fly. Who would play numbers given to them? Well, not initially. Once they realized they were holding the correct numbers, he would have to do it all over again. And then everything would start coming back to him. He decided to worry about these problems later.

He kept reading the information about the lottery prize claim process.

"Eight to ten weeks!" Ty involuntarily shouted out at his screen.

He couldn't believe how long it would take for the money to be sent. He assumed he could arrange for a direct deposit, or have it wired directly to his bank account, but that long? What was he going to do for the next eight to ten weeks? And that was after he finally sent in the claim forms. That reminded him, he might need to hire a security firm for protection.

Now that he knew how long it would take to get the money, he wanted to be smart about it. *Don't spend what you don't have,* he reminded himself.

He'd lived and worked for fourteen years without this much money. He could survive another two months without it.

That thought didn't help him sleep. There was still another lottery drawing tomorrow night, and it was most likely going to be bigger. It might be a good situation if the Powerball jackpot was split tomorrow. The chances were better that there could be more than one ticket with the winning numbers. This was the world's largest lottery jackpot, the number of tickets sold for this should also be a record. Even people who never played the lottery would probably have bought a ticket just to be part of history. He decided to watch the drawing live on TV tomorrow night. There might be a special on with more information about the drawing.

He tried to get some sleep by not thinking about all the possible outcomes tonight and after tomorrow night. He just needed to be cool, calm, and collected. There was nothing wrong with what he'd done. He was still going to be rich, but now maybe he was just getting greedy and that was when dumb things started to happen.

No, that's not the problem, he told himself.

He was proving there was something unique about this quantum computer and the software that made it work. He was also showing his ability to code a program that recognized a predictable pattern from perceived chaos, and that pattern could continue on into the future. Or was there something special about random numbers that might not be random at all? This work and its results were all a tribute to Yuichu and his team. That was what Ty was good at; making other people's creations look good.

He fell asleep thinking about beneficial problems to solve that didn't include gambling and chance.

Chapter 15

The reflection in the office window staring back at him highlighted his aging eyes and an undetectable slump in his six-foot gawky frame. Dmitry watched the operation from the fourteenth floor of an empty office building. At least, it was empty for now, as the inspectors were busy looking over far more critical infrastructure elsewhere. There were small cracks on the outer walls and some debris on the ground. It was mostly cosmetic, but protocol dictated that an inspection would need to be performed before it could be occupied and reopened for business.

It would be a week before an inspection team could show up. If he needed more time, a few hundred thousand yen could buy an additional three weeks, perfect for his needs at the moment. The office was dark, without power, but comfortable. The windows were clean inside and out with an unobstructed view of the disaster site below. Nobody could see in, and he could see out to everything, even at night.

His camera equipment continued to record the area with the high-resolution wide-angle video lens, while he continued to watch with his binocular telescope. Any time a new load of debris was hauled away from the rubble, he would press the remote shutter button, so his zoom-lensed camera focused on the payload. The two instruments were digitally tethered together to follow his eyes to wherever they were focused.

He had a second similar camera setup focused on the front gate of the Katoshi research campus, except that one was set to automatically take pictures of any new object detected that included people, vehicles, equipment, and anything else that entered the scene. The laptop connected to that equipment would immediately run license plate numbers through the local vehicle registration system when it detected them. It also ran searches on the system back at the embassy for any new faces that showed up in the view. His camera setup was configured to do the same thing at the collapsed building site, but he currently was doing this manually to keep himself busy.

He didn't mind being there on site, it reminded him of the good old days where stakeouts were done manually. In the good old days, he would have a comrade with him, but he was no longer a part of that agency. Besides, everything was chaotic in and around Tokyo at the moment. This whole operation could have been done from the comforts of his apartment, but the bandwidth in the entire area was unstable and slow. He secured the office space as soon as he was assigned to investigate the unusual activities at the site below.

Spotters near the American Yotota Air Base let the Russian embassy know that an American government plane landed at night there a few days ago. A large group of Marines from Kinser Marine Base showed up at the airbase in civilian clothing shortly thereafter. Then a group of vehicles left the airbase in different directions and routes and ended up at the same location below. It wasn't an earthquake cleanup operation; they were carefully searching for something.

There was no heavy equipment to move earth and rubble. No, the largest pieces of machinery were mini-excavators and small hauling vehicles. Almost everyone at the collapsed building site had metal detectors and gardening tools, hand digging into the ground or through the debris. He could understand the hauling away of equipment and computers, but why were they also concerned with collecting all the scattered documents. And why was the front gate lightly guarded?

This wasn't a military operation. The few weapons he noted were sidearms on a few of the Marines, and those were carefully concealed. Everyone wore civilian clothing. The plane that arrived a few nights ago was just a government transport plane that easily could've been providing supplies and relief for the disaster. It was either a very clever cover or a coincidence. His deduction was a bit of both, just lucky timing. The operation was drawing no public attention on purpose, and they seemed oblivious to casual observation, but there was something odd about what was going on below. Something was lost or destroyed when the landslide collapsed that building. Why were the Americans in charge of this operation?

The landslide made it very easy to observe and record all the activity at the building site down near the river. A large swath of land, trees, and shrubs were cleared away, opening the entire area for observation from the right angle. The activity at the other building was a different situation. It was still shrouded behind trees and foliage. He could see the hauling vehicles heading toward one of the still undamaged buildings with a load of debris, and they returned to the dig site empty. The whole spectacle was like watching a high-tech archeological excavation looking for a tomb or treasure. He assumed, in the other building, there were more people sifting through the fragments of material, maybe even extracting data from the computer storage devices. Lost information? No, they were also hauling all kinds of equipment, cables, and junk. He thought, at one point, he saw parts of a robot arm heading to the building.

Beeping sounded behind him from his laptop. With the slow transmission rates, the queries from the embassy were lagging behind real-time responses. There wasn't really anything interesting happening at the moment. He pressed a button on the touch screen controller of the camera equipment he was manually operating, and the camera took over watching the site below. He sat in front of the laptop to see an identified woman leaving the front gate.

"CIA! The CIA is here?" He instinctively looked up and then down toward the excavation site, not really focusing on anything.

The identification process was running about two minutes behind real-time due to the slow bandwidth. He received a dossier on the identified woman and started reading it to himself. If they had a dossier on someone in their database, then there had been some type of interaction in the past.

```
Name: Daniela "Dana" T. Jordan.

Maiden Name: Lancer.

Marital Status: Widow.

Military Status: Air Force, Retired.

Rank: Captain.

Military Specialty: Cyberspace Operations Officer, 2008-2014.

Service: CIA Analyst, Retired.

Service Specialty: Analyst, Computational Sciences, 2014-2019.

Note: No known field engagements or operations.

Current Status: Employed Intel-Q 2019-Present.

Specialty: Deputy Director, Advanced Computational Technology
Investments.

Education: Graduated Purdue University, 2008.

     Master of Science, Computer Science, and Mathematics.
```

Dmitry mumbled to himself as he read through the dossier. A couple of pictures of Daniela Jordan were included.

"Intel-Q? Why would CIA send in investment person to dig through collapsed research building in Japan, and what is she looking for?" He asked himself questions as he read through the dossier.

He was making mental notes to himself for his report back to the embassy. There were no other notable personnel at the site, so he assumed Mrs. Jordan was in charge of the operation. He didn't know why Mrs. Jordan was a person of interest in their system, but from his assessment of her, she was an analyst and a computer geek, not a field agent. A button pusher; a finance person.

"A counter of beans." He thought that was what the Americans called their money people as he continued to study the dossier.

It looked like she was spending the rest of her career working in the technology and finance world, but not fully removed from the CIA. From what he could recall from memory, Intel-Q invested in commercial companies for supplying technology and equipment to the different government intelligence agencies and military branches. Many of Intel-Q's investments were very commercially successful, but it was the classified versions of these commercial products that made them important to the intelligence community globally. He looked down at some of his equipment, wondering how much of it was influenced or invested in by Intel-Q.

"So, they invest in research here in Japan that is very important to them, but they did not expect earthquake to destroy it. One hundred and sixty people die in collapse of building, maybe research team gone too."

There was no report of any Americans lost in the collapse. Dmitry continued to deduce what was happening below.

"A salvage operation? Cryptography technology. Mrs. Jordan is a computer scientist and mathematician. They are assessing whether research and investment is a total loss," he continued to think through the situation.

"No remote backups anywhere? And they need to piece everything back together. Something was built and now is damaged or destroyed. This was a recovery operation." That was why they were collecting everything.

His report would include a lot of speculation, but he had a good reputation for putting loose pieces together to form a story worthy of deeper investigation or action. His deductions had been correct in the past, but it was his actions that got him in trouble. He began typing up his report.

***

Dana left the recovery operations at the destroyed research facility to head to one of Katoshi's fully operational corporate office buildings outside of the disaster areas. She needed to look up some company information.

Dana asked Dr. Lancer to work with chairman Nakatori to help her follow-up on a few of her leads. She wanted to look through the company's directories and personnel files. What other facilities would work on this device? Was it hardware or software related work? Heck, for all she knew, it could have been out for radiation testing, drop testing, or painting. Why did everyone think only five devices were made? Actually, a sixth unit could have been created after the initial five for non-functional testing. Then again, it could simply be a mock-up for marketing purposes. No, it seemed to be too early for that kind of concern. Some other division or department had a prototype quantum computer, and it might just be sitting in an abandoned laboratory waiting for Tokyo to come back to life.

"En route?" Why would it be "en route" around here? Everything was practically less than a day's train ride away unless it was on an airplane or shipped somewhere. Maybe she needed to find a research department in Katoshi Corporation outside of Japan. The company had over 150 different divisions in forty-eight commercial businesses worldwide. They made everything from information technology products to ships to manufacturing equipment to consulting. Where to start? She would look at every division that had some type of R&D group that might help with the development. There might be some divisions that would look at the device for applied quantum computing research. She doubted there would be any quality and stress testing going on at this phase. They were still a few versions away from production quality candidates.

From the information she had, they hadn't begun building any of the Mark 4 machines—not even close. Any planning for that machine would still be at the main research site.

No, she needed to track down this sixth unit, and she needed to find where it went and who else knew about it. If there was another team of researchers familiar with this product, they might actually have all the operational data for it, and they could continue developing it.

Dana had a pep in her step as she headed toward the nearest train station.

Chapter 16

Ty watched the TV and the time. The Powerball drawing was coming up soon, but he didn't know what to expect. He'd never watched any of the live drawings before on TV, but he had seen videos of it from time to time. It was basically a long commercial between shows at around 7:59 p.m. on the west coast. There were about fifteen minutes to go, and he was half watching something that didn't interest him.

It had been another long day of looking for things to do to occupy himself so he didn't dwell on tonight's Powerball drawing. He'd gone out for an extra-long run, then hit the gym. He worked on his cars for a while, washed them in his driveway, then backed them into the garage. That got him through lunch.

He researched other lottery games around the world so he had an idea of how he could pick additional tickets. They were all straightforward, and he could apply his program to the datasets to predict upcoming drawings if he wanted to.

He also started looking into other types of problems that could only be solved with a quantum computer. It was fascinating to learn what couldn't be performed today and why it seemed like the world was not advancing as fast as humanity could. He always considered himself one of those people who were pissed that people weren't commuting by air to work by now.

He spent the afternoon recoding his program to do all the continuous learning and validation testing steps automatically. It was fun going through those steps the first couple of times, but he didn't need to manually go through all that again. He would just pick a withholding value and the program would pull the last drawings based on that value from a given lottery dataset. His program will then process through those steps, retraining the models and making predictions through and to the final drawing. This gave him the final probability score, which was still garbage symbols, but at least it was the same garbage symbols, and the next prediction for an upcoming lottery drawing.

The program would score itself on the predictions and throw out an alert if it missed one. He didn't know if this function actually worked because it hadn't made a wrong prediction yet. There was also a function to notify him if the probability symbols ever changed. He wanted to implement these features outside of the virtual machine environment because he felt having the device check its own results was self-fulfilling.

He didn't try to fix any of the oddly behaving time problems, though he did attempt to figure out what was wrong with the strange probability symbols. Ty didn't push too hard to fix that issue, not wanting to break what was already working. The most valuable answer was the next predicted set of numbers based on the game. Finally, for good measure, he made a few copies of the USB flash drive and Tomahawk, which included the virtual machine and all his work.

"Okay, here we go!"

The Powerball drawing was on. The announcers talked about the new world record this jackpot was setting and the possible jackpot size at the next drawing if no ticket won tonight. The Powerball jackpot was now $4.407 billion. In less than a minute, the drawing was over and so was the show.

Tyson McNally, double jackpot winner, multi-billionaire. He knew the numbers as they were coming out of the hopper in the exact order he predicted. He just sat there blankly watching the screen as the next TV show began. He wasn't paying any attention to it.

The estimated lump sum cash value was $3.3 billion, which probably meant about $1.8 billion after taxes. That was if his was the only ticket. He sat there hoping there were other winning tickets to split the pot with, but that information wouldn't show up for several of hours.

What did he do? He sat and wondered what would happen to him. Would it be just, "Here's your money, have a great life," or was there going to be a long series of questions he didn't want to answer and investigations.

There had been many people who won multiple jackpots, but those were mostly small-time winnings. A million dollars here, a few hundred thousand dollars there, nothing in the billions or multi-billions of dollars. Of course, he didn't have to claim anything. The money could just get defaulted—absorbed into the system after a year or so if it wasn't claimed. The whole thing would disappear and assumed flushed down a toilet by accident or washed in the laundry in someone's pants pocket.

Ty wasn't feeling guilt, and it wasn't shame. He did the work to make these predictions. He thought about that. Could his algorithm run on a conventional computer and still be this accurate? This was the first time he'd tried this approach. He'd be surprised if anyone else thought of it or tried it. He knew if he ran his program on Tomahawk, it would take a long time to finish, maybe too long. Getting the prediction after the drawing was done wasn't really that useful. Could he recode it to run on a supercomputer or a high-performance cluster?

No, he had an advantage. He was using work assets, but it yielded promising results that could be used to solve future problems. A product? So, he actually used the results and played the lottery—that just proved it worked. He'd done that in the past for work and didn't win a thing, and nobody cared. The work he did then helped develop some new machine learning algorithms that were used in some of the company's products today to predict component failures.

The fact that he'd proved this algorithm and this quantum computer worked at making a prediction in the future, or "a" future, was a significant achievement in his mind. He was able to use the results physically; in reality. Nothing observable changed as far as he could tell. In quantum mechanics, the observation of a quantum phenomenon could change the results.

Much of quantum computing's challenges today was observing the results before the quantum fields broke down into noise. All the shielding from outside interference, isolation from reality, qubit error detection, and correction mechanisms were all part of an attempt to preserve the results of the qubits long enough to be usefully observed. Not only was he able to get the results out of this quantum computer, but he used the results in the real-world. Then, sometime later, those results still held stable long enough to become the past. Once the results were in the past, they could no longer be affected, right?

He didn't know how this was accomplished or how it was implemented. He just knew how to use it. That was the way this type of technology needed to mature, being able to be productive without having to know how it worked. Whatever Yuichu and his team did, they probably should be awarded the Nobel Prize in physics or something else—posthumous.

So, what if the device was returned? No big deal. They could work with it, reverse-engineer it—restart the project. He could probably be on the project resurrecting it. He was an expert, or at least knowledgeable in how to use it. That was a fact.

He should make sure he had the money he'd won in the bank first. He could also help others before turning the device over to Katoshi. He would definitely return it to Katoshi Corporate or what remained of KRF. The new executives at KSS wouldn't even know how to spell quantum computer. Originally, Yuichu's team would have crushed the Mark 3 devices after all the testing and development was done, being replaced by the next version, the Mark 4. It was just a part of their development procedures. But now, Q-Tip was probably the last one in existence, and those plans might have changed, if there were any plans at all.

"Wait a second! Who says I need to return it? I can still use it and work with it while I'm currently employed. I don't need to leave yet."

He'd see what happened during Monday's meeting with HR. Besides, he still had a couple of months to go before any money showed up.

He changed the channel, looking for some local news. He was interested in hearing how this was going to get reported when it was discovered that the two winning tickets were purchased from the same store. In the meantime, he had some forms to fill out and some phone calls to make.

***

There was no new activity at the recovery site. The response from the embassy came quickly. They knew what the search team was looking for, a quantum computer and information about it. This wasn't a secret mission, but it was interesting that the Americans were so interested in recovering it. It was also interesting that they couldn't find it. He looked up pictures and information about this technology. These machines were very large and very distinguishable. There could even be chemical traces to look for if it was destroyed. Plus, the materials and debris the Americans were recovering didn't look anything like what he had just learned of a quantum computer.

That couldn't be it, Dmitry thought to himself, continuing to read the response.

"Continue to monitor the situation and report any abnormal activity, or if the machine is recovered."

That was not a good use of his time. No, his instincts told him to follow Mrs. Jordan. She left the site about twenty minutes ago and hadn't returned. He suspected she would return eventually. So, he would do as he was told for now because he had to, but once he found Mrs. Jordan, he planned to tail her if she left again.

Meanwhile, he looked over his automated equipment and decided to let it do all the work for a while. There were enough triggers programmed into the equipment's operation to notify him if anything unusual came up. He began searching for Katoshi buildings that were still open for business. That was the course of action he would have taken assuming this facility was nonoperational.

***

Dana left the train station and started walking toward a large building a few blocks away. The train schedules were light, but at least this area was still open to civilian travel. It was good to get out of the dark recovery operations building and walk around outside for a while. If she had her running shoes on, she would have jogged around a few blocks on her way to the Katoshi Corporate headquarters building. Even though it was a Sunday afternoon, and a disaster recently shut down the city, corporate headquarters was open for business. The staggered work week schedule that all large Japanese corporations were following took some getting used to. Katoshi Corporation was on the Wednesday through Sunday work week, so this was a Friday afternoon for the company, with Monday being their Saturday.

After entering the lobby, she made a call on her phone. The lobby was nearly empty except for two security guards standing by a far wall and a receptionist sitting at the front desk. After a few minutes of waiting, a smartly dressed young woman met her and bowed slightly.

"Dana-san, please follow me." She gracefully raised her arm, pointing toward a door off to the side of the main lobby.

"Thank you." Dana slightly bowed back and walked toward the door.

She wasn't dressed for regular business, she was dressed for recovery business, and she could tell she was noticeably underdressed—almost dirty. It wasn't a concern, but blending in was one of the trademarks of a "company" employee, even a retired analyst.

Should have thought this out a little better, she noted to herself. At least there was no one around to stick out from.

Entering through the door, there were rooms on both sides of the wide hallway. Apparently, this was a back entrance into a conference area—the executive briefing center. She wondered if her clothes warranted entering from the side door versus the grand front entrance. Then again, her task required a bit of concealment from the general public. Luckily, there was no public around.

"Right here Dana-san," she heard from behind her.

She stopped to turn around.

The young woman was again pointing, this time at one of the conference rooms.

Dana opened the door and entered it. Inside was a handsome conference table with very nice chairs surrounding it.

"Please have a seat. Someone will be with you shortly. Would you like any refreshments?" the young woman politely and professionally asked.

"No. Thank you for asking. I'm fine," Dana replied.

The young woman bowed and closed the door as she left the room.

Dana took a seat at the head of the table and looked around. A standard customer briefing center conference room with a large display at the front of the room, and an empty catering cabinet for refreshments off to the side.

After several minutes, a young man dressed in a sharp business suit entered the conference room carrying a laptop. He quickly bowed and reached out his hand toward Dana.

"I am Takani Yoshi. I am from corporate human resources here at Katoshi headquarters. How may I be of assistance, Dana-san?"

Dana made a brisk bow back toward Takani, then shook his hand. They both sat at the corner of the conference table.

"I was hoping you could help me locate a research department or a department head that might work with your KRF organization. They might do additional development or testing of research coming from KRF. I'm looking for a device or research materials for some work headed by Yuichu Norigawa or Dr. Takashi, the general manager of KRF." Dana was trying to describe what might have been the case with the unknown department.

"Yes, Dana-san. I understand. We do not know of the daily interactions between divisions, especially the research and development groups. They are normally unstructured in their activities and record keeping. I am sorry. However, you may use our internal directory and look up internal personnel in our system if it would help. Our systems support English. I understand the importance of this joint venture between our organizations." Takani placed the laptop on the conference table, opened it up, and logged in.

"I will show you how to navigate through our personnel files and the hierarchy of our company. Then you may spend as much time as you need searching for your information." He began typing and navigating through the system.

"Thank you. That would be most helpful," Dana acknowledged respectfully. His English was exceptional. There was something about Japanese business culture and their professionalism that brought out the respectfulness in people.

Dana watched Takani navigate through the personnel files by divisions.

After drilling down through a couple of divisions, he looked at her and asked, "Would you like me to continue, or do you understand our systems?"

"Thank you again for the information. I think I can manage from here. May I have your number in case I have any questions, or to inform you that I am finished?"

"Of course, Dana-san." Takani pulled up a quick text application on the laptop screen and typed his personal mobile number into it.

"You may also text me if that is a more suitable communication method for you. Please let me know if I can be of any further assistance." Takani stood up, briskly bowed, and headed for the door.

Before leaving, he turned around. "Mrs. Jordan. If you need to leave without letting me know, please close the laptop and leave it on the table." He nodded as he was about to close the door behind him.

"Arigato gozaimasu, Yoshi-san." Dana bowed slightly and stiffly.

Takani looked at her and gave a deep approving bow as he continued out of the room and closed the door.

The Katoshi system, as with most Japanese systems, tended to be laid out differently than western systems. She always noticed information, detailed information, was more important than esthetics when designing web applications and human interfaces.

Dana began looking at the different research divisions within the Katoshi Corporation of companies. Looking for ties, collaboration points, integration of different groups, subdivisions, anything that would look like KRF would transport a research device outside of their facility. This would take a while.

***

Dmitry arrived outside the Katoshi Corporation headquarter building from the nearby train station. He assumed Daniela Jordan was inside looking up information, it was what he would do. This was the closest Katoshi building open for business. The fact that it was corporate headquarters only reenforced his hunch that this was where she was heading. Most likely searching through personnel files.

He bought a large coffee from the café across the street from the main entrance of the building and sat down at a table outside on the sidewalk. The foot traffic on the street was very light, but people were going about their business in this undamaged part of the city. Sipping his hot coffee, he reviewed the pictures of Mrs. Jordan on his phone, making sure he would be able to spot her when she emerged from the building. He continued reviewing her dossier.

Why would a button pusher analyst be in our system?

Their system had many agents from around the world in it, but those were mostly based on some type of interaction or operation in the past. He'd have to dig a little deeper into that history later. Right now, he was focused on the mission at hand.

He pulled out a small black device from his jacket pocket and set it on the café table with the lens pointed toward the entrance of the building. He then placed a set of keys next to it to conceal its presence. He was close enough that he could see the main entrance and the faces of everyone coming in or out, but far enough that the entire width of the building was within the device's view.

He opened an app on his phone, which synced up to the device and immediately showed a live video of what it was viewing. He turned his phone so the view was showing more of the width but fewer floors. He chuckled a few times to give the appearance of watching a funny video. Then he started touching the screen, cycling through different spectrums, searching through visual marks until he found what he was looking for.

On the first floor were several color spectrum profiles of people walking around, one person sitting at a desk, several people sitting in a circle with one person standing up waving their arms and walking around next to them—a presentation. Then he found the image he was looking for, a single person in a large space sitting and focused on something. He deduced it was a laptop display or tablet. The movement of the arms and hands suggested they were scrolling and reading through information.

Dmitry smiled again and chuckled artificially. It was a habit of his while tailing someone. Nobody seemed to notice you when you were watching dumb stuff on your phone by yourself. He reached in his pocket and placed a set of wireless earbuds into his ears to complete the ruse, then took another sip from his coffee. He touched a few buttons and focused in on the lone figure. Everything was being recorded and analyzed. If the lone figure in the room changed, he would be notified of it. There were certain nuances of human reaction that could signify surprise or satisfaction or other emotional body queues. He'd know if she found what she was looking for—or failed.

***

Dana was able to learn and understand the basic corporate structure of Katoshi Corporation. It was a standard Japanese business hierarchy. The research and development organizations started at KRF, then branched downward to subdivisions which took the advance research materials and began the productization process. The most advanced work was initiated at KRF, which made sense and why Intel-Q was working directly with them and corporate headquarters. Chairman Nakatori oversaw all of research and development, so that was why he and George were in close contact with each other.

She entered a search query for Ashito Takashi.

```
Ashito Takashi, PhD.
General Manager, Katoshi Research Facility.
Direct Report to Chairman Hashiro Nakatori.
Eight Direct Reports:
    Karishi Onito, PhD
    Suzuki Tanaka
    Matsumoto Yoshida, PhD
    Inoue Sato
    Saito Shimizu, PhD
    Yuichu Norigawa, PhD
    Kimura Yamamoto
    Kato Kobayashi, PhD
```

Dana recognized Yuichu Norigawa. He was directly in charge of this project from the start. She clicked on his name.

```
Yuichu Norigawa, PhD.

Department Head, Computational Sciences, Katoshi
Research Facility.

Direct Report to Ashito Takashi, PhD.

Ten Direct Reports:

     Sasaki Ito, PhD

     Mori Watanabe

     Ishii Hashigawa, PhD

     Aoki Sakamoto, PhD

     Mark Higgins, PhD

     Toshi Iwata

     Jens Boris, PhD

     Anki Namora

     Shitomi Hota, PhD

     Taizo Suzuki, PhD
```

This was where all the real work was done. She pulled up an internal company webpage and did some searching on Yuichu Norigawa. The first search result showed Yuichu Norigawa listed as one of the 159 employees who were killed. She looked at the memorial webpage and recognized other names from the list she was just looking at. She hadn't yet grasped the magnitude of the destruction at the recovery site until just now. She paused for a moment and collected her thoughts, then made a mental note to be more respectful to the site when she returned.

She clicked back away from the memorial webpage and selected the next search result. There was an internal company blog dating back a couple of years ago describing the release of a new product that Yuichu invented earlier in his career. There was a picture of him with an American standing behind the product on a display table. They were both happy and celebrating the announcement. It looked like they were in the U.S. in an exhibit booth at a technology tradeshow. The product looked like a pizza box server of some kind with about six mobile devices positioned around it. The blog stated it was the third time the two collaborated on a successful research product rollout together. The announcement was made by a subdivision of Katoshi called Katoshi Systems Services, and the name of the American was Tyson McNally, an employee of KSS.

"Director of Advance Product Development" was how Tyson McNally's title was shown in the article. She opened the personnel application again and entered Tyson McNally. Nothing. Employee not found. She searched for Katoshi System Services as a subdivision of Katoshi Corporation. A public webpage for KSS appeared as the only search result. From there, it was a website all on its own. Even the domain name changed from www.Katoshi.jp to www.kssinc.com. She looked at the company structure from the top down, there was only a brief mention of KSS. Katoshi System Services was a wholly owned subsidiary of Katoshi Corporation, but was completely incorporated in the U.S.

Revenues of the subsidiary had been declining over the years, but it didn't look like they were failing. It looked to her like revenue streams were being redirected away from KSS to other Katoshi divisions. Looking closer into the company, she found the executive management suite had been experiencing severe churn, including four CEOs over that last five years. All four CEOs were coming from failed companies and bringing in executives from those failed companies with them. Why would a successful company continue to hire failures to run their company? They were in the "business death spiral," some of which was self-inflicted, the other part might be planned above them. She could tell something was wrong, but that was no concern of hers, her immediate goal was to find Tyson McNally.

She reached for her phone and took a few pictures of the blog, the photo of Tyson McNally, and other information. These internal systems between Katoshi headquarters and KSS probably weren't integrated together. From what she gathered, KSS was only about a twenty-five-year-old company, and for a subsidiary, KSS only reported up through board members, not as a company.

She did a search on the internet for "Tyson McNally." It looked like he had a lot of followers on social media. He wrote a lot of blogs on technology. Smart man, nothing personal posted. Good, he still worked for

KSS in the U.S. Only a couple of pictures of himself. It looked like other people posted images of him speaking at conferences or posted selfies with him.

Hmmm, so he's popular and influential, but modest. Nice traits. Handsome in a scruffy looking kind of way.

"Here we go, more pictures with Yuichu and McNally. Looks like it spans about nine years or so." Dana finished looking through three pages of search results, including images.

"Perfect!" She had her lead. She was confident she knew where the sixth unit was sent, but she was going to need some help.

She got up from her seat and closed the laptop lid. She texted Takani that her work was done, and she would be leaving now and thanked him for all of his help. She left the conference room, walked out of the main doors of the EBC, and exited the building.

She looked up and down the street, then turned her face up at the afternoon sun. It felt good after being inside sterilized air for a while. Facing the warmth, she could see the lone guy sitting at the street café looking at his phone, smiling and sipping an empty cup of coffee. She turned and started walking toward the train station. She was followed. There was a fifty-fifty chance that in fifteen minutes, he was going to know what she knew, or she was going to be tailed.

After turning the corner, she could see in the distorted reflection of a store window that the man went across the street instead of tailing her. Dana grabbed her phone and called Tanaki.

"Yoshi-san. Could you please retrieve your laptop as soon as possible? I see… Yes, I understand… Please do your best and thank you again." She disconnected the call and made another while walking toward the train station.

***

His phone pulsed three times in his hand, notifying him that something interesting happened. The figure in the image appeared to pick up a phone and take pictures. He knew something was found, but what? Soon, the figure stood up and slapped their hand down on the table. Standing there, it looked like they were messaging on their phone. Then they walked, closing a door. Fifteen seconds later, out walked Daniela Jordan onto the sidewalk.

Picking up his empty coffee cup, he took a long sip from it while staring at his phone, smirking.

She looked up and down the street, then up at the late afternoon sun, then she started walking down the street toward the train station.

Dmitry smiled at his phone and nodded, acknowledging nothing. He watched over the top of the phone as she headed down the street and turned a corner. Grabbing his keys and shutting off the device, he placed the items into his jacket pockets. He crossed the street and entered the building's main lobby. The lobby was surprisingly empty. He walked over to a grand entrance to the executive briefing center and opened the door. Nobody was there either. He could see lights and motion across the way in a conference room with frosted windows for privacy. Remembering the way Daniela Jordan walked away from where she was sitting, he headed toward a right-side hallway.

Down the hallway, there were three doors on each side. Slowly, he opened each one and peered inside. When he reached the last door, he found what he was looking for. Closing the door behind him, he pulled out a USB device and plugged it into an available port on the closed laptop at the head of the conference table. Opening the laptop, Dmitry immediately powered it off, then powered it back on. The laptop never finished its normal startup sequence. Instead, it copied every file created or modified from the past twenty-four hours to the USB device. Most importantly, this included browser history and data caches, as well as copies of the applications that used the data.

After a few minutes, the process was complete. Pulling the USB device out and stuffing it into one of his pockets, the laptop completed its startup sequence. He closed the laptop and made his way to the door. He peeked out of the door to see that the hallway was empty as he stepped out of the room and began walking toward the executive briefing center's exit.

He stopped by the refrigerator to grab a bottle of Coke in the refreshment area. He held the refrigerator door open with his head inside as a young man in a nice business suit entered the EBC lobby and walked toward the conference room hallway. Grabbing the soda bottle, he closed the refrigerator door and confidently walked out. He emerged from the building and onto the street, standing where Daniela Jordan stood no more than fifteen minutes ago. He took in a deep breath, turned, exhaled, and walked toward the train station.

Chapter 17

Howard entered the CEO's office with a frantic urgency in his step. Qu-Cell Incorporated had been struggling to stabilize their system for nearly two years. They were in the early stages of adding 20 percent more qubits to their QPU architecture in an attempt to detect and correct the quantum decoherence they were currently experiencing. Their anticipated outcome would be to stabilize the QPU's results long enough to be observed.

It would take another two years just to see if it worked, but according to their simulations, it would be the right balance that got them to a minimum viable, stable product. This approach would also nearly double the number of patents they have already filed, and nearly double the current development cost. Their plan was to have the most predictable and stable quantum computer on the market by 2029, and that was just the hardware.

"Bob! Intel-Q is digging around the KRF site where that building collapsed during the earthquake in Japan. Not just Intel-Q, but George Lancer's team is directly trying to recover something from that disaster site." Howard sat down and crossed his legs.

"And how do you know this?" Bob looked like he was interrupted from something important but was now focused on Howard sitting in front of him.

"Ex-CIA is in charge of the recovery operations. A friend in Japan sent me a redacted status report. Apparently, the operation captured the attention of the Russians, and they sent an agent out to observe the activity." He held a manilla folder up by his head and placed it on Bob's desk in front of him.

"I get it, ex-CIA gets everyone excited. So, what the big deal? The U.S. is all over that country helping with earthquake relief. Why is this any different?" Bob hated probing for more detailed information.

"Because they landed at Yotota Air Base, gathered airmen and marines from Kinser Marine Base, and they're all in civilian clothing—no military markings of any kind. They aren't cleaning up anything, they are digging and hauling material from the collapsed building to another building. No heavy equipment, and there are armed guards at the front gate. They aren't hiding their presence there, but it seems like strange behavior. At least the Russians think so. They also think they're looking for a quantum computer of some kind." Howard switched his crossed legs.

Howard continued, "Look, we know George is heavily invested in the development of quantum computing. It's no secret he's hedged his investments in a number of companies globally, including us and Katoshi Corporation. Katoshi isn't known as a player in this space. Why would he send his team and the military there to dig around in the dirt? Unless there's something important to him there. Speculation is, they're not looking for a machine built like ours or everybody else's. Katoshi was on to something new—a different approach. If the intelligence out there is true, it could put us and everybody else out of business. But it appears the earthquake messed that all up," Howard explained, trying to connect the dots for Bob.

"Any patents filed?" Bob was following along and processing this information in the back of his mind.

"There's about a dozen patents filed and awarded, but these are mostly theoretical. They haven't filed for any of the implementation patents yet. That's probably what they're looking for as well—information."

"You mean to tell me they didn't have an off-site backup or a disaster recovery system in place? They're digging for data?" Bob gave out a half laugh, smirked, and slapped his knee. "That's tragically funny," Bob finished.

"Bob, we don't either," Howard told him, deadpan.

Bob stopped laughing cold.

"All the data we have is right here in this building too. We use compute cycles in the cloud, but that's purely transactional. All the results are transferred back here, then the virtual cloud servers are wiped clean. Everybody in the industry is keeping everything close and secure; everything's on premise. Especially with all the recent cloud security breaches over the past few years." Howard looked ashamed for mentioning that fact.

"Right now, we're only burning through investor money. Until we start making money—turning a profit—we're not set up to protect ourselves. Maybe IBM does, but they're a huge, profitable, diversified company. They can afford to protect everything. Hell! They use their own products for business continuity, then turn around and market and sell them." Howard sounded envious.

"Okay, so what's the plan? Is there a plan? Do we know if they had a working machine? Is that what they think they'll find? I can't imagine any piece of equipment surviving that disaster, let alone finding anything that still works." Bob was already thinking through ideas.

"KRF is pure advanced research. They don't have a business continuity plan, at least not for a huge disaster like what happened. They could have done so. They have the products in their portfolio to do so, like IBM, but they're Japanese." Howard shrugged, acknowledging he didn't understand the culture.

"Anyway, one way to look at this is we're still in business with our modified design going forward. Intel-Q would need to continue funding us until we can release our first commercial product. That's assuming the KRF project is unrecoverable." Howard thought for a moment.

"But if they find enough salvageable equipment or documentation to restart the KRF project? Then all bets are off. If the rumors are true about their technology, then I bet George redirects funding from everywhere and pours it into KRF. And lord knows what'll happen if they actually find one of those machines that still works." Howard was speaking through different strategic scenarios.

"Well then, we'll either have to figure out a way to keep them from finding anything at that site. Or find it ourselves, so we can reverse engineer it." Bob was beginning to think the KRF design might actually be the better path to take.

"Look Howard, we've been at this for years. We think we have a working quantum computer, capable of exhibiting quantum results, then another problem forces us to build a larger machine to counter the problems—fix another instability. This new recommendation from our scientists will be the fourth modification to the original design, just to add error correction capabilities. I'm not a quantum physicist, but it feels like we're going to chase this problem all the way into bankruptcy. I'd rather try something new, if we even had a new idea to try, but it seems like we've hit a roadblock and we have money committed to seeing this design through to the end. Whatever that end is." Bob's voice was stressed. He knew this next machine would find another way of not delivering what was promised.

"What else can your friend in Japan find out?" Bob was eager to look into exploring some new options.

"She has access to almost everything at the Russian embassy." Howard leaned forward in his chair.

"What do you have in mind?" Howard lowered his voice when asking that question.

"Look, they haven't filed any patents on their implementation, right? That means it's still up in the air. We should at least have a look at what it is. What they were doing. Maybe have a go at replicating it, incorporating parts of it into our machine, or outright change it—something. Our design is a money pit, and it's hard to see when it will ever be finished." Bob sounded frustrated running a company without a clear path to a working product or profitability.

"I'm just looking for ways to keep our options open. Do you understand where I'm going with this?" Bob leaned in and matched Howard's lowered voice.

"I do understand where you're going with this." Howard was looking Bob square in his eyes.

"It's going to require some petty cash to get more information. Then, if you actually want to take some kind of action, well, we're going to have to hire somebody who can hire somebody, probably who can hire somebody to do the job. Now do you understand what I'm saying? Neither of us should get our hands dirty for this." Howard poked Bob's desk with his finger as he stressed his last sentence.

Howard knew exactly what Bob was asking. He'd done this before a long time ago, and he was good at it, but he'd hoped he might have moved on past his past. He thought by being in the technology industry, he'd have a legitimate, boring career.

"Agreed. Let's start with more information. No point in diving in without knowing if it's worth it. Go make something happen and keep me updated," Bob said with a more normal voice as he leaned back in his chair.

Howard left Bob's office. This could be fun. He did miss the cloak and dagger lifestyle from his past a little. Maybe in the tech industry, it would be a lot more civil. After all, this was just business. In the old days, it was personal.

Chapter 18

A couple of local news stations arrived at the minimart in his neighborhood yesterday. News of the Mega Millions jackpot winner was announced after Friday's drawing. It wasn't a record lottery jackpot, not even for the Mega Millions game, but it was the largest lottery jackpot awarded in the state's history. Standard local news did a few interviews with employees, the owner, and a couple of customers from the neighborhood. He even recognized one of his neighbors on the TV. It was a good local piece with a couple seconds of national mentions at the end of news shows.

Now, Sunday morning, the minimart and the surrounding streets and neighborhood were overwhelmed with news crews, reporters, news vans, people, and street vendors. There was even a news helicopter overhead for a short time. The entire corner was jammed packed with people from everywhere trying to be a part of history.

Over seven and a half billion dollars in lottery jackpot money had just been won from this lottery retailer. Even cable news channels and national news sent crews to cover the story. The store owner, employees, some customers, and residents in the neighborhood were being interviewed again. Over half the people there were videoing the scene with their phones as citizen reporters and live streaming it to their social media accounts.

Ty watched the spectacle from his family room TV. The whole scene was kind of funny. There were women and men holding up signs saying,

"*Marry me—I'll sign a prenup!*" and "*Buy me a car, whoever you are!*" and "*Wanna go on a date?*" and "*I'm available!*" There was one teenager holding a sign saying, "*Adopt me please!*" It all felt like people were just having a good time, wanting to get interviewed and seen on TV. There were a couple of scary signs though that made him nervous: "*No one should be allowed to win this much $$$!*" and "*You Will Be Found!*"

He hoped nobody was assuming the same person won both jackpots. That would probably turn the peaceful gathering into something else. No, please just keep letting everyone think it was just two tickets from the same state, the same city, and the same store. It would be okay for everyone to think two people from around the area won for the time being.

Luckily, California was one of the last to join the growing group of states that allowed lottery winners to keep their identities private. He never understood why winners should be forced to reveal their identity—it sounded dangerous. The scene on TV made that very clear.

His attention focused back to the TV. A reporter was saying something he was dreading would come up.

"*There's a growing number of analysts speculating that both of these winning lottery tickets belong to the same person. There's no proof of this other than the two winning tickets coming from the same retailer. And since these two recent jackpots were so large, everyone playing the lotteries purchased tickets for both games at the time of their purchase. We'll have more on this story as it develops. That's all from me. Reporting live, this is Candice Hanes, back to you, John.*"

Ty's stomach twitched. Who cared? It wasn't against the law to win the lottery more than once. It wasn't against the law to use a computational machine to pick your numbers either. The only issue was the social pain-in-the-ass it would cause. That inconvenience should only last for a while, then the public's attention would drift to some other outrage or shiny object. It always did.

He did think about hiding his tickets in a better location, at least until he finally filed his claims and contacted all the professionals he needed to hire. That could take a few days. He should also figure out a way to hide Q-Tip. He got up off the couch and headed to his office.

He walked into the room and looked at Q-Tip. How could he hide that strangely shaped device? He had an idea. It was late Sunday morning; he decided to head to the hardware store.

***

Dana pulled out her phone after she boarded the short single-deck green car that sat between the two larger double-decker green cars. It was smaller with only twelve seats, and it was usually empty this time of day, even without a recent disaster.

"George!" She didn't wait for Dr. Lancer to answer his end of the phone.

"Dana, what's wrong?" He immediately sensed her distress.

"I was tracked to the Katoshi Corporate building by someone. Non-Japanese." Her voice was low, but above a whisper.

"So, I take it you lost them?" George's voice involuntarily matched hers.

"No, after I left the building and turned the corner, I could see him head toward the main entrance of the building. My guess is he was going to look at what I was doing on the HR system. He probably had a digital cache scrapper," she said as she now spoke calmly.

"Okay. Did you find something useful?" Again, George's voice matched hers.

"Yes. I have a lead as to where that sixth unit might be. I think it's in the U.S. I'm heading to Mountain View now." Dana looked at the time.

"I can land at Moffett Field in about nine hours. I'll brief my team to keep the recovery operations going at the site."

"Okay, but tell your team to remove as much as they can from the site and store it in the building. We only have until the end of the week to work the site, then we have to leave it. We have the operations building for as long as we need it." George reminded Dana of the time schedule they needed to be aware of.

"Okay, understood." She forgot about the deadline at the collapsed building.

"Do you need me to send some people to meet you at Moffett?"

"No, but if you can call Katoshi Systems Services and let them know I need access to their systems, that would be helpful." Dana thought about that for a moment. "Better yet, could you make a call to chairman Nakatori to get approval for my requests? It might sound less suspicious coming from him and have more authority."

"Dana, this isn't a mission, it's part of a larger project. So, somebody tailed you and wants to know what you're up to. The operation probably drew some attention. We're not hiding much. You're ex-CIA, you probably triggered their facial recognition system. It's probably the Russians.

They're always trying to find out what we're doing." Dr. Lancer chuckled to himself to where Dana could hear him.

"Funny, we should have sent out three other teams to dig around Tokyo. That would have kept them busy trying to figure out what's going on," George joked. "Be careful, take a deep breath, relax. Let me know what you find at KSS."

"Okay, will do. Talk to you soon." Dana disconnected the call.

She loved working with her father, even if it was professionally, especially after John died. Leaving the "company" after the "incident" was all part of "company" policy, but letting George hire her to come work for him took some political jujitsu to make happen. Keeping her married name helped ease the work environment, but it wasn't really needed. She'd earned her position and was highly regarded by her peers. By all accounts, she was next in line to take over should George decide to retire, though there was no indication that would happen anytime soon, which was fine by her.

George wouldn't come out and admit it, but she knew this project was important to him, and probably his last. She didn't want to fail him.

She made another call.

"Hey, Ed! I need you to take over the operations there at the site. I'm following up on a lead. I'll be in Silicon Valley for a day or two… Also, change of plans. Get as much material from the search site into the operations building. We don't have much time left at the collapsed building, but we'll have all the time we need in the operations building, so the priority is to suspend searching and start moving… Keep me up to date. Thanks, goodbye."

She made one more call.

"Don, this is Dana. I need the plane prepped. We're heading to Moffett Field… Fast… I should be there in about ninety minutes… Perfect, thanks… Hey Don? Is my stuff still onboard the plane? Great, thanks. See you then. Bye."

She disconnected the call. The train compartment was still empty, so she reclined her seat, leaned back, and closed her eyes before the next stop.

***

George saw that the call ended. He stared at his phone for a few seconds, then looked around his home office. Did he put his daughter in danger? He didn't take these sorts of things seriously; his background was mostly academic. Having the school's mascot stolen before a big game was a serious matter. Maybe there were people who did take these situations more serious—powerful people.

George made a call to his assistant.

"Jane, I need a flight to San Jose... Yes, I'll need to use company assets to get there... Thank you and sorry for doing this to you so late on a Saturday... I'll make it up to you," George disconnected the call and went to his bedroom to pack.

***

Back in the dark office of the abandoned building, Dmitry surveyed the recovery operations below. He stood close enough to the window to see the street area in front of the gate, but distant enough to not light himself up for people to see him from outside the window. He backed away and looked over his surveillance equipment, then sat down at his laptop. He unlocked it and inserted the USB device into an available port. An application popped up automatically and began transferring the contents of the digital cache scraper.

While that application was processing, he pulled up the logs of his camera and notifications. He looked at the front gate camera notifications. Seven objects were detected, five of them were people in the last hour. He began reviewing the images. The system couldn't identify anyone from the back, so he needed to examine them manually. She was not there. He went back two hours. Eleven objects detected—eight of them people. He looked at the one new hit; it wasn't her. Going back three hours ago only turned up Daniela leaving from the front gate. She hadn't returned yet or wasn't returning.

A few minutes later a carousel of images came up over the top of the surveillance application he was using, sorted by dates and times.

"Let's see what you find that is more important than coming back," he said to himself as he flipped through the carousel of image cards until he arrived at about an hour ago.

He read through the different HR screens and looked up company personnel at KRF, the Katoshi memorial webpage, and other applications. What was she looking for? There was a time period where she was looking for different research and development divisions within the company.

"Maybe she looked for other researchers at other divisions? Restart project. There are many quantum computer companies trying to make new machines," he talked out the scenarios as he worked.

Then he found the internal blog depicting two Katoshi employees smiling behind a table with a computer server and phones on it. Reading through the blog, he noted it was a couple of years old. American's and their product announcements. There was one Japanese and one American in the blog. Yuichu Norigawa. Why was that name familiar? He flipped back through the carousel to the internal company memorial webpage and found the name on the list. Then he flipped further back to find the company organizational chart. Yuichu Norigawa, PhD.

"So, he was head of project and died in the disaster. Now she is looking for other researchers not in the building during the disaster? Smart. But something…" He flipped forward through the carousel.

"Is she searching for this American? Maybe the two of them work together. Information is old."

He flipped through the work that Daniela did. Internet searches for Tyson McNally: social media, blogs, speeches, all junk. He was just a marketing guy. Not a quantum physicist. There were older articles with these two men, but nothing about quantum technology. He read through some of the older articles and blogs up to the point where Daniela stopped. He found other names in the articles with "PhD" degrees who worked for Katoshi in other research divisions and began searching through those names.

"Ah, now this is more interesting; physicists." He cross-checked these names against the Katoshi memorial page.

"This is good. Only a few of the names are listed. There are about five scientists who are still alive. She must have found someone to seek out."

He began typing up his status report and his suspicions to send to the embassy.

***

Ty backed his Tesla up into his driveway and opened the garage door. Unloading the contents from the trunk, he placed the materials in the middle of the empty parking stall left by his Tesla. Then he began rummaging through the storage cabinets of old computer parts he collected over the years, but never had the heart or will to throw out.

It was funny how a tech guy thought. Except for a few collectable relics like the original Macintosh computer, an Amiga, or an old Commodore computer, old parts just got older and more useless. It really became more worthless as time and technology advanced. He'd collected old computers and parts since he was a kid with the idea that it might be valuable again someday. Some of it came from his dad.

Well today, it was useful. His plan was to make props with all this stuff. He put all the storage bins in the middle of the parking stall and started sifting through everything. He had a bin with old stereo equipment in it, another with lights and LEDs; one had robot parts, another had motherboards and peripheral cards, and the last one had a little of everything in it.

After taking a quick inventory of what he had to work with, he took one of the twenty-four-inch-long PVC drainpipes and the end caps he purchased over to his workbench area. He loaded it into an old makeshift lathe he built a while back and turned it on. He began carving and sanding it into the shape he had in mind.

As Ty continued to work in his garage, digging through his bins of parts, painting, and assembling things together, he was also thinking about what he should do next with Q-Tip. After he gifted friends and colleagues with lottery tickets, and probably charities, then what? The device was too powerful to hand over to his company. No, they were too incompetent to realize what it was. As he thought through different scenarios in his head and played out storyline after storyline, he continued crafting his designs.

Then it dawned on him. Was it the device that was dangerous to have or was it his program? He had been modifying it here and there to make it more generic, not just to predict lottery numbers, but also stocks, other gambling games, simulators, weather—basically, anything that could be vectorized into a landscape of numbers in a time series dataset. It now also allotted for as many matrix structures as possible. He didn't know how far forward a prediction could be made or how long before it lost its accuracy or stability, but it was spot on for a quick result.

The applications for just this one program could be limitless. Weather predictions could be perfect. How far in advance? He didn't know, yet.

Then again, that was his thing, machine learning. He couldn't solve chemical analysis problems or protein folding problems. There was a whole list of challenging engineering problem he couldn't solve even with a quantum computer. But there were those who could but couldn't because they didn't have access to a working, low-cost quantum computer. This device needed to fall into the right hands, but until he knew whose hands those were, he needed to keep it from falling into the wrong hands. Destroying it wasn't an option either. He knew the future would be better with it than without it.

He kept working on his scheme for disguising Q-Tip while thinking about what the future held for him and humanity.

Chapter 19

Ty finished the disguises he was building by late Sunday evening. He'd cleaned up and had a pizza delivered while he sat on the couch waiting for the new episode of *Rick and Morty* to come on before heading to bed.

When Monday morning woke him, he jumped out of bed, showered, and took care of all his hygiene. He dressed a little better to face the day of phone calls and possible meetings. Tech formal, he called it: unfaded blue jeans, a nice, untucked dress shirt, comfortable soft shoes, and a sport coat he carried over his shoulder. He bounced down the stairs into the kitchen and placed his coat over the back of a chair at the kitchen counter. Thinking to himself, he fixed his normal breakfast of Pop-Tarts and coffee.

While his breakfast was preparing itself, he turned on the TV to the same local news channel to see if the lottery winning frenzy was still buzzing. He collected his breakfast and sat at the kitchen counter to watch the news. It wasn't really news; it was a morning talk show discussing events of the weekend. He checked the time, 7:03 a.m., which meant the show had just began. The title card at the bottom of the screen read, "Top discussion topic: Billions Won in Lottery Jackpots from the Same Store."

Good, he wouldn't have to sit through forty-five minutes of people sitting in a semicircle talking about other people's social media posts. Though, he bet they would discuss other people's posts if they related to the lottery jackpots. It had been like that for over a decade now, showing and reading social media posts instead of doing the journalism themselves. Even the social media platforms started formatting their systems to be TV optimized when displaying the messages while the talking heads discussed each one. The worst part was that people liked it, which changed the whole format of the news, at least, the opinion programs anyway.

Ty focused on the show because they were now covering the jackpots.

"*And of course, the big news this weekend was the winning of two very large lottery jackpots. The Powerball jackpot was a new world record amount of four billion four hundred and seven million dollars that one lucky ticket won Saturday night,*" the anchor in the middle of the four-person team announced.

"*That's right Phil, and on Friday night, a single lottery ticket won the Mega Millions jackpot in the amount of three billion two hundred and eleven million dollars. This wasn't a new world record, but it is the second highest amount for the Mega Millions multi-state lottery, and that puts that jackpot as the third largest jackpot ever,*" the woman sitting next to Phil stated.

Ty tried to guess which anchor would speak next.

"*But that's not the real news, is it, Janice? No, the real news is that both of these tickets were purchased from the same lottery retailer. A small corner convenient store in a neighborhood in the California city of Soledad.*"

His own personal ability to make a prediction still sucked; a fifty-fifty chance at picking who would speak next, and he guessed wrong. Well, at least he had a 100 percent chance of knowing who would speak last.

"*Well Tim, there was a lot of speculation yesterday as to the odds of that ever happening, and it's something like one in several billion. But even that's not the real breaking news to this story. The actual breaking news is that our sources have informed us that the two lottery tickets were purchased at the same time!*"

There was a pause in the conversation as though to let everyone absorb the information.

The same anchor continued, "*This has led many to believe that the total jackpots amount of over seven point six billion dollars was won by one person!*"

Ty nearly spilt out his coffee when that speculation was announced.

"Well, they're not wrong," said Ty, talking to his TV and the anchors.

"*We may never know for sure if this is true or not. Last year, California joined a growing group of states in the multi-state lottery systems to allow the winners to keep their identity private, which by the way, I support one* hundred percent. So, unless this person comes out publicly on their own, there's no sure way to know. Personally, I wouldn't tell the public. And I'd leave this show in a heartbeat!"

They all laughed together in agreement at the thought of winning that much money.

"Of course, that could never happen since I don't play."

The anchors all laughed again in unison.

"And here it comes," Ty grumbled.

"Opinions on social media seem to be all over the place as far as the amount of the jackpots and going public or not. Here's 'yougotafriendinme,' who posted this message, 'No one should be allowed to win this much money at one time. The lotteries should cap the jackpots at one billion dollars, then start a new jackpot. That's only fair.' And at 'marysmart' wrote, 'Whoever won should donate the money to charities. Who needs that much money anyway?' Here we have an interesting take from 'sonofdumbledore,' 'Somebody cheated! I don't know how, but this is a scam of some kind. Probably the government wanted the money, so they rigged the lottery. There's no way they would let a normal citizen win that much money.'

"Phil, what do you think about that last posting? Should a common citizen have access to that much money basically overnight?"

"That's a good question, John. Don't you mean over the weekend? That's a very good Vegas trip, wouldn't you agree?"

Everyone one in the semicircle laughed.

"It's not my place to say how much money someone is allowed to have. But I hope they are smart with it. That's an enormous amount of money. There are hundreds of stories about people winning the lottery and then ending up worse than before they won; they'd go from middle-class to wealthy to impoverished in less than two years. We read about it all the time."

This went on for another ten minutes before the show broke for commercials. Ty turned the TV off and headed to his office with his half cup of coffee in hand. His office now looked like a showroom of some kind. He brought down one of his acoustic-electric guitars from an upstairs bedroom and placed it in a stand next to Q-Tip. In the same corner as Q-Tip, he placed three more matte black cylinders on tripods and quadpods with LED lights on them, making different geometric patterns. In total, there were four devices standing there in the corner of different heights, but all the same circumferences. For one of the mock units, he gutted an old, cheap, beat-up guitar amp and placed it inside the homemade cylinder, including the speaker. It was about ten watts from an electric guitar starter kit.

Picking up the guitar, he plugged it in the repackaged amp and strummed a few chords, then a short rock-n-roll riff. It sounded like shit. He'd just hot glued everything inside the PVC pipe and stuck the controls through holes in the back of the cylinder. However, it was cool to see what was happening. It looked like he was trying to create a new type of guitar amp, and these were prototypes. He left a bunch of the excess parts outside on his workbench with stereo speakers and wires laying around. These four were nearly completed amps, but only one worked. If he weren't a new billionaire, he might actually try and develop these into real products. He probably still could if he took the time to design a better sound from them. He chuckled to himself, they looked like a bunch oversized Amazon Alexa's.

On his workbench was an old aluminum Apple workstation case. He removed all logos from it and mounted an old server motherboard inside, then hooked it all up. It would have run as a regular computer if he hadn't modified it. In the center of the large case, he mounted a thick aluminum plate on a stand. On that plate was a full, eight-point-four-ounce aluminum can of Red Bull that he'd cleared the labeling off of. The can had eight steel braided lines secured to it and to the underside of the metal plate. He'd used a lot of extra parts from some liquid cooling equipment he had laying around in his garage that included aluminum vanes and copper tubing routed around the inside of the case.

It looked very similar to the robot patient device he saw at the labs in Saitama laying on a lab bench with test equipment attached to it. He did the same thing. He'd connected several wires from all of the test equipment on his work bench to different parts inside the case. He actually connected an RGB LED strip of lights inside the case that changed colors between amber and green. He knew it seemed corny, but there was something about pulsing the light that finished the look he was going for. From a distance, it looked more like a new type of quantum computer than Q-Tip and its band of new-age guitar amps.

"Hide it in plain sight," he told himself.

He sat down at his desk and began to make phone calls, starting with his tax guy, Mitch.

"Ah shit, I forgot about the meeting with Scott this morning," A thirty-minute meeting reminder popped up on his laptop and his phone.

"I'll call Mitch anyway and schedule a meeting for later this morning," he said under his breath.

He still wanted to continue working for the time being, but there was a chance he was getting laid off this morning. It seemed disingenuous to beg to keep his job, but things would be a little easier if he continued to be employed at KSS for now.

He called Mitch using his speaker phone.

"Good morning, this is the office of Mitch McGregor. How can I help you?" The voice on the phone was pleasant to listen to for a Monday morning.

"Yes, good morning. This is Tyson McNally, I'm a client of Mitch. I have an emergency, and I need to talk to him right away." Damn! He didn't want to come across like he'd committed a crime, but he also didn't want to sound like he'd won the lottery either.

"I'm sorry, Mr. McGregor isn't in yet. Can I have him give you a call back?"

"Do you have access to his calendar? I'd like to schedule a meeting with him today; this morning if possible."

"Yes, let me take a look. Well, he has a thirty-minute time slot available at ten thirty this morning. Would you like me to schedule this time for you?"

"Perfect, yes please." That would work out.

"Okay, you're scheduled for ten thirty this morning. I see we have your email address; I can send the meeting details to you if that will work for you. May I let him know what this is concerning?"

"Yes, email is good. Um. I just got a huge bonus at work, and I don't think it got taxed correctly," he lied.

"I see. Well congratulations. We'll get it all fixed up for you."

"That would be great, thank you for all of your help. Have a nice day."

"Thank you, Mr. McNally. You have a nice day too. Goodbye"

He disconnected the phone call.

He looked at the list of names and numbers he needed to call today, but didn't really want to get started until after the meeting with HR.

***

Ty joined the online meeting with HR in progress.

"Good morning, Scott." It was funny that he sounded so glum.

"Mr. McNally. I hope you had a good weekend."

Artificial platitudes.

"I think I had a better weekend than I deserved." That was no lie. "Is there anyone else in the meeting?"

"No, just you and me. Sorry about that last time. Based on the way the last meeting was unfolding, I asked a couple of people to join me. The revelation that you have been poorly managed, well, I wanted some of my colleagues to hear it and voice their opinions."

This didn't sound like the Scott from the first meeting.

"I should apologize. That was a couple of years of pent-up frustration. I should have gone to HR sooner." Ty wasn't really caring how things turned out, except for Rick still getting whacked.

"Mr. McNally..."

"Please, would you mind calling me Ty? Unless there's some reason you have to address me that formally." It always made him uncomfortable.

"Sure thing. Just a professional habit until I become more familiar with someone. As you might imagine, I tend to get pulled into the unpleasant parts of this job more often that I want."

A professional hatchet man?

"So, what is this meeting about this morning?" He had things to do, people to see, and places to go.

"Ty, we realize you and your team are caught up in the organizational restructuring because of the incoming new executive team. Originally, the entire business unit from Byron Smith all the way down was to be reorganized and cut. That unit just wasn't performing, and when I say, 'wasn't performing,' it was costing the company over twenty million dollars a year to keep it afloat. And you're right, Rick Michaelson bares a lot of that cost due to his mismanagement. However, you were wrong in your estimate of how much he impacted the company's downturn. It's closer to forty-seven percent." Scott was going on and on about what was supposed to happen.

"So, how does this affect my team and I? I mean, you keep using words like 'was' and 'were.'"

"Effective immediately, you and your team are to be reassigned to me until the new executive team addresses the situation. I'd say the first chance they look at this is in their second quarterly executive meeting."

"Six months? We have six months until we find out whether we stay or are released?" What a screwed-up company.

"I'm sorry, that's the best that can be done at this time. Please continue doing what you are currently doing and send me your weekly status reports. I'll send you a reoccurring meeting invite later today for a biweekly status meeting."

"Can I inform my team?"

"Yes. And please schedule a meeting with them and include me later this week so we can go over the details in case they have any questions."

"So, is there anything else?" He was done listening to anyone talk from this company. He didn't know if it was because he didn't need to, or if he would feel the same way under different circumstances.

"No, I think that'll do it for now. I'm sorry it's like this, Ty. I will do my best to make sure this situation works out for the best for you and your team. In the meantime, please plan accordingly."

"Meaning?" He was struggling to maintain his composure.

Scott took a deep breath. "Hope for the best and plan for the worst."

"Understood. Goodbye." He left the meeting feeling wronged. Then he thought about it for a moment. This was exactly what he needed. He needed to get the ball rolling. He looked at his notes and began making phone calls.

***

The government Boeing 787 plane landed at Moffett Field in Mountain View and pulled into an unmarked hanger. The mid-morning sun shined, leaving a harsh contrast between outside and the dark hanger inside. Dana deplaned and filled out and signed a few forms with the special customs agent. She then got into a black, midsized SUV and sat there for a moment. She synced up her phone to the head unit of the vehicle, did a search on her phone for Katoshi Systems Services, and clicked on the address of their headquarters building. The map showed up on the large display screen in the middle of the vehicle's dashboard. She touched the start button on the screen, a route to KSS lit up, giving her the directions she needed.

She put her seatbelt on and looked around, then pressed the accelerator pedal. The electric SUV rolled forward smoothly and confidently. She drove out of the airbase through the main exit and turned left onto King Road, right onto Bushnell Road, then south onto the 101-Freeway southbound. A short fourteen-minute drive down the freeway was the Katoshi System Services headquarters building off the Lawrence Expressway. It was a good time of day to be on the 101-Freeway, as the traffic was very light, for 101 standards.

The building wasn't much to look at and was in need of being updated several times over. She estimated this was still the original façade from the 1970s.

It must be much nicer and more modern on the inside, she told herself.

That was mostly wrong. The interior had been updated at one time, probably in the 1980s.

How does a company like Katoshi Corporation let one of its divisions operate out of a building that looks like this? she wondered. *Then again, how does a company that still pulls in six billion dollars a year operate in a building that looks like this?*

The visitor lobby was dark and uninviting. She couldn't believe anyone would bring their customers into a place like this. Something was wrong. She wondered if she was in the right place. Walking over to the reception desk, she was greeted by a middle-aged woman who welcomed her and ask her to sign in—on paper!

"May I ask who you are here to meet with? Ms.?"

"Jordan, Dana Jordan." She was still signing the visitor's logbook.

"Oh! Mrs. Jordan! We've been expecting you. Give me one minute." She picked up the phone and dialed an extension number.

"Yes, Mrs. Jordan is here... Yes... In the EBC." She hung up the handset and looked up at Dana.

"Please follow me."

They walked through a set of glass doors into an open area with several conference rooms in a circular arrangement. They walked over to one of the conference rooms, where the receptionist asked her to have a seat.

"Scott Richardson is on his way and will be here shortly." She turned around and jumped in startlement. "Oh! Well, he's already here."

She felt the obligation to introduce the two. "Dana Jordan, this is Scott Richardson from our talent management department. Scott, this is Dana Jordan from... Um, I'm sorry, dear, I didn't catch where you're from."

"Intel-Q," Dana said as she looked at the receptionist forgivingly. Then she looked at Scott. "Good morning, I'm Dana, deputy director of advanced computational technology investments. Thank you for meeting with me, Mr. Richardson."

The receptionist excused herself from the room.

"Please, call me Scott. I must say we don't usually get calls from the chairman of the board. How can I help you, Mrs. Jordan?" He held out his hand to shake hers.

Dana took his hand and shook it. "Please call me Dana. I'm here looking to talk to one of your employees, Tyson McNally. Would it be possible to speak with him?"

"Tyson McNally? I just got out of a meeting with him. He doesn't work in this location. I mean, he visits from time to time for customer meetings or other reasons. Maybe once a month. He works remotely from home. He lives down in Soledad. He has a small lab here with some equipment in it, but that's just for research and development that he and his team access remotely."

"I see. Would it be possible to visit his lab while I'm here?"

"May I ask what this is about? You don't have to answer, I was told to get you anything you need, but this a little unusual." Scott seemed a little uncomfortable.

"No, not at all. I just want to ask him about some work he was doing with KRF. There was a joint project we were funding with KRF, and as you know, the earthquake destroyed one of the KRF buildings a few weeks ago. Mr. McNally was working with Yuichu Norigawa, head of development for this project. I just have a few questions to ask him about his level of contribution before I write this project off as a loss." That was mostly true.

"I see. Please come with me. His lab is near the data center." Scott led her out the door and down a hall.

The sound of whirling fans and forced air cooling were getting louder as they approached the main data center area. She could see the main doors to the data center, but they didn't go into it. Scott asked her to wait by another door on the opposite side of the hallway. The sign on the door simply said, "Advance Product Development." Scott poked his head inside an office door for a couple of minutes, then a woman came out after him.

"Hi, I'm Mary, I run the data center here. This is Ty's lab." She entered a code on the keypad lock to a loud *click*. Mary opened the door and the lights turned on automatically.

"I think it's been a few weeks since Ty or any of his team have been in here. They usually set up for their next project then work on it remotely for several months."

The room was on a raised floor; it was spacious and carpeted. The carpet helped dampen a lot of the equipment noise. In the middle of the room was a single row of racks with different types of servers, network and storage equipment mounted in it. The doors on the racks looked to be insulated for additional noise absorption. Against three of the walls were workbenches and chairs with different desk accessories in different areas. She suspected each person who worked in there had their own workspace set up. The only exception was one walled area that had different types of test equipment and tools set up and a shelf full of parts and cables stacked up in it. Most likely a common workbench area.

Dana walked over to the densely filled equipment racks. Basically, a standard set of racked computer servers, storage equipment, networking gear, and a console monitor and keyboard tray in the middle of all six racks.

A typical server room setup. Even though she didn't know what she was looking for, she was pretty sure this wasn't it.

"Mary. Does Tyson and his team keep any equipment in the main data center?" she asked while looking back at the two of them by the door.

"No. I know every piece of equipment in that data center. Most of what they do is software development on the equipment we sell. They try to keep everything in this lab. Most of the work they do is company confidential or highly sensitive. We jokingly call this room 'Ty's Skunkworks Lab.' A lot of great products have come out of this lab and from this team over the years. I don't know what kind of company this would be without them. In fact, I don't know why we aren't doing better in the market. These products are cutting edge."

"Really? I had no idea what this team did," Scott said, surprised he didn't know where the company's best products came from.

"Oh yeah! I can't wait to see what they've been working on and what comes next. In fact, everybody looks forward to Ty's brown bag lunch briefings. He'll spend an hour and half during a random lunch describing what's coming next. Anyone who wants to can hang out for another couple of hours afterward to learn more. Ty loves to talk about the work his team does. These briefing are always standing room only. Maybe if we could get a first-rate marketing team and a marketing campaign, we could turn this company around." Mary sounded like a huge admirer of Tyson McNally.

"I don't know why Tyson still works here. He could go anywhere he wanted, probably for twice the money. I'm just glad he works for us," Mary finished saying.

Dana looked around at the workspaces for any notes or manuals that might be laying around—nothing. The diagrams and scribbles on the large whiteboard on the wall didn't reveal anything useful either.

"Scott, would it be possible to talk to Tyson? Do you have his number or an email address I could contact him with?" She turned and looked at the two employees.

"Sure, I suppose that's alright." Scott looked hesitant.

Dana reached into her pocket and handed him her business card. "Like I said, I'm just following up on the type of collaboration he had with KRF on this project."

"KRF? You mean in Japan? The building that collapsed in the earthquake?" Mary questioned with concern.

"That's right. We are in a joint development venture with Katoshi Corporation to bring some new technology to market, but the earthquake destroyed a lot of the work, and I'm just assessing how much of it we have to write-off or restart." She wasn't ready to say "all of the work" just yet.

"The earthquake and the loss of so many people. Yuichu and Ty worked together on so many projects. They were pretty close friends." Mary was obviously upset at the mention of the KRF facility.

"Ty's number is right here."

Mary closed the door enough to show a sign that stated, "Please Contact Tyson McNally Before Shutting Anything Down or Removing Any Equipment from This Room at 831-555-4354 or Tyson.McNally@kssinc.com."

Dana made a note of both the number and the email address.

"Thank you. I think I've seen what I needed. Thank you so much for your cooperation. I hope we can continue with this joint venture."

Dana shook hands with Mary, then Scott escorted her back to the visitor lobby where she exited the building. She entered her SUV and looked at the battery levels: 98 percent capacity, estimated range, 350 miles. She looked up the city of Soledad on the navigation app of the head unit: 104 miles south, an approximately ninety-five-minute drive with current traffic conditions. She hit the "Start" button on the navigation app and the screen updated with the direct route to take. Then she turned on the SUV and began the drive south down the 101-Freeway.

Chapter 20

It was 1:30 in the afternoon. Ty thoroughly read through the California Lottery Winner's Handbook, which included more details on what he'd already read about. He did note the nearest Lottery District Office was in Milpitas, which was very close to his office, about ninety minutes away. He figured he'd drive up there tomorrow to officially claim his winnings.

Ty met with Mitch on the phone. Mitch was more excited than Ty was in hearing he won the huge lottery jackpots. It was a good meeting. Mitch was able to assure him that he could manage his tax situation. Mitch then helped him connect with a financial advisor at an accounting firm and a law firm that had experience with these types of financial windfalls, including several lottery jackpot winners as clients. The two of them attended several introductory meetings together over the phone and scheduled in-person meetings starting the next morning. He was grateful for Mitch's help and guidance in ushering him through all these professionals, though he was well aware he was a big fish.

He didn't like to think this way but keeping him happy was what everybody wanted to do. He'd just disconnected from his last call with the law firm and felt very good that everything was underway. He leaned back in his chair for a moment, then jumped up and decided to go for a run.

His phone vibrated on his desk with a number he didn't recognize. He decided to pick it up, thinking it was one of the firms he'd been in meetings with all morning, but just hadn't added them to his contacts yet.

"Hello, this is Ty." He turned on his speaker phone while he sat back down. He was more chipper than usual for obvious reasons.

"Hello, Tyson McNally? Hi, this is Dana Jordan. I worked with Yuichu and his department at KRF."

The mention of Yuichu turned his mostly upbeat day into a bit of a solemn moment.

"Yes, this is Ty. How can I help you?"

"When I say worked with him, I meant I mostly managed the project from an administrative and financial perspective. I was wondering if you had a moment to discuss the project Yuichu and his department was working on?

"Would you be willing to meet with me in person? I am currently in Soledad having lunch at a restaurant here in town. As you are aware, the research facility in Saitama was destroyed, including all research and equipment. Tragically, so were most of the researchers and developers, and all their knowledge. I am trying to piece back together their work to see if we can restart it or if we'll have to write it off as a total loss. It has come to our attention that you might have been part of the collaboration with Yuichu's team in working on this project. Any information or insight you might have would be an enormous help in assessing whether or not this work can continue."

"I'm sorry, who are you again?" Ty was interested in hearing more but wanted to be cautious in how he answered her questions.

"I'm sorry for not introducing myself properly. My name in Dana, Dana Jordan, I am the deputy director of advanced computational technology investments at Intel-Q."

"Thank you. So, what is Intel-Q?" He'd heard of Intel-Q but didn't really know what they were about.

"Sure. Intel-Q is a venture capital firm for the U.S. government. We invest in commercial high-tech companies and startups to develop technology the government uses but is also sold and used commercially. You've probably heard of some of our related work, like Google Earth, Spotfire, and MemSQL. We invest in companies for all the three letter agencies and all military branches. One branch we are heavily investing in currently is Space Force, as you might imagine. All of these investments are targeted for commercial consumption and productization. We get our investments back, plus interest, when a product or company successfully goes to market with the technology or product. There are special military specification needs for some of these products that the government pays a premium for. You've heard of ruggedized laptops, computer servers for submarines, data centers on an aircraft carrier, surveillance drones, SpaceNet? We helped get SpaceX started. That's us and more." She was providing the more favorable description from their website.

"Wow! I had no idea. Why isn't Intel-Q more popular or famous? And what's the point?" He was very impressed.

"You can look us up on the web, but that's not why we do this. Look, there are several reasons why we exist and do what we do. Two of the main reasons are that technology is moving very fast. One, it's hard for the government to keep up on its own, and two, it would be very expensive to supply everything the government needs if the government did it themselves. So, we outsource it. There's a lot of companies and products on the market that owe their start to us.

"Some of us like to think we're advancing technology by investing in people and companies; 'Innovation on a Mission.' It's more than just supplying to government with advance tools, it's moving the needle. What people and companies decide to do once they are successful is up to them. They can run their company however they want. We do put clauses in our contracts that if they end-of-life a product we still need, we get the patents, intellectual property, or source code back so we can seed another company to continue supplying it for us."

"So, you're the government?" he asked, legitimately concerned.

"No, not really. Think of us more like a civil service branch or civilian contractors."

"So, how can I help?" Ty was still guarded but wanted to know more.

"Well, could we set up a time and place to meet? I would like to interview you. I work better face-to-face."

He looked at the time. "Yeah, me too. Okay, would tomorrow mid-morning work? I was on my way out to run some errands for the rest of the afternoon, but I'm available all morning tomorrow."

"That would be perfect. Thank you for your help. Where would be a good place to meet?" Dana asked sincerely since she was unfamiliar with the area.

"Well, if you are comfortable with it, you could come to my home, and we could meet here. Otherwise, it's a ninety-five-mile drive to my work just to get a conference room."

"Oh, I'm fine with that. Thank you for offering your home for this meeting. This should only take an hour or so."

"By the way, if you don't mind my asking, how did you find me and my mobile number?" It finally dawned on him that she found him.

"As I mentioned, we are in a joint development venture with Katoshi Corporation. I found some blogs with you and Yuichu from a few years ago. So, I asked chairman Nakatori if it would be appropriate for me to contact you directly. You are an employee of Katoshi, right? I hope you aren't offended, but the chairman would also like to keep this partnership going if there is any chance of restarting this project. We've invested over a hundred million dollars in this project over the past few years." She thought maybe she sounded suspiciously off.

"Ah! Sure. No problem. Yes, I work for Katoshi Systems Services. I'll text you my address after this call. How about nine tomorrow morning?"

"That'll be great. Thank you, and I looking forward to seeing you tomorrow morning. Bye."

Ty disconnected the call. He looked at the time, 1:50 p.m. He decided to go to the Lottery District Office this afternoon in case it turned out she needed the device back or if anything weird happened—like it turned out everything about this was a government top secret project and all results from the device was top secret.

He'd run a few lottery predictions tonight when he got back for his team and a few others to cash in. Then, he'd help restart this project tomorrow. That would be a great way to honor his friend.

He stood up and stretched after shutting everything down, including Q-Tip. He decided to disconnect Tomahawk and take it with him as he went upstairs to freshen up before the hour and a half long drive up to Milpitas. He figured he could be there by around 3:30 p.m., register his wins, start the process rolling, and be home by dinner.

***

Dmitry figured out who Mrs. Jordan was looking for. Tyson McNally was a colleague and close friend of Dr. Norigawa, the head of research for this new type of quantum computer. When she didn't return to the recovery site, and after he researched all the associates of Dr. Norigawa, he deduced that the first blog of the two was the lead she ran with. He was so stupid for not seeing it. It was obvious. The reason everyone was still searching for information was because no one expected that a development manager for an American vendor of Japanese products could be involved in quantum computing research. At least he didn't initially, but there must be something different about this Tyson McNally person. The right person in the wrong place? It also appeared that she already arrived in Silicon Valley.

It was too late for him to catch up to her, but he was back in lockstep with her moves. The embassy found and provided him with information as to where Mr. McNally was employed and where he physically worked. His superior at the embassy requested that he keep tracking the progress of this operation. He interpreted that to mean continue pursuing the activities of Mrs. Jordan and now, Mr. McNally as well.

He sent a message to some old comrades in America.

***

Howard barged into Bob's office with a pleased look on his face.

"I got a name and address of someone in California that was working with the KRF team on that Intel-Q project. He works for KSS. A Tyson McNally." He was holding his phone screen toward Bob as if he could read the message from across his office.

Bob stopped what he was doing and looked up at Howard, who was about to take a seat in front of him.

"Let me guess, he lives in Soledad, California, but works in Silicon Valley?" he said flatly.

"That's right, how did you know that?" Howard stopped halfway down before sitting in the chair in front of Bob's desk.

Bob picked up the remote control and pointed it at the TV screen on the wall behind Howard and unmuted it. The audio came back on for a reporter holding a microphone with thousands of people behind her.

"...the frenzy here at this quiet neighborhood convenient store is still going strong for a second day in a row. The news that the two winning lottery tickets were both purchased here has everyone buzzing in this sleepy town of Soledad in Salinas Valley, California. Now, information that both tickets were purchased at the same time has just turned this place upside down. The chances that one person bought both tickets here is fueling all kinds of conspiracy theories, though this hasn't been confirmed, speculations are thick with anticipation that..."

Bob lowered the audio until it sounded like scratching on the wall behind Howard's head.

"KSS headquarters is that dump in Santa Clara off of the Lawrence Expressway, and this guy, Tyson, just used this device to win the largest lottery payout in human history."

Howard stared at Bob's face for a moment.

"This means that that quantum computer is fully functional. It works! Somehow, this Tyson guy just made it predict random numbers to win the lottery jackpot, *twice*! Do you realize how impossible that is? I don't know how he did it and I don't care. What I care about is getting that machine." Bob's eyes were dark and sinister, and his shoulders tense.

Howard realized what Bob was talking about. This machine just killed every quantum computer company in the market.

"What if the machine is at Tyson's house? We're assuming it needs to be in a large space, but what if it's more different than we think? What if it's running on house power in someone's garage, in a farm town in the middle of nowhere?" Howard finally turned his stare from Bob's eyes, glanced back behind him and pointed his thumb at the TV.

"Shit, that's even worse." Bob was thinking about all of the possibilities. "I want that machine, Howard! Get me that machine. Or let's find out how it works."

"Alright, we can look into obtaining it. I'll put a team together. Or do I put two teams together?" Howard looked back at Bob inquisitively.

"Good question. In the reports from your informant, are they still digging around at the KRF site?" Bob asked, looking back at Howard intently.

"Yes. My contact says they're monitoring the site for any type of discovery, and they're still recovering material from the collapsed building."

"Good, there's a chance no one else knows there's a working machine in the U.S. That means Katoshi thinks it is destroyed. Which also means the machine is not at the KSS building in Santa Clara." Bob rubbed his chin.

"I think you are right. That machine is in Soledad, and nobody knows about it, not even George Lancer."

"We have to move fast. I'm betting when Tokyo comes back fully online, they'll find out KRF had a recovery site at another research facility, they just don't know it yet because of the disaster. We need to get that machine in our lab before they know it exists."

"Understood. I'll get on it right now." Howard stood up from his seat to leave and looked back at Bob. "Just to be clear. We want Tyson too, right? I mean, he might be the only one left who knows how this device works." He was concerned about the intensity Bob was exhibiting and wanted a clear understanding of his intention.

"Ah, that's a great point. Yes, make him an offer. A really good one; equity in Qu-Cell if you have to. The whole nine yards if he fully cooperates."

"And if he doesn't?" He still wanted crystal clear clarity.

"Look, I'll let you make that decision based on how things go. This is the start of a trillion-dollar business. I think we can offer Tyson a few million dollars to advise us for a while, maybe a board seat; tell him anything. The main objective is the machine; Tyson is secondary."

"Got it!" Howard continued out of the office.

Bob sat back in his chair behind his desk. "Besides, the guy's already won billions of dollars. Brilliant!"

***

The text returned with a simple "Confirmed." Dmitry smiled and looked down at a video stream of the recovery site on his phone. They were still busy digging up material and transporting it up the hill to the other building. Now there seemed to be more people working at the site moving material.

He just sent a team to Tyson McNally's home to search it for information about this machine—there might be papers or a laptop they could copy—especially pictures or images of the device.

Dmitry was on his way to the airport, but it would be some time before he would arrive in America. This information might be valuable to Russian intelligence. If not, at least he was doing something he missed doing. He sat in his Narita Express seat and closed his eyes for the hour-long train ride to Narita Airport.

Chapter 21

Ty pulled into the weird cul-de-sac parking lot of the District Lottery Office in Milpitas. Cars were parked along the edge of the curb in a disorderly arrangement. It was nothing like he expected. He parked his Tesla in an open space between two other cars and grabbed his backpack before closing the door and locking everything. It was a very industrial park looking area. He followed the signs to the front of the building and entered.

The sign overhead made it very clear where he needed to go: "Winning Claims Window Here." There were a few people mingling around the lobby. He walked over to the counter, opened his envelope, and placed the filled-out claim forms for the Mega Millions and Powerball along with his signed winning tickets.

The woman behind the counter greeted him stoically. She looked at the forms and the tickets, looked up at him, and then back down at the forms. Her eyebrows raised and she took a big breath. She picked up the tickets to look at the backs, then inserted one of them into a machine next to her. The machine sucked in the ticket, then spit it back up. She did the same thing to the other ticket. Reaching down below the window counter, she grabbed two envelopes, one for each game, and placed them on the counter in front of her. She reached over and grabbed a large stamp and hit the tickets "RECEIVED" and the date stamped under it. She blotted the stamp again and hit the claims forms, then she pushed a couple of buttons on the machine and several slips were printed out. Collecting a grouping of forms and slips, she stapled the bunch together. She did the same thing to the remaining forms and slips and placed them in the envelopes. After sealing the envelopes, she signed two forms and hit them with another rubber stamp, then handed the forms to him.

"It will take eight to ten weeks to process these claims and wire the money to your account. Congratulations. Have a great day." She smiled at him with a "we're finished here" look on her face.

Ty backed up, turned around, looked at the forms he received, then started walking toward the exit. That was underwhelming. He was relieved and disappointed at the same time. All the information on the forms were correct. The women behind the counter didn't look phased by the amount or the two winning tickets—what a professional.

That wasn't as bad as he thought it would be. Maybe with the recent privacy changes, they put the confetti canons away and shredded the giant billboard checks. At least the process was underway, and his claims were in the system. No matter what happened from this point on, billions of dollars would show up in a couple of months. He felt a weight lifted off his shoulders in relief. He hadn't been aware of the stress this was causing him, but now that it was over, it felt over; though he knew this was just the beginning.

Getting into his car, he was relieved that there were no reporters lurking at the building, waiting for someone to show up to claim the jackpots, and asking tons of questions. Maybe they didn't expect anyone to claim their winnings this fast. He turned on his Tesla and made the long drive home through the Silicon Valley traffic.

***

Dana opened the door to her hotel room to two queen beds and threw her bag on the bed she wasn't planning to sleep on. Opening her duffle bag, she grabbed an outfit for tomorrow morning's meeting with Tyson and hung it up in the closet, then plopped her long, tired body down on the other bed. Her shoulder-length auburn hair spread out up over the top of her head. Using her feet, she kicked off her shoes onto the floor and closed her eyes for a moment. She was tired from jetlag and wanted to get some sleep right then and there. She laid down for a few minutes then sat back up. Something in the back of her mind was eating at her.

Tyson was so polite and upbeat on the phone. Why? It was pleasant talking to him. Was he hiding something? Probably, she was hiding something too. This project was very important to the government, to her, and to her father. So what? George told her how important the project was to the world as he envisioned it, so why wasn't it a matter of national security? She could have just brought in an FBI team and ransacked Tyson's home to look for anything related to project Shinsei. No, George wanted diplomacy; to be nice. *Interview him to find out everything he knows; don't push the issue.*

The machine wasn't at KSS headquarters, so that meant the sixth device must be in Soledad, either at his home or nearby somewhere. If it was at his home and he was using it, then the machine was small and had low power and environmental requirements; maybe set up in his garage. It would be game changing if it was; a true industry disruptor. If Tyson was using it, he was the only person in existence who could use it. She got that. Tyson might be just as important as the machine; no need to spook him with a retired spook.

She turned on the TV to listen to a little news and clear her head. With all of the "*quantum*" vernacular she had to endure recently, she planned to watch "*Ant-Man and the Wasp*" tonight; it reminded her what a fun movie it was. She needed her spirit entertained.

The news channels were buzzing about the small city of Soledad and the two lottery jackpots totaling seven point six billion dollars won from the same store this past weekend. Then the revelation that the two tickets were purchased at the same time and speculations that it might have been purchased by the same person.

She jumped up out of the bed. At that moment, she realized what was going on, though now she wasn't as surprised as she initially was. Tyson McNally did have the machine, or had access to the machine, and he just used the device to predict winning lottery numbers. Two sets of winning lottery numbers worth billions of dollars.

She resisted the urge to call him and call him out on what she thought was happening. Then she thought about it, there was nothing wrong with what he did. Actually, it really was a good use or test of the quantum computer's capability. The stability of the qubits was intact long enough to be observed and acted on. How did he do that? He got a prediction for a future event and it stuck, twice! She didn't think, nor anyone else, that was possible. Of all the hard problems that could be solved, forecasting the future was one of them, but predicting a random number wasn't. Twelve numbers to be exact.

She sat back down on the foot of the bed and thought about the discussion tomorrow. She wanted to talk about how he did it, but first she needed him to trust her. Get him to show her the machine and give it up willingly, to see the greater good possible, not the short-term decryption purposes. Possibly join the project to help resurrect it.

A text arrived on her phone. It was Tyson sending her his home address and a quick note, "See you tomorrow morning at 9:00 a.m. How do you like your coffee?"

She smiled and text him back, "Large and black. Do you like Pop-Tarts?"

A minute later he responded, "I've got you covered. Good night."

She chuckled a little. She looked at the time, it was 7:30 p.m. She made a call to her brother in the FBI.

"Dana! How the hell have you been? It's been a long time. What can I do for you?" The voice on the line was that of a large man and chipper as always.

"Hi, Jim! How's are those girls and Barbra?"

"The girls are great and keeping Barbra and I busy. What's up?"

"That's excellent to hear. We really need to grab a coffee sometime and catch up."

"Absolutely! It's been too long," the large voice responded.

"Hey look, I need a favor. I'm meeting this guy tomorrow morning to interview him about a project we are heavily invested in, and I was wondering if you could have a team sit at his house tonight and watch it."

"A guy, uh? You looking to see if he's attached?" Jim's laugh on her speaker phone filled the hotel room.

"No, no, nothing like that. I don't know, I feel like he needs to be watched tonight. I just arrived here from Japan this morning, but while I was there, someone tailed me for a while, and I just can't shake the feeling they might be looking to find this guy."

"Say no more, done. Hank and I are pulling an all-nighter tonight. Where are you at or where do we need to stake out tonight?"

"Hi Hank!" She yelled. "I'm in Soledad."

"Soledad? The lottery capital of the world? What the hell are you doing in that tiny city?"

"I'll describe it in detail to you over coffee later. Right now, I want Tyson McNally monitored until I can see him tomorrow morning. I'll text you the address. Whatever you do, don't alarm him, but let me know if anyone comes or goes."

"Alright. Hank and I will chill in front of your boyfriend's house tonight and keep all the ladies from visiting, but I can't promise anything for tomorrow night. Were about thirty minutes away, so we'll head over there now."

"Shit, Jim, quit trying to get me knocked up already." She rolled her eyes.

"I'm only trying to get you knocked up because I care about you. You deserve to get knocked up. Hell, if I weren't your brother-in-law, I'd knock you up."

A few awkward seconds of silence filled the phone connection.

"Oops, did I cross a line? Please don't tell Barbra I said that," Jim pleaded.

Dana heard a loud, burly laugh in the background bellow over her phone's speaker. She couldn't hold it in any longer either and busted out laughing along with Hank.

"Gotcha! That was funny. And I won't tell Barbra as long as you keep this guy safe tonight. Call me if anything looks out of place."

"Phew! Deal! What time is your meeting tomorrow?"

"Nine. I'll arrive a few minutes early and meet you."

"Well alright then. Hank and I will hang out until you arrive. Call us when you get close, and I'll meet you around the corner to give you a big hug."

"Perfect. See you tomorrow then. Good night."

"Good night, Dana. Great talking with you."

The phone disconnected. She couldn't quite put all of the pieces together, but she had a feeling something was developing. The feeling would probably go away once her meeting with Tyson was completed. She needed to convince him it was better for her to take possession of this technology. This would be a commercial product soon, available to the world, but at the moment, it was dangerous in the wrong hands.

She felt much better knowing Jim and Hank were going to spend the night watching Tyson's house.

***

Jim and Hank pulled into the neighborhood at about 8:45 p.m. It was peaceful and dark out. The community was a newer development, so the streetlights were spread out further than older neighborhoods, leaving dark stretches of road, and the streets were narrower. The address Dana gave him was up a slight hill on a corner; that was good for concealing a stakeout. Jim parked the midsized SUV a house and a half away, across the street in a dark patch next to a few other cars to get a wide-angle view of the home of Tyson McNally.

Jim turned the engine off and flipped the "stakeout" switch on. This prevented anything on the vehicle from coming on that would draw attention to it, like accidentally touching the brake pedal or bumping the horn. He then dialed the auto-tinting level on the windows to almost black so no one could see inside, while the two of them could see outside. An amber light under the dashboard lit up, giving the inside of the SUV a warm, undetectable glow. Hank instinctively set up the surveillance cameras and sensor network built into the government vehicle. Here they would campout for the night, taking shifts observing the neighborhood and the house for any activities. It helped that this looked like a quiet community and was well off any busy streets.

A light in a front window of the house was on as well as other lights in other windows. At the moment, they couldn't tell if someone was inside.

"Hank? Do we have that new sensor array installed?" He talked at a normal volume since the SUV was acoustically insulated.

"Yeah, I've been wanting to try this new equipment out. Everything should be set up and ready to go. I also picked up the new field kit. It's supposed to have the latest surveillance equipment in it." Hank was already reaching for the case in the back seat when he finished talking.

"Neat! I'd like to check it out, too, later. See if you can locate someone inside the house."

"Way ahead of you." Hank was already opening the case the handset was stored in and setting it up. They were briefed on the new equipment, but this was their first field usage with it.

He plugged the handset into a port under the vehicle's dash and turned it on. Hank used the controls to focus the sensors at McNally's house. The set of sensor arrays were mounted on the outside the of the government vehicle on the front, sides and back, and concealed in the body panels, undetectable. After a few seconds, the display showed the road on the corner of the SUV. Hank started moving his finger on the handset's screen and the camera began moving and adjusting itself to point toward the house; wherever the camera pointed, the set of sensors focused also. The view on the display now showed the front of the house. He adjusted the camera to zoom out some so it filled the display with the full shape of the home's front and several feet to either side of the house. He began cycling through different frequency spectrums, starting with infrared.

The display lit up like a flat panel lamp. Hank quickly adjusted another control and the bright light darkened to show the house again, but with glowing areas of pink, orange, blue, and yellow figures. A bright yellow and orange image in the garage showed in an empty patch of blue. Water heater. Hank made a note. Next to the water heater, the glow of two electric motors nearly cooled down, a thin, hot cord leading to a glowing red box, and a bank of batteries were charging. An electric vehicle charging? The roof outline glowed in pink and orange as Hank noted the attic was still cooling down from absorbing the day's heat. Hank made notes of other heat signatures in and around the house where he could—mostly rough guesses.

In the front where the window would normally be lit to the eye, the sensor only showed blacked-out blotches since the infrared sensor couldn't penetrate glass.

Hank switched to one of the new sensors that could scan in a different frequency spectrum. It was less intuitive but could penetrate more materials than infrared. He made some adjustments to the equipment and looked at the new color signatures. There was a glow of a pink, blue, black, and purple image hunched over with smaller images moving around next to it. This different color palette was the opposite of infrared and the figure that looked like a person was a blacked-out figure.

"I think I found him. It looks like one person sitting at a desk, working on a laptop, in the front room where the window is lit up. It doesn't look like anyone else is in the house." He circled the moving image on the display and touch a button. The isolated image sharpened up a bit and became more defined. It was human sitting down hunched over a desk; typing? They assumed this was Tyson. Occasionally, the figure would stop and move around the space, then settle back down again.

"Hey Jim! Check this out." Hank put the handset display between himself and Jim. In the display they could both see someone sitting at a desk, then the figure seemed to change position. The entire screen would turn white, emanating from a location near the figure, then subside. This pattern would repeat itself for about fifteen to twenty seconds and then stop.

"What the hell do you make of that? I thought this frequency spectrum's imaging only worked in a color palette of black, blue, red, yellow, and purple. Why would white show up and overrun the entire image?"

"I have no idea. Are you using the right palette? Defective sensor? Change sensors and see if we can see what's going on." Jim turned and looked at the house again.

"Good idea, I forgot this did a bunch of other different spectrums." Hank began adjusting the controls to set it for visualizing other frequency spectrums.

"Ugh! Some of these views look like someone puked after eating a Jell-O fruit salad." He adjusted the settings to see if he could clear up the display to be more useful.

Cycling through several different modes of viewing, he stopped. They both saw the movement in the psychedelic display.

"Put it back to thermal," Jim whispered.

"Way ahead of you." Hank was already tuning the thermal setting to enhance the images in the display.

"Okay, it looks likes two people approaching from the, uhm, shit! Where are we?" Hank grabbed his phone and opened up the compass app, then aligned digital needle to north.

"From the east, southeast. It looks like they're heading toward the opposite side of the house away from the where the figure is working."

"Yeah, I can't see a thing over in that direction. It's pitch black in that area." Jim was straining to see out toward the darkest part of the house's side yard.

"Do these new kits still pack good old fashion night vision gear?"

"Yeah. The case is behind you." Hank stayed focus on the display. He was recording everything since he turned the equipment on.

Jim reached back behind his seat and found the equipment kit. He slid it over toward the center and reclined his seat back. There he located a set of night vision binoculars. He put his seat back up, turned them on, and began scanning the area void of light.

"Got 'em. Two guys hanging around the corner of the garage. Hey, did you locate the breaker box when you thermally scanned the house?"

"Yup, they're standing right next to it, but it doesn't look like they've touched it yet."

"So, they're either going to wait until Tyson heads to bed to break in, or they're going to trip the main breaker and do it while he's still awake."

"Why did Dana say this guy needed to be watched?" Hank adjusted the image to make the area more defined.

"She didn't say. She said she felt like something might happen. She also said she was tailed in Japan before arriving here this morning; non-Japanese as she put it." Jim looked at the time, it was 10:38 p.m.

"So, what's the plan then?" Hank wanted to know how far they needed to take this.

"No idea yet. This was supposed to be a babysitting job and... Hey! Are you seeing that?"

"Got it. Two more figures came from the other side of the house. Who are these guys?"

Two more forms came into view on the thermal imaging display and stopped short of the other corner of the house outside of the lit window.

"It's another team. I can't tell if they're together. I'm going to call Dana. You got this?"

"Yeah, go for it. I have both teams in view."

Jim reached for his phone, called Dana, and put her on speaker phone.

"What've you got?" Dana answered the phone immediately.

"We've got two teams at the house. The first two guys showed up earlier and have been waiting out by the main breaker box, the second pair just approached the opposite side of the house. We can't tell if they're together or not. Who did you say this guy was?" Jim was back to using his night vision binoculars while talking.

There was a momentary pause on the line.

"That's Tyson McNally. I believe he won the two lottery jackpots this weekend."

"What?! You think this is the guy who won? Okay, so what? If he has any brains, those tickets should have been signed and locked away somewhere. Heck, he could have already turned them in or something. I get it, seven billion dollars, but still. These guys look like professionals. You think he's going to be kidnapped for lottery money?" Hank was still focused on the display and talking to Dana. "And why do you care?"

"It's worse than that. If I'm right, they're Russian or eastern European, or at least one of them is. I don't know why there'd be two teams there." Dana paused for another moment.

"She might be right. The new guys are smoking," Hank inserted into the conversation.

"Listen, I don't think they're there for the money or the tickets. They are probably going to ransack the place looking for a computer, a quantum computer. I think that's how Tyson won those lotteries."

Both Jim and Hank looked at each other, then back to their visuals.

"Okay, but neither team drove up in a vehicle, and they have no gear. I guess they're going to neutralized Tyson, then call in for help to haul away the machine." Jim was surmising the situation.

"No. This computer is small. It isn't like the typical quantum computers you see in the ads today. This one is very different. We've been working with Katoshi to develop it, but that research facility was destroyed during the earthquake in Japan. I think this one computer was shipped here before the disaster, and now it's probably the only one in existence. I'm guessing others have figured this out too and they're there to steal it. I just didn't think they would have figured it out this fast. But like you said, 'it's the lottery capital of the world.' Someone, some *ones*, were bound to put the pieces together."

"Okay, so what do you want us to do? We assume they're armed, but we don't know with what."

"See if you can scare those guys away, at least for the time being. I'll call Tyson and try to have him drive away from the house." Dana was thinking through a plan in real-time. "Jim, I'm thinking of using that new FBI data center in Morgan Hill to stay overnight?"

"How do you know about that facility? That's an FBI sec—oh right, never mind." Jim caught himself after saying it. Of course, she would know about it. Intel-Q helped design and fund it.

"Yeah, I think we can use it. I've been there a few times. It's still under construction, but it's a about a year away from being finished. So, when do we start operation saving private McNally?"

"I'm going to call Tyson and let him know you'll be coming to the door after those guys are gone. I'll meet you at the house."

"Okay, sounds like a plan," Jim said as he put the binoculars down and began getting the SUV ready for work.

"I'm heading there now."

The line disconnected.

Jim started the SUV and rolled closer to the house, then made a sharp left turn, situating the SUV to point directly at the front of Tyson's home. He flipped a switch on the console and an intense light flooded the entire front of the two-story house and the surrounding area. Then he pushed another button and a loud siren pulse blasted through the thick night air. Hank watched on the display as the two teams were stunned and hurt by the sudden intense illumination and sound. Blue and red lights flashed in a random pattern in the front grill of the FBI vehicle. He looked up at the scene now that everything was lit up.

Both teams scrambled and ran toward the shortest distance to the cover of darkness. Other homes began to light up as the commotion drew curious neighbors to their windows and front doors.

"Wow! That was easy," Hank said.

"Can you see where they ended up? Scan for heat signatures." Jim was looking around as well.

"Nothing showing up on my end, but the thermal camera has a limited range. I think it's safe to say they bugged outta there." Hank shut the equipment down.

Jim parked the SUV in front of Tyson's home. The two agents got out and headed to the front door. Tyson was already waiting for them at his opened front door.

"Tyson McNally?" Jim asked in his FBI agent voice.

"Yes, can I help you? What is that all about?" Ty was obviously surprised by all the attention. He could see his neighbors watching from their front doors and windows.

"Special Agent Jordan, FBI, and this is Special Agent Hughes." Jim and Hank held up their wallets, opened to show their badges.

Ty looked at the badges and the agents and again asked, "So, what can I do for you? Is something wrong? And what's going…"

Ty stopped mid-sentence and looked back at agent Jordan. "Agent Jordan? Um, any relation to Dana Jordan?" He asked, baffled.

"Not anymore. It's complicated," was all Jim had to say.

Just then, Ty saw and heard an electric SUV pull up behind the parked FBI SUV. A tall, beautiful woman stepped out as she looked up toward the front door, at the agents and him. She walked up to the front door. Her hair was pulled back, but still at shoulder length. Her long legs climbed the couple of steps through the front yard and onto the front porch.

When Dana reached the door, she smiled at Jim and Hank, then looked at Ty, still smiling.

"Hi Tyson McNally, I'm Dana Jordan. We spoke on the phone earlier, and just now. Sorry I'm a little early for our meeting." She reached out her hand.

"Good evening. Please call me Ty," he said as he took her hand and lightly shook it. "It's nice to meet you."

"May we come in? I can explain what's happening without your neighbors watching us." She turned to glance at all the looky-loos.

"What, no badge?" Ty looked at Dana, waiting for an explanation.

"Sorry, no. I'm not an agent of any kind. I can explain once we're inside." She wanted to apologize, but not right then, not right there.

"Ah, sure. Come on in. Please have a seat if you'd like." He turned on more lights and pointed toward the front living room chairs and sofa as the three of them entered the house.

"Hey, sorry to ask under the circumstances, but is your restroom available? It's a government emergency." Hank smiled at Ty. He knew Jim would be wanting to go, too, right after him.

"Yeah, sure thing. It's right there." He pointed toward the room behind them.

"Thanks," Hank said as he turned and headed to the latrine. This was much better than relieving himself into a bottle in the SUV.

"Ah, really quick, am I under arrest?" Ty asked, looking at all of them with a bewildered look on his face.

"No, we were just making sure everything stays peaceful. Dana will explain everything," Jim said, watching where Hank went.

"Okay, then, that's cool. Special Agent Jordan. There's a restroom at the top of the stairs if you need to… you know—go." Ty motioned toward the hall and upward.

"Thank you." Jim didn't hesitate as he started down the hallway.

Would anyone like something to drink?" He wasn't going to offer them anything if he was going to jail.

"That would be great. Water if you have any," Dana responded.

"Water would be great too," Hank yelled as the door to the bathroom closed. Jim also acknowledged affirmatively.

"Three waters?" she asked politely.

"Be right back." Ty turned and headed down the hall to the kitchen. He was thinking to himself how beautiful Dana was and how fit she seemed, but two Jordans? They must be divorced the way Agent Jordan sounded—somewhat bitterly.

Ty returned with four cold bottles of water and coasters. He'd also brought out an unopened bag of Doritos and some small plates with napkins, all on a tray.

"Oh, you didn't have to go through all that trouble," Dana said as Ty placed the tray on the coffee table. "Thank you."

"I have other snacks if you'd like something else. I'm kind of big on junk food. Did you want any Pop-Tarts? Strawberry, blueberry, brown sugar cinnamon?" He smiled at her. "I usually only have them for breakfast with my coffee."

"No, thank you. Same here. This is more than enough, though I'm sure the guys will appreciate it. By the way, you have a beautiful home here." Dana looked around and up at the high ceilings.

"Thank you. I actually don't get a lot of visitors." Ty wanted to say, "*It is now that you're here*," but opted to not be that kind of moron.

"Do you live here alone?"

"Yes. My wife died over seven years ago from cancer, and I've just never moved out," he said by accident. He hated mentioning that; he felt like people made it seem okay for him to live like a hermit in a big house.

"Oh, I'm so sorry to hear that. I'm also a widow. My husband died at work." She took a deep breath.

So, not two Jordans. It was—complicated.

"Sorry, that's not entirely right. I'm an ex-CIA analyst and my husband, John, was a CIA field agent. He was killed during an operation six years ago. CIA policy states that I should leave the agency due to a conflict of interest. So, I don't know if I'm ex-CIA or retired CIA. I joined Intel-Q after a that, and I've been there ever since." That was too much information, she told herself. She never did that.

"I'm sorry to hear that. I was able to stay at work after Janet died. The way I got through it was to pour myself into work. I actually didn't mind staying in this house after she passed, even though it's too big for a single person, it has everything I need. Plus, I was too busy to move out and into something smaller."

Ty held up his thumb to point back toward the FBI agents at the bathroom.

"Agent Jordan says it's complicated. I..." Ty let the incomplete sentence trail off with a hanging question in the air.

"Oh, Jim? He John's brother; my ex-brother-in-law? That doesn't sound right. We still consider ourselves in-laws, maybe closer than that. It's like we're real brother and sister since John... Um, sorry about that." Dana looked down at her opened bottle of water, then took a drink and looked up.

Their eyes locked momentarily. Their deep gaze was broken up when Hank returned to the living room. He grabbed a bottled water.

"Thank you." He mock toasted toward Ty and sat down on one of the chairs.

Jim returned and grabbed a water bottle and two coasters, tossing one at Hank.

"Thank you." Jim held up the bottle and sat down on the sofa next to Dana.

"So, now that we're all here, let me explain," Dana started.

***

Howard got up and turned his light on, then answered his phone.

"Well? Do you, have it? ... What do you mean someone saw you and you left? ... Get back there and get me that computer. ... Did they identify themselves? ... Security?! Police?! He's probably hired himself some rental cop security firm. I thought that was something you could handle. ...

Then get it done! Get more guys if you have to. Yes, I'll pay for them. I want that device secured tonight."

He disconnected from the call and texted Bob that everything was still a go, but he needed to adjust the plan.

Chapter 22

Dana explained what Intel-Q and Katoshi Research were working on and that somehow, Yuichu must have built a sixth unit, just to send it to Tyson. She explained that the plan was to commercially make this technology available to the world, but in the immediate term, a special version of it would be used by the CIA.

"Ah, that must be why that folder existed. It was empty of course, but I saw the framework of something I shouldn't have access to," Ty said, putting the pieces together.

"Yes, that's possible. We had a team directly from Intel-Q working at KRF on those algorithms, but they were back here in the states when the earthquake struck. Yuichu must have very high regard for you, Ty," Dana said, looking down at her water bottle.

"We worked together on a number of successful projects in the past. I was under the impression this project would follow the same process, though I knew this would be the biggest one I've ever been part of."

Dana could tell Tyson was still sad from losing his friend.

"So, how did you do it? How did you program a quantum computer to correctly pick random numbers? I think that's how these people eventually homed in on you."

"Would you believe it if I told you they were picked in order?"

"That's amazing! So, it isn't just correctly choosing random numbers, it's predicting the numbers as they would be drawn?" Dana was genuinely excited and impressed about how this worked.

"Something like that. It's using a fully quantum machine learning algorithm. I've trained it on the number patterns from previous drawings with a time dimension, but I don't think it's learning the pattern statistically. I think it *knows* the next sequence of numbers. There's a multiverse theory in quantum physics that everything that could happen, has happened. It's just a matter of aligning the resulting outcome with the present request. I think this machine can do that as well as solve many other classical hard problems." Ty couldn't stop talking about all of the possibilities he thought of doing with this technology.

"In the right hands, I think many engineering and mathematic challenges could easily be solved. It would launch a new age in... human... evolution..." His voice trailed off as he stepped down from his soapbox.

"I'd love to see it." Dana looked at Ty.

"I would love to show it to you. It's in my office." Ty felt good about sharing this information—this responsibility—with Dana. This could be the *right hands* he'd been looking for. Intel-Q and KRF could actually restart this project, for Yuichu.

Besides, he made several other lottery predictions earlier this evening and sent them to his team and others before all the commotion started. The idea of Q-Tip falling into the wrong hands made him shiver, especially if he could have prevented it.

Jim and Hank were sitting there listening to the two of them go on about quantum computing theory. Jim looked at Hank and Hank looked at Jim, and they both started cracking up. Dana and Ty stopped talking and looked at the two agents, puzzled.

"What's wrong?" Dana asked Jim and looked over at Hank.

"You two. It's like sitting here listening to Stephen Hawking chatting with Albert Einstein. Nobody else understands a word you're saying. Nerds."

"My voice sounds like Stephen Hawking?" Ty sounded offended that his voice sounded robotic.

"No, no. I'm mean, the words you two are using. It's like—"

The house went dark. Jim and Hank instinctively grabbed for their guns, then turned their phone flashlights on to assess that everyone was accounted for. Jim looked at the time. It was 1:30 a.m.

"I think our friends are back. Everyone, get down on the floor."

"I'll call in backup." Hank already had his phone up to his ear and was tilting his head sideways so the light in the back of the phone was pointed toward the floor.

"Dana, are you packing?" Jim whispered, knowing the answer.

"No! You know I don't do that anymore," she whispered, pulling her phone out and turning on her light. She was squatted down next to Ty and was assessing the situation with Jim and Hank.

"Alright then, you and Ty should go upstairs and find some place safe to ride this out." Jim was in charge and making decisions, however, their equipment and weapons were back in the SUV, which limited their options.

"Our heavy gear is back in the SUV," Jim stated as he worked on a plan.

"I have a gun safe in my stairwell closet."

All three of them turned and looked at Ty.

"What? I went through a gun building phase a few years ago." He seemed ashamed and worried that he'd get arrested afterward.

"I stopped because I couldn't keep up with all of the gun restrictions and 'compliance' California was ordering. So, I put them away and got into archery last year."

"What do you have?" Hank didn't care and was eager to have something more than his Glock at the moment.

"For this situation, four AR15s with different accessories, three 1911s, and a six round tactical twelve-gauge pump shotgun with two sets of home defense rounds." Ty had other weapons, but he didn't think anyone wanted to use bolt action hunting rifles or .22 anything.

Dana looked at Ty with adoration and pity, and Ty caught her eyes in the shadows of the phone lights.

"I was just looking for something interesting to occupy my free time. I wasn't ready to see anyone yet, and I can only play so much Xbox before—"

They all heard the footsteps outside and saw the shadows pass by the front window.

"Can you open that safe quickly!" Jim whispered.

"Yeah, it's down the hall with a biometric lock. It's actually a good place to hold up in."

"OK, you two head there now. Hank will lead, and I'll cover the back. Stay low."

The four of them duck walked down the dark hallway. They all set their phone lights to the lowest setting and even placed their fingers partially over the light to dim it even further. Just before the stairs, they reached a recessed doorway.

"Right here," Ty whispered to Hank.

Hank opened the door, and they all entered the closet space inside. Off to the side of the closet was a short doorless opening that Ty led them into.

It was uncommonly large inside, five and a half foot-high space under the midlevel loft used as a storage area. Ty affectionately referred to it as a California basement. They turned their lights up and faced the Winchester gun safe. Hank stayed back at the opening between the closet door and the opening to the extended storage space. Ty placed his thumb on the biometric sensor and the safe clanked. He turned the handle and the safe opened, its internal lights illuminating the compartment.

Inside, on the left side of the safe, there were weapons, ammunition, magazines, and accessories stacked neatly. On the right side were documents, boxes, and other miscellaneous valuables. Lining the inside of the safe's door were handguns and magazines.

"I like this guy," Jim whispered to Dana, though everyone heard him.

At that moment, the smashing of the front door could be heard throughout the house and in the storage space.

"We have a problem." Hank poked his head inside the short doorway.

"They've got night vision goggles on," Hank said, matter of fact.

"Oh, then they're going to love this." Ty grabbed one of the AR15s then reached for a light on one of the built-in shelves and clicked it onto the picatinny rail along the underside of the barrel.

He handed the AR15 to Hank with the barrel pointing up. He then wiggled his trigger finger and showed him the location of a button on the trigger guard. With his palm covering the end of the light, Ty pressed it. The entire storage space lit up with a blood red glow as Ty's hand looked like a wizard's magic red hand casting a spell. The 2,000-lumen light source shined through his hand, then he turned it off. He turned on the holographic sight, then gave Hank two full 50 .223 round double width magazines.

"This is dialed in to one hundred feet," Ty said, pointing to the holographic sight.

Hank looked at Ty with approval and took the rifle and mags, inserted one of the magazines into the empty receiver, then pulled the charging handle slowly; quietly.

Ty did the same thing with another AR15 and handed the rifle and magazines to Jim.

He looked at Dana and asked, "What's your preference? AR15, shotgun or 1911?"

Dana looked at Ty, then inside the safe. "Shotgun," she whispered.

Ty looked at her in awe.

"Excellent taste. May I suggest the buckshot, buckshot, slug arrangement instead of the rock salt, birdshot, buckshot default, madame?" he said with a mock accent, but worry in his eyes.

"That sounds perfect." Then she looked at him straight faced. "Ty, these guys are serious. They're professionals with military gear. If they're here for the machine, then there's a good chance they are also here for you; possibly you alone."

There was another crash of wood and wall being mashed in as the house shook. This time the sound came from the side door of his garage.

"Okay, that's gotta mean there's at least two two-man teams; maybe more," Jim assessed.

"Hank, how long before reinforcements arrive?"

"Probably another ten minutes before locals show up, sirens blaring," Hank whispered for everyone to hear.

"Got it. Can you hear anything?"

"Not yet." Hank continued to monitor up and down the vacant hallway. He turned off the light on his phone and switched to using the camera in night mode. He flipped between the front and rear cameras, peeking around the corner of the hallway closet door. His eyes were adjusted to the darkness. The moonlight peeping in from the windows lit enough to make out shadows and outlines with his naked eye.

Ty finished quietly setting up the shotgun with the shell pattern. Then he mounted another light on the barrel's picatinny rail. He showed Dana where the light button was located, next to her trigger finger, then handed her the shotgun, barrel up.

Before letting go of the shotgun, he whispered, "I know. I'm scared and angry, but I'll be okay. They can try and take the device. It's useless without other components. I hid them before you all came into the house. However, I would really like for this project to restart; to continue on."

Ty let go of the shotgun as Dana held it next to her. He grabbed a pair of 1911s from inside the safe's door. He gently and quietly slipped two magazines into the receivers, then pointed them downward and cocked the slides to load up the first rounds. These two guns already had lights mounted under the barrels, though with far fewer lumens.

Jim looked at Ty and all the weapons.

"You and I are going to have to have a little talk when this is all over."

Ty smiled back at Jim a little nervously, either from the current situation or from the aftermath; probably both.

Footsteps and shushes could be heard down the hallway toward the front door, then a door opened from behind the kitchen—the garage team. Both teams were closing in from both ends of the hallway with them in the middle. Hank could make out the team at the front of the house.

"Three-man team at the front end of the hallway. They're armed; two with handguns, one with an assault rifle. Another team is coming in from the back garage door. I don't know how many yet," Hank whispered toward the other three.

"Got 'em. Another three-man team at the other end of the hallway, same weapons configuration." Jim crawled up behind Hank.

"The garage team is closest," Hank said at half a whisper toward Jim over his shoulder.

Jim could see the video image on Hank's phone.

"Alright, you two, stay in here with guns pointing at this doorway. Hank, you take the garage team. I'll hit the front door team. Hit them with the light; six shots, center mass, and we're back. Okay?"

"Got it. On three, two, one, go!" Hank whispered.

Both agents sprung from the closet doorway, still in crouched positions, simultaneously pressing the light button with the rifle barrels pointing in opposite directions up and down the hallway.

Screams could be heard from all over the house as cries of agony and pain filled the once dark space. Then the crack of equipment hitting the tiled flooring as the night vision goggles were cursed and thrown to the floor by the intruders. The intense light from the two AR15s filled the house like lightning that never flashed. This effect blinded and disoriented the now goggle-less intruders.

The two FBI agents opened fire at the men. The front man from each team took the full barrage of shots like a human shield, while the other two behind them scurried off to the sides and out of view of the narrow killway. Inside the storage space, the shots were loud and sharp as they exploded next to the opened closet door.

Ty was a little disoriented. He'd never actually heard one of his AR15s fired without hearing protection on, let alone two AR15s.

The only return fire came from reflexes from the blindness and the pain as the men shot aimlessly at nothing while falling. Jim and Hank retreated back into the closet entry, out of view of the invaders and back to safety. They both turned off their high-intensity lights.

"I got the front one," Jim said.

"Same here." Hank picked up his phone and began monitoring the hallway again.

They could see the two bodies lying on the floor at both ends of the hall. They couldn't tell of they were dead or alive. Then, the body from the garage team began sliding out of view—dragged by his foot.

Voices over radios could be heard. One of the intruders dodged into Ty's office at the front of the house. The voice over one of the radios could be heard echoing though the hallway, saying, "Hold them down, I think I found something!"

"They're in my office!" Ty whispered.

Hank could see what looked like beams of light flashing from a side opening near the front door, near where the bathroom was. "They're searching for something," he said over his shoulder while still staring at his phone display.

Then a loud open chord rang out from that same direction. Like an acoustic guitar being kicked or thrown to the ground.

"I got it! Package secured. Let's get out of here!"

"Roger that! Meet you at point two. We'll cover you from there."

The conversation was overheard by everyone.

The garage team could be heard leaving back out through the garage door in the back of the kitchen.

Hank watched as the second body was dragged out of view from the other end of the hallway. A few seconds later a heavy vehicle approached and screeched to a stop in front of the house. They heard a metal door slide open, and the unmistakable sound of a suppressed firearm firing—eight silenced shots and the sound of escaping air as tires released their last gasps.

Heavily booted footsteps could be heard outside from the front of the house, then stopped.

"Ready!" A voice shouted.

Gun fire rained through the hallway, tearing at the walls and plaster and studs in a cloud of dust and debris. Shards of floor tile shot through the air in front of Jim and Hank, spraying them with travertine chips as they threw themselves back, retreating further into the closet space, out of the line of fire and shrapnel.

The multiple firing of guns began to decrease until it was one gun firing into the hallway. The shots stopped, the galloping of running boots fading away, then the sound of a sliding metal door crashing shut, and a large engine vehicle pulled away fast into the darkness of the surrounding neighborhood.

Chapter 23

Sirens filled the dark, early morning air. Red and blue strobing lights seemed to hit every window in the once-quiet neighborhood. The power to the house was restored by Tyson. Jim told him to use a paper towel to flip the switch on; they would be dusting for fingerprints there later. Hank was talking to one of the local police officers as he took notes. Neighbors were still looking out of their windows or opened front doors. The ones wearing clothes stood out in the open, while the ones wearing less stood behind their doors, showing only their heads.

Ty thought they had a right to see what was happening. This was a quiet neighborhood; he was a quiet neighbor. Now this, this was never going to go away, and the neighborhood would be telling this story for years; especially if they heard about the lottery tickets.

Dana walked up to Ty and touched his arm. Ty was fine; actually, too fine. He wasn't shaking or nervous or in shock. He was scared at the time, but he never felt crippled by it. All he thought of was protecting Dana, then he laughed to himself; him, protecting the CIA, good one. But what did that say about him? Did it excite him a little? Psychopathic tendencies? This should have shaken him, but he was calm.

"Are you okay?" she asked him out of real concern.

"Yeah, I feel fine. How about you?" That seemed like a dumb question to ask her. She was trained for these situations.

"I'm good." She could tell he expected more from her than she did.

"Look, I was a CIA analyst, not a field agent. I've never been in a firefight like that. Not a real one anyway. I just analyzed data for other agents to use."

Ty looked at her. Was she trembling? Without thinking, he wrapped his arms around her, and she held him back. Her trembling began to subside, and she exhaled a long, heavy breath, like she had been holding it during the entire ordeal. They stood there, embracing, while the buzzing of police activity ignored them.

Moments passed and they released each other. His shirt was wet on his shoulder where a tear landed. Ty reached into the closet and grabbed a jacket hanging there covered with dust and debris. He shook it off and put it around Dana's athletic shoulders.

"Want to go see what that machine looks like?" He was able to look her in the eyes more comfortably than before.

"What? They took it with them. It's gone. I had no idea the lengths someone was willing go through to obtain it." She though he was joking trying to cheer her up.

"Wanna bet!?"

Her eyes lit up when she saw his face brimming with an *"I'm pretty smart"* look on it.

He took her to his front office. Jim and Hank were doing their FBI stuff with the local police. They both glanced at the two of them as they walked past and nodded their way. More police with big cameras and gloved hands were scouring the place, taking pictures, and collecting bits and pieces from the scene.

When they entered the office, Ty looked around at the damage. It wasn't too bad. His guitar was knocked over and laid on the ground, strings down, which he was about to pick up, then decided to leave it for now. The surface of his workbench was bare, including his test equipment and gear; basically, everything he attached to the fake quantum computer. Near his guitar stood four upright black cylinders, untouched.

Ty held up his hand toward the standing matte-black monoliths.

"There you go. I present to you for your inspection, Q-Tip." A shy smile on his face held the look of satisfaction.

"What? That's a quantum computer? All four of them? Q-Tip?" Dana looked at them, then back at Ty, confused.

"Only one of them. Third one from the left. The only one on a pentapod."

Dana walked over to the four standing cylinders and crouched down in front of Q-Tip. She looked at it carefully, stood back up, then pointed at it while looking at Ty with a crooked smile on her face. "This one?"

"Yup. You should see what it looks like when it's powered on, but maybe don't stare at it when it's processing. I haven't figured out the time dilation yet. It's quite disorienting."

"What's 'Q-Tip'?" She asked with a puzzled expression while looking around at the inside of his office. "But. So. What did those guys take? What did they get shot for?" She was still confused.

"I built a decoy and laid it out on this workbench." He waved his hands over his now empty workbench where the imposter once sat.

"When I was at KRF back in January, Yuichu showed me a Mark 2 device in one of the labs. It looked like an old PC case on its side with all kinds of test equipment and wires attached to it. It looked like a robot having surgery under the lights laying there. I built something similar out of junk from my garage based on what I remembered from that visit."

Ty grabbed his phone and opened up the photo app. He showed her some pictures of the fake.

"Is that an old Apple Mac Pro A1289 aluminum case?" She pointed at the device in the pictures.

"Yeah! Great eye!" Ty was admiring her more by the minute. He wondered what she thought of him.

"I cleaned everything up, scraped off logos, put a motherboard in it, and hooked everything up. It would have run as a server if it was turned on. I put some copper tubing together from some old liquid cooled gear, some steel braided lines, some RGB LED light strips and a Red Bull can in the center. I didn't even empty it." He was pointing at a top view of the inside of the decoy.

"I hooked up all of my test equipment to it, and they took all of that too."

"So, what are all of those?" She pointed to the cylinder statues.

"More decoys. I hid the real device in plain sight." He finally decided to pick up the guitar; it rang through the makeshift speaker amp now that the power was back on. He strummed a chord before setting it back on its stand; it was knocked out of tune. "Only one of them works, but I actually like the way it looks. It needs a lot of work, and the sound is horrible, but I just threw it all together Sunday afternoon.

"After they made the announcement that both tickets were bought from the same store at the same time, then speculation that it was bought by the same person, well I got paranoid. Not for my safety or the money, but for the machine itself. After this morning, maybe now, my safety a little too." He looked at Dana, then glanced around at his office.

"Oh crap!" He was looking at his desk.

"What is it? What's wrong?" Dana looked in the same direction with fear.

"They took my work laptop. I liked that MacBook." He sat down at his desk chair and reached far under the desk. He pulled out Tomahawk and set it on the desk's surface.

"This is Tomahawk." He introduced the laptop to her. That was stupid and nerdy. And that's why he never got a second date, he thought. "Sorry, I name things as part of my projects." He pointed to the external GPU on the shelf behind him. "That's Bazooka," he said sheepishly. *Will you please just stop before she runs away?*

"So, Q-Tip?" She pointed at the cylinder.

"Yeah, and his band of imposters. I didn't bother to name them all—for now." He smiled at her.

"Cute. I can see it." She smiled back at him.

"I don't know. It just came out and it stuck. I didn't want to go with another weapons name."

Shut up Tyson. The voice in his head was trying to abort the dork conversation he was having.

"The software on this laptop is probably more valuable and more important than the device itself." Ty placed his hand on Tomahawk.

"The tendency for people—programmers—will be to write programs like they're used to, on traditional computers. This software allows for that. That's how the quantum computing revolution will get supercharged, by tapping into what everyone already does and knows. Just look at me, I did it." Ty stood up and picked up Tomahawk.

"So, even if they managed to take the real device, it would be worthless without this. Or best case, it would be lethargic." Dana pointed at the laptop.

"Mostly. This is what's really important." Ty pointed specifically at the USB memory stick plugged in the side of Tomahawk.

"Oh no!" She said with a sudden awareness. "Once that team takes that decoy to whoever hired them, shit's going to hit the fan. They might actually come back here looking harder for the real one—Q-Tip." Dana looked at the time, it was 4:20 a.m. "This time with a larger and more heavily armed team."

"I was betting that if anyone broke into my house to steal it, they weren't going to be a quantum physicist. I hadn't thought of them coming back." Ty began smiling at a thought.

"What's so funny? This is serious. Whoever sent that team knows some bad people and will probably show up with more of them, even if the FBI is guarding this place." Dana's concern pierced through his smile.

"I'm sorry. I know this is serious. I just had a funny thought of a scientist examining that decoy and opening the central component, the Red Bull can. They might let all of the 'quantum serum' out." He laughed again at the imagery.

"Do you just put the word *quantum* in front of everything?" She rolled her eyes and laughed too.

"I know! Right! You watched *Ant-Man and the Wasp*?" He was beside himself.

"Of course, hasn't everyone?" she asked sincerely. "I was watching it again last night. I love that movie."

Ty stood there looking at her, wishing he could have been there watching the movie with her.

She stuck her head out of the office and called Jim to come over. As Jim walked in, Hank followed him into the now tight office.

"I think we have a problem," she announced to the guys.

"Oh, and what's that? Those guys got what they were looking for and we don't have a clue as to what they were driving or where." Jim seemed agitated.

"Well, no they didn't. This is the real machine." Dana point to the group of matte black cylinders in the corner.

"Ty here hid the real device in plain sight. What those guys took was a decoy he built that was laying up here on this workbench along with some test equipment. All of it garbage, but very convincing in the dark. They didn't send a scientist or engineer to steal the machine; someone sent a bunch of mercs," she explained.

"Hey, it was very convincing in the light too," Ty protested in jest.

"Sorry, not important right now." Dana smiled back at Ty.

Jim looked around at the situation.

"So, if they were willing to hit this place for a pile of junk, they're just as likely come back stronger for the real thing. Is that what you think?" Jim looked at Dana to see if his assessment was right.

"That's not quite what I think will happen." She was thinking this through. "By the time they realize they stole a fake, they'll have to know the real device was moved out of here. They know law enforcement of some kind was here last night to pick off two of their own. We really do need to get this device out of here and to a safer place. The Morgan Hill data center would be perfect." She was walking around the office.

"It's four thirty in the morning. Whoever they have to examine that fake probably wouldn't do so until later this morning. That should give us enough time to transport this one out of here. If they're stupid enough to try and search this place again, we should have a team here waiting for them. We could get some answers if we caught them here." Dana continued pacing while thinking out loud.

"I'm on it. I'll get a team here to watch the place for a couple of days." Hank was already on his phone as he was talking.

"Okay, then let's get moving." Jim agreed with Dana's take on the situation.

"Problems is, we don't have a ride. Both vehicles were disabled. And it will take a while to repair or replace them." Jim said as he and Dana looked at Ty.

"So, what do you drive?" Jim smiled at Ty.

"Follow me," Ty said as he smiled and led them toward the garage.

Hank stopped what he was doing with the police and followed them.

Entering the garage from the kitchen entrance, and turning on the light, they could see the broken door jam and the smashed-in side garage door. The damage wasn't as bad as it sounded. *My senses must have been heightened when all that craziness went down*, Ty thought.

"What do you think?" Ty was proud of his girlfriend and showed her off.

"Oh my god!" Dana gawked.

"I know, right!" Ty was beaming and couldn't wait to take her for a ride.

"You have a Model S P100D with Ludicrous Plus mode?" She walked up to the black Tesla. "Do you know how fast this car is? Well of course you do, you have one." She was in awe.

Ty couldn't believe she was infatuated with the Tesla when his beloved M3 ZCP was right here.

"I was referring to the M3 Z…" He was genuinely hurt as his voice trailed off.

"Jim and I will take the reject and escort you two in the Tesla to Morgan Hill," Hank said with a playful smirk on his face.

"Fine. Let me grab this box." Before he grabbed the old packing material, he closed the side garage door and took a cordless drill and some screws from his workbench, then sealed the door shut. Ty grabbed the shipping box that Q-Tip arrived in a few weeks ago and dejectedly walked back into the house with it.

***

Dmitry watched the police activity from down the street. The three men in the car with him were asleep while waiting for the operation to be continued or aborted. The men in the sedan behind him were awake and alert; they were also observing the activity and assessing the situation. They were scared off earlier with the extremely bright lights hitting them before they could start their mission. They regrouped back at the cars and watched as another operations team struck the house before them. That was good luck for them. They would have been shot, caught, or both if they would have continued their mission last night. Who could have anticipated such well-armed law enforcement would be meeting with Tyson McNally at that hour. It was probably the FBI or NSA questioning him. Whoever they were, they were professionally trained for tactical situations.

Homes in the quiet neighborhood began to light up. Front doors and windows were opened to see what all the noise and lights were about.

They watched the other team carry two bodies away from the house and something that looked like a computer enclosure, along with equipment, then loaded everything into a van and took off. Before Dmitry could start the car and follow them, the police showed up as the full-size van disappeared. Leaving at that moment would have drawn unwanted suspicion, and they would have easily been caught and questioned. No, the second priority was to take Tyson McNally if the device wasn't at the house, and he was still there.

For now, he would wait to see what happened next. There might still be an opportunity to salvage this mission. Moscow would be very pleased with him if he managed to bring them a quantum computer genius. They might even forgive his deliberate misinterpretation of their orders.

If this worked out right, they might even reinstate him back as a foreign security service agent. It wasn't fair they blamed him for the incident with the CIA years ago. The intelligence was flawed. He did what he had to do to complete that mission, which in the end, by most measures, was successful. But the international mess it created needed to be pinned on someone down rank. That meant he was blamed, shamed, demoted, re-identified, and reassigned. That covered everyone else's ass but his. His redemption would be celebrated throughout the FSS community.

He smiled with self-satisfaction as he continued to monitor the home of Tyson McNally.

***

Jim helped Ty break down his weapons and store them back into his safe.

"This is some quality hardware. You built these?" Jim asked curiously.

"Not the shotgun. Just the 1911s and the AR15s. It seemed like something interesting to do, you know, being a gunsmith. Technically and mechanically, it's a fun challenge, but once they're built, tuned, and dialed in, there's not much left to do but shoot them. I'd start another one, and so on, until I ended up looking like a doomsday nutjob. So, I stopped and locked them up." Ty was worried where the conversation was going. "I never thought they'd ever get used like this."

"Well, I for one am glad you had them available. When all this settles down, give me a call; I'll see about getting you an exception for them. You might have to take a few FBI weapons classes, but I'll get you signed up."

"Thanks! That would be useful. All those California restrictions just turns them into garbage." He locked the safe and they both left the California basement and joined the others in his office.

Ty disconnected and disassembled Q-Tip, and packed everything back into the box exactly in reverse order from how he'd unpacked it. As he walked back into his office with Jim, he took the packing tape he retrieved from the closet, and he sealed the box. It was ready to go. He placed Tomahawk and a few accessories into his oversized laptop backpack and zipped everything up.

"Mind if I put on some fresh clothes before we head out?" Ty asked. The anxious sweat was getting ripe on him as the morning sunrise started to brighten the sky.

"Sure, we have time. We'll try to head out in about ten minutes. Let me check with the police to see how much more time they'll need," Hank said as he and Jim were getting ready.

"Do you need anything before we head out?" Hank looked at Dana.

She was on her phone reading and messaging someone or some ones.

"Yes, I want to stop by my hotel room and grab my stuff. It's less than ten minutes away and it's on the way to the freeway." She looked up and put her phone away.

"Hank, go grab our gear out of the SUV. I'll wrap up here. The sooner we get to Morgan Hill, the better I'll feel." Jim coordinated the makeshift team.

"I'm on it. I'll start loading up the car. You want the other car armed?" Hank asked on his way out.

"Yeah, get something for them too. Better to be over prepared. We don't want to find ourselves in a situation like earlier. We got lucky," Jim said as Hank continued heading out to the FBI SUV.

Ty returned to his office in a fresh set of clothes and a jacket. "Does anyone want a coffee for the road? Let me rephrase that. I'm making myself a coffee for the road, would anyone like one too?"

Dana and Jim looked over at him and immediately nodded. "Yes please. Black," they both said simultaneously.

"And if you don't mind, a black one for Hank as well. Thanks, it's been a long night," Jim requested appreciatively.

"Anyone up for some Pop-Tarts?" Ty added. He could tell everyone looked haggard, worn, and needed some fuel.

"Oh man! You were reading my mind, but I didn't want to impose." Jim looked like someone just offered him an "Old Timers" breakfast from Cracker Barrel.

"Anything specific? Sorry, I don't have anything frosted."

"Hank and I will take strawberry if you have them, otherwise anything unfrosted would hit the spot."

"I'll help you out." Dana followed Ty to the kitchen.

"I'm so sorry all of this is happening to you. All of these different circumstances have just culminated onto you, and you don't deserve any of it." She was walking at his side down the shot-up hallway, avoiding the large chunks of debris on the broken tiled floor.

"I mean, your beautiful home, look at it." She was observing all the damage from the gunfire.

The two of them reached the kitchen. Ty went to the pantry and grabbed several boxes of different favored Pop-Tarts. He pointed at a cupboard next to Dana for her to open. When she opened the cupboard, she found dozens of travel coffee mugs with different company and tech conference logos on them.

"Thanks for that, but I think I'll be alright. All of this can be fixed up and I don't think anything important was damaged. The way I see it, if it wasn't for the earthquake, I would have never met you." He closed his eyes tight and pursed his lips.

Oh crap! What are you doing Ty? Too soon. She's just doing her job, and you're just another assignment. Once all of this is over, she'll move on to her next assignment, and you'll be a note in her status report. And that's why you're still single. He was beating himself up in his head as he opened his eyes to start loading Keurig pods into his custom coffee maker.

Dana looked at him with her tired, hazel eyes. His eyes caught hers at the same moment. She leaned over and she pressed her lips to his for what seemed like hours. His eyes were closed again, this time serenely. When she gradually pulled away, his eyes opened to see her opening her own eyes slowly, almost in unison. It felt like time stopped. His head was swimming with calmness. When he regained his focus, he half thought it would be noon outside.

He didn't know what to say or do next. So, he did what he did best in these situations—he'd screw it up. "Look, I—"

She put her hand on his lips to keep him from finishing whatever he was about to say.

"I'm sorry for doing that. I've never thought... I'm not like..." She paused for a moment, looked down, and inhaled deeply.

"When John died, I had to move on, I poured myself into work; a new career; an adjusted life. It was how I managed my grief and anger. That was over six years ago. I haven't seen anyone seriously since then. I didn't have the desire to look." She paused again, still looking down at the logoed travel cups.

"I'm happy you did. I would like to do it again." *Jesus! I should just shut up!* He tried to hide the anguish in his head. "What I meant was—is— I've never met anyone like you. I know we've only just met, and you're here on an assignment, but I'd really like to get to know you more. Um, when this is all over." *Better. Decent recovery.* His shoulders relaxed a bit.

"I'd like that too." She gave him a tired smile. Then she looked around at the task in front of her. "But first, we need to get to Morgan Hill." She was focused again and rejuvenated. She hadn't even had her coffee yet.

The two of them finished making coffee for everyone and wrapped the toasted Pop-Tarts in paper towels to-go.

They handed Jim and Hank their coffees and Pop-Tarts. In exchange, Hank handed Dana an already loaded, FBI issued 9mm Glock and two additional clips.

"Thanks for the gun loan, but we'll be using government issued hardware from this point forward. Just in case. And thanks for the breakfast," Hank said as he also handed Ty a Glock and took a sip of coffee.

"It'll be easier to explain and less paperwork if you use one of these instead of your homemade brands. If it ever comes to that." Hank bit off the corner of both pastries.

The local police crew were finishing up in the house. They installed a new police lock on the front of his broken door. The officer in charge of having it installed handed Ty a set of keys.

"This is for your protection and remains the property of the Soledad police department. You have thirty days to have your door repaired. After which time you will be charged fifteen dollars a day to continue using the lock." He was pointing to the front door.

"Call this number and someone will come out and remove it for you." The officer handed him a business card. "We're just about done here. Do you have any questions?" He looked at Ty, then the two FBI agents.

"No. I think I'm good for now. Thanks for getting here quickly." Ty shook the officer's hand.

"We'll be in touch." The officer then shook both Hank and Jim's hand, turned, and left the house with the rest of the departing police crew.

Jim looked at the three of them.

"Well, ready to get this show on the road?" Then Jim took a long sip from the coffee cup.

"Let me load up my stuff." Ty turned and went into his office and came out with his backpack on and the box in his hands. He headed straight to the garage with the three of them following him.

He loaded the box in the rear passenger seat of the Tesla and strapped it in with the seatbelt, then he put his backpack down on the floor in front of it. After closing the car door, he walked over to the kitchen door and pressed the button to open the garage door.

He pointed at the M3 and threw the keys to Jim. They began loading their stuff into the car.

As the door rolled up, his friend and next-door neighbor was walking up toward his front door. He stopped as the door finished opening.

Hank and Jim instinctively pulled their guns and were both pointing them at Ty's neighbor, Tim.

"Dude! Shit! Wait!" He backed up with his hands in the air.

"Wait! It's okay. He's my next-door neighbor. He's lived here longer than me."

Jim and Hank both lowered their guns and put them back into their holsters.

"What the crap, Ty! What's going on? Are you Okay?" Tim was shaken by Jim and Hank's reaction and stayed where he was, his hands still partially lifted

Ty walked out of the garage and asked Dana to join him.

Jim and Hank looked carefully out of the garage door beyond the driveway. They both looked up and down the street as they took a few steps out of the garage. The brightening sky was starting to blanket the neighborhood in fresh sunlight to start everyone else's new day.

"Hey Tim, sorry about that. I hope you're okay. They're the FBI." Ty pointed toward Jim and Hank, then embraced Tim in a quick man-hug.

"Yeah, I'm good. I nearly shit myself though. What happened last night? We've been up all morning. I came over to check on you now that all the police cars have left." Tim was waving his hand over the neighborhood as he spoke.

"Tell Maggie, I'm okay, and that everything's fine. Some people tried to rob me last night and things got really crazy. I gotta go do something with—" He stopped mid-sentence.

"Ah, sorry. Tim, this is Dana. Dana, this is my friend and neighbor, Tim."

Dana and Tim shook hands.

"Nice to meet you, Tim."

"It's nice to meet you." Tim looked at Ty, then back at Dana, then back at Ty with his eyebrows raised.

"It sounded like a lot more than crazy was happening inside your house last night." Tim now looked a little confused and concerned.

"I've gotta go do something with Dana up north. I don't know when I'll be back. Can you watch over the house until I return? There might be some FBI guys stopping by to watch over the house later. I don't know what to expect," Ty explained.

"Sure thing. I can do that." Tim glanced inside the garage at the two agents loading up the M3.

"You're going to let someone else drive your girlfriend?" he asked as they man-hugged each other goodbye.

"It's complicated. I'll explain everything later."

"You're still going to compete in the tournament next month, right?" Tim yelled as the two headed back into the garage.

"I'm planning on it." Ty gave Tim a last finger-point from the garage. He looked at Jim and Hank, then at Dana. All four of them loaded up into the cars.

"Hopefully that'll ease a little of the anxiety in the neighborhood. There's going to be a ton of rumors flying around for weeks about last night," he tried to explain.

It was then that Dana realized he was just a regular guy. She looked at him with admiration and concern. A great guy with extraordinary talent, but just a regular guy caught up in something he shouldn't be caught up in. She felt this was partially her fault, and she would never forgive herself if anything happened to him. He was right, the earthquake was both a tragedy and a blessing, but much more of a tragedy. She was determined to make sure he was safe and protected and get him through this mess. They needed to get to Morgan Hill.

"Mind if I drive?" she asked Ty, though she wasn't actually asking.

"Um, sure, no problem. Wait! Do you even know how to drive an automatic?" He laughed at his inside joke, then realized how stupid that sounded, since no one else ever got it.

She busted up laughing. "I guess we're going to go get your future ex-ex-wife!" she blurted back.

They both looked at each other with their wide eyes locked.

"What happens in Vegas!" they said in unison and laughed.

She needed that. It energized and lifted her heavy mind.

"I loved that car!" She opened the driver side door and got into the black Tesla.

He got into the passenger seat and buckled up.

Dana let Jim and Hank pull out first. The M3 growled out of the garage. Jim revved the engine as he pulled ahead of the Tesla toward the driveway and out onto the street. Dana pressed the accelerator and the Tesla rolled forward. Ty touched the garage door button on the large center screen and checked to make sure it was closing.

Dana handed Ty her phone. "Call Jim."

Ty looked at her already unlocked phone and opened the phone app. One of the top recent numbers listed was Jim Jordan, which he touched to initiate the call.

"Yeah? Everything good?" Jim was looking back at the Tesla as it was leaving the driveway.

"Let's keep this line connected until we get to Morgan Hill," Dana said while approaching the M3.

"Good idea. Lead the way," Jim acknowledged and waited for Dana to pull ahead of him and Hank.

"I'm heading to the hotel first."

Dana pulled up to the M3 and signaled for Jim to follow her to her hotel. The two vehicles accelerated down the street and away from Ty's home with only the raspy exhaust of the M3 being heard.

***

Dmitry watched the police leave the house after they had finished their work and talked to nearby neighbors. He bumped the two sleeping men behind him and the guy next to him to wake them up. He looked in the rearview mirror at the other sedan behind him. The men in that car were awake and watching the scene unfold in front of them along with him.

Dmitry had a trace ran on the two disabled vehicles in front of Tyson McNally's home. The smaller vehicle had a civilian license plate and was registered to a small, private rental company. He could not determine who was renting that vehicle. The larger SUV, that was an FBI vehicle. That was how Tyson McNally survived last night's assault, and how two men died. The FBI were here protecting him. This changed everything. It would not be a simple matter of overpowering and grabbing Tyson McNally. How did he have FBI connections? Dmitry's planning needed to be carefully and thoroughly thought out.

He picked up his phone and called the other vehicle on his speaker phone so everyone could hear the plan.

"Put your phone on speaker. Are you seeing this?" He spoke with his phone up near his chin.

"Da, all of the police cars have left. Now what you want us to do?" The deep, rough voice spoke professionally.

"How are your men?" Dmitry looked in the rearview mirror as the men in the sedan all nodded their heads, indicating they were ready to go once he gave them the plan.

"We are all ready to execute your orders." The driver in the other car was looking forward at the rearview mirror of Dmitry's car, where they caught each other's eyes.

"Okay good. We will approach the front and back of the house. Your team will neutralize everyone and take Tyson McNally. You know what he looks like, yes? Be careful, there are FBI agents protecting him. Also, I need time to search the house. Your team has suppressors installed, yes?"

"Da. You want we should restrain him or remove him?" the leader of the other car asked.

"Better to restrain him unt—" he stopped talking mid-word. "Wait, someone is coming." Dmitry watched as one of the neighbors walked up to the house, stopped on the driveway, then walked further up the driveway and stopped again. Dimitry was not in a good position to see that part of the house. Why were his hands in the air?

He watched as Tyson McNally and Daniela Jordan walked out to greet the neighbor. The three of them talked for a few minutes. So, Mrs. Jordan was there talking to Tyson McNally. He watched the three of them. Tyson and the neighbor briskly embraced, then the neighbor returned to his home. Both Tyson McNally and Mrs. Jordan turned and walked back toward the garage. A couple of minutes later a silver BMW drove out of the garage and waited on the street in front of the house with two men inside it. They must be the FBI agents. Then a black, four-door sedan pulled out of the garage. He saw Mrs. Jordan driving and Tyson McNally sitting in the passenger seat. It pulled in front of the BMW, and the two vehicles drove off with the black sedan leading.

"Change of plans. We follow those two cars," Dmitry said into the phone.

"Da. We will follow you," the deep voice from the other car responded.

The black and silver convoy drove nearly out of sight before the two sedans pulled away and began tailing them from a distance, careful to not to draw attention. Dmitry was formulating a new plan as he followed the two cars.

Chapter 24

Traffic was picking up as the city of Soledad woke up. The two sedans took turns leading and getting close to the silver and black cars, then retreated, careful not to weave through traffic. One car would approach them or even pass them, then turn into a parking lot, letting the other car tail them. They coordinated their locations so the trailing sedan could catch up and the ruse would start over. They only went two times through this cycle before the two cars they were tailing pulled into a hotel parking lot and stopped at the entrance. Dmitry's teams drove past the hotel and turned into two separate parking lots beyond the hotel. The closest car kept a lookout on the two stopped cars. The female driver of the black car left the car and entered the hotel.

After a couple of minutes, an unmarked police SUV pulled up alongside the small BMW and stopped. It appeared there was a conversation taking place.

After a few more minutes, the woman returned with two bags, which she placed in the back seat, then walked between the gray BMW and the black SUV and stopped for a few minutes. Then she walked back to the black car and entered the driver seat.

"We have a trouble. They are on the move again. Now they have an unmarked police escort with them; a black SUV," the deep voice updated over his phone.

"Okay, good. That might help. Let them pass you. I'm going on ahead. I think they are going to go north on the freeway." Dmitry had the start of his plan. "Once we are on the freeway, you will take out the police SUV by shooting the tires out. Take out other vehicles to block the traffic behind you. I will be out in front of everyone and will stop and block the traffic ahead. Then, we will approach them and take them out. It will be a long stretch of road with no exits. This will be on my signal. Do you understand? You need to block two lanes and the shoulders so they cannot escape." Dmitry would have rather had more time to plan a kidnapping like this, with everyone involved seeing the same plans and maps, but the plan changed and continued to change. They needed to move fast and think en route.

"Da. I will make traffic mess behind them, and you make traffic mess in front of them. After they are boxed in, we attack. On your signal."

"Good. I am going on ahead to the freeway to get further north ahead of them. You stay behind and keep tailing them—carefully. Wait for my signal."

With that, Dmitry pulled out of the parking lot and headed to the northbound 101-Freeway onramp.

"They have left the hotel and are heading to the freeway. Gray BMW, black car, and unmarked black police SUV. We are following them now," the rough voice announced.

***

The two-car caravan pulled up to the hotel entrance.

"I'll be right back. Keep the engine running." Dana looked at Ty and smiled.

"Ha! Now that's funny right there." Ty smiled back as he watched her walk into the hotel lobby then disappear inside somewhere. He couldn't help but wonder how this might end or if it would end. He wanted to be himself, which didn't always end well for him, but he also didn't want this connection to end yet. There was something there.

"Put her clothes back on, McNally. That's my sister you're undressing. Well, my sister-in-law, mostly. My sister-in-law until she gets married again. You get the picture, lover boy," Jim's voice bellowed over the phone as he watched Ty from his other car.

"I wasn't undressing her. I was thinking about undressing her. Shit! Sorry about that. I crossed the line. It sounded funnier in my head before I said it." It was too late to save this one. Better to just apologize and take the beating.

"Relax, Tyson. I can tell she sees something in you. What it is, I haven't a clue other than you're both a couple of nerds. She's been a bit of a recluse since my younger brother was killed. But I haven't seen her this genuinely upbeat in a long time. Even when she visits the kids, I can tell there's some darkness she's hiding. Just be yourself, I think she likes that." It sounded like Jim was protecting his younger sister but wanted her to be happy too.

"But don't use that bit about undressing her. That does cross the line. For everyone." Hank jumped into "the talk."

"Technically, Jim brought it up."

"Fair enough. I'll give you that one." Jim didn't apologize but did acknowledge the breach in etiquette.

At that moment, a black Ford Explorer pulled up alongside his M3. Ty could hear the windows slide down over the speaker phone.

"Are you special agent Jordan and special agent Hughes with the FBI?" the passenger side officer asked.

"That's right. And you are?" Jim showed them his badge.

"I'm officer Gomez and this is officer Jenkins. We're here to escort you to Morgan Hill. It's a pleasure to assist you, sir." There was a respect in the officer's voice that Ty could hear on the speaker phone.

"Thank you, officers; the pleasure is all ours. We appreciate your help." Jim was appreciative and respectful back.

Ty thought he must watch too many movies, because he thought local police and the FBI didn't get along very well. Hollywood bullshit.

"We need to escort that Tesla in front of us. We'll lead. If you could cover our six, we'll keep that car in between us the whole way up the one-oh-one." Jim explained their plan to the two officers.

"Do you have a mobile number, officer Gomez? We'll add you into our phone connection so we can all stay in communication."

"Yes sir," Officer Gomez replied.

The officer gave his number and Jim entered it. A faint ringtone could be heard, then a clicking, and a three-way call was established between the three vehicles.

"Good morning! I'm Ty," Ty jumped in and greeted the officers.

"Ty? McNally? Is that you?" Officer Jenkins was surprised to hear Tyson's voice and name on the phone.

"Yeah. Hey, thanks for your help, Ted."

"I thought this was your car. Why are you in that car? You're letting someone else drive your girlfriend? How did that happen?"

"It's a long and complicated story. I'll tell you about it at the next tournament."

"That's our package. And what tournament?" Jim interrupted the chit chat.

"Archery tournament," both Ty and Ted said, almost simultaneously, even with the phone connection lag.

"Hey? Was that your house that was shot up earlier this morning?" Miguel asked for the both of them.

"Yeah, like I said, it's complicated."

"We heard about it—" Officer Gomez stopped as Dana walked out of the hotel with her bags.

She opened the driver's side back door and placed her bags behind the seat, closed the door, then walked between the vehicles to join the conversation.

"Good morning officers. What going on?" She leaned over to a height somewhere between the low M3 and the high SUV.

"Hank called the Soledad chief of police this morning and asked for an escort to Morgan Hill." Jim was throwing his thumb at Hank.

"Excellent idea, Hank." She bent over further to look at him directly.

"Officers, thank you." She stood up to thank the officers.

"Let's get going. The sooner we get there the better." Dana turned and got in the Tesla.

She pulled forward slowly, while Jim maneuvered around to get in front, then the black SUV brought up the rear. The three vehicles pulled onto Front Street and headed toward the freeway onramp in tight formation. The convoy approached the 101-Freeway northbound onramp, made the hairpin turn onto the freeway, and sped up to seventy miles per hour. Traffic for this area and time of the morning was sparse and mild for California. The caravan was able to stay tightly together and maintain their speed. If their intention was to not draw attention to their formation, they were failing miserably. The three vehicles looked like they were in their own seventy miles per hour traffic jam, and every car that passed them, or they passed, knew they were a team on a mission. This had the desired effect of telling everyone to "stay out!"

They mainly stayed in the right lane and passed slower vehicles as a train in the left lane, then returned to the right lane. The farming communities of the northern Salinas Valley and the farmlands they cared for stretched for miles in all directions between small towns and cities along the 101-Freeway.

"Jim, there's a problem up ahead. Traffic is stopped about three miles ahead. Jackknifed semi," Ty's voice announced on the phones. He was monitoring traffic conditions on the Tesla's console and his phone.

"He's right. We're just getting reports in now. Complete freeway blockage," Officer Gomez confirmed.

"Thanks for that. Any alternate routes or exits before we get there?" Jim responded.

"Nope! Nothing that I can see. These maps are usually up-to-date," Ty inserted.

"Then this is no accident," Hank announced.

"Do y'all see that dirt service road on the right there?" Officer Jenkins' voice came through the call. "There're paths to that road all along this freeway. The farmers use them to get from one field to another; sometimes they need to use the freeway shoulder, but mostly those dirt roads. There's probably three more of them before we get to that traffic. We could use it to bypass the traffic. They're pretty well maintained, but we won't be doing seventy miles per hour on them."

Jim was already slowing the convoy down.

"Excellent. Officer Jenkins, please lead the way. Take us as close as you can to the traffic jam before we get off the freeway." Jim was just starting to change lanes to get behind the convoy when a silver sedan approached in the left lane. He waited for the car to pass them, but it matched their speed instead.

"Look out!" were the last coherent words that could be heard on the connected phones, late by split seconds as the black police SUV was already swerving in the rearview mirrors of the cars in front of it. Gunfire could be heard outside the car windows before the warning scream, then gunshots came over the lagging phones. Thumping, cussing, screeching, and grunts were the only sounds coming over the speaker phones as the officer tried to regain control of the crippled vehicle while their phone was thrown around within the SUV.

The view from their rearview mirrors showed the black SUV swerving then spinning in the middle of the freeway and coming to a stop upright, perpendicular to the road.

"Dana! Punch it!" Jim yelled over the phone. She was already speeding, pulling away from the sluggish, overweighted sedan. Jim swerved into the left lane to let the Tesla speed ahead of him, then he pulled the M3 up behind her. The two cars reached 130 miles per hour in a few seconds, then 150 miles per hour after a few more seconds.

"Ted! Miguel! Are you alright?" Ty screamed into the phone.

There was an unbearable silent pause.

Muffled yelling, groaning, fumbling, seatbelts unbuckling, and scratching could be heard, then a clear, frazzled voice. "Yeah! We're fine! Get out of here! That car behind you is heavily armed! They shot out our tires. There's an exit road about two miles ahead of you. That should get you around the traffic then back on the freeway. Gomez is calling in support from Salinas, north of you right now. Good luck!"

"Roger that, Jenkins! Thanks!" Jim replied as the two cars continued to accelerate away.

"Jim! The speed limiters are disabled on these cars, but this Tesla is going to need more distance to stop at these speeds when we reach that exit road. That car will stop on a dime," Ty yelled into the phone.

"Understood. Keep an eye out for that dirt road and let us know when to turn off," Jim responded.

Ty pulled up a satellite view of their current location on his phone. They were traveling at a 160 miles per hour and still accelerating. Excessive speed warning notices were lighting up red all over the navigation app, but he found what he was looking for, an unmarked dirt road up ahead, in one mile.

"Found it! Less than a mile ahead! We're going to need about five hundred feet to stop in order to make that turn under control. I'll count it down," Ty announced.

Dana and Ty could both see the traffic ahead, nothing but stopped cars and people standing around outside of their vehicles.

"We're approaching the stopped traffic. We're going to start braking in three, two, one—now!"

Dana slammed on the brake pedal with both feet and pressed her hands forward on the steering wheel. Her hair flung forward toward the windshield, hiding her face from the side. The Model S's four calipers grabbed their discs tight while the anti-lock braking system torturously screamed and pulsed, letting the tires continue to roll, keeping the car in a straight, controlled line. The Tesla's regenerative braking system and gearboxes could be heard squealing and storing the enormous amounts of converted kinetic energy into the batteries. The time it took for the electric vehicle to go from 167 miles per hour to zero seemed to take forever. Their high-speed sprint worked as they pulled away from the pursuing car, giving them time to navigate the sharp right turn ahead. Their restraining systems held tight across their chests, including Q-Tip in the back seat, locking them safely in place.

The M3 ZCP shot past the Model S in the left lane before Jim slammed on the brakes. The M3 was lighter and factory equipped with a competition braking system that included oversized cross-drilled discs and calipers designed for much larger, heavier racecars from BMW. The maneuver was executed perfectly. Jim began his stop further down the freeway as the Tesla shot past it, continuing its stopping process. The M3 stopped well before the Tesla came to a full stop just ahead of the dirt road exit and ahead of the M3. Before reaching the Tesla and the exit, Jim yanked the e-brake handle at the last second, which pitched the car sideways, leaving it perpendicular on the freeway and pointing directly toward the dirt road exit.

"Dana, get off the freeway. We're right behind you," Jim yelled.

The Tesla dropped down onto the dirt road exit, crossing a dry drainage ditch bridge, then turned left up the service road.

"Ready!? Here they come," Hank announced.

The oversized, over-stressed, heavy sedan was coming up the freeway directly toward the M3. They hadn't started their stop yet, which meant they were going to attempt to ram the two agents. They were still over a thousand feet away and closing in fast when Hank pulled out a M110 sniper-equipped rifle. With the passenger-side window down, he took two shots at the driver's side windshield, shattering it and blinding the driver; if he was still alive, he wouldn't be able to see. Next, he shot three rounds into the engine grill, causing steam to shoot up and out of the engine bay, disabling it. Finally, he shot at the front driver's side tire, hitting it on the second shot as it exploded. That was good enough to throw the car into an uncontrolled swerve that sent them into the concrete center divider, which launched the car into the air. When it hit the ground, the sedan tumbled several times and stopped in an exhausted heap in the middle of the freeway less than three hundred feet away from them.

Before the sedan even came to a full, shattered stop, Jim punched the accelerator, leaving the freeway and catching up to Dana and Ty in the Tesla.

"Nice shooting, Hank! You've been working on your left side, I see." Jim was navigating the zigzag maneuver onto the dirt road.

"I thought it would help since I sit shotgun the most." Hank put the M110 in the back seat and grabbed a more tactical M16.

"Okay, we're clear from behind, but we don't know how many there are up ahead of us," Jim said over the still connected phones.

There was no room to maneuver around to the front of the Tesla yet, so Jim stayed behind it far enough to avoid being blinded by the dust. The dirt road was a mix of pea gravel, dirt, and patches of grass. There were many drivers and passengers in the stopped traffic on the freeway to their left. The stranded drivers, who parked their cars to stand on the freeway while they waited for the traffic to clear, watched the two dusty cars approach.

"Do you see that?" Dana called out over the phone. "People are running down into the ditch and running away from the accident."

They all could see why; there were two men with rifles running up toward the big rig on the freeway shoulder ahead of them. They reached the big rig and began shooting their automatic weapons. They were sitting ducks. Dana and Jim tried to speed up carefully. The cars didn't handle as well on the patchy dirt road as they do on the well-paved freeway. Rounds were peppering the ground around them. They were too far out of range for the shooters to be accurate with those weapons. A round managed to hit the M3's rear taillight as they barely navigated past the main barrage of gunfire and the crippled big rig.

"Ty? How soon to the nearest path back onto the freeway?" Jim asked calmly.

"Uh, about another mile and a half. Looks like all dirt road until then. I'll count us down." Ty zoomed into the satellite view of the navigation app to inspect the road ahead as he informed both Dana and Jim.

Even with all-wheel drive and traction control engaged, the Model S struggled to stay under control. Both cars became squirrely if they exceeded fifty miles per hour on the pebbly dirt road. The last thing they needed was for one of them to spin out and end up in the ditch.

The other half of Dmitry's team caught sight of the two cars racing up the service road. Abandoning their position on the other side of the big rig accident, they ran for their dark-gray sedan, jumped inside, and began their pursuit of their fleeing target. They accelerated as fast as the lumbering, loaded sedan could take them on the freeway. The two cars on the dirt service road were a good three thousand feet ahead of them, but the sedan was starting to close that gap. The armed men, one in the front passenger seat and the other in the back seat, switched to semi-automatic weapons and were aiming more carefully as they began firing at the dusty convoy.

They were still missing their mark, but as the sedan gained speed over the trapped convoy, the distance closed, and their aim improved.

Dana drove the Tesla as far to the right-hand side of the dirt road as she could safely manage. Jim drove as close to the rear of the Tesla as he could and hugged the left side of the road in order to cut off the angle of the gun fire. This maneuver would only work for as long as the sedan remained behind them.

Dana looked at the control console and touched the settings button. She pressed and held the Ludicrous Mode button for five seconds. The screen began a warp-speed starlight streak animation for a couple of seconds. An acknowledgement notice appeared, asking if she wanted to continue and a warning about accelerated component wear, with two options: "No, I want my mommy" or "Yes, bring it on." Touching the "Yes, bring it on" button, the setting screen came back with an indicator showing the batteries heating up; this process took the batteries to fifty degrees Celsius. The batteries were already at forty-three degrees but would still take some time to reach their Ludicrous-ready state.

"This is going to be close," she told Ty and Jim.

"I'm going to shoot out to the far-left lane. At this rate, it looks like I'm going to cross behind them. That should slow their gunfire down for a few seconds. Then we'll disappear. You can catch them from behind." Dana was watching the "Max Battery Power: Heating" indicator and the dirt road ahead.

"We've got another thousand feet to go! About twenty seconds. And it's going to be a zigzag ninety degree turn in the dirt," Ty yelled out.

"Come on, hurry!" she urged the batteries to heat up.

"Coming up to the side road in three, two, one—now!"

Dana and Jim both hit their brakes hard as the cars slid and fishtailed on the pebbly dirt road. She jerked the steering wheel to the left and caught the intersection at the very beginning of the opening, then headed diagonally across the junction toward the paved shoulder of the freeway. The sedan, with the two gunmen perched out of their windows, shot past the front driver corner of the Tesla as the gunmen recoiled back into their sedan; they assumed she was trying to ram the side of their car. Far down the freeway, the driver finally applied the brakes.

As soon as the front tires of the all-wheel drive Model S hit the solid traction of the paved freeway shoulder, the Tesla grabbed the road and was under control again. Dana continued at a forty-five-degree angle to the far left lane of the freeway just as the battery heat indicator displayed "Max Battery Power Ready." The car embraced the road in the left lane under control as she gunned it.

The Model S's front and rear electric motors and gearboxes screamed as it accelerated from forty miles per hour to eighty miles per hour in under a second, throwing Dana and Ty back into their seats. Never screeching the tires, they were at 115 miles per hour when they passed the sedan, still pinning the two into the backs of their seats. The sedan already stopped braking and was desperately trying to regain their speed when the sure-footed Tesla shrieked passed them like they were parked. Their feeble attempt to slow them down by swerving into the left lane was comically late.

"Damn it! I overturned the corner and spun it in the dirt. We'll catch up to you as soon as we can." Jim was pissed. He misjudged the turn with the dust flying and ended up in the wrong position approaching it. He was going to have to catch everyone from a dead stop.

The Tesla was at 155 miles per hour and still accelerating when the g-force and the car reached a comfortable equilibrium. The force subsided enough to release Dana and Ty from the backs of their seats. By the time the car was at a 172 miles per hour, the sedan could barely be seen behind them in the rearview mirrors.

"That was awesome! Nice driving, Dana." Ty turned and looked back at the road behind them.

"Nice car!" She smiled back at him.

"I had no idea this car could do that! Everyone kept telling me how fast it is, but I've never driven it like that." His back was sweaty from exhilaration.

"I don't think anyone is going to catch up to us at this point. Jim and Hank will take out the guys tailing us once they catch up to them," Dana said just as gunfire could be heard over the phone.

Several more shots could be heard, then the sound of screeching tires and the uneven, throbbing concussion of metal on concrete of a car flipping at high-speed fading away.

"Okay! Those guys are toast! Slow down so we can catch up to you," Jim said.

Dana put the Tesla back into Sport Mode on the settings screen and the batteries attempted to cool down. She slowed the car down to seventy miles per hour to let Jim and Hank catch up to them. They were still forty minutes away from reaching their destination in Morgan Hill.

Chapter 25

Dmitry realized his plan was a bust when too many cars were stopped behind the big rig and piling up. They forced the truck to jackknife perfectly, too perfect; it blocked the entire width of the freeway. It would have been better to allow the cars to slowly pass through or around the wreckage, somehow funneling everyone through a choke point and lessening the traffic buildup. Instead, the standing traffic forced and forewarned the remaining two cars to use the service road.

When he saw what was happening, he stole a car from someone in the stopped traffic, drove around the front of the jackknifed big rig through the dirt, and headed up the freeway to formulate a new plan, leaving the rest of his men to stop the remaining two cars on their own and abduct Tyson McNally. If they were successful, they were to meet at a designated rendezvous. Dmitry did not believe he would be meeting his team there. From the conversations over the phones, it was an inexcusable failure.

He was speeding north on the freeway, trying to come up with a new plan to abduct Tyson McNally from his protectors before he disappeared into hiding with more protection. Tyson McNally was with the CIA and the FBI. Where were they going?

"They must be heading for the FBI office in San Francisco. There, they could protect him from me; but not forever!" He struck his hand on the steering wheel in frustration, shouting at himself.

He continued on toward San Francisco. There he would wait for Tyson McNally to arrive. He would be better prepared this time. He grabbed his phone and made a call.

***

The guards at the front gate checked their credentials, then the cleared personnel roster before letting them pass. The Tesla and the M3 entered the parking structure of the yet to be fully opened, new FBI data center building that didn't look like a data center building. It was more than just a data center, though that was its main purpose. It had abundant office space for normal FBI business—too much office space, too many windows. There were rumors of making it a full time FBI office to offset some of the load at the San Francisco office, but those plans wouldn't happen for several years. The primary purpose of this building was to stand up a modern data center to host a private cloud infrastructure for the FBI, second only in size to CIA's data center in Langley, Virginia. The two data centers would use each other as recovery sites. That was the rumor anyway.

Dana parked at a charging station, while Jim parked the M3 behind it in an unmarked stall on the ground floor of the parking area. It seemed mostly empty; just a few cars parked near the elevator entrance. Ty got out of the Tesla and stretched his long, stiff body, then walked over to his M3, inspecting it for damage. The only thing he found was a shot-out driver side taillight. *That should be easy to fix*, he thought. *Expensive, but easy.*

Then he inspected his Tesla. It was dusty, but unharmed. He grabbed what he needed to charge the car from the glovebox and plugged the Tesla in.

"Nice, it's free," he said to himself.

"What a fantastic driving car! Wasn't this called "the ultimate driving machine!" at one time?" Jim yelled at Ty from across the way as he climbed up out of the driver seat. Hank was also pulling himself up out of the passenger side. "However, we're going to have to have another little chat about those mods you've programmed in these cars." Jim smiled at Ty and winked at him. "Later, of course."

The convoy finished the rest of their journey nonstop at an average of seventy miles per hour without any additional issues. Dana got out of the Tesla and stretched her lean arms skyward, then bent down at the waist, knees locked straight, and put her palms on the ground for several seconds. She straightened up, gracefully throwing her hair back in perfect style. Blessed with low maintenance hair. She checked the time.

"Not bad, it's only nine fifteen. Do you need any help?" she asked Ty.

Ty was already unloading the box from the back seat and grabbing his backpack.

"No, I think I'm good. It's really not that heavy, just awkward to carry." He placed the box on the ground, then closed the back door.

"Here, use this." Hank was pushing a flat cart he found near the elevator entrance.

"Oh, that'll work perfectly." Ty loaded the box onto the cart and was ready to go to wherever they were going to.

They headed into the entrance where the elevators were. Jim pushed the button to call the elevator. The door behind them opened immediately. They let Ty enter first, then loaded up after him. Jim pushed the button for the main lobby. When the doors opened, they were welcomed by a beautiful, spacious, empty lobby. It was about three floors high, with white marble floors and a glass wall with glass doors at the main entrance. Out front, there was a circular driveway with flag poles and a monument of some type in the center circle. The lobby echoed their footsteps as they entered. There still was no furniture or plants or anything, but there were a few throw rugs by the front doors. Dirt tracks and black skid marks on the white marble was the main evidence that the building was still under construction on the inside.

There was a counter with people there, which was where they headed. Jim had been here several times before, but the last time was several months ago, and it wasn't nearly this complete then.

"Good morning, can I help you?" the woman behind the counter greeted them.

"Dana Jordan here to see George Lancer."

Jim looked surprised for the first time and looked at Dana.

"Oh yes, he's expecting you. Let me sign you in first. He's on the fifth floor, room five-one-two-seven."

"If you're an agent, may I please have your badge."

Jim and Hank pulled out their wallets and handed them to the woman. She placed one of them on a scanner for a second. She then pulled out a slip and placed it in a clear plastic sleeve attached to a black lanyard.

"Special Agent Hughes."

Hank walked up to the counter.

She handed him his badge and the lanyard. The visitor badge had his picture printed on it along with his name and rank.

She repeated the same process. "And Special Agent Jordan." She handed Jim his badge and the lanyard.

"Make sure these are visible at all times while you are in the building. They should get you in just about every security door," she instructed, then looked to Ty and Dana. "May I have your driver's licenses or other form of identification."

Ty pulled out his wallet and his California driver's license, then handed it to the woman.

Dana pulled out her Intel-Q employee badge and handed it to her.

She scanned the employee badge and handed it right back to Dana.

"Make sure this is visible at all times. It's already programmed to get you into everything," she instructed.

She scanned Ty's driver license and a slip printed out. She placed the slip into a clear plastic sleeve with an orange stripe and a bright-orange lanyard. She handed the lanyard and his driver's license back to Ty.

"Make sure this is visible at all times. And one of you three must escort Mr. McNally at all times."

Ty looked at his badge. It had his picture and his name on it, then in big bold letters, "CIVILIAN," at the bottom of the badge.

"Let's go, civi," Hank joked as the three of them headed to the lobby elevators.

"Oh dear! I forgot. That box and your backpack needs to be inspected before you can take them in."

Two gentlemen stepped out from behind the counter, halting their progress.

"That won't be necessary, Mrs. Langston." George Lancer was briskly walking up to the counter from the elevators.

"Dr. Lancer. I'm sorry, I can't let something like this in without it being inspected. You know the policy." The woman was nervous about her current circumstance.

"Ah, you are so right. That's my fault. I shouldn't have put you in that position. Please forgive me." George was embarrassed that he was caught subverting authority, again.

"Hello, Dana, I'm glad to see you're alright." He shook her hand professionally.

"Jim, Hank. It's so good to see you boys again." He shook both of their hands vigorously and put his other hand on their shoulders.

"And you must be Tyson McNally. It's a real pleasure to finally meet you. I've been reading up on some of your work and blogs. I'd like to talk about some of it sometime if you don't mind." He shook Ty's hand warmly with both of his hands.

"Please, you can call me Ty. It's nice to meet you too, Dr. Lancer."

"Oh, please. You can call me George."

"Well then, can this be opened up here for the inspection?" Dr. Lancer clapped his hands and rubbed them together.

"Sure. That shouldn't be a problem, as long as they're gentle with it." Ty explained.

"How about it then? Is this a gentle inspection?" Dr. Lancer looked at the two gentlemen standing between them and the elevators.

"Yes, it should be. We're just checking for unauthorized devices and materials. You can assist us if that'll make you feel better." The taller of the two guards explained.

"Perfect. Where do you want me to take it?" Ty said with relief in his voice.

"Right through here," the taller guard said, then stepped out of the way of the door they were standing next to.

"Ah, would it be alright if I watched?" Dr. Lancer sounded like a kid waiting to open birthday presents.

"Sure, no problem, Dr. Lancer. I'll inspect your backpack while you assist with the box," the shorter of the two guards said.

Ty handed his backpack to the guard, while the other escorted him through the door. He left the box on the flat cart and began opening it like he did at home when it first arrived, only this time, he did it a lot faster, being careful not to cut his hand. When he reached the last layer of packaging, he pulled it back, exposing the matte-black cylinder with the rounded corners still in the box. The window portal was facing up.

George let out a gasp. "So that's how they did it," he said, astonished.

"What is it?" the guard asked.

"That, my boy, is the future. This computer is the future," George answered matter-of-factly.

The guard shrugged and checked the accessories packages.

"Okay, this is fine. You can go ahead and go in. Looks like your backpack is cleared too."

"What? No x-ray or other scanner?" Ty asked a little sarcastically.

"Already did that when you walked up to the counter. You were all scanned. The two special agents are armed, which is okay for them. Your box is shielded, so we have to hand inspect it. And your backpack? Well, we're just practicing. It's a new facility and we're not getting a lot of visitors yet. Thanks for your understanding and cooperation," The taller guard said.

Ty smiled with his eyebrows raised, then placed the packing foam back on top of Q-Tip and closed the aluminum cover. He folded down the box flaps and placed his backpack on top to keep them closed. The five of them headed to the elevator.

The elevator took them directly to the fifth floor. The area was clean but empty, no plants, furniture, or signs, just numbers on doors. As they walked down one of the wide halls, it dawned on Ty that this didn't seem like a building with a large data center in it.

"George? Where's the data center? I mean this building doesn't feel like it could host a big data center. It just seems like office space." Ty was looking around and gauging the strange spatial sensation.

"Ah, you are correct. This 'building' is mainly office space and FBI administration stuff. Eight floors of office space, interrogation rooms, holding cells, and glorious bureau bureaucracy. There's even a completely insolated thirty-meter, eight lane shooting range on one of the floors somewhere." George waved his hands around in the air.

"Eight floors below ground level, that's the data center. That doesn't even include the one floor worth of reenforced concrete shielding you have to go through before you get to the first sublevel. Five floors of server floorspace and three floors of offices, support staff, maintenance, power and cooling. That's currently where all the main construction work is still underway. You should see the control room when it's done." Dr. Lancer continued his tour as they walked.

"It's very similar to the NSA's Utah data center near Bluffdale we built about a decade ago, plus there's this eight-story FBI building on top of it. Both data centers are plugged into the Switch SUPERLOOP fiber network. So, while the Utah data center was designed to store exabytes of data, this facility is designed to process that data with a future equivalent of one thousand EXA-FLOPS of computational capacity combined, though very little of it will be used for scientific computing. It'll take years to build it out to that capacity. Most of that projection is based on current technology development trends and roadmaps. You can think of it as a single enormous computer system spanning three states." George held up a finger for emphasis.

"And it will be ninety-nine percent emission free, all renewable and stored energy. There's a network of pipes and conduits further underground and all around the underground facility for shallow geothermal heating and cooling using both air and liquid mediums for both facilities. This data center will be processing data for all the U.S. intelligence agencies. So, while it's unofficially referred to as the FBI data center, it's only called that because this FBI building sits on top of it. It's literally two functions stacked on top of each other." He stopped and opened a door and let everyone in. "Here we are."

The office was large and spacious, but poorly furnished. There was a good-sized conference table with four chairs around it, a cheap looking desk and chair, and a matching wall shelf. A folded laptop, a manilla folder, and a multi-function phone set were the only items on the desk. There was a large screen TV mounted on the wall near the conference table. A small refrigerator sat next to the shelf. The carpet was clean but looked temporary.

"Sorry, this building isn't scheduled to open for another year or so. Nobody's really 'supposed' to be using it yet, but you know, FBI stuff happens." George was air quoting with his fingers.

"Please have a seat. Anybody want something to drink? You know Intel-Q is going to occupy some office space in this building too." He continued to talk while he walked behind the desk and opened the refrigerator door.

Ty parked the flat cart with his stuff on it in the corner out of the way and sat down next to Dana.

"Looks like bottled water and sodas," Dr. Lancer said while looking inside the refrigerator.

"Water please," The four of them all said in unison, while Jim and Hank sat down at the conference table.

George grabbed five water bottles and the chair behind the desk. He dragged everything to the conference table, placed the bottles in the center of the table, and joined everyone.

"So, what would you like to talk about?" George opened, leaning back in his chair.

Everyone just looked at each other, confused.

"I'll start," Dana volunteered.

"I have a few quick updates. Ed found documents indicating the start of procedures to recover the data from the KRF building site. Apparently, they did have a disaster recovery plan. It's hosted at two other research facilities in Japan, but since the earthquake, they've both been closed and powered off awaiting inspections. They should be able to restore their research data in a couple of weeks. That doesn't help much with the destruction of all that equipment. It will take a while for them to get back up to speed, but they can restart. Then there's the issue of the researchers." She stopped and looked a Ty solemnly.

"There are a few scientists who weren't at the facility when the disaster struck, and they've been with their families. They know most of the work and could pick it back up, but again, it'll take some time and resources. Combine them with our own scientists who are working on this project, and I think we can get everything back up to speed." She looked over at the box in the corner and pointed. "But maybe some of this can be accelerated now that one of the units survived, and Ty here knows something of the operation of it." She touched him on his arm as a gesture of focus, but it looked more like affection.

"Um, yes, a little. I've only been working intensely with it for about the last week. When I heard about the earthquake, I stopped working with it and was, um... you know, taking care of other work business." He was listening to Dana's update and assessment of everything that had been going on. Not that it was any of his business, but he had no idea how much time, money, and energy was being spent on this... this project?

"Do you mind if we step back a little." Ty hoped he wasn't out of line. "I get it. Quantum computing is a big thing. It's going to be a big market and a lot of money is going to be involved. Dana explained your role in this research. But why all the cloak and dagger and shadow operations? I mean, won't the commercial markets finally figure this out and put it out there? Heck, it might be a commodity in ten or fifteen years."

George cringed when he heard that timeframe. "Good point. But that's because you've had access to that device right over there. Even just for a week, it's changed your perception; your thinking of what it could do. It's accelerated and expanded your understanding of what's possible. I'll bet you've been thinking of new ways to solve hard problems beyond gambling and predicting random numbers."

Ouch. Ty looked down, a little embarrassed.

"Think about what could happen if a hundred million developers and domain experts had access to a device like this for a week, a month, a year! You've probably thought of solving chemical engineering problems, impossible math problems, physics challenges, energy, space, the environment. Imagine an electric car that you recharge once a year; or maybe never. Space travel as a common activity; like traveling to Europe. Hell, colonization of other planets." George paused and looked around at everyone, then he continued.

"What if global poverty and hunger were eradicated?" And with that, he calmed down. "None of that will happen if a quantum computer sells for twenty-five million dollars apiece. And they're as big as a motorhome." George took a deep breath.

"Do you realize we're only using a small fraction of a sixty-four-bit CPU today, and you won't see a one-twenty-eight-bit CPU in your lifetime.

Even if there were, we would still be stuck on the same problems, trying to solve them the same way. It's not just processing, number crunching, and data, it's mentality. Most problems today are solved with 'brute force' calculations—iterate through every possible combination of calculations until one works. Do that as fast as you can. That approach is useless in problem structures that involve infinity or extremely large values. So, we constrain our problem sets or down-sample data or summarize or create shortcuts or give up or just get close. In many cases today, 'close enough is good enough'; we represent a value with a number we can work with. We end up with a 'horseshoes or hand grenades' problem set. It'll get us close, then we'll adjust.

"We still can't represent real numbers without truncating or rounding them in order fit our current computing technology, and it doesn't look promising for any future technology based on 'ones and zeros' processing. We, as humanity, will never be accurate enough for the challenges that need to be solved. Therefore, humanity will be stuck like this for another century unless something breaks this cycle. Like that over there." George pointed to the box. "The universe is analog; we need to process in analog, not digital. Imagine being right, instead of being close."

Everybody at the table was mesmerized by Dr. Lancer's speech. It was Ty who broke up the mood though with another question.

"I've been following some of the developments in quantum computing. What makes this one different than the other guys, besides the size and power requirements? I mean, that's really important, but aren't the big companies far along? They keep making big claims..." Ty answered his own question. "I know. I knew it before I even said it—marketing. More funding."

George smiled. He liked this guy.

Ty continued. "To be honest, the device is amazing, but I think the real innovation here is in the software; the programming language to use the device. I picked it up immediately."

George banged his hand on the table, which made everyone jump in their seats.

"That's the key, isn't it?! When I said, 'a hundred million developers,' I didn't mean new quantum computing developers, I meant existing classical computing developers. That programming language, um, QtPython I think, with its translators and converters, is what will accelerate this process. I tried to teach it for twenty years before I realized how slow the process to adopt it would be. Fun point, did you notice the program file extension name '.qtpy?'" Dr. Lancer asked Ty directly with a look of satisfaction.

"Ah, yeah?"

"It's pronounced 'cutie pie!'" Dr. Lancer chuckled and slapped his knee.

"Nerds." Jim laughed, in a respectful way but still rolled his eyes.

"Okay, I gotta ask the trillion-dollar question. Why does this device work, and the others don't, or kind of do, or whatever they're claiming? I mean jeez, Yuichu explained a little of it to me, but he described more of the why and not the how," Ty asked.

"Ah, excellent question. The other companies and their quantum computing technology are chasing a never-ending cycle of shielding away outside interference and creating isolation, while wasting capacity on error checking and correcting. We still invest in them in case they reach some kind of equilibrium, but I have my doubts. They bring their new, larger designs online, process some algorithms for a while, make announcements and claims which get the media excited, then it all breaks down into noise, and they can't repeat their results. The current capabilities available for commercial use is a combination of classical computing with some quantum processing. This helps keep the calculation stable long enough to be useful." Dr. Lancer was waving his hands around animatedly, describing the highs and lows of the state of the industry.

Dana was fixated on George. She never heard him describe the problem, this project, the research, the reasons like this before. Did she not ask the right questions? Was she not listening close enough? She knew his goals and why this was important to him, but he was sharing something, probably for the first time, with everyone here. Was Ty pulling something out of him that her father was holding in?

"Yuichu and his team figured something out about outside *interference*, and for that matter, outside observation. You may not realize this, but the Mark 1 device was a huge traditional chandelier type of device, just like everyone else's. It was noisy, and I mean loud. Everyone in the lab needed to wear headphones, then noise canceling headphones, and other hearing protection. Finally, one of the technicians installed an environmental frequency canceling device in the center of the lab up on the ceiling. Two things happened, the noise level diminished dramatically, and their device started working. That's when chairman Nakatori called me." Dr. Lancer was pointing at the ceiling.

Jim ignored a call, not wanting to interrupt Dr. Lancer, and texted the caller back, while Hank leaned in so he could see what was being written.

"This was a few years ago, just after that new trade agreement was signed allowing the U.S. to work more openly between friendly countries like Japan. We decided this would be a good project to jointly work on, so we started funding this concept. Basically, the idea was, stop shielding out the interference; instead, use it. Let the interference in and cancel it away. The Mark 2 explored a very wide spectrum of frequencies and mechanisms to cancel it all to a zero level. It couldn't be sustained for long periods of time, but it worked beautifully when it did work. The Mark 3 used outside samples of interference and some light shielding. But it was the Mark 2 that let them start looking at ways to make programming it easier, instead of spending all their time and energy making the device work."

Jim thought this was as good a time as any to interrupt. "Um, I think we may have a problem. I've been texting with Officer Jenkins in Soledad."

"Oh, how is he? And Miguel?" Ty instinctively jumped in.

"He said they're fine. No injuries. Just a messed-up police SUV." He appreciated Ty's concern for his law enforcement friends. "Thanks for asking. It looks like one of those guys on the freeway got away before we approached the truck accident. The report says one of the armed men waiting for us suddenly pulled someone out of their stopped car at gunpoint, drove around the big rig, and hightailed it north." Jim paused and looked around the table at everyone's eyes. "I'm guessing it was the leader. He left his guys to finish the job if they could, but he either had other plans, or that plan was blown up. He's probably regrouping."

"How many agents are in this building?" Hank asked, looking at Dr. Lancer.

"I have no idea. I only got here last night. Let me call downstairs and ask." George started to reach over to the desk for the phone.

"That won't be necessary. Hank and I will go down to the lobby and assess what's available. Does that phone work?" Jim was pointing to the desk.

"Yes. The number is on the phone."

Hank was closer, so he got up and dialed the number shown and the phone rang.

"Okay, perfect. We'll be back shortly," Jim said as he and Hank left the office.

"So, what's happening?" Dr. Lancer was surprised at the agent's concerns.

"I told you about the break in at Ty's house last night. Well, on the way here this morning, we were ambushed on the freeway by another group. We think it's a different operation from the house break-in operation. Jim and Hank think they're eastern European, maybe Russian." Dana hadn't got to that part of her update earlier.

"Could it be that person who was tailing you in Japan?" George was now very concerned for his daughter's safety. It hadn't dawned on him just how dangerous this assignment was getting and that he may have inadvertently put her in grave danger.

"Ty, full disclosure here. Dana is my daughter." George felt a wave of relief as he let Ty know the truth.

"It's not a secret, but it's also not widely known. Jim and Hank know, but then, they work for the FBI, not me." He looked at Dana as her eyes were starting to well up.

"Thank you for trusting me enough to tell me this. She is an incredible woman. She's already saved my life."

Dana got up and walked around the table to give her father a hug. George wrapped his arms around her and squeezed her tight. The agony of acting professionally around each other all the time was stressful.

Ty could see it in their embrace. He thought there must not be enough opportunity to see each other outside of their jobs. That didn't seem right. If you're the right person for a role and you perform your job well, it shouldn't matter the relationship. He never understood the broad-brush policies painted on everyone because a few bad people abused a situation.

Ty stood up and grabbed the cart. He opened the already opened box, pulled out the pentapod stand, extended it fully, and placed it on the conference table.

George and Dana released each other as they both wiped their eyes, then focused on what Ty was doing.

Next, he carefully cradled the matte-black cylindrical computer and placed it on its stand. Just like before, the device slowly began turning itself on the threaded stud until it reached the bottom, it bounced back a half turn, then settled. He gently gave the cylinder a controlled, firm twist, it clicked and locked in place. Grabbing the base, he situated the device so the portal window was facing the three of them as best he could.

"This is Q-Tip!" Ty held his hands up, formally introducing the device to the both of them. He saw George smile at the cute nickname.

Continuing, he pulled out the induction power adapter, found an outlet in the wall next to the conference table, and plugged it in. He placed the brick up on the table, then plugged the jack into the back port of the device. The brick's LED light went through its normal sequence until both sides were green.

Grabbing his backpack, he took out Tomahawk and placed it on the table in front of his chair. Then, taking an HDMI cable from his backpack, he connected the TV on the wall to his laptop. Finally, he connected the optical fiber cable to the laptop and to the back of the device.

"That's all there is to it. Full mechanical and electrical isolation from the power to the optical communication cable to the stand. Would you like a demonstration?" Ty finished setting up the device and held his hands out gestured toward Q-Tip like he successfully performed some magic trick.

"Yes! I was scheduled to visit KRF in a month for a live demonstration, but this will do perfectly." Dr. Lancer was giddy.

His and Dana's eye were both bright and clear again, and they were sitting on the edge of their seats.

Ty opened Tomahawk. The mirrored display showed up on the TV screen in sync with the laptop display. Unlocking the laptop, the display showed a shutdown and powered-off virtual machine. After powering on Q-Tip, he clicked on the screen to power-on and start the virtual machine.

After about a minute, everything was initialized and ready to go. The device was lit up to its normal, spectacular ready state. As he suspected, it started up faster than the first time it initialized. It looked amazing. Pulling up a terminal window, he typed in a command and an application window popped up.

"Are your phones working right now? Do you have a signal?" he asked as part of a bit of showmanship.

"I'm connected to the building's Wi-Fi," Dr. Lancer offered, like he was volunteering to be part of the act.

"Perfect! Do a search on the lottery in Japan. I think it's the Takarakuji Loto six," Ty said.

"Okay, got it. The pot is at the beginning of two hundred million yen. It just reset last night," Dr. Lancer provided.

"Oh, perfect. Excellent. That means she won. Last night, before everyone showed up and shot up my place, I was making more lottery predictions in different countries. I sent these numbers to Yuichu's wife, Mikito, and told her to play them before Monday night's drawing. I think it was almost six hundred million yen. Don't tell me the numbers drawn."

Ty started clicking the controls in the application. It was just datasets of numbers and matrix counts.

"Now before I click start. You can either watch the device or not. Actually, if you don't mind, this is the first time I've done this with more than just myself, so I'd like to try something; to validate something.

George, you look away. Don't watch it for this run. Dana, go ahead and watch this window." Ty pointed at the window panel on Q-Tip.

"Got it," They both acknowledged together.

Ty clicked on the start button, then watched the device. He wanted to share this feeling with Dana. The portal began its hypnotic opening and closing, like an eye sleepily trying to focus on something that wasn't there. That blinking you do when you've had a great night's sleep and it's time to wake up... then the "eyelid" abruptly stopped mid-cycle, snapping Dana and Ty out of their joint daze.

"Whoa! That was so weird. How long was that...? What happened?" Dana was coming to from the experience.

"What do you mean 'what happened?' The program took a few seconds to run and there are the predicted numbers displayed right there. The timestamps are screwed up and you've got garbage for your probability." George looked down at his phone, then up at the predicted lottery numbers, then down again. "Good lord. They're in the order drawn?!"

"Yup. I grabbed the lottery history dataset yesterday. Basically, everything except last night's numbers. It just gave you the numbers you see here, which are the numbers that were drawn as they were drawn. This equipment is off the grid, so nothings been updated. Actually, if these numbers haven't been drawn yet; the result don't exist; the device and the weird experience is different. I can't explain why or how, yet." Ty was pointing between the big screen and the numbers on Dr. Lancer's phone.

"I don't think it's making a prediction, statistically; it feels more like it's aligning an existing outcome to a present request. Every possible combination already exists somewhere, sometime, some-verse. Some requests take longer to align." Ty didn't know how to explain it any deeper.

"What Dana and I experienced together is some kind of time dilation. Wall clock time, system time, execution time, and the internal timer in your head get out of sync, but only if you observe the device processing. That's why I asked you both to observe it differently." Ty felt vindicated that he wasn't the only one experiencing this. He could now cross "brain tumor" and "madness" off of his list of possible maladies; now he had witnesses.

George was deep in thought, trying to understand and follow Ty's explanation.

"This pattern can be repeated across any number of use cases. Stocks and investments, weather predictions, fuel burn rate, and others. I can't even begin to comprehend everything; the possibilities." Ty was starting to sound like Dr. Lancer.

"I keep thinking there's a bug in the packages somewhere screwing up the time functions and figured the probability garbage output is another bug in the fully quantum machine learning package. But now I'm not so sure. It could be a mismatch between the analog and digital systems that hasn't been calibrated yet," Ty continued.

"Okay, let's do it one more time and this time we'll reverse observations. George, search for OZ Lotto. This is the Australian national lottery. I already sent these number to one of my guys who lives there. If I'm not mistaken, they've already had their drawing for this week too."

Ty configured the application again for the OZ Lotto game.

"Now, Dana and I will look away. George, you watch the device."

Ty pressed the Start button.

Dana and Ty looked in each other's eyes for a moment when the blue light in the room stopped pulsing. It was just a few seconds. George was coming to, dazed and confused, but not debilitatingly.

"What the…? It feels like I've been watching the device for ten minutes. How long did it take?" George was trying to regain his focus.

"About four seconds?" Ty looked at Dana to confirm.

She looked at George and nodded with excitement.

"Yeah, between the two of us, it was about four seconds. The timestamps never seem to make sense, and the strange probability symbols haven't changed once. So, I assume that's *quantum* for one hundred percent."

"*Ant-Man and the Wasp!*" Ty and Dana both said it at the same time, looking at each other and laughing.

George was even more confused. He didn't understand how he was feeling. Radiation leak of some kind was all that he could come up with.

The phone on the desk rang and broke up the demonstration. George pushed the speaker phone button to answer the call.

"Hi Jim, what's going on?" George assumed it was Jim; no one else would be calling this number.

"If I said it already, I'm sorry, but we might have a problem. There are no other agents in the building. There are a handful of security guards, including the two we met earlier, but that's it. Hank and I are the best armed people in the facility."

"That doesn't sound promising," George replied, not grasping the whole situation.

"If I'm running an abduction operation and this was my third attempt, my first instinct would have sent me to the FBI office in San Francisco." Jim was playing out terrorist scenarios over the phone line.

"What do you mean 'abduction' operation?" Ty yelled from across the office.

"Ah, sorry, Ty. My gut tells me this team watched the operation at your house last night after they scurried off the first time. They probably saw the other team remove that decoy machine. They couldn't leave because the police arrived shortly after that team left, so they just watched. Since they don't know where the machine is, I'm guessing their new priority is you. That's why they staged an ambush on the freeway this morning, but it was a last-minute plan; with no advance planning, they blew it. They don't know we have the real computer, but they know you're with us. At least for the time being, they— he—doesn't know where 'us' is." Jim's voice sounded emotionless over the phone's speaker.

Ty thought about this for a moment. Why would he be a priority target? The money? He didn't have it yet. It could be two and half months before he had it. Then again, they might not know that. It couldn't be for his knowledge. He didn't invent the machine; he only knew how to use it. Then again, they didn't know that either.

"Hank and I are working on a plan. There're only construction workers here and a skeleton staff manning the facility. If they do come here armed like they were on the freeway, we wouldn't stand a chance." Now Jim sounded worried for the first time.

Chapter 26

They had not arrived yet. They were not coming to this location. He miscalculated. Maybe they went to a local police station at one of the larger cities along the freeway. Could they have gone all the way to the Sacramento FBI office? That was a much farther drive. If it was him, he would not be out in the open that long. Too much exposure. No, they were somewhere between Soledad and here. Maybe they changed cars, or into one different vehicle. That would be a smart move. Dmitry was looking for a larger black sedan and a small, silver sports car. That was all he had been looking for to enter the San Francisco FBI building's parking entrance. He was carefully looking into every vehicle entering the building, but they still could have slipped by. He had men posted at corners around the block of the FBI building, watching everybody walking in and out and around, driving around the area.

Dmitry never could have predicted the target's cars would be so fast or that the large American sedans his teams were driving would be no match for them. He wouldn't underestimate these people again. To start, Dmitry had his men find faster cars.

It was necessary to upgrade because if Tyson McNally and his babysitters were on high alert before, they would be even more so after the failed hijacking attempt on the freeway. Dmitry would need every advantage he could get.

The bigger problem at the moment was that he had no idea where Tyson McNally and his team were. They should have arrived in San Francisco already, but knowing someone was tracking them; they changed their plans? Dmitry knew they must have stopped somewhere between here and Soledad, but where?

Dmitry pulled out his phone and made a call.

***

"Shit! *You*, are full of horseshit!" Bob was beside himself as Howard and Dr. Gurski stepped back out of the way of Bob's tantrum and flying tools. Dr. Gurski just proclaimed the device he was examining was not a quantum computer, not even a little bit. It was an old SuperMicro workstation motherboard with other stuff mounted on it; glued to it. When Bob challenged his assessment, he pointed to the center upright cylinder canister.

"That is a can of soda," he said as factually as he could muster.

Bob went ballistic. He still didn't believe him. Two guys were killed retrieving this machine. It was heavily protected; how could it be a fake? Who would protect a fake like that? It looked authentic.

"Turn it on!" Bob demanded. "See what happens when you plug it in and turn it on." Bob wanted results and answers, not more setbacks.

Dr. Gurski took a deep breath and exhaled. He looked at the workbench and sifted through one of its tool drawers. He poked a hole in the side of the cylinder with a sharp punch tool; liquid squirted out under pressure all over the internal components.

"What did you do? That's not what I asked you to do! What are you doing?" Bob panicked, thinking the fluid was important to the operation of the device, and now it was ruined.

Dr. Gurski stuck his fingertip into the pooling liquid and licked it. He smacked his lips a few times. "Red Bull." He took a bigger swipe of the liquid and tasted it again. "Sugar-free Red Bull. That's an eight-point-four-ounce aluminum can of sugar-free Red Bull. In fact, this is an old Apple Mac Pro aluminum server case." Dr. Gurski was done.

"You have been fooled. I hope you did not pay too much for this box of used parts, but now I have real work to do. We are close to finishing our newest improvements. If you will excuse me." He turned and left the room, letting the security door close behind him.

"What the fuck, Howard? How did your guys take a box of junk?" Bob was leaning on his hands, straddling the fake quantum computer on the workbench with his shoulder up and his head down.

"Hey! They lost two guys to heavy firepower. There were professionals in that house protecting McNally and this, this fake. Or maybe they were just protecting McNally." Howard was trying to calm Bob down by lowering his voice a few notches.

"The power was out, there was chaos, it looked legit to these guys. It wasn't like they could ask, 'Hey? where's the quantum computing machine?' They grabbed what looked like a new type of computer to them and the attached test equipment; they even grabbed the only laptop in the room."

Howard failed to calm Bob down, but Bob was already exhausted on his own.

"Hey, how about that laptop? There might be some information in it that could lead us to some breakthroughs. It's a slower process, but it's something to look into. It looks like a Katoshi asset, so it could contain data on the real machine." Howard was trying to salvage the situation and cover his own ass.

Bob looked up at Howard, then over at the MacBook sitting on a desk.

"That's good thinking. Yeah, if the real machine isn't at that house, maybe he was accessing it remotely from this laptop. Maybe he was just building a marketing prop for a trade show exhibit booth or something. There might still be code on it, documentation, designs, plans… This might still be worth the effort." Bob was standing upright again, energized.

"It's probably locked. I can get one of the developers to crack it." Howard picked up the laptop and peeled the Katoshi System Services asset tag off. "I'll get one of our best guys on it and get back to you after we've scanned it for information. In the meantime, you need to relax, calm down. There's no way to trace what happened at that house back to us. I was very careful; there were many layers of indirection and middlemen. It cost a lot, but it could be very well worth it."

Howard held up the laptop toward Bob and shook it.

"Good! I'm going back to my office. Let me know as soon as you find anything," Bob said. He didn't care as much about getting caught or being in a scandal as he did about losing money; *his* money. Right now, he was losing a lot of money and there was no turnaround in sight—except for this new little glimmer of hope. He let the security door close behind him as he exited the "Special Projects" room, leaving Howard standing by himself next to the fake quantum computer and holding the laptop.

***

Dmitry only miscalculated because he didn't have all the information. His digital tracker informed him of the new FBI data center that was under construction in the city of Morgan Hill. He didn't have this information before, but if he did, he would have gone there instead. It was an excellent place to hide. There was already a new building there with guards; that was smart.

Now he needed to go there with no detailed information and no time to properly plan. More than an hour's drive to get there gave him some time to think of a plan without knowing what he was planning for. That was the FBI's territory; they knew the landscape. He was at a disadvantage, and he never liked working with a handicap.

He studied the navigation map. There were no updated images of the area to show the physical location of the new construction. Just an address that appeared to be located in the middle of farmland. He would make do with this information. He needed to find Tyson McNally before he disappeared.

***

Jim and Hank were on their phones calling in backup. It was a bit touchy since the facility was still supposed to be undisclosed, but they needed to disclose it. This whole situation felt impossible. They were in an FBI building; it was theoretically one of the safest places to be, but it was empty, which made it one of the most unsafe places for them. Should they leave or stay? If they left, they were exposed. If they stood their ground there, they were undermanned and lightly armed.

Jim was making huge assumptions while trying to make a plan. It was best to assume whoever was looking for them would soon know this place existed and they were already here. It was safe to also assume whoever was looking for them was still looking for them, and "they" were after Tyson. "They" may know or not know the machine was with them in this facility. He was also assuming, since they were able to find Tyson's home, eventually they would find him here.

They could all leave. There was a possibility they hadn't found this place yet and that would give them a head start. The Sacramento FBI office was almost three hours away. Then again, someone could be watching this place right now. Jenkins reported that a lone guy carjacked someone and headed north. He didn't hit them again on their way to Morgan Hill. Why? Was he regrouping? Getting another team together? A larger team? Most likely, he was planning something more carefully this time. How long would all of that take?

All agent Jordan knew was the longer they waited around without a plan, the less likely their chances of getting through this were.

"What've you got?" Hank was walking up to Jim after finishing a call.

"All the guards at the gate are armed and on high alert for anything. Nobody is schedule to visit here for the rest of the day, so if anyone shows up, they're not supposed to be here. However, these guys aren't trained for this. These aren't the real guards they'll have once this facility comes online." Hank was going through his mental checklist.

"All of the other guards are on high alert as well, but they're from the same security agency."

"I called in a few favors to some old army buddies of mine from SJPD. They can get two cars here in a little over an hour. That's the best offer I could find with discretion." Hank looked dejected.

"We'll take it." Jim looked past Hank's eyes for answers or ideas.

"So, we're going to stand our ground here?" Hank wished he had a better plan to offer.

"I'm not sure. We could hightail it to SF or even SAC if we need to. The problem is, will this guy ever stop? We can't keep hiding Ty. No, I feel like we need to just end this. Then the issue is where and how; let him come to us, or go get him?" Jim was still just grasping at possible ideas with nothing to plan on.

"There's a good chance he only knows this place exists, there's no way he can know it's empty and basically unarmed." Hank was brainstorming now too.

"Have the main gate guards barricade the gate," Jim said while still thinking of a plan.

"No can do. The vehicle barriers haven't been installed yet." Hank spoke like it was just par for their situation. "Nothing about this building is ready for a siege." Hank was waiting for the next question to say "no" to.

"Shit. Okay, have them build a barricade with some of the construction materials around here. They can do that, right? Or is that not ready to be used too?" The air around Jim was thick with frustration.

"Yeah, they should be able to handle that." Hank didn't need to snap back at his longtime partner and friend. That would only make things worse and make Jim feel bad about his outburst. He'd wait until later to rub it in his face—when this was all over with.

There was a moment of silence. Jim knew he just snapped at his partner for no reason, but now was not the time to hug it out. He'd let Hank rib him about later.

"I keep trying to figure out where this guy is at. Shooting north up the one-oh-one, for what? He had to believe we were on our way to the SF office. Everything points north. He has to be at the SF office—or was there." Jim snapped his fingers. "Get on the line with SF and have them pull surveillance footage from around the building and the block. See if they can find anyone staking out the place; it could be more than one car. Maybe we can find out who this guy is, and possibly if he's still there or is on his way here."

"Got it! So, were standing our ground?" Hank asked flatly.

"For now, yes. Let's plan on it and be ready to adjust if called for. I'll go get the guards to build a barricade." Jim turned and headed out the front main doors.

Hank got back on his phone.

***

Ty tried to shake off the thought of being abducted. He didn't know as much as people gave him credit for. Computer scientist? Check, but there were tens of thousands of computer scientists more qualified than him. Data Scientist? Check, same problem. Quantum physicist? Not even close. Quantum computer scientist? Maybe a good user. Billionaire? Got that covered, at least, in a couple of months.

"Ty. Ty. Tyson!" Dana snapped him out of his thoughts.

He must be tired; it was a stranger night and morning than he was used to. Was he still only up from adrenaline?

"Yes, um, sorry. Where was I?" He focused back on Dana's eyes.

"I asked if you sent predicted lottery numbers to everyone you knew."

"No, just my team of three people and Mikito, Yuichu's wife. So, four." Plus, he didn't know if he could forecast a prediction beyond the upcoming drawing. He'd thought of using the predicted results and feeding them back into the model to see how far he could go before the models and the results started to drift. He also ran out of time.

"Why would you do that?" Dana was asking for no apparent reason.

"Well, for Mikito, I think it should be obvious. If I had more time, I would probably do it several more times. Japan has a cap on their jackpots. I guess I could just send Yuichu's family a check, but…" He pointed at Q-Tip.

"I have, had, this." He gave her a crooked smile.

"I know, I know; with great power, comes great responsibility." Ty said half-heartedly.

"Spider-Man!" They both blurted out, then chuckled together for a few seconds before quickly returning to being serious. Bad timing, but it helped ease the tension.

George jumped out of his seat at the outburst, but seeing his daughter laugh a genuine, happy laugh delighted him. He was pretty sure she liked this guy. He liked this guy too.

"Look, one thought I have is, if this device becomes easily available, then lottery drawings, the way they're structured today, are dead. This device could end all games or businesses of chance based on perceived random guessing. So, I thought I'd use it while the opportunities are still available." Ty shrugged his shoulders innocently.

Dana thought about that for a moment. He was right. This could end a lot investing based on risk. People would just know the answer. This was a true social and moral dilemma.

"Whoa, there's a lot more than lottery games that could be impacted." She looked at George and Ty.

"I know. But only if there's a history of data to learn from. What I don't know is if that's good or bad. My gut tells me, in the future—the one Dr. Lancer is describing—it could be a good thing, but there will be a lot of angst over it." Ty sounded like he had thought a lot about this.

"Did you just use the word 'angst' in a conversation? Who talks like that?" Dana smiled at Ty.

Ty smiled back with a little, "*angst* is a perfectly good word" smile, then continued to answer her initial question. "The other three are the guys who work for me or *used* to work for me. We were all about to get laid off last week because of the incompetence of the current management, mine especially, and executive teams that keep rotating though at my company draining the life and funds out of it. It's unrecognizable. I managed to delay it for a couple of quarters, maybe, but I have my doubts. So, I sent them a parting gift—a better severance package. They deserve it. Especially after everything we've done for this company." Ty's voice sounded strained and frustrated.

She could tell the topic upset him. He'd been more than upbeat about everything that happened to him so far, but this, this hit a nerve.

"I don't know if I told you this, but I was at KSS yesterday before driving down to Soledad. Mary, your data center manager, she's a huge fan of yours. Actually, it sounds like you and your team are well respected there." She thought for a moment about some of the financial reports she came across at Katoshi headquarters.

"Also, you may or may not know this, but there's something fishy going on between KSS and Katoshi Corporate. I ran across some reports back in Japan that didn't make any sense, like revenue streams for KSS were being diverted or redirected to other Katoshi divisions. Your products seem to be strong offerings in the market, you have low overhead costs, yet your financial statements show you're losing money. None of it made sense, but it's not my job to go and fix a company's strategy, so I just ignored it."

"So, the rumors are true," he mumbled to himself. "I kept hearing stories of us being internally sabotaged, and for such a petty reason. So, it's not a conspiracy theory; it's a conspiracy fact." He was starting to lose his cool. This wasn't fair. Screwing with people's lives, a whole company, because someone got butthurt years ago by someone who wasn't even there anymore.

"So, they bring in these serial failures that know nothing about the industry, let them run the company into the ground, have them lay off another batch of employees, collect a huge bonus on their way out the door for doing a crap job. All the while, everyone left works their asses off to keep the company afloat. Then, they intentionally make us look bad in the books." Ty took a deep breath and held it for a second before exhaling.

"I'm sorry. I've been working there for a long time, and I hate seeing the company crapped all over because someone's ego got bruised. Good people are getting hurt over an offhanded comment; years ago!"

"Well, I can ask around, if you think that will help. I'm well connected in Katoshi," Dr. Lancer said. He was genuinely concerned about what he was hearing. They needed to do business with this company, the U.S. government needed to do business with this company, but if they were manipulating their financial statements, that would never happen, and the whole project might be at risk.

"Thanks, but I think I'm going try and do something more meaningful than pump out products for an unappreciative company. I want to make an impact on the world. The world you're describing." Ty looked at George with admiration. "I always felt that I could turn the company around if I were in charge. It's a good company, but I don't have the political and business acumen to fight an internal corporate vendetta."

Dana could see the anxiety this one subject was causing him. He really seemed to care about people more than himself. He'd been shot at, chased, his house broken into and destroyed, and he'd stayed in pretty good spirits, but this depresses him.

"You could make a big impact by being at that company. We'll need a stable presence there to make this proj—"

Jim opened the door, interrupting George. Hank followed him into the office with a large equipment bag hanging over his shoulder and they both sat down in their seats. They glanced at the device erected on the conference table, then ignored it.

"What's the update? Jim, you don't look so good. Are you alright?" George asked, worried.

"We got an identification on the leader, and there's a good chance he's on his way here now," Hank said with a grim tone.

Jim was looking down at his phone, motionless, emotional. He looked up at Dana with red eyes, filled with rage and sadness.

"What's wrong?" Dana alarmingly asked. That anguish in Jim's face, she'd only seen it once before.

Jim looked over at George and put his phone on the table.

"This is Dmitry Petrov, an alias for..." Jim's voice broke as his throat tightened, he tried to finish his statement and say that name. "For Mikhail Ivanov." After saying the name, Jim's mix of emotions turned to complete rage.

Dana put her hand over her mouth and looked at the picture on the table. Her eyes became bloodshot, a haze of gloss covered her eyes, but not from a tear. The hand covering her mouth clenched into a fist. She looked up a Jim and Hank.

"Are you sure it's him?" Her voice was coarse and deep.

"Confirmed identification at the airport and from the FBI building in SF. They crosschecked with Langley for us. He was demoted right after, um... that... er... the incident." Hank stumbled on his words.

"And he's been stuck in low-level, third-world embassy duties around the world since; with new identification, faked death, everything. Full government cover-up. That's the new Russia for you, no more convenient disappearances." Hank laid out the information they had so far.

"They pulled surveillance footage and found him scoping out the FBI building in San Francisco and the surrounding block with four other cars. As of twenty minutes ago, all five cars are gone. They agree with us, they think he's on his way here after it looked like he received a call. That gives us about thirty-five minutes if the freeways are clear. San Francisco is sending us agents, but no ETA yet. Helicopters are currently reassigned at the moment." Hank was doing all the talking for now.

"They gave us a profile on him. He's looking to get back in good with the FSS and he's looking for a prize to present to them." He pointed toward Ty with his palm up.

"FBI policy states that we get pulled from this assignment, but that's not an option." Jim finally was able to speak up again, but his shoulders were still slumped and his head down.

Dana got up and walked over to Jim, bent down, and wrapped him in an embrace, which he returned, then straightened up. When they released their hug, Jim pinched the bridge of his nose, starting from the outside corners of his eyes. When he finally let go, he looked at Hank and George, then held Dana's shoulders, nodded, and stood up.

Jim turned to Ty and looked him in the eyes. "You've probably already figured out there's some newly discovered history here. It's more than complicated. I would have died to protect you because it's my job and my duty, and I would never have regretted it, but now I need to thank you. However the universe saw fit to involve you, you've managed to bring that cold-blooded murderer back from an easy life for me to properly pay him back."

Ty felt very awkward. It was true, the sense that this epic backstory was something out of a Hollywood action movie was giving him a feeling of unworthiness. He didn't deserve this attention or this devotion, but he appreciated it.

"You'll have to forgive me if I ask an insensitive question, but what happened? Who is Mikhail Ivanov and what did he do?" Ty tried to look like he was ashamed for asking, but he really hadn't connected the dots.

"He killed my younger brother," Jim said stiffly.

"And my husband," Dana continued his sentence.

"And my son-in-law," George completed the response, looking bitter and upset.

Jim cleared his tight throat as best he could.

"John was on a routine assignment in the Ukraine, digging up non-sensitive intelligence for the current administration. The Ukrainians gave the U.S. permission to search their records and documents. It wasn't even national security material. A lot of it was public knowledge, even public record if you knew how to find it. John was good at finding information, too good. So, they sent him and an undercover team, just to protect any innocents. Mikhail Ivanov was assigned from Moscow to watch him and his detail, to make sure he found what he was supposed to find, and nothing more. Well, John did find what he was supposed to find, and he read it. He realized it was a plant, a fake to throw off the analysis. So, John did what

John does; he did his job. He found the real information, which wasn't public. The information he discovered would have thrown the assumptions politicians were trying to prove upside down. It's like the old saying goes, 'Those who protest the loudest are usually the ones who are the guiltiest.' Mikhail was ordered to retrieve the information from the U.S. detail. Instead, he just killed John and everyone he was in charge of. It was an international mess, and all three governments covered it up."

Jim stood there, breathing heavy and shaking his head. He turned his head up with his eyes closed. Then he continued.

"I understand the cover-up a bit; I don't pretend to understand the politics, but why did he just go rogue and kill everyone? He had a bit of a reputation for disobeying orders, taking shortcuts, twisting his interpretation of orders. A maverick, but nothing in his character profile would point to that kind of behavior. He killed eight people in cold blood. Reports say he made John watch before killing him last. What kind of psychopath does that?"

Jim pulled out his 9mm Glock and checked the clip. "This is a vague account of what happened; it's all classified. I was able to get this much information as a favor from an old friend in the CIA. He let me keep everything I could remember." He holstered his gun. "So, now we know who we're dealing with. He's been out of the FSS for a long time, so he's probably tapping into his old network and connections, but there are no ties back to the FSS. It sounds like he's doing this on his own. No orders, no direction, no directives."

"So, now that we know the who, 'and the *who*,' the why, and the what, how are we going to handle this?" Ty asked. He wanted to help, but he didn't know what to do or how to help.

Chapter 27

Ty's grabbed his phone when it double-buzzed and chimed with a priority notification with his location app. He had been expecting the notification since earlier that morning. His laptop had been opened and it attempted to join an unknown Wi-Fi network. The notification was part of a two-factor acknowledgement that made him accept the connection of his laptop to a new or unknown Wi-Fi connection from his phone. The notification gave him the geolocation of his laptop at the time and location of the request and the option to accept the attempt. This app he created served as a security mechanism in case his laptop was stolen and someone else opened it. It would attempt to join the local Wi-Fi network and issue an alert over its built-in 5G connection, asking to allow the unknown new connection—or not.

"Hey guys! My stolen laptop just showed up. It notified me that it's been woken up and is on another network in Santa Clara!" He didn't think it was pertinent to the problem at hand, but it seemed like it was an issue he wanted to bring up.

When Ty mentioned where his laptop was located, Jim was in the middle of trying to figure out what they were going to do next; to prepare for Mikhail's arrival and take him and his team on.

Mikhail didn't know exactly where they were other than that they were most likely at this undisclosed facility. He couldn't know this FBI building didn't have any other FBI agents in it, or there was only a skeleton staff of security guards and construction workers. Jim thought this could be an advantage for them, but in what way? Jim assumed Mikhail was after Tyson; what if he could give him a quantum computer instead.

"Hey, Ty! Where exactly in Santa Clara is your laptop?" Jim asked, as more information might be useful.

"It looks like it's near the corner of Scott Boulevard and Bower Avenue. Why?" Ty asked, looking closer at the map on his phone.

"Can you pinpoint the address?" Jim looked at the time.

"The building... it looks like..." Ty typed in a few search queries. "It looks like the address is for Qu-Cell Inc. I've never heard of it." Ty looked up at the group sitting around the table.

"I know that company. That's Bob Hendrick's company. I've invested forty million dollars into their R and D for a quantum computer. They're doing what everyone else is doing, building a larger QPU to compensate for the instability of their system. I was considering dropping them from the next round of funding," George jumped in, joining the conversation.

"It's about a thirty-minute drive to Santa Clara up the freeway. If we go fast, we could get there in a little over twenty minutes." Jim was now looking at the ceiling of the office as he thought of a plan out loud.

"What if we brought Mikhail to the fake device. If we could somehow let him know we're heading there to retrieve it, we could have an ambush ready for him there." Jim offered up the idea and was now looking at everyone around the table.

"What if we announced the machine was there?" Ty proposed to the planning committee.

"And how, pray tell, do we do that?" Hank sarcastically asked.

"Twitter, TikTok, Instagram, Facebook, Parler, LinkedIn, and so on. I have over sixty-five thousand followers on Twitter alone, most of them are in the valley. It's been a while since I've posted anything. That will cause these platforms to send out an announcement that I've posted something. People will think I'm announcing something new we've been developing." Ty was still thinking through the idea in real-time.

"People will see it. If these guys are monitoring social media, then maybe they'll pick it up too. Problem is, there could be a lot of innocent people showing up at that location." He thought about it more. "It could also ruin that company, uh, Qu-Cell?" Ty let that last observation sink in a bit. He knew there must be a few sleazebags there if they broke into his home to steal the machine and his laptop—with goons—but he would bet there were more good people there than bad.

"How about if you don't announce the address or the company name? Just that intersection. There's got to be dozens of buildings in that area and a bunch of tech companies nearby," Dana said. She could see in Ty's eyes that hurting good employees of a bad company was an emotional problem for him.

"Hey! That's a good idea. It'll keep the crowds down or at least dispersed in the area." Ty was thanking Dana with his eyes for pulling him out of a hole he didn't fully think through.

"You know, if Mikhail wants the device more than Ty here, then he could figure out where it is." Jim's mind finally had some useful information to work with.

"How many companies in that area are developing this type of technology?" Jim asked the table, expecting someone to start looking it up for him.

"Two! Qu-Cell and Intel," George said off the top of his head. "I would count Intel out of this, but Bob always struck me as a little underhanded given the right circumstances. And Howard, his COO, has a questionable background. Those are the only two companies in Santa Clara developing quantum computing technology. There are several other companies in the valley, but they are all further north or south in other cities. These are companies with active R and D projects on location with suitable development labs. We have some level of funding or insight into all of them, so I keep an eye on all of them." George turned and looked at Ty apologetically. "Sorry my boy, but we don't consider KSS as doing active R and D into this technology. That's KRF in Japan."

"Why are you looking at me? I'm hearing all of this for the first time. I know of the few big names in quantum computing, but I had no idea this many companies were working on it." Ty wasn't offended. He'd only learned Katoshi Corp. was working on quantum computing a few months ago.

"So, what's the plan?" Dana inserted, getting back on track.

"Well, let's see. If Mikhail is monitoring social media and we tailor the post for him, he might find Qu-Cell without you telling him." Jim had his plan.

"Ty, do you have pictures of that fake device you built?" Jim asked.

"What is with the fake device?" George finally had to ask.

"Sure, here." Ty pulled out his phone and opened the photo app. He took about six pictures of the decoy.

"I personally like this one the best." Ty put his phone down in the middle of the table for everyone to see.

"I built this decoy and put it in my office in case someone figured out what I did with the lottery and tried to take it. It's loosely modeled after the Mark 2 I saw at the KRF lab back in January." Ty was swiping through the six pictures on his phone for everyone at the table to look at.

"Brilliant! It obviously worked." George smiled.

"Well, I also didn't think anyone would send in a quantum physicist to steal it. Plus, it was dark and there was a lot of chaos going on," Ty added.

"Use this one. It's obscure enough but gets the idea across." Jim pointed at a picture.

"Okay. I'll also include a map of the intersection." Ty began typing up his announcement.

"Did the surveillance footage grab any license plates?" Dana asked Hank.

"Actually, they got us five plates. The one with Mikhail in it, and four other cars staking out the block around the building. No one in those cars were recognized, but when Mikhail left, the other four cars left. They think the five cars were together and are heading here." Hank looked at the time. "I'd say we have about ten to fifteen minutes."

"Did you find out if any of the surveillance equipment here works?" she asked.

"Yeah, not the full suite, but enough to spot these five cars approaching," Hank answered. "There isn't much equipment installed inside the building yet, but the outside is covered."

"I'm going to redirect some agents coming here to that Santa Clara address. I think they can be there before our bad guys show up, assuming they can figure this out in time." Jim was already dialing his phone.

"Okay, I'm done and ready to tweet this message. All of my platforms are linked together, so this one message should be on all my social media sites in about a minute. Here's what I have:

Ty McNally
@TyMcNallyOnTech

Dear Twitterverse #IndustrialEspionage

My home was robbed by armed & desperate men last night. Laptop & new SPECIAL DEVICE stolen. Laptop beacon location currently in area of Bowers Av & Scott Blvd, SC, CA.

Pic of device

If you see it? DM me

#Reward #NewTypeOfComputer #Disruptive #WorldChanger

10:50 AM · APR 8, 2025 · Twitter for iPhone

Ty looked around the table at everyone. "Any suggestions? Changes? I don't know if this is going to work, but some people will engage. I'll probably get a lot of direct messages back with questions in a few minutes. I can fake the ruse for a while. I guess we could announce the equipment has been recovered, um, you know, when this is over?"

Nobody said anything for a minute.

Dana looked at Ty with a heavy heart. He fell into the middle of a very dangerous situation all by accident—by an act of God. He was in over his head and he didn't have any responsibility or training to deal with this. She needed to make sure this plan worked.

"That's perfect. If his network is watching, they should contact Mikhail with this information. They might do some research into it and identify Qu-Cell," Dana finally spoke up.

"My guess is this will work, but it will only break them up. I'll bet half of his team heads to Qu-Cell, and the other half keeps coming here. We won't know which group Mikhail will be in." Hank shared his opinion, then began looking closer at the surveillance footage on his phone. "Taking on half of them improves our odds here though," he added. "If we can figure out what type of car he was in at the SF office, we might be able to spot it with the equipment here."

"Okay, post your message, Ty." Jim turned to Ty to have him send it. It was like the official start of the incomplete plan.

"Done! Let's see if he bites." Ty was watching for responses on his phone.

"Got it! It looks like Mikhail is driving a silver or gray Ford Mustang. If we get on the streets again, it'll be harder to outrun him. I'm working on the other cars," Hank blurted out, not following the current conversation.

"Where is the surveillance equipment for this building?" Dana asked, wanting to know the status outside.

"Security office is on the lobby floor. The two guards who inspected your stuff are there monitoring the cameras. They're up to date on the situation," Jim responded.

"Shouldn't they know the plates and make of the car?" Dana was getting frustrated waiting for something to happen to them. She wanted to act on something.

"Good point. We'll know if he's here or heading to Santa Clara." Jim reached for George's desk phone and dialed the security office extension.

"I don't think we should be in here huddled together like this." Dana was ready to head downstairs and wait at the front door for Mikhail Ivanov to arrive.

"Calm down, Dana. We'll know something if any cars try to enter the facility. Nothing is allowed in here." Jim was trying to get a handle on things.

"What if they don't enter by car? What's that outside, construction fencing?" Dana asked. There really wasn't a complete plan, not even an incomplete plan.

"Outside of the fencing is a concrete barrier. The main gate is the only way in," Jim tried to console Dana.

"Hank, maybe you should post up on the roof with that M110. You be our eyes and first line of defense. George and Ty, you should stay in here." Jim pulled out a Glock from his holster and handed it to Ty.

"Hopefully, you won't need this, but if you have to use it, there'll be less paperwork to deal with." He winked at Ty as he handed him the gun.

"Dana, let's go down to the lobby and see how everything looks." Jim handed her a Glock and an M16 with extra magazines from the equipment bag. "Maybe you'll get to use this."

They both held onto the Glock together for a moment, her hand overlapping his, before Jim let go.

Dana looked Jim in the eyes and nodded. She turned and locked eyes with Ty for an extended period of time. Less than awkward, but noticeably affectionate as she gave him a "this has to be done before there's an *us*" look.

"Stay here and stay safe." She was now looking at her dad, reassuring him everything was going to be okay. "Ty, please protect my dad."

She put the extra ammunition into her jacket pockets and loaded a round into the chamber of each gun as the three of them headed out of the office.

Ty nodded and watch Dana leave the office and closed the door. He looked at George and smiled, then began shutdown on Q-Tip to pack it away.

"I think the demonstration is over for now.

Chapter 28

"Bob? I think you need to see this." Howard was in Bob's office looking through the blinds and out of the window toward Scott Boulevard. "Have you ever seen so many people walking around here before? They're on both sides of the street." Howard motioned for Bob to come over to the window.

"What the hell? It looks like they're all looking around for something." Bob was now standing next to Howard, observing the weird spectacle outside their building.

"Why are they all walking so slowly?" Howard asked, not expecting an answer.

The two men left the window and sat back down.

Howard crossed his legs before starting. "No luck with that laptop so far, but we're still working on it. I've got a couple of people looking into it." Howard's status didn't have a lot of confidence behind it. Luckily, Bob didn't seem to be paying much attention.

"Fine, keep at it," Bob responded automatically.

His mind was a hundred miles away and not totally engaged with Howard at the moment. Bob was contemplating his exit strategy. His company wasn't going to succeed at bringing a commercially viable quantum computer to market for another six years, if that. Without repeatable and observable results to demonstrate consistently, he wouldn't be able to secure another round of funding. Plus, they were burning money faster than he could bring it in. The current course of action from his scientists was to sink more money into their design without a guarantee that it would work.

Worse, without these positive results, the valuation of his company wasn't worth what had been invested—what he'd personally invested—not even close. If he sold the company today, it would just be considered a building full of expensive parts. An inventory closeout sale. A "dumpster dive" for companies scrounging around for cheap intellectual property. At this point, he would be fortunate to get 10 percent of what he had personally invested back. There wasn't a more dreadful feeling of owning something that you owe more on than what it's worth. Unlike a home that's underwater, at least you still have the benefit of a place to live. This was just a dead weight on his life.

Riding it out would personally cost him at least twice what he'd already invested, and he was already over leveraged in loans. Riding it out to see if the next design was the one that pulled them out of this technology death spiral didn't look promising. As far as return on invest went, this was a huge bust.

Bankruptcy would end the pain, like cutting off a gangrene foot; you'll survive, but you won't be the same. He shuttered at the thought of failing, yet again. He needed a way out.

"Shit! Bob, we have a problem." Howard was holding his phone up to show Bob what was being displayed.

"All those people outside; they're looking for us! It's all trending right now. They're looking for Tyson's laptop and that prop computer. It's a flash mob search!"

"Well, let's get rid of it." Bob snapped out of his brooding thoughts.

"I don't think it's that simple. That's one of the new MacBook's with the built-in 5G network service. We must've triggered a beacon or something." Howard was extremely nervous.

"Hide it in one of our isolation rooms. That should block the signal," Bob instructed, also very anxious.

"Okay, but I think that someone, Tyson McNally, already knows where it's at. He sent out a tweet that hit every social media platform and it's gone viral. His message shows a map of this area, but I bet he has the exact location and didn't share it, just the general location. This is turning into a media spectacle. It must be a publicity stunt or something." Howard got up to look out the window.

"There are thousands of people on the streets looking around or walking slowly."

Bob picked up his TV remote and turned on the television in his office.

***

"What do you mean, 'you find it'?" Dmitry and his crew had just arrived in the city of Morgan Hill when his phone rang.

"Da, the computer you are looking for, it is the virus on social media. At TyMcNallyOnTech said it was stolen from his home. He is offering a reward for information of it and laptop. It does not say it is quantum computer, but picture of it is not a normal computer. And he used hashtag, 'new type of computer' in tweet." The thick eastern European voice on the phone was that of an excited young man, probably attending an American university.

"So? That does not mean you found it. It means you know *about* where it is." Dmitry wanted more information and was getting impatient with his young digital tracker.

"That is true, but location is Santa Clara and drop pin is at street intersection Bower and Scott. There is only one company that is doing quantum computer development in area. Company name is Qu-Cell. I forward you address. You can do what you want with information." The young man hung up.

Dmitry slowed his car down as he led his team off the freeway. Then he pulled into a shopping center parking lot as the four cars followed close behind him. He did not expect Tyson McNally to seek help from the internet to locate the quantum computer and his laptop. That laptop would contain useful information about the machine. It must have a location security feature in it to have its location known. That would have to be disabled as part of his new plan.

He would not underestimate Tyson McNally again. He would send two cars back north to retrieve the machine and the laptop from Qu-Cell. This company must be desperate to have sent heavily armed men to Tyson's home to steal the equipment. By his assessment, two men were killed in the process. He divided his men; he would take the other two cars and eight men with him to the new FBI building and directed the remaining eight men to Qu-Cell in the other two cars.

If he could obtain Tyson McNally and the machine with the laptop full of information, then that would solidify his reinstatement and status with the FSS.

***

"It looks like it worked." Hank announced over the multi-phone connection.

"Only three cars are coming down the street, including the gray Mustang. That must mean Mikhail is in this group. At least we only have to deal with half of them." Hank was able to connect his phone to the surveillance system and was monitoring the area while also overlooking the area from the roof of the eight-story building. He took his M110 rifle and scope and zoomed into the window of the lead Mustang.

"Confirmed. Mikhail is in the forward Mustang. I can't hit him from this distance." Hank panned into the windows on the other two cars following the Mustang.

"Including Mikhail, it looks like there is a total of nine men in three cars. He must have thought we were going to make a run for it; they've muscled up with a Camaro and a Charger. I won't have a clear shot until they're near the main construction fence opening. That's if he approaches the main gate." Hank was providing a play-by-play of everything he was observing to the others over his phone. He zoomed out and was watching the three cars drive slowly down the street. It looked a little like a modern American muscle car club cruising down the boulevard: Ford Mustang, Chevrolet Camaro, and a Dodge Charger.

"If it were me, I would make a few drive-by passes to assess the lay of the land before making any kind of move. Maybe drive around the block a few times." Hank was still watching the three-car motorcade cruise by. The new facility was similar to the San Francisco FBI office building in that it took up an entire city block, only this block was larger.

"Thanks Hank. Keep us posted and keep the line open." Jim's voice sounded a little relieved at the news of a smaller team showing up.

***

In the main lobby of the building, Dana and Jim were checking on the personnel they had available. Civilians were sent to the lower subfloors for protection. Reinforcements were still several minutes away, but they were on their way.

Jim wanted this to be over before they arrived. He would gladly endure months of investigations and inquiries for a chance to end this right here. There was no "by-the-book" policy that covered this situation.

Dana and Jim headed out the front door and positioned themselves on both sides of the marble monument in the center circle of the roundabout driveway. The three bare flagpoles behind them stood tall and fresh, waiting for the first flags to be hoisted. The bright white marble was new and had that new marble smell. Dana and Jim leaned in close to the nonweathered monument, their M16s loaded and ready. They were situated about two hundred feet from the main gate in a straight line through to the main street entrance, which was another two hundred feet away.

"They're coming back around. They just circled the block and now they're coming back down the main street slower this time. They've also changed order; the Mustang is now in between the Charger and the Camaro," Hank reported over the phone.

"Confirmed. Mikhail is still in the Mustang, the cars just changed positions. I still don't have a clear shot." Hank sounded defeated again. Hank was an exceptional marksman, but he would not be able to hit a moving target from this distance.

"If they approach the main gate, I'll have a better chance of making this shot." There was a pause over the line. "Correction, it looks like they put the heaviest car forward and there's just the driver in it. All the other men are loaded up in the Mustang and the Camaro. I think they plan on smashing the barricade at the main gate with the forward car." Hank now sounded anxious.

"They've stopped short of the entrance. They're stopped next to the construction fencing so I can only see the roofs of the cars." Hank was narrating the details.

The Dodge Charger turned left into the middle of the four-lane street, then made a U-turn and accelerated straight into the main entrance, gaining speed and momentum. The large vehicle collided with the makeshift barricade at nearly sixty miles per hour, smashing through it and flipping itself over as barricade and debris scattered and flew everywhere. The car landed on its side and slid for several feet, pointing toward the main building entrance, with sparks shooting out from the metal on concrete connection. Before the dust and wreckage settled, the Mustang and Camaro sped onto the driveway, swerving back and forth. The two cars approached the destroyed barrier at an angle, clipping the roof of the Charger hard enough to knock it back on its four wheels, clearing the path for both cars to charge the main building's glass doors.

Dana and Jim turned and emerged from both ends of the monument, their M16s aimed down the main driveway, and began firing at the lead Mustang, hitting it in the front grill and windshield. Jim adjusted his aim to attempt to hit the front tires. Dana began shooting at the Camaro. From the roof came shots that hit the windshields of both cars. The two vehicles kept coming, steam spewing from the engine compartments and liquid pouring out from underneath. Though the three shooters couldn't stop the charging vehicles, they kept the barrage of bullets flying.

From the right side of their vision, a black sedan shot out from the parking structure, faster than a car should travel in the close quarter, curving driveway. Electric motors and gear boxes streaming with an increasing frequency. The four-door sedan hopped the rounded curbs of the roundabout driveway, taking the curving road in a straight line. Sparks shot out from the undercarriage as the chassis bottomed out on top of the highpoints of the curbs. The black Tesla Model S was heading straight at the steaming lead Mustang for a T-bone strike. The Camaro was already pulling up along the other side of the Mustang. The Tesla continued to accelerate and adjusted its trajectory to ram the Mustang ahead of its driver side door.

"Tyson! Stop! What are you doing? Please, no!" Dana screamed at the black, streaking, electric missile as it struck the Mustang violently and with enough force to slam it into the side of the Camaro, disabling both cars for good. The Tesla slid sideways and pinned the Mustang, sandwiching it between the Camaro and the Tesla, all three cars were steaming or smoking in a parallel formation—a dead heap.

Moments passed before crippled, disoriented bodies began struggling to escape the Mustang and the Camaro through broken windows and deformed car body sheet metal; there was no movement coming from the Tesla. Deployed airbags were deflating.

Tears were running down Dana's red face when she saw a body moving in the Mustang's driver's side window. Just a hand reached out at first, then two arms trying to pull himself out of the wreckage.

"You bastard!" Dana screamed and stood up next to her white marble shield. She lifted the shaking M16 and began shooting toward the clawing driver.

The body retreated like a slimy snail back into its protective shell. Gunfire began coming from different sides of the disabled cars. Nothing was on target, but they both took cover out of instinct.

The volley of trading bullets went on for a minute. It was a standoff between crippled and disoriented bad guys and emotionally shaken good guys.

"Hank! Shoot the Tesla near the firewall! Into the driver side floorboard!" Tyson's voice yelled over the phone that was sitting on the grass between Dana and Jim.

"Got it!" Hank began firing into the Model S's carriage in front of the driver's seat. He had a clear view and emptied his magazine into the battery modules.

"Hank what are you doing? Stop! Tyson is still in there!" Dana looked up to the roof of the building where Hank was perched. There she saw two heads overlooking the edge of the building.

"I'm up here on the roof with Hank. Sorry, my phone crashed when my car slammed into that Mustang," Ty's voice came over the grass muffled phone.

"What? How? Why are you up there?" Dana was confused with relief and fury and flooded with conflicting emotions.

"Get ready!" Tyson yelled again as he pointed down toward the wreckage.

Dana and Jim both turned to look at the cars as the Tesla began spitting out a blue tinted smoke under high pressure, then flames shot out like a flame thrower. The entire pile of cars became surrounded in the thick toxic smoke and fire. Thermal runaway overcame the battery modules as the fire increased its heat to almost three thousand degrees. The tires were the first to ignite, then body panels started to deform and melt. The flames shooting out from under the Model S engulfed the trapped Mustang.

A body frantically clawed out of the driver's window again with disregard for any other danger. It was a desperate act of survival to escape the flames and smoke. Desperate cries could be heard as the heat increased

Dana and Jim stood up from behind their marble cover and walked toward Mikhail Ivanov. They each pulled out their Glock 9mm pistols. Henchmen escaped from the windows of their cars and struggled to run away, leaving Mikhail wriggling on his own to escape and face his past. His squirming stopped as the two approached; he could see them through the toxic smoke and flame.

On the roof, Hank was watching Mikhail's face through the crosshair of his scope, then he lowered his rifle to watch family retribution through his own eyes.

Dana and Jim looked the struggling Mikhail in the eyes. Mikhail recognized the two, even though they never met. He realized what he was facing. Dana was the first to fire, hitting Mikhail square in the chest. Jim followed with a round in the neck. While they continued to walk closer, they both emptied their guns into the dead body, every round hitting flesh somewhere before the toxic flames fully overwhelmed all three vehicles. The gruesome sight was washed away with an intensely cleansing, smelly fire: justice, execution, cremation. Mikhail Ivanov, currently known as Dmitry Petrov, who was made nonexistent on paper six years ago, was now nonexistent in real-life.

After her gun stopped firing, she let her arm drop and watched as the car fires continued to burn. She was no longer crying, and her face was no longer red with anger. She turned to look at Jim, who also dropped his gun down to his side and was staring at the burning body as charred parts began to break off and crumble on the ground. He finally turned to look at Dana, his eyes red, swollen, and glassy.

There was an unacknowledgeable satisfaction stewing inside him. The gruesome sight made sure he didn't celebrate outwardly. His gratifying emotions inside came out as sadness because he'd still lost his younger brother, and this only made him realize how much he still missed him.

Dana embraced her big brother after she finally dropped the gun on the ground. Jim embraced her like a big brother would. He shuttered slightly as the tears began running down his face and landed on her broad shoulder. Jim had known John his entire life and now there was finally closure for himself, his younger brother, and his younger sister-in-law.

The growing sounds of sirens blaring and tires screeching broke up the emotional embrace. The escaping henchmen were too injured and disoriented to run away effectively, and they surrendered easily; they probably hoped they'd receive care and have their injuries tended to properly.

Ty and Hank ran out of the glass doors behind them. Hank and Jim gave each other a huge, burly man-hug. Jim wiped the tears dry from his face in order to man-up. He had let out enough emotion for one day, and he was ready to be special agent Jim Jordan again. Although there was a weight lifted from him that he'd been carrying for six years, he felt grounded and confident in his abilities.

Dana turned to look at Ty with joyful anger on her face. "What the hell did you do? What happened? Where's my dad?" She didn't wait for Ty to finish running to her, she ran into his arms, and they embraced.

He could tell there was something different about the way she held him; she seemed lighter, less guarded. He didn't really understand it all, and he didn't know if that was even important right now. All that mattered to him was that she was safe, uninjured, and holding him like she didn't want to let go; all he wanted to do was hold on to her.

After a couple of minutes, the two of them were joined by Jim and Hank in a four-way hug. Jim broke away first and slapped Ty on the shoulder a few times. The four of them stood there looking at each other, smiling as an FBI car arrived and police cars drove up as close as they could to the burning heap of metals, plastics, chemicals, and electronics.

George finally came out of the building to join them.

"Oh my! You don't see this every day," he said.

Dana left the group and hugged her father in a tight embrace.

"So, what was that?" Jim finally spoke up and asked Ty.

"It's an Easter egg in the recent Tesla software." Ty showed Hank and Jim his rebooted phone.

"About two years ago, Elon Musk hinted on Joe Rogan's podcast, "the Joe Rogan Experience," that there's an Easter egg in the new software release you could enable if you accepted the waivers. Elon wanted to use his car as a remote-control car, you know, like an RC car. It's a special mode in the Smart Summon software feature that allows you to remotely drive your car using the onboard cameras and steering through a special mode in the phone app. It's limited to nonpublic streets and disables the collision avoidance features. Elon's become a huge fan of the video game Forza and online racing, and he wanted to race a real car on a track remotely." Ty finally had the app loaded and was showing it to them, though the connection to his car was currently unavailable.

"After the three of you left the office, I heard Hank describe what was happening over the phone. I went down to the garage and disconnected the Tesla, put it in Ludicrous plus mode, and drove it to the exit of the garage. While the batteries were heating up, I ran back in and went up to the roof with Hank. It was a good vantage point to remotely drive from." He was pointing up to the rooftop.

"I thought I could stop them from breaking through the barrier by using the car to block them or ram them. With the batteries extra hot, the thermal runaway effect of the damaged battery modules worked faster than I'd read about."

Jim and Hank looked at Ty and shrugged their shoulders.

"Nerd," was all Jim could say as they both hugged Ty.

"I loved that car," Dana said behind him as she let go of her father and turned toward the guys again.

"I might have to get another one. That car is—was—awesome. Especially with you driving it." He looked at Dana again as she leaned in and kissed him passionately. Ty wrapped his arms around her and pulled her into an even deeper kiss.

When they finally released each other, he opened his eyes slowly and looked deeply into her opening eyes. No words could explain the connection the two of them were feeling or experiencing. So, Ty did what he did best in situations like this, screw it up.

"At least now you have to take a ride in my M3." He smiled at her.

"I would love that."

Chapter 29

"What do you mean the FBI and police are in the building?" Bob was frantic and yelling at Howard.

"They just arrived and entered the lobby flashing badges and started wandering the office cubicles with guns." Howard was looking out of the window toward the intersection of Scott Boulevard and Bower Avenue. There were TV news vans parked at the intersection and reporters were interviewing a few of the thousands of people on the streets. Traffic in all four directions was halted.

Then the lights went out. Instantaneously, the emergency lighting system engaged and illuminated everything in an alien-green glow. "EXIT" signs were lighting up over every doorway that led outside. Gunfire was heard out in the rear shipping and receiving dock, then it went quiet.

The door to Bob's office smashed opened with a huge-booted foot.

"Hands in the air!" commanded the armed officer.

"What is the meaning of this?" Bob blatantly protested with his hands stuck up in the air.

Howard also had his hands in the air, but his head was down in defeat. He knew they were screwed, though he didn't know why there was gunfire sounds coming from the shipping and receiving dock. Nobody in the company really knew what happened or what they did.

The officer put handcuffs on Bob and Howard, then led them out of the office and into the main lobby where six other men were handcuffed and sitting on the floor against a wall. As the officer sat Bob and Howard down on the opposite wall, two other men were being carried out on ambulance stretchers, their wrists handcuffed to the rail of the rolling beds.

"What the hell is going on?" Bob demanded.

"These eight men were here to break in and steal some equipment. They're Russian sleeper operatives recently activated. Do you know anything about that?" an FBI agent standing next to Bob asked.

It startled Bob as he turned and looked up at the agent. "I have no idea what these men were here to steal. It could be anything. We are doing quantum computing development here. Everything here is priceless." Bob was pleading his case that they were the victims.

"Interesting. It seems they were here to steal this laptop and this, this case of junk." The agent was pointing to a MacBook being carried away by a police officer and an aluminum computer case being carried away by another police officer. Following behind them, then stopping before entering the lobby, was Dr. Gurski.

"Thank you, Dr. Gurski, you've been a big help. We'll contact you if we have any further questions." The two shook hands, then Dr. Gurski turned and left.

"Apparently, your chief scientist is a big fan of *at TyMcNallyOnTech*. He recognized the, the, whatever that is, in the picture he tweeted. And that message, well that's why there are so many people outside. In about five minutes, you two are going to be famous."

Chapter 30

Tyson McNally looked out of the window down to the Potomac River flowing across the landscape of Fairfax County and Maryland. Sitting at the large conference table between Dr. George Lancer and Dana Jordan, he turned his attention back to the droning sound of murmurs in the large room. Others sitting at the table were George's direct reports and a few of their direct reports, seated most of the way around the large table. There were empty seats at the far end of the table, but everyone was huddled near the front to listen to their boss and their boss's boss. The meeting hadn't started yet, so everyone was just chatting with each other, sharing content on their phones, or taking notes. Dana was informally interrupting various side conversations around the table and would introduce Ty to them, professionally and stoically.

It had been over a week since the events at his home and Morgan Hill; unfortunately, life for him was returning to some level of both normalcy and abnormalcy.

Ty was at home making phone calls, gathering quotes to repair his home, and talking to his new lawyers, new accountants, and his old tax guy, Mitch. They were all upset with him for claiming his lottery winnings without their guidance. It wasn't a good idea to just walk into the lottery office and present winning tickets for billions of dollars without a team representing him. For him, the whole process was underwhelming and overhyped. They also scolded him for having all that money wired into one bank account.

They convinced him to open up several accounts across several banks and split the money among them, at a minimum. He agreed and would let them guide him once the money showed up. That was still over two months away; he had time. Every time they tried to get information from him as to why he did what he did, all he provided them was, "It's complicated." That was an understatement; this whole experience would make a great movie someday.

This trip to Langley, Virginia, was at the request of George to have a discussion about the future. What really got him to stop what he was doing and listen was when George mentioned Dana would be in the meeting. Dana hadn't been very connectable over the few days since Morgan Hill; just few text messages acknowledging his test messages. She needed to get back to Japan and close out the operation there and get processes going in restarting project Shinsei with Katoshi Corporation. Now here she was sitting next to him in this conference room.

She met up with him in the lobby before the meeting and gave him a warm hug and a professional kiss, but didn't really say much more than, "I'm glad you're here."

That wasn't satisfying enough for him. He wanted more and he wanted her to want him just as much as he wanted her. There was so much to talk about, then she disappeared.

It was confusing and frustrating, but he felt like he couldn't push the matter. The two of them had only been in each other's presence for less than twenty-four hours, but it seemed like they shared so much more. There was a connection like he'd never felt before, not even with Janet; the connection must have been unidirectional. It must have been the circumstances; one of those situations people find themselves in that artificially and temporarily drew them closer together for the moment. Without the surrounding circumstances, the connection was lost, for some.

Ty's mind was wandering while his body was in autopilot, nodding at people he didn't know and smiling for no apparent reason. He wanted to talk with Dana, do stuff with Dana, be alone with Dana.

"Okay, I think we can get this meeting started. Everyone, please. Let's get started." George stood up from his chair, which helped draw everyone's focus.

Ty snapped out of his internal funk and looked up toward George along with everyone else.

"So, if you haven't already met Tyson here, *Ty*, let me start. Ladies and gentlemen, this is Tyson McNally. Ty here has been instrumental in helping us recover some lost research as well as proving that quantum computing really works on real problems repeatably and can perform imaginable and unimaginable feats." George looked down toward Ty and smiled, then he looked at Dana and nodded.

"Let me spare you the gory details, there'll be plenty of time for that and formal introductions later. We have a lot to discuss, and I need to put Ty on the spot."

Ty's attention spiked and his face flushed with all the unwanted focus turned to him for some unknown reason.

"Ty, my boy, I, we, want you to run Katoshi Systems Services as CEO and CTO." Ty heard what George just said, but he didn't *understand* what George just said. He didn't even notice Dana's hand on his shoulder, or the clapping going on in the room. He parsed in his head the words he thought he heard a few more times and tried to process the statement—the request—in different ways; each approach he took, it all sounded like the same thing. Time for verification.

"What did you just say?" he asked, not realizing his mouth dried out, and his tongue was starting to stick to the roof of his mouth.

Ty had heard the term "double take" before, he'd even used the term in some casual conversations or posts before. He now realized he'd never used the phrase correctly as he did a "double take."

"We would like for you to be the chief executive officer and the chief technology officer at Katoshi Systems Services," George spoke slower this time to help let the statement sink in better.

"How can you do that? KSS is owned by Katoshi Corporation. They appoint their own CEOs, or at least, approve them. Maybe not recently, but they're supposed to, it's their company." Ty finally understood the request, but still didn't believe it. It didn't make sense, and all he could see were objections and obstacles.

"True to a point. KSS needs to be fixed if it's going to be the sole developer and supplier of quantum computing equipment and services to the U.S. government, and probably the rest of the world, for the next five to ten years. I've been in communication with Katoshi Corporation through Chairman Nakatori and he agrees. Whatever the internal spat between the other divisions and KSS was, it's been resolved; they've cleaned it out. The chairman and the CEO of Katoshi Corporation were unaware of it, and they've put an end to it." George was in his element, explaining everything.

"We're not doing this for you, we're doing this for us, for our needs. Our needs, needs you to get KSS back on track so we can do business together. Katoshi Corporate and Chairman Nakatori will invest in KSS to get it back to previous revenue levels of four years ago, which includes new buildings and a research campus, and Intel-Q will invest in Katoshi Corporation to build the supply chain needed to mass produce these machines and the software. This is under the stipulation that you, Tyson McNally, are in charge of putting KSS back together. We've also come to an agreement to move half of the quantum computing research and development operations to KSS from KRF. They are starting the process of identifying researchers and scientists familiar with the project to be expats to start operations at KSS." George paused for a moment to let it sink in.

"There's a lot of work to do and we're asking for a minimum five-year commitment to see this through. After five or ten years, we'd like to see the software and the hardware open sourced." George was now looking squarely at Ty, not expecting an answer, but more questions.

"You know I don't have to work anymore." Ty tossed that little fact out in the open to see what would happen.

"True, but is that really what you want? Could you impact the world by buying and building more cars or competing in archery tournaments?"

Ouch! Ty didn't expect to be put on the spot. He wanted to do something big, but he didn't know how to start. He wanted to be smart with his money, but there needed to be a plan, a strategy, a vision. He could do all that, but then he needed help executing it. It would be stupid of him to pass up this opportunity, this gift to change the world, to shape the future, to improve the human condition.

"We will help and advise you. I will help you." There was something in Dana's voice that pierced through the fog in his head.

Ty turned to look at Dana. Her hand was still on his shoulder, and for a moment, he forgot she was still sitting next to him. This was the definition of an overwhelming moment.

"Ty, I believe this opportunity needs your international experience, passion, your vision, and your moral compass. I believe you and I see a similar possibility for the world, for the future of mankind. I also believe not needing the job makes you perfect for the job; you'll need to take risks to do the job right without fear of repercussions. You can still invest personally where you want. You can create startup companies if that's what you want to do; you can buy a company. You can serve on boards of companies you believe in. It's not unprecedented to be CEO of multiple companies as long as you have the right staff." George knew he was getting too lofty trying to convince him to accept this offer, but he could tell Ty was thinking about it.

"You could start by acquiring Qu-Cell to set up your new quantum computing research campus. It sounds like it's going to be a steal." George winked at Dana and Ty and smiled.

"They might even be able help you figure out what's happening with that strange hypnotic timing feeling you get when the machine operates." George rolled his eyes, acknowledging the shared experience.

"I'll do it! I accept, but I don't know how to start or what to do next." Ty had a nervous confidence that made him want to push through the unknowns.

"Excellent! Thank you, Ty. Congratulations! You won't regret this. You might actually enjoy it. We'll address your questions shortly, but first, I have an announcement to make." George shook Ty's hand energetically with both hands.

"I'd like to announce that Dana Jordan, my daughter, will be leaving us here at Intel-Q. She will be starting her own consultancy practice and her first client is Katoshi Corporation, advising them on the new economy of quantum computing. She will still be working with us and KSS and will act as a conduit between us to move this business forward into the new future. Please…" George proudly gestured toward his daughter and led the applause.

Everyone in the room stood up and applauded.

"As you are all aware, Dana was to be my replacement when the time came, but now, I'll be looking to groom a couple of you to take her place, so be nice to me."

Laughter filled the room.

Ty looked at Dana.

"We're going to be working together?" If Ty's smile was any wider, it would have come off as disturbing.

"All of this was her idea," George bent over to loudly whisper to Ty. "With a little detailed help from me, but make no mistake, this is an excellent idea. It's perfect!"

"I wanted to tell you, but there was so much to do and work out. There are a few things you need to know about me, but only now I'm in a position to tell you. I couldn't before. Let's talk after this meeting." Dana put her hand on Ty's hand and squeezed it emotionally, then picked up her pen.

"Alright then. Let's continue on with this meeting." George rubbed his hands together as he sat back down in his chair.

"This meeting isn't over?" Ty looked at Dana.

"Not quite. Get used to it or change it if you want." Dana looked back at Ty.

He wanted to kiss her right there, but he felt the urge subside immediately; professional displays of affection were never his thing.

"Would you invite our guests in please." George gestured with his arm to whoever was closest to the door.

George's executive assistant, Jane, escorted into the conference room eight people. Chairman Nakaktori and two of his assistants, and Hashito Yamamoto, CEO of Katoshi Corporation, and his two assistants, and two Katoshi lawyers.

"Now, let's get down to quantum business," George announced as the executive team took their seats at the far end of the table.

Ty and Dana erupted out laughing as they both pointed at each other.

"*Ant-Man and the Wasp*!"

Epilogue 20 45

Lancer 1, the first of the new Norigawa class spaceships, quietly lifted off its launchpad on stunning balls of blue light coming from its thruster control booms and the large main thruster under the fuselage. The blue light made the night sky and ground below light up like a blue sun. This was the first spacecraft to use the photonic-based propulsion system to launch from the ground, complete a space mission, and land in the same place to be reused over and over again. Now it would be the largest and heaviest single object to ever leave Earth's orbit from the surface. Its seven-month mission was to deliver the crew, passengers, and supplies to the Mars Deep Space Staging Base, return without recharging, and land in the exact same spot. A product of SpaceX, there were six more under construction with the next two ships ready for missions by the end of the year.

The short, snub-nosed wide-bodied fuselage smoothly cleared the one-hundred-meter launch towers by an additional two hundred meters then stopped ascending. It hovered there for a short ten seconds, tilted to a forty-degree angle pointing directly at the full moon, then the spacecraft began moving upward slowly.

President Musk wanted this photo opportunity of Lancer 1 crossing the face of the fully illuminated lunar surface on its way to Mars. A supermoon like this wouldn't be this close to Earth for another fifty-six years, and the air was clean and crisp.

"Ground control, this is Lancer One. Did you get that?" The flight comms were being piped into the viewing lobby over the sound system for everyone to hear.

"Lancer One, this is ground control. Not yet. Continue at your current speed and heading for ten more seconds and then hold position on my countdown; five, four, three, two, one, hold."

The voices over the sound system were soothing and sultry. Too bad they were synthetic. Ty thought quantum computers flying mankind everywhere was strange enough, but quantum computers talking to each other so humans could enjoy their conversations while riding along and watching just seemed patronizing.

Lancer 1 stopped dead center, silhouetted by the surface of the full moon. An array of cameras and sensors focused on the moon and the spacecraft. The images were fed to the walls of the viewing lobby for all the invited guests to watch, while also being live streamed globally to the three Moon-based communities and the base on Mars. Some of the guests were already taking selfies of themselves with the images on the giant video walls in the background, while others took turns handing their phones to one another to take their group pictures and videos.

"Lancer One, this is ground control, you may begin maneuvers."

"Roger that ground control. Commencing maneuvers."

Additional lights of blue lit up at different places on the fuselage as the confident spacecraft began posing for its audience and the ground-based instrumentation.

Staff and guests could watch the performance outside on the observation deck or inside on the video walls of the lobby.

Ty stood on the observation deck holding Dana's hand watching Lancer 1 perform its vain maneuvers. He would have bet that if the spacecraft had arms, it would have flexed for the cameras.

Lancer 1 completed the sixty second exhibition, pausing at different positions for cameras to capture thousands of images, video, and sensor reading. Some in 3D, others in different spectrums. Then the space craft stopped posing and hovered.

"Lancer One, this is ground control. That was beautiful. You are a go to proceed with your mission at your discretion. President Musk, his guests, and the world would like to thank you for your service and the performance, and wish you a successful mission and return. Ground control out."

"Roger that ground control. Our pleasure. Lancer One out."

With a brilliant blue flash, Lancer 1 left the scene, leaving only a stunning, clear, unobstructed view of the full moon. It was officially beginning its seven-month mission, lighting the night sky as it left Earth's atmosphere.

Ty was still holding Dana's hand, their heads craning skyward admiring the blue glow of Lancer 1 as it left Earth's atmosphere. There was no toxic exhaust trail to follow; only the recognizable blue lights made it impossible to lose in the sky. Their son, Nikola, was in front of them, talking and laughing with a beautiful young girl, and pointing at the blue glow. Their younger teenage daughter, Ada, was socializing with the other teenage girls, oblivious to the commotion quieting down.

President Musk walked up to the Ty and Dana, put his arms around both of them, and laughed. "It's amazing to think you were able to make all of this possible because you used a quantum computer to win the lottery."

AUTHOR BIO

This is K. A. Wood's first novel, which he refers to as a "tech action novel," though it could have easily been called a "nerd's action novel." He describes *Quantum Ball* as "a technology action story with a touch of magic," with the understanding that magic is just yet-to-be-explained technology.

An avid reader of science fiction, fantasy, and action-adventure novels, he always felt he could write unique stories with his own style, experiences, and perspective. He is often found holding conversations using movie, TV show, and book quotes.

He is much younger than his forty-plus years in the computer industry suggest. He started working on large computer systems as a junior in high school as the teacher's technician in his school district's only computer science program.

Growing up on '50s and '60s science fiction and horror movies, his childhood dream was to become a mad scientist as an adult. He got close, but he was never that mad at anything.